The Poison Maiden

The Poison Maiden

Paul Doherty

W F HOWES LTD

This large print edition published in 2008 by
W F Howes Ltd
Unit 4, Rearsby Business Park, Gaddesby Lane,
Rearsby, Leicester LE7 4YH

1 3 5 7 9 10 8 6 4 2

First published in the United Kingdom in 2007
by Headline Publishing Group

A CIP catalogue record for this book is available
from the British Library

ISBN 978 1 40741 328 0

Typeset by Palimpsest Book Production Limited,
Grangemouth, Stirlingshire
Printed and bound in Great Britain
by Antony Rowe Ltd, Chippenham, Wilts.

Moira and Brian Carter dedicate
this book to our grandchildren
Elizabeth, Thomas, Jonathan,
Megan, Zoë, Jake, Sarah, Katie and Alex

HISTORICAL PERSONAGES

ENGLAND

Edward I: warrior king
                          [died 1307]

Eleanor of Castille: first and most
                          beloved wife of
                          Edward [died 1296]

Edward II: son of the above
                          [crowned in 1308]

Peter Gaveston: royal Gascon
                          favourite, Earl
                          of Cornwall

Margaret de Clare: wife of the above

Isabella: daughter of Philip
                          IV of France,
                          Edward II's
                          Queen

Margaret Queen Dowager:	second wife of Edward I, sister of Philip IV of France
Thomas of Brotherton Edmond of Kent	Margaret's sons, half-brothers to Edward II
Robert Winchelsea:	Archbishop of Canterbury
Aymer de Valence, Earl of Pembroke Thomas, Earl of Lancaster Guy de Beauchamp, Earl of Warwick Henry Bohun, Earl of Hereford Henry de Lacey, Earl of Lincoln Gilbert de Clare, Earl of Gloucester	Great Lords
Roger Mortimer of Wigmore:	Edward II's lieutenant in Ireland
Roger Mortimer of Chirk:	veteran fighter, uncle of the above

Hugh de Spencer:	nobleman, loyal to the crown

FRANCE

Philip IV:	King of France, 'Le Bel'
Joanna [Jeanne] of Navarre:	wife of the above, now deceased
Louis, Philippe, Charles:	sons of the above
Enguerrand de Marigny Guillaume de Nogare Guillaume de Plaisans	} Philip's principal ministers and lawyers

AVIGNON

Clement V:	pope, continued the papal exile in Avignon

THE TEMPLARS

Jacques de Molay:	Grand Master of the Templar Order
William de la More:	Master of the Templar Order in England

SCOTLAND

Robert the Bruce: skilled Scottish war-
leader against the
English

FOREWORD

In the spring of 1308, England was on the brink of civil war because of the new King Edward II's total reliance on his favourite, Peter Gaveston. Edward had just married Isabella, the daughter of Philip IV of France who seized the opportunity of his daughter's marriage to meddle in English affairs. This account of what happened next is based on historical sources. A commentary is provided at the end to explain its startling revelations. The quotation at the beginning of each chapter is from the *Vita Edwardi Secundi* (The Life of Edward II), the authorship of which is still debated.

PROLOGUE

Thus today the will conquers reason.

Vita Edwardi Secundi

'What will you have to say for yourself when the wind no longer stirs your hair? When your gullet is dry and you can utter no word, your bloodless face is white and your eyes are set in their gloomy sockets? When your mouth cannot be moistened and inside it your tongue stiffens against the roof of your mouth? When blood no longer courses in your veins? When your neck cannot bend or your arms embrace? When your foot cannot take a step? What does that putrid dead body reply now? Let him say what vain glory has to offer him now . . .'

I listened to Prior Stephen's funeral homily on the man I had killed as I nestled in the shadow of the great rood screen in the cavernous nave of Grey Friars, the Franciscan house that lies between Stinking Lane near the Shambles to the south and the Priory of St Bartholomew to the north.

1

I, Mathilde de Clairebon, also known as Mathilde of Westminster, in the Year of Our Lord 1360, the thirty-third year of the reign of Edward III, am still killing to protect myself. I have no choice. I am old and wasted, well past my sixtieth summer. My courses have long dried. My blood is sluggish, my bones ache, my muscles protest, but that is only the flower; the stem is still as strong and tenacious as ever, as is the root that defines me. The great Aquinas, quoting Aristotle, claims that 'being' is only being when it relates. Our relationships, he argues, define us, bring us into being and, in so many cases, make us murderers or the victims of murder. I am no different. I, Mathilde, formerly handmaid, henchwoman, counsellor, physician and even lover of Isabella, once Queen of England. Now I'm a relic, a survivor. Two years after my mistress died, I shelter amongst these cold grey stones. Isabella lies buried here in her marble sarcophagus, a majestic table tomb that stands in the choir to the right of the high altar. They buried her in her wedding dress, clutching the heart of her husband, Edward II, whose reign she so brutally ended. However, as in life so in death: Isabella also lies near the tomb of her great love, Mortimer of Wigmore, hand-fast in life, soul-fast in eternity.

The new father prior, the deliverer of sermons of doom, his fur-lined cowl framing a narrow, anxious face, favours me. He allows me to write my memories, my confession in a cipher only God and I understand. So close, so subtle is the cipher that even the most skilled clerk in the king's secret chancery cannot understand it. They could spend their time in purgatory trying to break it, yet still fail. Oh, the king would love to know! He hungers for my secrets, whetted by his own mother's fevered babblings as she lay in that cold, grim chamber at Castle Rising with the babewyns, griffins, gargoyles and other stone-sculpted grotesques staring down at her from the walls. She talked to those from the past. Names I knew well. I have watched them parade and posture in the sun before slipping into the dark: Philip IV, le Bel, the beautiful King of France; his helpmates, those demons incarnate, Marigny, Plaisans and Nogaret. Other sinister shadows gather. Chief amongst these is Clement V, pope, usurer and destroyer, shitting blood as he died, his corpse abruptly bursting into flames as it lay before the high altar of some church. Next to him, Edward of England screaming at the cross after his beloved Gaveston was executed. They all congregate: pictures, legends, frescoes in my mind. So many memories! Streets, havens of darkness, torchlight glinting on the weapons of hooded, visored assassins as they slip through a doorway intent on murder. Battlements prepared for war, packed with *armures de fer*, pots of flame brightening the darkness, the ominous silence broken by the creak of leather and the clatter of armour. Men, hearts full of fury, determined to hold fast against the dark mass of

3

enemy approaching the walls. Churches with their hallowed light and shifting gloom; before their rood screens, coffins containing the corpses of the murdered, all draped in black and ringed by purple candles, tended by bedesmen telling their paternosters whilst in the shadow-filled transepts the priest is silently garrotted by those who plan more murder. Soaring castles overlooking battlefields soaked in bloody snow. Forests and woods alive with men moving silently round those they've left hanging from the outstretched branches of oak and sycamore. Towns burning. Gallows set up before cathedral doors. The pestilence slinking across a blighted landscape. The dead choking filthy ditches. The living on their knees in desperate prayer as Abaddon, the Angel of the Bottomless Pit, cuts the cords and empties the sack of God's anger on to the land. I have also lived in a world of secrets, of amorous lechery thronged by the Judases and Losengiers, those betrayers of courtly love.

I may be dried and shrivelled as an ancient plum. My hair is grey and wiry, my skin a leathery brown; nevertheless, I have lived life to the full, drunk, even guzzled from the goblet of life. So why do I write? Well, every soul has its song, the very essence of its being, and this is mine. My confession to God. My discourse with myself. After all, aren't the most intimate and enjoyable conversations those we have with ourselves? I have seen history unfold. I have watched in mounting apprehension

4

God's justice come to fruition. I have, the good Lord assoil me, witnessed the effect of that hideous curse Jacques de Molay, the last Grand Master of the Temple, hurled from the roaring flames and bellowing foulsome smoke that burnt his flesh to a cinder on the Île-de-France and sent his soul fluttering like a dove towards God. A few words screamed out, yet that curse spread like a thick shower of arrows up and across God's heaven, barbs cutting the air before falling on their victims. All this was helped by my mistress. She who became the Virago Ferrea – the Iron Virago, Isabella la Belle, the new Jezebel, the Destroyer of Kings, the Usurper of Princes, the Ouster of Thrones, the Shatterer of Lives, God's anger incarnate. Isabella, mother of the one I call the Accursed, her son Edward III, bloody-handed, falcon-faced and hawk-hearted. Age has steeped him deep in villainy. He has drenched Europe in blood, blackened God's sky with the sooty smoke of funeral pyres. Gog and Magog have risen and stalked the world. Edward and the Annihilation, the Great Pestilence, siblings who have roamed the earth hand in hand. Once I was a famous physician who witnessed all this; now I am a recluse, a pensioner no better than a servant girl. How times change! Fortune's wheel spins so dizzily. Edward ordered me here to be with Isabella, his beloved mother, now interred beneath that cold, ornate sarcophagus.

'As in life, so in death, Mathilde,' he mocked,

5

full red lips curling in derision. 'Look at you,' he hissed. 'Grey-haired, grey-eyed, grey-souled. Yes, Grey Friars will suit you well. You have my permission to stay there. I could give you more, greater reward?' He smiled and stroked my hair as if I was one of his limner hounds.

At the time I steeled myself. I stared over his shoulder at his Luparii, his wolf-men, the knights and clerks of the king's secret chamber. They would have cut my throat if Edward had lifted a finger. Yet he dare not do that; well, at least not publicly. He probably knows what pledges I have lodged with powerful churchmen up and down this kingdom. They protect me. I smile, they have no choice! I know all about their secret lives. Edward recognises this. On that particular day he curled his finger round one strand of my hair, tightened it and pulled.

'Mathilde,' he whispered, 'they say you were once beautiful.'

'Sire, they say the same about yourself!'

'Ever quick.' He tugged on my hair again, then withdrew his hand. 'Swift as a lurcher!' he breathed. 'I can see the traces of what you once were. Mother told me: your hair black as night, fair-skinned, tender-eyed, slender and willowy as a wand.'

'Vanity of vanities,' I mocked. 'All things pass, sire.'

'Then tell me, Mathilde,' the king leaned closer so I could smell the fresh fragrance from his quilted jacket; his gold-ringed fingers edged towards my hands, the skin now dark and spotted like that of a toad, 'tell me whom you trust.'

'Put not your trust in princes,' I quoted. 'In mortal man in whom there is no help.'

The king drew back, amber eyes gleaming, lips white-spittled like those of an angry cat.

'See,' he quoted menacingly back, 'they lie and wait for your life, powerful men band against you.'

'I shall hide my face from them,' I retorted, 'and see what becomes of them, for they are a deceitful brood with no loyalty in them.'

'Take your psalms, take your prayers!' Edward taunted. 'Go and wait for your God. Shelter in the shadow of Mother's tomb, but remember, Mathilde, one day I will know the truth.'

'What is truth?' I smiled. 'Pilate asked the same question, though he didn't wait for an answer. In that way, perhaps,' I taunted, 'you do differ from him.'

'I am no Pilate!' he yelled. 'No innocent blood sullies my hands.'

He would have struck me, but his gaze caught the gift, Isabella's gift, I always wear: a silver brooch with a Celtic cross studded with gems that clasps my cloak. Edward's clenched fist, his *main de fer*, hovered over me.

'Go,' he whispered. 'I withdraw my love from you.'

He is so desperate to know the truth! Especially as he has wasted so many opportunities to discover it. He killed gentle Mortimer, gave him 'a fair trial', or so he proclaimed it: Mortimer was gagged throughout before being hanged at the elms overlooking Tyburn stream. Isabella never forgave her son for that, and Edward always regretted it. He could have learnt so much! My mistress certainly reminded him of that. For twenty-eight years she baited and taunted her 'beloved son' about her secrets. On her deathbed she deepened the murky, mysterious gloom by babbling feverishly about her life. She betrayed herself in words and phrases that flew like darts to sting the king's pride.

I am old. I consider myself cunning. In truth, I can be as foolish as the next. I thought Edward would leave me buried alive in Grey Friars, for both I and the prior are solemnly bound by the king's own writ. I am never to leave here. I was wrong. Edward is, if anything, his mother's son, so any struggle with him is *à l'outrance*, to the death. In this case, mine. He decided that if he could not learn my secrets, perhaps he should close my mouth for ever so that no one else could either. So, back to that funeral of the man I killed. An anchorite arrived here, a self-proclaimed recluse, a hermit who called himself Rahomer. I was suspicious about him from the start. For fifty years I have dealt with the Judas coven, the traitors, the suborners, the perverters of the truth, spies of every countenance and kind. Despite Rahomer's mildly ascetic looks, scrawny hair and watery eyes, I recognised the cuckoo in the nest.

He did his best with his sanctimonious gaze, the prim set to his lips, his hands ever clutched in prayer. I am a physician; I study signs and symptoms. Rahomer was slender, a man who, by the colour and texture of his skin, the set of his teeth and the smoothness of his fingers, was a child more of this world than the next. The good brothers had no choice but to accept him. Anyone who came with letters close, confirmed by the secret seal of the king, carried complete royal approval for his arrival at Grey Friars.

Our pigeon-toed hermit made himself at home. He was granted the ancient anker-hold built into the south chancel wall of the priory church. It has two windows. The internal one overlooks the sanctuary; the other gazes out over God's Acre with its decaying forest of crosses and headstones. Rahomer, dressed in brown and white like a pied friar, wandered everywhere, paternoster beads wrapped round his fingers. He proclaimed he was a lay brother dedicated to a stricter rule, so the Franciscans simply accepted him for what he pretended to be. Prior Stephen was different. From the occasional sharp glance at our sanctimonious toad's pious gestures, Father Prior was not convinced. I certainly wasn't. Now and again I drew Rahomer into conversation. I acted the witless old woman who wandered the friary eager to talk to anyone. I asked if he had ever read the *Anciente Rewle*, a spiritual reflection on the life of an anchorite. He replied that he had, but he stumbled over the words and his shifty eyes never met mine.

Now my chamber at Grey Friars is a cavernous, stark cell with crumbling stone walls, a stained raftered ceiling and a dusty floor covered with rushes. It stands off the small cloisters overlooking some wasteland, a deserted, quiet place. I would often sit near the cloister garth studying the grotesque faces of the gargoyles and wondering who they reminded me of. The good brothers were ever courteous. They left me alone. Master Rahomer did not. On occasions I'd return to find my papers had been disturbed. Someone had entered my chamber secretly, carefully sifting my belongings. I suspected, by mere logic, our self-proclaimed holy anchorite, so I brought him under closer scrutiny.

Rahomer was accustomed to receive visitors at the anker-hold window overlooking God's Acre, men and women desperate for spiritual advice. They must have been, to consult that reed shaking in the wind. Ecclesiasticus is correct – pride and arrogance lie at the root of all sin. In my experience they are also the cause of many a spy being hanged. Master Rahomer concluded I was what I looked, a grey-haired, stooped old crone. Isn't it strange how people dismiss the old as if they don't even exist? He never reflected about me. I did about him. He had one constant visitor, a man garbed in brown fustian, obviously a royal clerk despite this clumsy disguise. Such intrusion I expected; murder I did not.

The anchorite arrived around the Feast of St Peter ad Vincula; by Michaelmas he was trying to kill me. Rahomer was a malicious soul, biding his time and striking silently. I eat in my own chamber; the refectorian leaves my food on a stone ledge outside. On that particular day I had attended solemn high mass. Afterwards I waited until the sanctuary was empty so I could approach Isabella's tomb and talk to her, as is my custom, so I was delayed in my returning. When I did, I picked up the tray and studied the platter carefully. I have a horror of rats, a relic of the Great Pestilence as well as hideous imprisonment in a French dungeon. I recognised traces of my old enemy: the splayed five-clawed toes, the slight gnaw marks, the hard black pellets; my tray had certainly been visited by vermin. I was surprised: the refectorian always covered the platters with wooden lids, but on that occasion two of these were missing. I decided not to eat and left the food to be collected. I was about to enter my chamber when I heard a scuffling, a scrabbling in the far corner of the hollow-stone gallery leading down to the small cloisters. I plucked a walking cane from my chamber and went over to investigate. I poked and prodded. The scrabbling was repeated, followed by a hideous squealing, and a brown rat, thickset and furred, sped out of the shadows only to roll on its side, paws thrashing the air. It had been poisoned.

I returned to the tray. The bread and cheese had

been left covered. I examined both but could detect no taint. The potage of meat and diced vegetables was cold. I sniffed the bowl, and immediately recognised an old acquaintance: the magnificent glistening purple monkshood. Its red berry smell conceals the most deadly poison, particularly the juice crushed from the roots and seeds. If consumed, monkshood scours the organs of the belly like a sharpened steel rasp. Master Rahomer, and I was sure it was he, had chosen well. What could I do? I am no pug-nosed brawler in a London runnel. My opponent had a soul as narrow as a coffin, hard black with malice, and a conscience unbending as iron. He intended to kill me, yet to whom could I appeal? Who would defend me?

Before Vespers that very evening, I stole round to the anker-hold. Rahomer was standing at the ledge, hacking at his teeth with a toothpick. His surprise and consternation at my abrupt appearance were both his judge and jury. I gabbled about how unwell I felt. Rahomer smiled, nodded understandingly and added that perhaps I should retire. I did, but not to my chamber. I returned to Isabella's tomb. I leaned against the statues carved on its side and whispered my terrors and fears. I do not dread death; it is just that my confession must be made before I go. I crouched there in the shadows and waited for the reply. It came, Isabella's voice echoing through my soul.

'Mathilde, *ma petite*, I cannot defend you now.

Nobody can, except yourself. This man will kill you, so strike first, strike hard!'

I went into God's Acre and harvested a yew tree, its needles soft and fat, the berries shining red. I mixed up a paste. The following morning I stood by the priory postern gate and bought a bowl of sweetmeats from a baker taking a tray down to a nearby tavern. I mixed in the yew paste and left the bowl on the anker-hold ledge as a gift from some visitor or pilgrim. Rahomer ate it before Nones. He was ill before Vespers and dead before Matins the following morning. *Sic transit gloria mundi* – thus passes the glory of the world. To all intents and purposes Rahomer died of a falling sickness, a sudden failure of the heart. His corpse was dressed for burial and placed under a purple drape on a funeral trestle before the great rood screen. Father Prior sang the requiem mass and delivered that sermon. I listened to it scrupulously and helped shoulder Rahomer's corpse out to be buried in the poor man's plot. One day I will join him there, though at God's invitation, not the king's. I wondered if I should ask Father Prior to send a copy of his funeral homily to the court, but decided against it. You don't cast pearls before swine!

Three days later Father Prior summoned me to a meeting in his wood-panelled chamber. I sat on a faldstool, aware of the faces of angels, saints and demons staring down at me from the paintings, frescoes and triptychs that decorated his parlour.

He sat in a window seat, threading Ave beads through his fingers, a youngish-looking man, certainly a good one. I, Mathilde of Westminster, have, in the words of the old proverb, 'lain down with wolves and woke howling'. I can recognise a wolf when I see one! Father Prior, however, was a good shepherd; he was truly concerned for me. He referred obliquely to the sudden death of Master Rahomer. I rose, walked over and pressed my fingers against his lips. He looked startled.

'Father Stephen,' I begged, 'please do not ask about him. What you don't know cannot harm you.'

He gently removed my hand. 'Be careful, Mathilde. Tomorrow, the Feast of St Dionysius, Magister Theobald, Advocatus Regis, one of the king's most skilled lawyers, a priest of the Royal Chapel, is coming here to question you.'

'Father,' I stepped back and smiled, 'he'll not be the first.'

Magister Theobald swept into Grey Friars shortly after the Jesus mass. He demanded to see me in my own chamber with its thick walls and narrow windows; an eavesdropper would certainly have found it difficult to listen in. He was a porky man, with a balding head, his plump face shining with oil from the ripe fruits of good living. An urbane, cynical soul with pebble-black eyes and sensuous jutting lips under a sharp, hooked nose. He settled himself on the great chair that Father Prior had provided, while I, like some sinner come

14

to judgement, perched on a cushioned footstool. He was arrogant, so I waited. A man deeply impressed by himself, Master Theobald had only one uncertainty: why someone as important as himself had been chosen to question someone like me. He soon discovered the reason.

'Magister,' I began, 'why are you here? Why do you want to question me? On what authority?'

'My child . . .'

'I'm not your child.'

'My daughter . . .'

'I'm certainly not that, Magister, nor your sister, nor your mother.'

'Mistress . . .' Magister Theobald breathed in deeply, nostrils flaring, eyes rounded. 'According to the law—'

'According to canon law,' I interrupted, 'this is church land. I am a relict in a priory of the Franciscan order.'

'Why are you a recluse, Mathilde?' Theobald shifted his ground.

'Because I chose to be. Do you want to hear my confession?'

'Why, Mathilde, are you in God's grace?'

'If I am, I ask God to keep me there. If I am not, I ask him to return me there. Do you want to hear my confession?'

Magister Theobald moved uneasily. He became more formal.

'You are Mathilde de Clairebon, born near Bretigny?'

'You know I am.'

'You joined your uncle, Sir Reginald de Deynecourt, senior preceptor in the Order of the Temple. He was a physician general in Paris?'

'You know that too.'

'You acquired whatever medical knowledge you have—'

'You make it sound like an insult!'

'You did not attend a faculty of medicine?'

'My knowledge of medicine is as great as any practitioner. It is based on observation and treatment.' I smiled. 'Take yourself, Magister Theobald. You like claret, hence the vein streaks in your nose and cheeks. You sit uneasy on cushions and wince slightly when you move: piles? The veins in your arse are extended. You have difficulty at the stool. You should drink more water and eat fresh fruit and vegetables not smothered in some rich sauce. You have wax in your right ear and sometimes the catarrh, hence you find it difficult to hear. You act as if you are confident, yet if so, why are your fingernails so frayed? What do you want me to tell you, Magister? How juice extracted from a bucket full of snails covered in treacle and hung over a basin during the night will cure a sore throat?' I laughed. 'There are practitioners of physic who would recommend that. Or if you have the gout, take a young puppy all of one colour, cut him in half and lay one side hot, the flesh steaming, against the soreness? Or a field mouse, skinned and made into a small pie,

16

then eaten, its warm skin bound against the throat for nine days, will cure a cough? I can distil such a potion, though the cure will kill.'

Magister Theobald held up a hand. 'Mistress, you were in Paris when Philip le Bel destroyed the Templars?'

'Yes.'

'He destroyed your uncle?'

'Of course. I had to flee. My uncle thought the safest place was in the household of Philip IV's daughter Isabella. She was about to travel to England to marry her betrothed, Edward, Prince of Wales.'

'Were you safe?'

'Philip and his coven, Marigny, Nogaret and Plaisans, overlooked me until it was too late.'

'And you,' Magister Theobald pointed a finger, 'you waged war against them?'

'I had no choice, as I would against any man who threatened me.'

Magister Theobald pursed his lips at that.

'Do you believe the Templar curse?'

I stared back.

'Were you not helped by a former Templar?' Magister Theobald stared down at the small scrolls half concealed by the folds of his robe. 'Ah yes, that's his name: Bertrand Demontaigu – the priest-knight.'

I caught my breath. Just the mention of his name by another made me start.

'You loved him?'

'Yes,' I replied slowly. 'I say that because he is now beyond all temporal power.'

'He was a priest?'

'I loved him, Magister. Where is the sin, the crime in that?' I leaned forward. 'Have you ever loved, I mean truly loved?'

'I am a priest.'

'Where in scripture does it say that that stops you from loving?'

'A scholar,' Magister Theobald mocked. 'Mathilde, you should have entered religion!'

'I never left it.'

'Taken vows.'

'I have, as solemn as any sworn by you.'

'Mathilde, Mathilde.' Magister Theobald rose to his feet and walked across to stand over me. 'Why do you not speak to the king?'

'Is that why you are here, Magister, to learn what I know? To urge me to confess?'

'To confess?'

'Come, Magister.' I gestured with my fingers. He leaned down, and I whispered in his ear one petty hint about Isabella's great secrets. He drew away, pale, eyes all startled.

'I don't believe—'

'Oh do, my child,' I teased, 'believe me. If you told the king what I have just told you, you would not live to see the first Sunday of Advent next.' I shrugged. 'An unfortunate accident, a contagion or something you ate, squeezing itself down your throat and depositing in your belly a feast of toads that, as you die, will rumble like a fire blocked in a chimney.'

Magister Theobald backed away and sat down.

'I'm trying to protect you, Magister. Go back and report that I am as obdurate as ever.'

The king's advocate wiped the sheen of sweat from his face. 'The old queen,' he muttered, 'she babbled so much when she died.'

'Leave that!'

'One thing.' Magister Theobald drummed his fingers on the arm of his chair. 'The Poison Maiden – who was she?'

'Ah,' I smiled, getting to my feet, 'tell his Grace the Poison Maiden is not far from me, or indeed from him.'

Magister Theobald stared back, perplexed.

'My child,' I bowed, 'I have said enough.'

I left and returned to the sanctuary, where I knelt beside her tomb, cooling my hot face against the marble. I stared down the nave and thought of the Poison Maiden. It was time to return to my confession.

CHAPTER 1

The said [Peter Gaveston] was the closest and greatly loved servant of the young Edward.

Vita Edwardi Secundi

Winter's spite was spent. Candlemas had come and gone in a glow of light through dark sanctuaries, chancels and chantry chapels. Edward of England had scarcely been crowned a month, yet already the Great Lords, as they called themselves – Aymer de Valence, Earl of Pembroke; Henry de Lacy, Earl of Lincoln; Bohun of Hereford; Beauchamp of Warwick; and de Clare of Gloucester – were mustering for war. The roads and lanes into London surged with fighting men of every description. Archers dressed in quilted jerkins over homespun shirts, around their waists leather belts with scabbards for sword and dagger, their green serge leggings and crude ox-hide boots caked in mud. Their helmets and neck cloths glistened in the sheen of the spring rain, and against their shoulders were longbow staves, the precious twine concealed in a leather sleeve to protect it against the wet. Behind these marched masses of foot in their leather jerkins, heads and faces concealed by conical helmets with broad nose guards. Crossbowmen followed armoured in kettle hats and hauberks; men-at-arms marched in leather jacks and quilted gambesons, coats of scaled armour, the iron skullcaps on their heads laced beneath the chin. They all carried round shields or targes, in their belts shafted axes, clubs and daggers. All these troops streamed towards Westminster, the retinues of the lords who hoped to unfold their war banners in a blaze of arms: dragons, castles, chevrons, martlets, griffins, bears and lions of every colour. The troops mustered in the fields and wastelands around Westminster, impatient for their masters, conventicled in nearby St Peter's Abbey, to issue their defiance of the Crown.

Across the narrow road, protected by fortified gates and crenellated walls, lurked their intended victim: Edward of England, with his golden hair and olive skin, two yards in height, a prince of striking appearance. His finely etched face was made all the more remarkable by a straight nose, full lips and a generous mouth, and his slightly drooping right eye, a legacy from his father, gave him an enigmatic, mysterious look, as if he was constantly weighing what he saw and heard. As well he might. The Great Lords were demanding the arrest and trial of Edward's favourite, the man he called his bosom friend, his dear brother, a new

21

Jonathan to his David, the Gascon, Peter Gaveston. The Lords thought different. In their eyes Gaveston was the alleged offspring of a witch, a commoner unjustly exalted by the king to the earldom of Cornwall, a premier lordship of the kingdom, a public display that the favourite was the king's heart and soul. Gaveston had also been given in marriage Margaret de Clare, the king's own niece. He was allowed to display extravagant arms dominated by a gold-scarlet eagle. In the eyes of the Great Ones, Gaveston, despite his dark hair and splendid physique, adorned by costly robes of silk, velvet and damascene, was a cockatrice. He was compared to that fabulous two-legged dragon with a cock's head and face whose stare and breath were fatal to all it glared at. In a word, Gaveston was a blight on the kingdom. He was that mysterious, fabulous beast, with the head of a man and the body of a lion protected by porcupine quills and a scaly tail, which roamed the land dealing out death and devastation. He was a marined, a merman, neither one thing nor the other. The Lords wanted him dead. Resentful at his hold over the king, his elevation to power, his marriage, his wealth, his wit, not to mention his skill at arms, they were truly jealous of Gaveston. They wanted him gone and had come fully armed to the Parliament at Westminster to achieve that.

To strengthen their case, the Lords had summoned old Robert Winchelsea, Archbishop of

Canterbury, back from exile to sanctify their proceedings. The leading earls met the archbishop in the hallowed precincts of the abbey. They muttered behind their hands how this was God's work, that Gaveston was not only the offspring of a witch but a badling, a sodomite who had captivated the king's heart and trapped his body in sinful, unnatural lusts. Satan, they argued, lurked in the shadow of the Crown. Winchelsea, with his scrawny hair, bony face and eyes all animate ready to fight, was only too eager to play the role of the 'Prophet of Wrath in Israel'. He had swept into London, which he dismissed as 'a city without grace, having men without faith and women without honour', a veiled warning to the capital not to support their king.

Edward and Gaveston laughed when they heard that, but sobered swiftly enough. Winchelsea, exiled by the old king for his meddling ways, proclaimed himself ready for martyrdom, eager to follow in the steps of Becket, to be the vox populi, if not the vox dei – the mouthpiece of righteousness come to judgement. In the end, however, denunciation was one thing, war was another. No one dared draw the sword. If Edward unfolded his standard displaying the royal arms, to go to war against him was high treason to be adjudged immediately. So the Lords hesitated. What was to be done next? Edward and Gaveston retreated deep into the Palace of Westminster. A host of retainers and servants, whitesmiths, blacksmiths, coopers, jewellers, masons, tilers and craftsmen followed. These were joined by petty clerks of the household, those of the pantry, buttery and kitchen, not to mention the royal clerks of the wardrobe, exchequer and chancery as well as those from the courts of king's bench and common pleas. A packed throng of liveried royal servants protected by the Kernia, Gaveston's wild Irish mercenaries, together with royal troops, knight bannerets and a host of Welsh archers. All these took up close guard along the walls of the palace, at King's Bridge and Queen's Steps, as well as the Great Gate and the postern doors to the royal quarters. The abbey scaffold in nearby Gallows Lane became busy, swiftly adorned with the corpses of malefactors, footpads and foists who'd dared to creep close to the royal household eager for rich pickings. The king had vented his rage and frustration on such lawbreakers, whose corpses froze, drying hard in the cold spring air.

I have read the chronicle accounts for those opening months of Edward's reign. They all depict it as a time of bloody change. Philip IV ruled France. Pope Clement V sheltered in his palace at Avignon, feasting himself and his court of cardinals on swans, peacocks and boar meat, guzzling like parched men on the rich wines of the south. A time of change also. Death and Destruction, those two gaunt riders on their pale skeletal horses, were already emerging from the boiling mists of time. Death, as one chronicle declared, was a knight on horseback carrying a square shield, in the first quarter of which was depicted a grinning ape, indicating how, after his death, a man's executors laughed at him and spent his goods. In the second quartering was a lion, symbolising the ferocity of death. In the third, an archer signified its swiftness, and in the fourth was a scribe writing down all the sins to be judged before God's tribunal. Flood and foul weather blighted lives; Pride and Pestilence prepared their ambush. One monkish chronicle declared: 'God is angry. He will no longer hear us and, for our guilt, grinds even good men to dust.' According to another writer, the times were so dreadful, Antichrist himself was already born and had reached his tenth year, a boy of great beauty. Grisly, mysterious incidents were carefully recorded. The earth turned barren due to blood being spilt. Trees creaked after they had been used as gallows. Cliff-faces were scored with the claw-marks of Satan. There were storms and floods. Eclipses, shooting stars and signs in the heavens. Monstrous births and violent visitations. People ate the bread of sorrow and drank the waters of distress. Looking back, all I can say is that the preachers and the prophets of doom had it wrong. Matters were to turn much worse! Evil was burgeoning like a plum ripe to rottenness, and as with all mayhem, once released, it followed its own destructive course.

Edward and his lords were bent on confrontation. The king withdrew into the spacious grounds of the palace at Westminster, where he had built a splendid hall that he nicknamed 'Burgundy', laughingly calling himself the King of Burgundy, and recreating there his favourite childhood residence: those chambers above the gatehouse at King's Langley. Burgundy Hall was a stately, majestic manor house of costly stone and timber with a slate-tiled roof. It was built round a quadrangle and boasted a long hall with chambers above, and alongside, half-timbered, half-stone extensions above a maze of cellars. It was a veritable jewel with its oaken framework, the elaborately carved verge boards of the gables, the vein-like tracery of the windows, the slender pinnacle buttresses. It was as if the king wished to create his own make-believe world and hide from the rage seething around him. He, Gaveston, the queen and a shrunken group of royal supporters, led by the old king's general Hugh de Spencer of Glamorgan, sheltered there.

Edward and Gaveston played and waited, ignoring the gathering furies. In Scotland, Bruce threatened his northern shires. From Avignon, Clement V fulminated how the English king should harass the Order of the Temple to destruction as Philip of France had. Close by, a mere arrow shot away, the Lords decided to stay and take up residence in the sacred precincts of Westminster Abbey. Philip, scenting victory, the opportunity to turn Edward into his minion, re-entered the mêlée, dispatching his own envoys to England. They arrived mouthing peace but planning for war. A vicious brood: the Abbot of St Germain, a pompous nonentity, together with the French king's evil familiars, Guillaume de Nogaret, Guillaume de Plaisans and, prince amongst those serpents, Enguerrand de Marigny. These three demons, at their master's behest, had destroyed the Templars, browbeaten the papacy and were now determined to bring Edward of England under the ban. In the king's palace itself, hiding in the shadows, was Isabella la Belle, not yet fourteen, but still possessed with the mind of a veteran intriguer. A true daughter of her father, nevertheless Isabella hated him as the cause of her own mother Jeanne de Navarre's sudden and mysterious death, as well as for the abuse perpetrated on Isabella by her three brothers, those scions of Satan: Louis, Philippe and Charles. In public, she played of the role of her husband's enemy, united with her father in his dreams of a Capetian hegemony, of bringing all Europe and its rulers under his iron sceptre. She was publicly aggrieved at her husband, deeply resentful of Gaveston. Ah well, that was how the tongues wagged. In private, Isabella plotted her own path with me in her shadow, like an archer notches his bow as he hides behind the shield of another.

I was close to both queen and king. In truth, I had no choice. Both my mistress and I were of the king's mesnie, his household, members of his own private chamber. There was one other. The beat of my heart, the light of my life, the passion of my soul, Bertrand Demontaigu, his black hair lined with grey, his sallow face redeemed by the most beautiful eyes and courteous ways. A Templar priest, the son of a French knight and an English mother, Demontaigu, after the sudden, brutal destruction of his order, had also hidden away in the shadow of the queen's retinue, acting as one of her household clerks. His previous role as a messenger of the Temple had saved him from being marked and hunted down by Alexander of Lisbon and his Noctales. These were ferocious bounty-hunters dispatched through Europe by Philip of France and Clement V to pursue, capture and kill any surviving Templars. Demontaigu! Even now the very thought of him sends my blood fluttering. He made me feel whole and good. Above all he made me laugh, saying our relationship was one of autumn and spring, for he had reached his thirtieth summer whilst I was just past my twentieth. He and Isabella brought purpose to my life. I repaid both with undying loyalty, whatever their sins, whatever their faults. Yet that is what love does, surely? Blinds us only to the good.

The spring of 1308 was a time of acute danger, made even more so when the Poison Maiden emerged to make her sinister presence felt. How did it begin? Let me tell you as I would describe two knights preparing for the joust. They mount, armed and helmeted, their destriers paw the earth and snort, the tourney ground falls silent except for the jingle of mail and the clatter of arms. The trumpets shrill. The red cloth falls. The knights lower their visors, couch their lances and raise their shields. The warhorses move in an ominous rumble. The charge begins, slowly at first, then the heart quickens as the earth shakes and the combatants bear down on each other in a fight to the finish. So it was. I can only recall what is important, what pricks my memory. Think of walking down a dark passageway, stone-walled, hollow-sounding. You pause and look back. You see the darkness but your eye is drawn to the flickering torches, the glow of light they throw – so it was with my life, my time. Danger did not threaten at every heartbeat. I was usually immersed in a tedious list of mundane tasks: supervising the pantry, ensuring the cooks and fleshers bought good meat and fresh fish. I went down to the slaughterhouse to check that the quails, partridges and pheasants were properly prepared and cured. I ensured old rushes were burnt and the freshly cut sprinkled with herbs. The laundry room was also my responsibility: how the linen of both wardrobe and bedchamber was washed to freshness and properly stored in aumbries, coffers and chests. I dealt with petitions, a licence for a man to crenellate the walls of his manor house, protection for a merchant going abroad, pardons to outlaws who had committed crimes and were now willing to purge themselves by military service in Scotland, the grant of offices and benefices, safe conducts for alien merchants to travel safely from Dover. I managed the spicery accounts as well as those of both the buttery and pantry. Above all I dealt with a myriad of ailments, including those of my mistress, whose monthly courses always brought her pain and discomfort. I treated these with great burnet, marjoram and camomile. She also suffered from rashes, a legacy of upset humours when she was a child. I soothed these with soap water and special potions distilled from herbs. I also dealt with the ailments of others: catarrh, stomach cramps, cuts, bruises and injuries. In the most serious cases, or when in doubt, I would recommend a visit to the physicians at St Bartholomew's or St Mary's Bethlehem. I acted as Isabella's clerk in the queen's secret chancery, my quill pen cut to my liking; or, escorted by Demontaigu, as her confidential messenger to various parts of the city. I loved such occasions, sitting cowled and hooded in some London tavern, be it the Swan in Splendour, the Honeycorn, or the Bell of Jerusalem. I would chatter to Demontaigu like a child. He would listen carefully. Sometimes he would touch me lightly. I would respond. He rarely talked of his priesthood. Occasionally he mentioned his hunger for silence, for a normal, restful life away from the hurly-burly of court life. People took him to be what he was, a clerk in priestly orders. He would discreetly celebrate his

Jesus or morrow mass just after daybreak, when the bells of the palace and the abbey were clanging. I would kneel at a prie-dieu and stare at those hands grasping the singing bread or the sacred goblet. I'd bow my head and blush at my waking dreams of the night before. *Deus meus!* Tears sting my eyes. My heart grieves at the sheer loss, the thought of such bittersweet memories.

Nonetheless, the tourney was about to begin. The lists were ready, the knights emerging from the shadows, the cut and thrust of secret, bloody battle almost imminent. So it was that on the Eve of the Annunciation in the Year of Our Lord 1308, deep in the royal enclosure at Westminster Palace, murderous mayhem emerged on to the field of life. (I will not hurry, but describe it as it was.) On that bleak, cold day, Isabella and I were cloistered with the Queen Dowager Margaret, Isabella's aunt, sister of Philip IV, widow of Edward I of England. Margaret had been married to that great warlord for eight or nine years and borne him four children. The eldest of these would die most violently at Isabella's hands outside the gates of Winchester, squatting, chained like a dog, until a condemned felon, in return for a pardon, struck off his head. Edmund of Woodstock, Earl of Kent, the most handsome man in England, half-brother to a king, uncle to another, a prince of the blood, son of the great Edward and saintly Margaret, slaughtered like a pig! Who says the Furies do not pursue or that the sins of the father, or the mother, are not visited upon the next generation? Yet that was the path I was about to follow, blood-soaked and violent. Others walked with me: great lords, princes of the royal house, bishops and ladies, knights and generals, all brought down, lower than hell. But that was for the future.

On that Annunciation Eve, Isabella and I had to while away the hours as well as flatter the queen dowager. We sat on faldstools round the great-mantled hearth of the queen dowager's solar near the Painted Chamber in the Old Palace of Westminster. A harsh, cold day even though spring was three days old. A fire roared in the dark, vaulted hearth. The logs crackled red in the heat. The herbal pouches split to give off puffs of summer smells and drive away the iron-cold feel of winter. We shared a jug of hippocras, heating it with a fiery iron and mixing in nutmeg, whilst we plucked at crushed honey-coated sweetmeats from a mazer fashioned out of vine root which, the queen dowager had solemnly assured us, came from the Holy Land. I remember that mazer well: gilded with silver and displaying the Five Wounds of Christ against the IHS insignia. I sat staring at it whilst the flames roared, the charcoal braziers crackled and the torches, candles and lantern horns sent the shadows dancing, a fitting prologue to the horrid murders about to slip like a horde of ghosts into our lives.

At the time my mistress and I were utterly bored, though Isabella schooled her lovely features like a novice. She crouched, head slightly down, the folds of her gauze veil hiding her lustrous hair, her fur cloak, still clasped about her, slightly opened in the front to reveal a woollen dress of dark blue, its lace fringes resting on the fur-lined buskins protecting her feet. Next to her, Margaret, the queen dowager, was garbed like a nun in dark robes, her face and head framed by a pure white wimple. Around her gloved fingers were a pair of ave beads with gorget of silver and a gold cross. A serene face, cold as clay; those heavy-lidded eyes, square chin and bloodless lips recalled the stony features of Margaret's redoubtable brother. I always considered her face to be chiselled out of marble, and even then I wondered if her soul reflected her features. Margaret, the devout, the holy one! Even her drinking cup depicted scenes from the passion of Thomas à Becket. Around the rim, as Margaret had tediously told me on at least three occasions, were the pious words: *Of God's Blessed hand be He that taketh this cup and drinketh to me.* On the wall behind her was painted: *God who died upon the Rood. He bought us with His Blessed Blood upon that hardy tree.*

Oh yes, Margaret, the saint, the bore, the empty head. Ah well, I should have been more prudent and reflected on the adage: *Cacullus non facit monachum*: 'the cowl doesn't make the monk'. Or in her case, the wimple the nun! On a stool at the far side of Margaret sat the queen dowager's constant companion and kindred spirit, Margaret de Clare, sister of Gilbert, Earl of Gloucester, and wife to Peter Gaveston. An ill-matched pair surely, or, perhaps, one fashioned in heaven, for de Clare did not interfere in Gaveston's affairs. She was whey-faced, redeemed only by expressive eyes and an ever-petulant mouth. De Clare adored the queen dowager, and imitated her in every way, particularly her piety and her public passion for relics and pilgrimages. I deemed both of them pious simpletons, but then I was green in matters of the heart, whilst experience is the harshest teacher. Isabella secretly dubbed them 'the great Margaret and the lesser' or 'the Holy Margaret and the even holier'. She could mimic both to perfection: their sanctimonious expressions, dull looks and monotonous gabbling about the sanctity of a shard of shin bone.

On that particular day, despite her innocent looks and questioning blue eyes, Isabella had been teasing them both about the so-called glories of Glastonbury Abbey, where the bodies of King Arthur and Queen Guinevere had allegedly been found during the late king's reign, together with the magical sword Excalibur and the mystical Grail Cup of Christ. The two saintly Margarets (and I write as I saw at that moment of time) warbled like songbirds about visiting Glastonbury later in the spring and wondered if her grace would like to join them. My mistress, as she later informed me, bit back her screamed reply. Due to the Lords, she could scarcely leave Westminster whilst her household exchequer was empty; she simply lacked the silver to travel. Of course, as always, she behaved herself, winked at me and innocently asked if the revenues of the good abbey had greatly increased due to their miraculous discoveries. The queen dowager was on the verge of a new homily about the mystical rose bush at the abbey, a sprig she claimed sprouted from the staff of Joseph of Arimathea, when Guido the Psalter intervened. He and Agnes d'Albret were also of the queen dowager's entourage and were usually present whenever we met her. From the start I was wary of Agnes, a young woman just past her twentieth summer, tall and slim, a mop of fiery red hair framing a peaked white face with slanted green eyes and a pert, mischievous mouth. She was dressed in a high-collared tight-fitting kirtle of tawny sarcanet, and sat throughout the dowager's sermon studying me carefully, as well she might. She was a kinswoman of both the Abbot of St Germain and Marigny, who had just arrived in England and were lodged elsewhere in the abbey precincts. She seemed friendly enough, though she must have known about the deep rancour between myself and the French court.

Guido the Psalter acted differently. An apothecary, a leech, his real name was Pierre Bernard, a Parisian who'd allegedly left France due to an unfortunate incident at the Sorbonne when a magister was stabbed during a tavern brawl. Guido had fled for sanctuary to England, where he successfully petitioned the queen dowager for protection against her brother's law officers and won a place in her household. A most resourceful man, he was both minstrel and jongleur; Guido was also skilled in leechcraft, an apothecary learned in matters of physic. I had met him quite frequently since his arrival in England after the coronation of Isabella. He seemed a lively, merry soul, with his sensitive, smooth features and close-cropped black hair. I was fascinated by his long fingers, white as lily stalks. Guido claimed he could feel pain from a patient merely by pressing his fingertips against the flesh. I did not believe him. Yet he was no jackanapes or counterfeit man. He openly mocked superstitions such as the power of the emerald being such a protection against poison that if a toad looked at it, its eyes would crack. He also quietly confessed that the queen dowager's interest in relics and elaborate pilgrimages were tedious in the extreme. Oh yes he did, clever man! Ah well, the scriptures rightly say, 'Judge not and ye shall not be judged.' I say, judge and he shall be truly surprised! On that day Guido caught my eye, winked, and when his mistress paused in her description of the mystical rose of Glastonbury, swiftly intervened.

'I have an even more wondrous story,' he declared, 'about a land inhabited by pickled fish-men, an eel-faced, beetle-browed race, very warlike, who live on raw flesh. They are opposed by mermen stoats, who, in their upper parts, resemble men, and in their lower, weasels—'

Abruptly the door was flung open, and Edward and Gaveston, swathed in heavy cloaks, swept into the chamber, furred hoods pulled back, their hair laced with rain. Both strode across, pushing their way through to the fire. They were followed by Hugh de Spencer of Glamorgan, a strange-looking individual with his receding hair tied in a queue at the nape of his neck, his ruddy face unshaven, his deep-set eyes glaring furiously around, mouth all aggressive as if expecting to confront the king's enemies there and then. Old de Spencer! I was there when they hacked his body to bits outside Bristol and fed it to starving dogs. Thomas, Earl of Lancaster, the king's cousin, followed, silent like a shadow, his pinched face tense under tangled hair. When Lancaster was taken out to execution, little boys threw snowballs at him. However, that was all for the future. I promised to tell the story as it unfolded from start to finish. I suppose it all began then, when the king strode into that chamber. We rose to greet him. He unbuckled his cloak, let it fall to the ground and thrust his back-side towards the fire.

'The royal arse,' he declared, bowing at both the queen dowager and Isabella, 'is frozen as hard as a bishop's heart!'

Gaveston slipped quietly on to the vacated stool next to his wife, his beautiful face wreathed in that infectious smile. Gaveston was truly handsome, his hair neatly cut, his face oiled and sensitive. He was graceful in all his gestures. He also bowed at the two queens and impishly blew a kiss in my direction before seizing his wife's silk-mittened fingers and lifting them to his lips even as he patted her affectionately on the thigh. Agnes, Guido and myself immediately withdrew from the circle but the king, still rubbing his backside, beckoned imperiously at us.

'No, no, Mathilde, and you, Guido. My ladies.' He bowed once again at the two queens, who sat staring up at him. I caught the questioning look of adoration in Margaret's eyes, as if completely bemused by her royal stepson. Edward sniffed noisily. 'Guido, Mathilde, I have need of you. Langton is in the Tower, he has an ulcerated leg. He mistrusts the leeches and once again has asked for you, Master Guido. I have agreed, but,' he continued, right eye almost closed, 'to show my deep concern, Mathilde will also attend on him. Thus my Lord Walter Langton, Bishop of Coventry and Lichfield, cannot whine to his fellow bishops that he has been ill treated.'

A short while later myself, Guido and Bertrand Demontaigu left King's Steps aboard a royal barge pulled by eight liveried oarsmen. A page stood in the prow tending the lantern horn and blowing noisily on a trumpet to warn off other craft. We sat in the stern shielded by a canopy emblazoned with the royal arms. Above us a blue, scarlet and gold pennant snapped in the breeze, proclaiming that this barge was on royal service. Demontaigu sat muffled in his cloak. He kept his distance as if he was a relative stranger, the royal household clerk he pretended to be, acting as if resentful at being plucked from his comfortable chancery chamber for this cold journey along a mist-hung Thames. He was armed with sword and dagger. These he placed across his knees, grasping them close, then glanced quickly at me, those lustrous dark eyes full of merriment. He murmured that famous prayer of travellers and pilgrims:

'Jesus welcome you be,
In form of bread as I see thee,
Jesus' holy name.
Protect us this journey.
From sin and shame.'

Guido heard this and laughed softly. He said he feared neither God nor man. On reflection, he was telling the truth. He was certainly dressed for that journey like a popinjay, in a puffed jacket and a richly embroidered cloak, gifts from the queen dowager, who appeared to have more than a tender regard for him. Demontaigu, as if tired of listening to Guido's praise of his mistress, asked about Langton and why he was imprisoned in the Tower.

'Hatred,' Guido replied. 'Walter Langton, Bishop of Coventry and Lichfield, was the old king's treasurer. Time and again he tried to rein in the spending of Edward when he was Prince of Wales. He often had violent confrontations with the prince over his lavish expenditure as well as his friend-ship with Gaveston. When the old king died,' Guido pulled a face, 'Langton fell.'

'Even though he is a bishop?' Demontaigu asked.

'He could be pope of the whole world!' Guido replied drily. 'The new king hates him. Langton was stripped of dignity, wealth and office and committed to the Tower.'

'Why?' I asked, staring into the bank of mist that swirled like a host of ghosts across our barge.

'The king regards him as a meddler who will side with the Lords. Langton is fiercely opposed to Gaveston.'

'But so are others.' I wiped the river spray from my face.

'True.' Guido nodded. 'The other reason is treasure. The king's exchequer is empty. Rumour has it that Langton owns over fifty thousand pounds of silver, besides a hoard of gold and precious jewels. Some of it is Templar treasure, lodged with him by the order before it fell. The king has asked for this. Langton claims such wealth is a myth, that he is poor as a friar. Searchers from the royal exchequer have ransacked his properties but cannot find any trace. Hence my lord Langton stays in the Tower until he remembers where he has put his money.'

Guido leaned forward and shouted at the captain of the guard to make more speed. I stared across the water. The Thames ran dark and strong; a sharp, biting wind forced my head down but it also stirred the mist to break and reveal the other craft along that busy river. Oystercatchers, fishing smacks, barges and boats full of produce thronged the waterways as they headed for the wharves of Queenshithe, Garlickhithe and Timberhithe. Cogs from Bordeaux, sails furled, manoeuvred to dock at the wine wharf, whilst a flotilla of powerful war cogs, flying the colours of the Hanse, made their way up to the German enclosure at the Steelyard. The air reeked of oil, fish, tar and spice. These odours mingled with the stench from the great loads of refuse, excrement, offal, dead animals and rotting food disgorged into the Thames by the gong barges as well as the city rivers of the Fleet and Walbrook. Now and again the dangers of the time manifested themselves. Great high-sided war barges flying the various-coloured pennants of the Lords and packed with men-at-arms and archers, made their way ominously down to Westminster.

'God preserve us,' whispered Guido, gesturing at them. 'Lincoln, Pembroke, Winchelsea and the rest are determined on Gaveston's trial. My mistress has interceded, mediated, pleaded.' He sighed noisily. 'It is of little use.'

CHAPTER 2

Walter Langton, bishop . . . formerly Treasurer
of the Lord King of England.

Vita Edwardi Secundi

Guido fell quiet as the bells of myriad churches along the north bank of the Thames – St Peter the Little, St Martin, All Hallows the Great and others – tolled the Angelus. We passed Downgate. Above us reared the gloomy mass of London Bridge, its rails adorned with the severed heads of Scottish chieftains who had been hanged, drawn and quartered at St Paul's or Smithfield. Pickled and preserved, they were displayed as a warning to other rebels. The arches of the bridge yawned like the cavernous mouth of some great beast. The water surged faster, full and furious between the starlings. The captain of the barge shouted orders; one last pull and the oars came up and we shot like an arrow through the watery darkness. I sat tense and only opened my eyes when we entered calmer waters and glimpsed the brooding walls, turrets and gatehouse of the Tower.

We left our barge at a grim-looking quayside and made our way under the massive Lion Gate, across drawbridges spanning a stinking moat and through the Barbican, which reeked of the animal smells from the royal menagerie. A close, narrow place, with blind walls and cobbled pathways, all under the watchful eyes of royal troops who manned the crenellations, towers and gatehouses. Time and again we were stopped as we proceeded deeper into the royal fortress. We crossed the outer bailey, busy with men-at-arms wheeling out and readying the great engines of war, the catapults and trebuchets a sure sign of troubled times. At the entrance of the inner bailey we met Sir John de Cromwell, the stone-faced constable. He was dressed in half-armour, clearly anxious about the crisis at Westminster but too politic to ask. He was the king's officer, and he told us in a blunt, terse fashion how his task was to ensure that the Tower remained loyal to the Crown. He took us across the rain-sodden green, where huge ravens and hooded crows prodded at the ground with cruel yellow beaks, and up into the four-square Norman keep.

Langton's chamber, a cavernous cell with a small ante-chamber, lay next to the Chapel of St John the Evangelist. It was a well-furnished room with lancet windows, some shuttered, others screened with horn paper. Turkey rugs warmed the floor and large paintings hung on hooks to offset the grimness of the walls. One in particular caught my attention, *The Parade of the Seven Vices led by Pride*: a mighty bishop stood admiring himself in a mirror held up for him by a grotesque-faced horned demon. I wondered if Gaveston had insisted that the painting be placed prominently beside the good bishop's bed. Langton himself looked unabashed by his imprisonment or his surroundings.

The room was stifling hot. A fire blazed in the hearth; braziers and chafing dishes crackled and spluttered. Langton, stretched out on the great bed, was dressed in a simple gown, a thick fur cloak over his shoulders, legs and feet already bared. He was impatient for treatment. Guido and I immediately scrutinised the angry-looking red ulcer. The open sore looked clean, with little infection. I recommended it be washed in salt and wine, then treated with crushed ale-hoof or ground ivory as well as powdered moss mixed with grains of dried milk. Guido, surprisingly, as physicians rarely concur, offered to prepare the recipe and asked the waiting Cromwell to bring the necessary ingredients from the Tower stores. I stood back and studied Langton. A burly, red-faced man with popping eyes and a codfish mouth, he had a swollen belly, fat, heavy thighs and short, muscular arms. I found it difficult to imagine him in episcopal robes. Yet for all his weight, he was quick and lithe in his movements. He turned and stared closely up at me,

I caught the cunning in his soul, the scrutiny of a sharp, twisting mind.

'You must be,' he scratched his thinning grey hair, 'Isabella the queen's little shadow.'

The statement proved how much he knew about the doings of the court.

'Give my most loyal greetings and rich blessings to your mistress, girl.'

'I will, Father,' I retorted. 'As I give you hers and mine.'

Langton stared at me, threw his head back and laughed raucously. Then he flapped his heavy hands, beating the coverlet either side of him.

'Very, very good,' he chuckled. 'Well, girl, let Master Guido do his business, although your soft touch,' he leered at me, 'would also be welcome.'

'Master Guido's hands are just as soft.' I bowed and left Guido to his ministrations. Servants arrived with mortar and pestle, a bowl of hot water and phials of powder from the Tower stores. Guido tactfully walked me away.

'My lord bishop believes in the natural order of things, Mathilde. You are young and female.'

'If he wants,' I whispered back, 'I can go into London and secure the services of a sixty-year-old physician who might prescribe *oleum cataellorum.*'

Guido glanced quizzically at me.

'Live cats boiled in olive oil,' I murmured. 'It won't cure him, possibly kill him, but will keep his honour intact.'

Guido spluttered with laughter. I patted him

gently on the shoulder and walked out of the antechamber. When we had first entered, I had noticed the clerk cowled and hunched at the chancery desk. He was still busy poring over some manuscripts in the light of capped candles. Demontaigu had placed his war belt on a stool nearby and apparently gone into the Chapel of St John. From the chamber behind me Langton's voice bellowed at Guido. I was about to join Demontaigu when the hooded figure turned abruptly. A peaked white face peeped out of the hood, deep-set eyes and bony features dominated by a nose as hooked as a scythe.

'Mistress,' his lips hardly moved, 'I understand you are from the king. I must go back with you.' The words came more as a hiss than a whisper.

'Must, sir?' I drew closer, aware of my voice echoing. 'Why must?'

'My name is Chapeleys,' the man gabbled. 'I am a clerk.' He glanced quickly at the chamber door, tilting his head towards Langton's bellowing. 'I am his clerk but I am no prisoner here. I must see the king. I have information.'

I gestured towards the other door. He followed me out into the gloomy recess.

'Why?' I asked. 'Why now?'

'It is urgent,' Chapeleys insisted. He drew so close I could smell his fear. 'I am no prisoner,' he repeated. 'I can come and go as I wish. I must see the king.'

I glanced back at the half-open door; the glow of

candlelight seemed to have followed us. I became acutely aware of the massy grey stone, the hollow, empty feel of that forbidding place. Chapeleys must have eavesdropped on my conversation with Langton and decided to seize his opportunity. The bishop was the king's enemy, and therefore, by implication, mine. I glanced at Chapeleys' peaked face.

'Why are you so frightened?'

'I have information,' Chapeleys retorted. 'His grace must know it.'

I pointed to the stairwell. 'If you are free to go, monsieur, then go, take your cloak. You have money?'

Chapeleys replied that he had.

'Go to the Palace of Westminster,' I declared. 'Let no one see you. You know St Benedict's Chapel in the Old Palace?'

Chapeleys nodded.

'Stay near the Lady Altar,' I insisted. 'I shall meet you there immediately on my return.'

Chapeleys scurried about, and a short while later hastened out cloaked and hooded. I glimpsed the poignard pushed into the sheath on his waist and the small leather chancery pouch that he raised before slipping down the stone staircase. I stood and listened. Langton was still bellowing at Guido. I walked into the Chapel of St John, lit by a host of candles glowing around the statue of the Evangelist. Their flickering light illuminated a grisly wall-painting of St John being boiled alive, though he emerged unscathed from his torments. Demontaigu was kneeling before the statue of the Evangelist, hands clasped, head down. I went over and joined him.

'*Mon coeur.*' My hand brushed his.

'How is Langton?' He turned.

I shrugged. 'Another fat shepherd bemoaning his lot.'

Demontaigu smiled. I quickly told him about Chapeleys. He put a finger to his lips and drew me deep into the shadows on the other side of the statue. For a while he just crouched staring into the darkness.

'Mathilde,' he turned, 'you called me *mon coeur*; so I am, as you are mine.'

'Even though you are a priest?' I teased, blinking back the tears.

'What I am, Mathilde, is not what I feel. To be close to you is to be . . .' He paused.

'Loved?' I asked, aware of my question echoing around that cavernous chamber, its juddering light bringing the frescoes to life.

'Loved!' he agreed. 'To be with you is to feel a fullness I have never experienced before. Oh yes,' he winked, 'I have said enough.' He grasped a tendril of my hair. 'Sometimes, Mathilde, I believe in nothing except you. You are my God, my religion.' He stroked my cheek with a finger then his hand dropped away. 'Oh Mathilde, I know that I am also a priest, a Templar whose beloved order has been destroyed. I and my companions are being hunted

48

down like rats in a barn. A year ago we were the glory of Europe; now the kings of the earth have turned against us. No, listen, Mathilde.' He brushed aside any interruption. 'Alexander of Lisbon and his Noctales are back in England. They act on the authority of the pope; Philip of France has seen to that. They hunt not only us, but our treasure, our relics. For now, Mathilde, don't be anxious, I am safe. I have explained that being a *nuntius*, a messenger of my order, I rarely stay in one place long enough for Philip's agents to acquaint themselves with me. Others are not so fortunate; they must keep to the shadows.' He glanced quickly over my shoulder. 'You also know that when we can, we strike back. Now one of our serjeants, a Frenchman named Jean Ausel, and others have arrived in this country to wreak vengeance. Ausel is an assassin, a skilled killer, a warrior. He also searches for our treasure, some of which – indeed, a great deal of which,' Demontaigu added bitterly, gesturing at the door, 'was held by Langton before he fell. If Ausel were here, Mathilde, he would kill Langton. Now Chapeleys wishes to flee. I wonder if he knows something about the lost treasure.'

'Bertrand,' I asked, a nameless fear almost choking my breath, 'what is going to happen?'

'I cannot say, Mathilde,' he replied hoarsely, 'but Chapeleys is a symptom of the times. Men are choosing sides. Langton has chosen his. If he was free he would go along with Winchelsea and the rest. This business at Westminster, the king and his lords, they spin like two hawks locked in flight and neither can break free. The king will have to go to war, yet he has no strength. Gaveston could be arrested and killed, Edward would never let such a matter rest. Meanwhile Philip of France is meddling furiously. We still have friends close to Philip's secret chancery. They claim Philip intends to bring about a revolution in England.'

He shook his head at my exclamation.

'The French king is casting his net far and wide. Rumours shed no light, but gossip from Philip's secret chancery claims that he is using someone called the Ancilla Venenata.'

'The Poison Maiden?' I exclaimed.

Bertrand lifted his hand. I listened. The faint hum of conversation had died. We clambered quickly to our feet. I left Demontaigu in the chapel and returned to Langton's chamber. Guido had finished and was washing his hands at the lavarium just inside the doorway. Langton was making himself comfortable on the bed. I quietly prayed that he would not call for Chapeleys, but he was more concerned with his goblet of wine. Guido dried his hands, turned and bowed. Langton fluttered his fingers and we were gone.

Cromwell and a group of archers escorted us back down through the Lion Gate. The constable made his swift farewells and we walked on to the quayside. The afternoon was drawing on. Stinking, vulgar gusts of smoke billowed across from the nearby tanning sheds. Assayers of the Fish were arguing with oystermen; these had brought in their catches and were waiting to unload baskets on to the quayside. The assayers, however, insisted that they check the baskets to ensure that the oysters were fresh and not the remains of the previous day's haul. The oystermen were furious in their own defence.

A line of fleshing carts was also off-loading supplies, messy hunks of freshly slaughtered meat. Blood swilled across the cobblestones, and the butchers had to fight off a pack of hungry dogs as well as a crowd of beggars who scrambled on all fours hunting for scraps. River pirates, four in number, were kneeling on the edge of the quayside, nooses around their necks. An undersheriff bellowed out their crimes to a crowd of curious bystanders as a Crutched Friar, hand raised in blessing, moved from man to man to give absolution. I caught the words *ad aeternam vitam* – 'to eternal life'. The undersheriff heartily agreed with this. The friar had scarcely finished when the red-faced law officer simply kicked each of the condemned men over the edge of the quayside. The drop to the water below was long; the nooses around the prisoners' necks tightened brutally. I could hear the strangled gasps and groans as the undersheriff bellowed how the corpses would hang for three turns of the tide and would not be released for burial until then. As we continued to push our way through the throng, a carrying voice caught our attention. Demontaigu paused and whirled round.

'Hurry if you wish,' the voice bellowed. 'Listen, sons of Esau, *vilior est humana caro quam pellis ovina* – man's flesh is more worthless than sheepskin.'

A preacher dressed in garish rags advanced through the throng towards us. He was of medium height, hair cut close about a lean, sun-darkened face. Beside him scampered a hideous beggar on all fours, wooden slats fastened to his knees, one more in each hand, his filthy face half hidden by matted hair.

'Know ye,' the preacher paused before us and pointed at the beggar, 'how low he is, yet when a man dies, he is lower than this: his nose grows cold, his face turns white, his nerves and brain break, his heart splits in two. Oh so repent! If not today, then tomorrow at the darkening hour. Go to church with all your brethren. Be not hanged like Judas! Confess your sins!' The preacher swept away, the beggar clattering beside him.

Guido muttered some witticism and hastened down the river-stained steps to the waiting barge.

'Ausel has delivered his message,' Demontaigu whispered.

I glanced at him in puzzlement.

'Tomorrow,' Demontaigu murmured, 'around Vespers, the brothers will meet at the Chapel of the Hanged.' He would say no more. We hurried down and climbed into the barge. The ropes were cast off and we made our way back to Westminster.

The journey was uneventful. Master Guido made us laugh with his mimicry of Langton – so sharp and accurate I almost forgot about Chapeleys. Langton's man was a chancery clerk, so the guards would admit him into the palace precincts. To be sure, Westminster Palace has changed; it is always changing, and that is the problem. New buildings, old buildings, wings added to this or that. Little wonder the king had built Burgundy Hall, his self-contained manor house. Some of the palace buildings dated back to the Conqueror's time and even before that. A warren of dark winding passageways, outside staircases, makeshift bridges and countless outhouses ranged around yards and gardens. A host of names described this cluster of buildings, which extended further than a large village: the Pastry Yard, the Paved Passage, the Royal Buttery, the Privy Kitchen, the Inner Court, the Outer Court, the Fish Court, the Fleshers' Court, the Boulevard, the Vintners' Ward: a maze of buildings, baileys, out-houses, chancery and exchequer offices. I found it bewildering. Demontaigu, however, had carefully studied the tangled spread. He knew its secret ways and forgotten postern doors because, as he explained, a fugitive like himself must always be prepared to flee. Such words chilled me. I asked him about Ausel, but he shook his head and led me across a garden, still frozen hard, in through a sombre-looking doorway, down a dark passageway, up a staircase and into the gloomy Chapel of St Benedict.

The chapel was no more than a square vaulted room, where flickering sconce torches illuminated the wall paintings, most of which were of birds and symbols from Scripture: the phoenix, the pelican, the mermaid. I recall one painting: an owl mobbed by magpies, an allegory on how the idle busybodies and gossips of this world mock wisdom. I wondered if Chapeleys was a wise man. The small chancel was hidden in gloom, but the Lady Chapel to the right glowed in candlelight. Chapeleys was sitting there on a stool, staring up at a statue of the Virgin depicted as the Queen of Heaven embracing the Holy Infant. As soon as he saw us, he leapt to his feet and shuffled out of the half-light like some timorous mouse. He looked askance at Demontaigu until I introduced him as one of the queen's clerks.

'I must see the king, I must see the king!' Chapeleys glanced around at the silhouettes dancing against the walls. A rat scuttled across the chipped tiled floor. Fingers to his lips, he moaned and clutched the chancery pouch more tightly, as if it was a talisman against the menacing gloom. I could not calm him or make sense of the clammy dread that held him fast. I explained that he could not see the king immediately – it was the Eve of the Annunciation and that night Edward intended to feast and celebrate in the great hall, a gesture of friendship towards the Great Lords and the French envoys. In truth, it was a mere sop to prolong matters even further.

'Yes, yes.' Chapeleys nodded. 'What then?'

'You can stay with me,' Demontaigu declared. He was studying Chapeleys curiously as if assessing his worth. 'You are Langton's clerk?'

'Of course I am!'

'His treasure,' Demontaigu took a step forward, 'you know where his treasure is?'

Chapeleys would have scuttled away if I hadn't grasped his arm.

'Monsieur,' I gestured with my hand for Demontaigu to stand back, 'the questions my friend is asking will be repeated when you meet the king. His grace will demand answers. But for the moment, no more questions.'

Chapeleys seemed comforted. He followed us out of the chapel and down into an empty court-yard. We crossed the grounds, up into a wing of the Old Palace where Demontaigu lodged.

'It's safe here.' Demontaigu, breathing heavily as we reached the top of the stairs, pointed down the ill-lit passageway. 'My chamber is in the corner. It was once part of the royal quarters, so the door is secured by bolts and lock.'

Chapeleys appeared reluctant.

'There is no other place,' I explained. 'You will be safe. I swear that, Master Chapeleys.'

At last he agreed, and Demontaigu unlocked his chamber. The door was heavy, reinforced with iron studs and metal clasps; the hinges were of thick, hard leather. The lock, probably fashioned by a skilled London craftsman, was fitted in the door so the key could be turned from both the outside and the inside. Demontaigu locked it behind us and pulled the bolts across, then stood back, aware of how he must not frighten this cowed clerk any further.

'Look, sir!' I pleaded. 'You will be safe.'

Chapeleys stared around Demontaigu's chamber. In the poor light, it looked like a monastic cell, the walls lime-washed, a crucifix hanging above the cot-bed, the windows all shuttered. Demontaigu opened two of these whilst I took a tinder and lit the capped candles and lantern horn. Chapeleys went round patting the wall, even checking the shutters; finally he moved into the far recess. Demontaigu's chamber was unique. It stood on a corner, and in one wall was a small window-door about five feet high and a yard across. In former times it must have been used to draw up supplies from carts waiting in the yard below. Near this a great iron clasp driven into the wall held one end of a coil of rope that could be used to escape from the chamber if a fire broke out. Chapeleys satisfied himself that the window-door was barred and bolted, then came back and sat on a stool, staring around. He still clutched his chancery bag. I was tempted to ask him what it contained, but the man was sorely affrighted.

Demontaigu left, saying he would bring some bread, cheese and a jug of wine. Chapeleys kept to his own musings as I walked around. I sat on the bed, stared at the crucifix, then across at the chancery desk and its high-backed chair beneath one of the windows. Everything was tidy: no parchments, nothing out of place. I went across and lifted the lid of a chest. Inside there were some scrolls and books. I picked one up, a beautifully covered psalter, but hastily put it back, feeling guilty at such intrusion.

The chamber was stark and very austere; apart from the crucifix, nothing decorated the walls. The drapes on the bed were neat, the bolsters carefully placed. On a small table beside the bed was a cup, a candlestick and a night light; on a stool near the door more jugs and cups. Demontaigu was both a priest and a soldier, and the chamber reflected this. Yet it wasn't cold; there was something warm and welcoming about it, safe and secure.

Demontaigu returned. I had bolted the door behind him, and as I now drew these back, Chapeleys jumped to his feet as if expecting a horde of armed men to invade the room. Demontaigu made him sit at the table and poured him a goblet of wine; he even cut his bread and cheese, treating him as tenderly as a mother would a frightened child. I watched carefully. At first Chapeleys was reluctant to eat, but at last he took a generous swig of wine and seemed to relax. Demontaigu pushed a brazier closer to him.

'Listen, man.' Demontaigu crouched beside Chapeleys, hand resting on his arm. 'You may sleep here. If you must,' he gestured at the dagger still pushed in Chapeleys' belt, 'carry that close. Once we leave, do not open that door to anyone except myself or someone we send. Do you understand?'

Chapeleys, his mouth full of bread and cheese, nodded.

'I will see the king?' he spluttered.

'Tomorrow morning after the Jesus mass,' I reassured him.

Chapeleys, a little more comforted, undid his cloak and let it fall over the back of the chair. Demontaigu followed me to the door.

'I must go,' I said, staring up at him. 'My mistress waits. We must prepare for the banquet tonight. You will come?'

'I am one of the household,' he replied smilingly. 'I must be there. I will settle this anxious soul, then return to my chancery office.' He lifted my hand, kissed it and opened the door, and I slipped out into the cold darkness. I made a mistake that night. I thought Chapeleys was safe. In fact he was no more than a condemned man, waiting for execution to be carried out.

The banquet later that evening was a splendid affair. Edward had agreed to it at the request of the queen dowager.

'On that evening,' he proclaimed, 'all animosity and hostility will be set aside. We will entertain both the French envoys and the leading lords to a splendid feast in the great dining hall at Burgundy.'

I spent the time before the banquet helping my mistress to prepare for it. Isabella was determined to look magnificent. She did, in a gown of white satin decorated with roses, a crimson girdle around her waist, a golden chaplet of silver lilies with a net of gold sewn with pearls over her magnificent blond hair. She and her husband, also gorgeously attired in a gown of blanched damask embroidered with golden lions, led the principal guests into the hall. Behind them strolled Gaveston, dressed in purple and white silk, holding the hand of his wife Margaret. He bowed to the left and the right as if he was the most favoured person on earth. The rest followed: Queen Dowager Margaret in a high-necked dress of dark green, a white veil framing her prim features; behind her, the principal lords, Lancaster, Lincoln, Pembroke and Hereford, clustered around Robert de Winchelsea, who was garbed in plain brown robes as if he wished to proclaim his austerity and asceticism to all. The Grande Chambre of Burgundy Hall was ablaze with light from hundreds of beeswax candles fixed in their spigots and holders. A range of great Catherine wheels, lowered on pulleys from the raftered ceiling, their rims holding a host of more candles, provided further light. The walls were covered with tapestries and hangings depicting lions and eagles, clear homage to the king and Gaveston, in gold, green, violet and red, whilst silver crowns and golden leopards intermingled with painted scenes from the great romance of Tristan and Isolde. At the top of the Chambre, the royal table on the long high dais was covered by a gorgeous canopy of cloth of gold fringed with silver tassels. The table itself was sheeted with ivory-coloured damask. On this the silver and jewel-encrusted goblets, cups, mazers, bowls and jugs shimmered brilliantly around a magnificent salt cellar carved in the shape of a castle and studded with precious stones. On either side of the dais were ranged two other tables similarly adorned, with a fourth completing the square.

To the left of the tables a fierce fire roared in a huge, elegantly carved hearth. At the far end of the Grande Chambre, above a moulded wooden screen, a loft housed the royal musicians, who, with lyre, fife, harp, tambour and other instruments, played soft melodious tunes. These were soon drowned by the blast of trumpets announcing the beginning of the banquet. Winchelsea intoned the grace, bestowing his 'Benedicite' in a peevish voice. The trumpets blared again and the royal cooks paraded into the hall carrying the main dish, a huge boar's head, its flared nostrils and curving tusks ringed and garnished with rosemary and bay. While the cooks circled the tables, a boy in the music loft carolled the famous invitation:

'The boar's head in splendour I bring,
With garlands and herbs as fresh as the spring,
So I pray you all to help me sing
And be as merry as birds on the wing.'

The feasting began. Napkins of white linen worked in golden damask and decorated with flowers, knots and crowns were shaken loose. Cups glittering with jasper, agate, beryl or chalcedoni were brimmed from the finest casks of Gascony wines. The fluted, silver-edged glasses set before each guest were filled with sweet wines such as vernage and osey. Dish after dish streamed from the kitchens: white broth with almonds, leg of mutton in lemons, capons in deuce, aloes of beef. The king intended to impress his opponents with this display of royal lavishness. The 'only blemish in the cream', to quote the old proverb, were certain rank smells and fetid odours plaguing the galleries and passageways of Burgundy Hall. I had also noticed these, whilst just before the feast, Isabella had complained loudly about them. She rightly declared that they had been noticeable for the last three days, and insisted that the easement chambers, latrines, sewers and garderobes be cleaned and purged.

The Grande Chambre had been specially perfumed against this, but other matters soon demanded my attention. I sat at the table facing the dais and watched the drama being played out. Edward, his golden hair now crowned with a jewelled chaplet, was deep in conversation with Gaveston on his right. On his left, Isabella sat like a beautiful statue, staring unseeingly down the hall, playing the role of the vulnerable, neglected wife to perfection. Next to her the two saintly Margarets were passing something between them. They lifted their hands in unison as if carolling the Alleluia. I quickly surmised they had found a new relic. The French envoys had been separated and placed amongst the great English lords. I recognised the portly Abbot of St Germain. He had the balding head and shiny face of an overweight cherub. I was more interested in my enemies, led by Marigny, lean of face and red of hair. Even from where I sat, I could almost catch his cynical glance, those lips ever ready to curl in derision. Then the other two demons: Nogaret the lawyer, the constant smile on that bloated bag of a face belied by the pursed lips and contemptuous eyes; and next to him Plaisans, Nogaret's alter ego, an angry-faced man who reminded me of a mastiff with his jowly jaws and aggressive mouth. The rest I knew by sight. Winchelsea the Prophet, with his lean face, sunken cheeks and darting eyes, sat next to Lancaster and Despencer, whilst Lincoln, a white-haired and pleasant-faced courtier, listened intently to Nogaret and Plaisans. I glimpsed Marigny lean back and snap his fingers. A shadow deeper than the rest stepped forward and filled the Viper's goblet. I recognised the dark, handsome face of Alexander of Lisbon, leader of the Noctales. Dressed in black like a priest for a requiem, Alexander apparently also served as the Viper's cup-bearer. I smiled to myself. Marigny apparently trusted no one! I glanced down my own table to see if Demontaigu had also glimpsed his enemy, but he was deep in conversation with a servitor. I wondered about the meeting planned for the morrow at the Chapel of the Hanged.

'You are not eating, mistress?'

I turned. Agnes d'Albret was smiling at me. She pointed to my bowl of white almond, the silver trancher with its strips of beef. I grasped the silver-edged knife and cut a slice.

'I am glad I sit next to you,' simpered Agnes, determined on making conversation. She touched the red pimples at the side of her mouth. I recommended camphor and vinegar mixed with celandine water. 'Wash three times a day,' I smiled, 'and keep your face free of powders and unguents; they pollute the skin.' Agnes was clever. She used her petty ailments to draw me into conversation about my knowledge of physic, my days in France, as well as my service with Isabella, who, whenever I glanced up, still sat as if carved out of marble whilst her husband roistered with Gaveston. The lesser courses were served. I was prudent about what I drank, as was Agnes, who, in mocking tones, speculated on the king's problems and his love for Gaveston. I kept my own counsel. I recognised Agnes to be a shrewd and subtle soul hiding behind a constant smile while she watched and judged. A scholarly mind as well: she could comment knowledgeably on *Tristan and Isolde* whilst referring to the wonders of Friar Bacon's *Opera Maioria* and his reputation as a possible sorcerer.

I was relieved when, just before the frumenty was served, jesters and tumblers appeared: those *joculatores*, small dwarves, male and female, whom Edward and Gaveston loved. These cavorted around the hall, jumping and tumbling, whistling, singing and farting raucously. They introduced themselves as Henry the Horny, Matilda Make-love, Griscot the Groper and Mago the Mewler. These *minstrelli* – little servants – could do what they wanted. They aped Winchelsea's pious walk, one standing on the shoulders of the other, and, just as the archbishop looked as if he was about to take offence, they turned their attention to Edward and his favourite, imitating the way the pair of them sat, drank and ate as if joined at the hip. The entire assembly burst into laughter, led by the king and Gaveston, who pelted the dwarves with precious items and sent them scattering around searching for these prizes. The frumenty was then served, followed by tarts and quinces. The king left his seat to circulate amongst the guests. Agnes and I had risen to join our mistresses when a serjeant-at-arms, his royal livery rain-soaked, slipped into the hall. He immediately went across to Demontaigu, who been accosted by master Guido. From Demontaigu's expression, I could tell some major hurt had occurred. He spoke briefly to Guido and beckoned me across. Agnes followed, intrigued by the interruption. I had no choice but to let her. Demontaigu didn't wait. He and Guido hurried from the hall out into the kitchen yard. Men-at-arms stood about, their torches spluttering in the wet.

'It's Chapeleys,' Demontaigu murmured when I joined him. 'He is dead. Hanged himself!'

CHAPTER 3

The leading men of the Kingdom hated him [Gaveston] because only he was favoured by the King.

Vita Edwardi Secundi

'Who is Chapeleys?' Guido asked.

'Sir,' Demontaigu gestured back at the door, 'I must ask you to return. You too, Mistress Agnes. This concerns me. A man sheltering in my chamber has died. Mathilde, Ingleram Berenger has asked for you to attend.' Demontaigu didn't wait for an answer, but spun on his heel.

I made my apologies to Guido and Agnes and hurried after him.

'Bertrand?' I asked. 'Ingleram Berenger, he is a physician, the royal coroner.'

'Precisely!' Demontaigu snapped. 'He did not ask for you, but *I* need you, Mathilde. Come, you'll see.'

It was a freezing cold evening, a stark contrast to the warm splendour of the Grande Chambre.

65

Once we'd left Burgundy Hall, Demontaigu guided me by the elbow down needle-thin alleyways, across derelict gardens and deserted yards, dark as a devil's mouth except for the flickering torches of the men-at-arms hurrying before us. In the far distance, on the corner of a building, I glimpsed torchlight and the glitter of armoured men. I soon realised it was the outside of Demontaigu's chamber. I drew closer and glimpsed Chapeleys hanging by his neck from the window-door, open above him. An eerie, sinister scene. The corpse hung slack about a yard from the ground, arms and legs swaying slightly as if the man was still alive. I reckoned the drop from the window-door was at least another two. At first glance, to all intents and purposes, Chapeleys had opened that small window-door and, with one end of the escape rope clasped to that ring in the wall, fashioned a noose with the other, slipped this over his head and stepped into eternal night. The men-at-arms staring up at the corpse let us through. I peered at the grisly scene. Chapeleys was still wearing his oxhide boots. In the murky gloom I could not make out his face. Ingelram Berenger, a plump, white-whiskered, fussy little man, came bustling forward, mopping his face with a napkin taken from the banquet.

'Master Bertrand,' he blustered, 'a guard found this.' He gestured at the corpse. 'A hanging! Suicide! God knows why it happened.' He rubbed his stomach. 'Not a night for such hideous scenes.'

'You've not entered my chamber?' Demontaigu asked.

'Of course not.'

'It should be locked and bolted from the inside,' Demontaigu murmured. 'Master-at-arms,' he turned to one of the soldiers, 'bring a ladder. I will go up from the outside and unlock the door; you can join me there.'

The master-at-arms brought a long pole-ladder. Demontaigu insisted that for the moment the corpse be left. He laid the ladder against the palace wall and climbed up. Master Berenger left two of the men-at-arms on guard whilst we hurried round into the building and up the gloomy, freezing staircase. By the time we reached his chamber, Demontaigu had opened the door. He ushered us in.

'Locked and bolted from the inside,' he whispered to me.

I glanced quickly round. Nothing looked as if it had been disturbed. The drapes on the bed were slightly creased. The empty platter and goblet still stood on the table. I glimpsed the chancery pouch and hurried across to where it lay on the floor between the chair and the still gleaming charcoal brazier. I pulled back the flaps. It was empty. I glanced at the brazier and noticed the charred scraps of parchment littering the top coals. Chapeleys had apparently burnt whatever he'd brought. There was no sign of any struggle. The cup and platter smelled untainted. The lock and bolts on the door were untouched. I examined the ring in the wall. The thick hempen rope was securely tied to it. The bolts and bars of the wooden door looked unmarked, with no sign of force.

Berenger stood in deep conversation with Demontaigu. The king's coroner eyed me darkly when he learnt who I was. In the end, however, he seemed satisfied with what Demontaigu had said and became very dismissive.

'A highly nervous man,' he declared. 'Master Chapeleys' humours must have been deeply agitated and disturbed by all these present troubles. He must have taken his own life.' He shrugged. 'God knows what Holy Mother Church will say about that.' The fat coroner spread his hands, clearly anxious to return to the festivities. 'There is little more I can say or do,' he pleaded. 'Perhaps . . .'

Demontaigu offered to take care of the corpse. Berenger was only too pleased to agree and promptly disappeared. Demontaigu ordered the men-at-arms to go back to the corpse and guard it. Once the chamber was cleared, he bolted the door.

'Nothing,' he exclaimed, gesturing around, 'nothing untoward.'

'Except the contents of his chancery bag have been burnt.'

'Chapeleys may have done that himself when he decided to take his own life. The door was locked and bolted.' Demontaigu shook his head. 'I cannot believe anything else. Chapeleys was under strict instruction not to open that door to anyone but ourselves or someone . . .'

'When you left him?'

'I brought some wine and a platter.' Demontaigu sighed. 'I scarcely talked to him, then I left for the chancery office. I did some work there and went direct to Burgundy Hall.'

'And Berenger?'

'I told him Chapeleys was a clerk much agitated by the present crisis. A man, perhaps, given to morbid thoughts.'

'Everything indicates suicide,' I agreed, 'yet we know that is not true. Chapeleys was truly frightened but he wanted to live.' I walked over to the writing table. The quill pens had recently been used. The inkpot was unstoppered. I searched the chancery bag again but it was empty. I went down on my hands and knees. Chapeleys was a clerk. He would write and perhaps reject what he'd written. I was proved correct. Under the table near the far leg lay a twisted piece of parchment. I picked this up, smoothed it out and glimpsed the scrolled letters. I slipped it into the velveteen purse on my belt. Demontaigu hurried across but I held a finger to my lips and gestured at the door.

'Not now. Let's first tend to the corpse.'

Demontaigu went across to the window-door and shouted at the men-at-arms to be ready. He then told me to help him hold the rope. He sliced this expertly, took the strain and gently lowered the corpse. The soldiers, using the ladder, grasped the body and laid it out on the cobbles below. A macabre sight! The cadaver sprawled on its back. In the shifting pool of torchlight, Chapeleys' white face seemed to stare up at me in reproach. I diverted myself by re-examining the knot in the noose which the soldiers passed to us.

'A clerk's doing,' I murmured. 'As they fasten the twine of a pouch containing a bundle of manuscripts, twice tied, the ends slipped back through the knot.' I rose and scrutinised the chamber once more.

'Nothing out of place.' Demontaigu voiced my thoughts.

'And that is the refrain the assassin wants us to repeat,' I replied.

We left the chamber and joined the men-at-arms, who carried the corpse across the palace grounds into the mortuary chapel of St Margaret's, the parish church of those who lived and served in the palace. The Keeper of the Death House was waiting. He merrily welcomed, as he put it, his new guest into the Chamber of the Dead: a long, barn-like structure lying between the corpse door of St Margaret's and God's Acre, the parish cemetery. The walls inside gleamed with lime-wash, studded here and there with black crosses. The carefully scrubbed floor, set with pavestones, was strewn with crisp, freshly cut rushes. Mortuary tables, neatly arranged in three long rows, stretched from the door to the far wall. Most of these were, in the words of the keeper, a lay brother from the abbey, occupied by his special guests.

'It's the gallows, you see,' he intoned mournfully. 'They have to be cleared before the great feast, felons and villains! All quiet now, washed and anointed, ready for God.'

Chapeleys' corpse was laid on a table near the door. The men-at-arms were eager to be gone from such a gruesome place; it reeked of death and decay despite the pots of crushed herbs and boats of smoking incense placed on sills and ledges. Demontaigu also asked the keeper to withdraw. The lay brother would have objected, but the silver coin I drew from my purse and the promise of some lady bread and meat, the leftovers from the lavish royal banquet, sent him scrambling through the door, which he slammed noisily behind him.

We turned to Chapeleys. In the light of the oil lamps and guttering wall torches, his face had a livid hue, eyes popping, tongue jutting out of his protuberant mouth, the skin a hideous, mottled colour. Demontaigu crossed himself, leaned over and whispered the words of absolution into the dead man's ear. Afterwards, with a phial of oil he must have taken from his chamber, he swiftly anointed Chapeleys from forehead to feet whilst whispering the solemn invocation to St Michael and all the angels to come out and meet the dead man's soul. We then stripped the corpse down to its pathetic soiled linen undershirt and drawers. I carefully examined the flesh for bruises and cuts but could detect none. No binding or force to the fingers, hands or wrists could be traced; nothing but that deep, broad purple-red weal round Chapeleys' throat and the slight contusion behind the right ear where the knot had been fastened. I studied the discarded noose I'd brought with me; the slipknot was expertly done, still tight and hard. I searched amongst the dead clerk's possessions. His wallet held a few coins which I left on the mortuary table. The dagger was still in its sheath and slipped easily in and out. I sat down on a stool and stared in exasperation at Demontaigu, now covering the corpse with a death cloth.

'Who knew Chapeleys had arrived at Westminster?'

'Nobody,' he replied, 'at least to our knowledge.' He gathered up the dead man's possessions in a bundle, came across, and stood over me. 'Mathilde, I recognise the problems if it was murder. Who knew Chapeleys was in my chamber at Westminster? Who killed him? How so expertly, so quickly? How did the assassin get in that room, attack an armed man who would certainly have resisted, and overcome him so soundly, so expertly, with no sign of force or disturbance. He then arranged Chapeleys' hanging and disappeared just as mysteriously. Chapeleys may have admitted him into the chamber, but why? He was frightened, under strict orders from us to be vigilant. And if he made a mistake why did he then not resist?' Demontaigu paused at a knock on the door. The Keeper of the Dead shuffled in.

'If he took life by his own hand,' he murmured, gesturing at the corpse now covered in a shroud, 'he cannot be buried in God's Acre.'

'Come, Brother.' Demontaigu picked the coins up from the table. He went over and thrust them into the lay brother's hands whilst placing Chapeleys' meagre possessions at his feet. 'If no one claims the corpse, and I doubt they will, these are yours. Why cause a fuss?'

'How did he die?' the keeper asked.

'I do not know, Brother,' I insisted. 'That is the truth!'

'When did he die?'

I glanced back at the corpse. The flesh was cold but the limbs were still soft. The freezing weather had drained the warm humours. The keeper's question was pertinent. Had Chapeleys been killed before the feast or during it? Had someone from our banquet slipped away and carried out the dreadful act? But if so, how was it done? I simply shook my head.

'Brother, I am unable to answer that.'

We were about to leave when there was a disturbance outside. The door was flung open and an irate Berenger strode into the chapel. Servants followed, carrying another corpse under a cloak. The keeper, clucking his tongue at how busy he'd become, hastily directed the bearers to an empty table. A grey-haired woman followed, sobbing uncontrollably; others entered, led by a young man who looked terror-stricken, his pimply white face sweating as he loudly

73

protested his innocence. As the keeper went over to console the sobbing woman, Berenger shouted for silence. Something about the distraught woman caught at my heart; she reminded me of my own mother. I went across, pulled back the cloth and stared down at the corpse of a young woman dressed in a faded green gown. Long auburn hair hid her face, which tilted sideways. I pushed the hair back and stared at the horror: once comely, her face was the same livid hue as Chapeleys', mottled and slightly swollen, eyes popping, tongue sticking out due to the garrotte string tied tightly round her soft white throat. I drew my own dagger and cut the cord; the corpse jerked as air was expelled and, for a heartbeat, silenced the clamour in the death house. Another young woman, black hair tied tightly back behind her head, lean, spiteful and full of anger, pushed her way through. She screamed accusations at the young man, who simply flailed his hands and shook his head. Once again Berenger shouted for silence.

'What happened?' I asked.

'The dead woman is Rebecca Atte-Stowe.' Berenger apparently decided to swallow his pride and speak to me. 'She was a serving wench in the buttery and pantry.' He gestured around at the clamour of accusation. 'She was found as you have seen her, in a storeroom where the maids keep their aprons, caps and gloves for use in the kitchens. Anyway, she was to help with the feast but hadn't been seen since the Vesper's bell.'

I stared down at the corpse. 'She must have disappeared shortly before the banquet began.' I went over and pressed my hand against her face; the flesh was cold. I lifted an arm; it was still supple. 'She's probably been dead for some hours,' I declared. I beckoned Berenger away from the shouting and crying. 'What's happening?' I whispered. 'That black-haired woman so full of fury?'

'Anstritha, Rebecca's friend. She maintains that Robert Atte-Gate, a groom from the stables, was sweet on Rebecca. Earlier today he and Rebecca quarrelled . . .' Berenger's voice faded away as if he was already bored by the proceedings, more concerned that once again he'd been disturbed in his pleasures by sudden, mysterious death. I returned to the mortuary table and scrutinised the poor girl's fingers. The clamour continued behind me, rising to screams and shouts.

'It's not me! I've done no crime!'

I whirled round. Robert, his face sweat-soaked, had retreated from the rest, drawing a dagger from his belt.

'Put down your weapon!' Berenger thundered, 'To draw a dagger on a royal officer in the king's own palace is treason. If you don't hang for murder, you will for that!'

Anstritha cackled with laughter. Robert lunged towards her but stumbled. The men-at-arms seized him and dragged him outside. Berenger declared he'd done more than his duty for one evening and followed. Anstritha, her face full of malicious glee, almost hopped to the door. The rest filed out, leaving Rebecca's mother sobbing over the corpse. I went and put an arm around her shoulders.

'What happened?' I asked softly. 'Do you really believe Robert murdered your daughter?'

'No,' she whispered through her tears.

I picked up the cut garrotte string, fine twine like that of catgut. 'Nor do I,' I murmured. 'This is more the work of a skilled assassin than a stable boy, but why should your poor Rebecca be his victim?'

The mother could not answer that. Demontaigu and I gave some money to the keeper and left. We walked away from the Death House. I paused and stared up through the darkness, listening to the sounds of the night: the barking of a dog, the creak of a cart, the slamming of doors and the ringing of bells. I stared around. Here and there the blackness was pierced by lights flaring at windows or peeping through shutters.

'Tomorrow,' I whispered.

'Tomorrow?' Demontaigu asked.

'Sufficient for the day is the evil thereof,' I quoted. 'Bertrand, I am tired. My mind teems; it swerves and shifts without reason.'

Demontaigu escorted me back to Burgundy Hall, where the laughter and music showed the festivities were continuing. He kissed me on the brow, clasped my hands and whispered at me to join him for his Jesus mass. As he hurried away, he murmured something else.

'Bertrand,' I called. 'What did you say?'

He turned and grinned. 'You, Mathilde, are honey-sweet.'

I went through the gatehouse, past the guards, still enjoying the compliment as a chamberlain ushered me up the stairs, along the gallery to my mistress' lodgings, a collection of chambers consisting of vestibule, antechamber, parlour and bedchamber. I was primly informed that the queen had retired but had been asking for me. Isabella was in her bedchamber, a dark-panelled room with heavy oaken furniture: tables, stools, aumbries and chests. The large bed was a stark contrast, brilliantly adorned with blue and gold drapes and coverlets fringed with silver. Isabella was sitting at a small table ringed in a glow of candle prickets with a chafing dish full of burning coals providing warmth. She was dressed simply in a white shift, shoulders and feet bare. I noticed the red scratch marks on her right arm; the skin looked irritated. She was more concerned in fashioning small images, using the candle flame to soften the wax, pushing it intently, decorating the figurines with scraps of cloth, parchment and small items of jewellery. I recognised the signs. Isabella was deeply agitated. She glanced up as I went to curtsy.

'I have been looking for you, Mathilde. I had to tend to myself, though I did talk to Marie.' She pushed back her hair.

I curtsied to hide my own agitation. Isabella was referring to a maid who had died some years ago but returned to have conversations with the queen whenever she was troubled.

'Has Marie left?' I asked. Isabella did not answer. She beckoned me forward. I excused myself, returned to the parlour and brought back a small pot of precious oleander. I sat on the stool beside her and, without bidding, treated the rash on her arm. Isabella watched me clean the skin and spread the paste.

'I should add a little witch-hazel to the water you wash with,' I murmured.

'Never mind that,' Isabella snapped.

I glanced up. My mistress had lost that girlish look. I glimpsed the mature woman she would be, long-faced, mouth set, eyes unwavering in their stare.

'Where have you been, Mathilde? I needed you! I looked for you.' She pinched my arm. 'You did not tell me.'

'I shall now.' I described what had happened. At the mention of the Poison Maiden, Isabella picked up a waxen figure crowned with a piece of parchment, I recognised it as her father, a pinprick through its middle. She held it over a candle flame and began to pummel it with her fingers. After I'd finished speaking, she sat staring at the effigy.

'I must tell his grace all this,' she declared. 'I am to join him later. Strange,' she smiled at me, 'only twice have I heard the Poison Maiden being mentioned: something my father said years ago, a chance comment, nothing else . . .'

'And the second?'

'Stranger still, a remark my husband made at the banquet this evening. He asked me: "Isabella, are you the Poison Maiden?" then turned away laughing. Oh, by the way,' Isabella picked up another wax image, 'Marigny demanded to know why I retained you. Why I did not send you back to your mother at her farm near Bretigny.'

'And?' I kept my voice steady.

'I told him that what I did was my own concern. My lord Gaveston overheard; he said you were a loyal subject of the English Crown whose favour you enjoyed.'

'And the Viper?' I tried to curb my fear. Marigny's reference to my mother, a widow on a lonely farm, was a brutal threat.

'Oh, he just smiled in that nasty way of his and walked away.' Isabella touched my cheek. 'Don't worry: they hunt more majestic prey – my husband.' She picked up a piece of wax, warmed it over a candle flame and began to mould it. 'They believe they can remove Gaveston but they are wrong, that is not the truth. Why is it, Mathilde, that people claim truth speeds like an arrow? Truth is more like a snake. It uncoils and slithers backwards and forwards. Or like a painting on a wall – it doesn't come in one flow but drop by drop. Only after a while do you realise what is forming.'

'Mistress?'

'I'll not speak in parables.' She laughed. 'The Great Lords and my father demand that Gaveston be put away, but Gaveston is not just my husband's favourite; he is his home. Do you understand?'

I shook my head.

'I've realised a truth!' Isabella continued passionately. 'I have been reflecting on it. Home is not a place, Mathilde; it's more a hunger, here,' she tapped her chest, 'deep, deep in the recesses of the heart. It is a completion, a fullness, a peace. I have no home, Mathilde. Father sees me as a marriage pawn, as he did my mother. He never truly protected me against my brothers but let me float like a feather in the breeze or grass on the surface of a pool.' She picked up an effigy and pressed the head. 'I have no home. Edward has, and I envy him that. I understand his love for Gaveston. Gaveston is his father, mother, brother, sister, friend and lover. He is Edward's reason for living. So the king and his favourite will fight to the death to protect what is theirs. God save me, I understand them! I'd do the same. Winchelsea and others of his coven believe I'm outraged. In truth,' she let the wax fall from her hands, 'I couldn't care. Edward is a good lord. Gaveston respects me. Neither do me any hurt—'

'But . . .' I interrupted. Isabella's face turned fierce.

'One day, Mathilde, I shall find my home, my resting place, and I shall never give it up, never!' She touched her arm. 'I thank you for your news. Now I must prepare myself.' She rose and patted me on the shoulder. 'I shall remember what you said.'

I helped Isabella anoint herself and dress. The hour candle had burnt another ring before the chamberlains arrived. Isabella, as beautiful as an angel, kissed me passionately on the cheek and swept out. I secured the door and doused all the candles except that which marked the hours and another on the table near the bed. I sat down and stared at it, reflecting on what Isabella had said. I fully agreed. My hatred for Philip and his coven sprang from their destruction of my home in Paris, their savage persecution of the Temple and the ghastly, humiliating execution of my dear uncle. Now they threatened what I had left: Isabella and Demontaigu were my new home. I doused the candle next to the bed and lay down, wondering when this, my new home, would be free of all danger.

The next morning Demontaigu celebrated his mass, long before the Prime bell tolled. I had slipped across the dark, freezing palace grounds and knocked at his chamber door. He had already prepared the altar. Once I arrived, he celebrated his low mass, reciting special prayers for the souls of Chapeleys and Rebecca Atte-Stowe. Afterwards, whilst he cleared the makeshift altar, I went down across the kitchen yard to beg bread, cheese, salted bacon and a jug of ale from a heavy-eyed cook. We broke our fast and returned to the mysteries confronting us. I sat at Demontaigu's chancery desk. The cold seeped through the shutters, rain pattered against the horn-covered windows and the abbey bells pealed out announcing the day.

'These problems concern us,' I began. 'Chapeleys was a high-ranking clerk in Langton's household; that good bishop is important to the king. Chapeleys was desperate to share something with our royal master. He surrendered himself to our care but died in our custody, here, in your chamber. Berenger may wash his hands, but the King will not be pleased. So . . .'

I dipped the sharpened quill into the ink and wrote as I spoke.

'Primo: what did Chapeleys know? Secundo: why was he so frightened? Tertio: how did he truly die? Quarto: who, apart from us, knew he was here? Quinto: how could an assassin enter and leave through a door that remained locked and bolted from the inside whilst the window-door appears to have been opened only by the victim? Sexto: if his death was an assassin's work, why did Chapeleys, still vigorous and armed, not resist? Septimo: if Chapeleys was under instruction to be careful about opening that door, as well as being so frightened, he would scarcely admit the assassin. So, and we now move back in the circle, how did the assassin gain entry and commit such an act, so swiftly, so quietly? Octavo: did Chapeleys burn the contents of his chancery bag or was that the work of the murderer?'

'I cannot answer any of those questions,' Demontaigu replied. He had pushed forward a prie-dieu and was kneeling on it as if before an altar. I raised my hand in mock absolution. 'And the scrap of parchment?' he added. 'That is the only thing we discovered here.'

I took the twisted piece of parchment from my wallet and studied it.

'Very little here,' I said, and handed it over. 'Nothing but two entries: what looks like an unfinished word, "basil", probably basilisk, the mythical beast, a dragon-like creature with deadly stare and breath; and a circle surmounted by a cross with the letter "P" in the middle and the Latin words, seven letters in all, *sub pede* – under-foot.'

'Scribblings,' Demontaigu mused, getting to his feet. 'Chapeleys must have sat here thinking what he would say to the king and wrote down those entries, but he was distracted. He didn't burn it, he threw it on the floor. Yet surely, if he was about to commit suicide, he would have destroyed that with any other documents he carried? No!' he concluded. 'He must have been murdered. He must have been sitting here scribbling, wondering when we would return. He heard a knock on the door and answered it. He must have been re-assured he was safe, but what happened then?'

For a while we discussed the problem until the abbey bells marked the passing hours.

'Bertrand,' I picked up my cloak and swung it around my shoulders, 'my mistress is with the king. She will attend mass in the Chapel Royal, break her fast with him, then return to her chambers. I must be there.'

'Later,' Demontaigu asked, 'at Vespers time, you will accompany me to the Chapel of the Hanged?'

'If I can,' I smiled, 'though God knows what this day will bring.'

I left Demontaigu's chamber and made my way back to Burgundy Hall. Guards were clustered at the gateway, talking heatedly with two women and a man. I recognised Rebecca's mother from the previous evening. As soon as she saw me, she ran forward and grasped my arm.

'Come, come, mistress,' she declared, and introduced the other two, an old white-haired man and woman, wiping the tears from their leathery faces on the backs of dirt-grained hands, their clothes all ragged and threadbare. 'These are Robert's parents. We have come to beg a favour, all three of us,' the woman continued. 'My daughter is dead, foully murdered, but mistress, I would swear on the Gospels that Robert is innocent. I ask you to intercede for him, please.'

I patted her on the shoulder and went across to Ap Ythel, captain of the royal guard.

'Has her grace returned?'

The Welshman took off his helmet and wiped the drizzle from his face.

'No,' he replied, nodding at the supplicants. 'They have been here some time, demanding to see you.'

'Where is their son lodged?' I asked. 'Do you know?'

'Probably in the Old Palace gatehouse; that is where they keep prisoners.'

I stared up. The clouds were breaking under a strengthening breeze. Somewhere a bird sang, a sweet sound evoking memories of my mother's farm.

'I could send one of my men with you.' The captain of the guard pushed back his chainmail coif. I felt sorry for the supplicants. Isabella would be some time, so I accepted the captain's kind offer and, using the queen's seal, gained entry to the soaring gatehouse and the dungeons below. Robert's was a dark, fetid cell, its straw black with slime. Huge cobwebs festooned the walls; the only light seeped through a barred lancet window high in the wall. Robert squatted, loaded with chains. He hardly moved, just lifted his head and moaned. The men-at-arms had not been gentle. Bruises had bloomed a deep purple around his mouth and on the side of his head. I crouched down beside him.

'Robert, listen,' I whispered. 'You will not hang. What happened?'

'Nothing!' He shook the chains. 'Nothing at all! An ordinary day! We quarrelled as we always did, then Rebecca left. The next thing I knew was the alarm being raised after her corpse was discovered.' He sobbed for a while, then pushed himself up. 'I'm innocent, mistress, but what's the use? I drew a knife on Berenger, he'll see me hang.'

'I don't think so.'

Once outside, I asked Rebecca's mother to take me to where the corpse had been found. As we hurried through the drizzle, I caught the tension from the men-at-arms and archers deployed in yards and baileys. The stables were busy. Farriers hammered at the forge. Grooms trotted out destriers. Saddlers were busy with tangled harness. Knight bannerets, Edward's own personal retainers, were everywhere supervising matters. I asked one of the men-at-arms, a Welshman, what the matter was. He just pulled a face and muttered how there were rumours that the Lords might launch a sortie to seize Gaveston.

'If that happens,' he murmured, 'there'll be swordplay and bloodshed enough, mistress.'

CHAPTER 4

The great men were summoned to discuss peace: they arrived in London with an armed force.

Vita Edwardi Secundi

S omewhere a trumpet blared. My blood chilled. Would it come down to that? I wondered. A bloody affray here in the palace grounds, men-at-arms fighting as the Lords tried to seize Gaveston and drag him off? Arraigning him for treason? What then? Edward would unfurl his banner. Civil war would rage in a fight to the death. What would happen to Isabella, to me? Why should I be worried about the death of a servant maid? Yet one glance at that anguished mother's face, and I knew it was important. We reached the huddle of Old Palace buildings, outhouses, wings and lean-tos. Rebecca's mother led us down a stone-paved passageway, dark and hollow-sounding, reeking of dirty clothes and rotting vegetables. At the end was a narrow chamber; inside, nothing but broken coffers and chests. Rebecca's mother explained how the maids and servants came here to leave their possessions and take whatever livery they had to wear to serve in the kitchens and pantries. She pointed out the pegs on the wall where they hung their clothes. In the far corner was a recess; she gestured towards it.

'Rebecca,' she whispered, 'she was found there by a kitchen boy.'

I went in. It was dark, nothing more than a large corner smelling rather stale. I turned and came back.

'Was there anything missing?'

'Not that I know,' the woman replied. 'Just poor Rebecca's life.'

'So let me understand. Your daughter came here and prepared herself for service. There would be others present.'

'She was late,' the mother replied, 'I remember that. If she was late when she came in, there'd be no one else here. No one saw her.'

I closed my eyes and reflected. Rebecca would come in and the assassin would strike. I did not believe the murderer was Robert. He was a man who could scarce tie a knot in a hurry, never mind use a garrotte string so expertly. I walked back down the passageway and out into the yard. I stared around and realised the building was not far from Demontaigu's chamber, scarcely a stone's throw away. The Old Palace was such a maze, it was easy to lose any sense of direction. Now lawyers move on evidence but sometimes the heart can proclaim the truth. I passionately believed that in some way, Rebecca's death was connected with that of Chapeleys, though how and why remained a mystery.

'What will you do, mistress?' Rebecca's mother clasped her hands as if in prayer. 'What will you do?'

'I shall see the queen.' I smiled. 'Don't worry, there is hope yet.'

When I returned to Burgundy Hall, I was surprised to be informed by Ap Ythel that not only had Isabella returned, but his grace and my lord Gaveston were also in the queen's apartments. I gathered up my skirts and hurried up the stairs, running down passageways, brushing past guards and surprised chamberlains. I almost burst into the queen's apartments. Edward and Gaveston were there, dressed in dark green silken cote-hardies over red leggings, their feet pushed into leather boots. They slouched in their chairs like two young men eager and fresh for the day's events, totally unaware of the great dangers threatening them. The king clambered to his feet and, seizing my hand, kissed my fingers. Gaveston gave me the most mocking of bows. Isabella came out of her bedchamber wiping her hands on a napkin. She stood, folding the napkin, staring coolly at me. I felt as if I was in the presence of conspirators. Now you may question how a leech and apothecary should be admitted into the secret councils of the king. I too was a member of his inner chamber, someone who could move in and out, speak to him as you would to a brother or sister. However, in the end, for those who speculate on court ritual, the charges against Edward when he was deposed included the allegation that he conversed and related to people of the common sort. I am proud to be included in that number. Oh yes, nineteen years later, during the hurly-burly time, I was interrogated on why he had discussed Negotium Regis, royal business, with someone of my ilk. I answered, why not? I was in his chamber, the confidante of his wife, Queen Isabella. I also had no illusions. If the king went down, what little hope did I have? I had no choice but to support him. Oh the Articuli Damnati, as well as the Ordinances of the Lords, accused Edward of 'taking counsel where he should not have'. In truth, that was prompted by malicious jealousy. The Great Ones regarded themselves as the king's God-given councillors. Edward disagreed, and for all I know, so did God.

'Come, come.' The king shook back his hair. He grasped me tightly by the hand and led me to the narrow table with four high-backed chairs placed around it. In the middle was a tray bearing a jug of white wine and a mazer full of sweetmeats. Edward and Gaveston sat at either end, Isabella and I opposite each other. At first the king seemed expansive, still drunk from the night before, eyes glittering in the candlelight. Gaveston was more subdued.

The favourite collected four goblets from a side dresser and poured the wine, studying me carefully. I concealed my own surprise. Of course, in the intrigue swirling round Westminster, everyone was suspect. Edward slumped in his chair as he realised what lay before him. For a short while the mask slipped: the king rested his head on his hand, blew his cheeks out and glanced under his eyebrows around the table.

On that March morning, the Feast of the Annunciation, Edward finally shrugged off the bonhomie of the previous evening when he'd swept into the Grande Chambre of Burgundy Hall. Now he looked tired and harassed. The *secretum concilium* began quietly enough.

'What do we have?' Edward murmured. 'Pierre?' He glanced down at his beloved, the man whom Winchelsea called 'the king's idol'. 'What do have? What can we do?'

'At the moment, very little,' the favourite replied. He leaned his elbows on the table, cupping his face in his hands. 'We have a few knight bannerets,' he explained languidly, 'companies of men-at-arms, archers and my Kernia. Burgundy Hall is well fortified, protected and provisioned.' He wiped his hands on a napkin. 'Even though these foul odours and the smells of the midden curl everywhere. However,' he glanced up, 'the Lords have brought their retinues to lie at Westminster Abbey. From what I gather, more arrive every day. They have the support of Holy Mother Church; the bishops

91

deeply resent Langton's detention in the Tower. They have united behind Winchelsea, who regards me as Satan incarnate. Rumours abound that our good archbishop intends to excommunicate me with bell, book and candle.'

Gaveston continued grimly, 'The Lords seem well resourced with gold and silver. We have little, and because Westminster is virtually under siege, no sheriff or bailiff dares to present his accounts or deliver his monies at Easter. Langton was treasurer; undoubtedly he amassed a fortune which, sire, should truly belong to you, but no one can find it. Langton lodges in the Tower. He is gambling that he can hold out longer than you. He may well be right.'

Gaveston tapped the tabletop. 'The Lords have been joined by the envoys,' he bowed smilingly towards Isabella, 'of Philip of France. They demand, as a matter of honour to you, madame, that I be removed—'

'Trust me, my lord,' Isabella interrupted. 'My honour is not my father's main concern.' She shrugged prettily. 'Indeed,' she continued, 'I doubt very much if he is bothered at all about me or my status.'

'But you will continue to act the part?' Edward asked testily.

'My lord,' Isabella retorted, 'I have been acting the part for as long as I can remember.'

Gaveston smiled boyishly at Isabella, who blushed slightly.

'My lady is correct.' Gaveston rose to his feet to refill the four small goblets. He served Isabella, the king, then myself, before taking his seat and sipping thoughtfully at his own goblet. 'Philip of France is more concerned with the Templars. The Abbot of St Germain carries letters from him and Pope Clement. They demand the total destruction of the order within the power of England, be it in Carlisle or Bordeaux in Gascony.'

Gaveston glanced quickly at me. I wondered if he knew Demontaigu's true identity. The king's next words chilled me.

'Philip may be in the market to barter one for the other,' he said softly. 'The destruction of the Templars for Pierre's safety. But I cannot agree to that.'

My heart skipped a beat.

'I cannot do it,' the king insisted. 'Not that I have any great allegiance to the Temple.' He waved a hand. 'I am kept close here at Westminster. If I issue letters authorising the destruction of the Temple, the Great Lords would simply seize their property and estates in towns and shires. I would not profit. What use is that to us?'

'So how will this end?' Isabella's voice was surprisingly sharp. 'The Great Ones will gather in Westminster Hall or the abbey chapter house. They will draw up a bill, articles of condemnation, they will attempt to put my lord Gaveston before their council. They may even indict, attempt to try him.'

Edward nodded in agreement. 'They will,' he whispered. 'Yes, they will . . .' He put his fingers to his face, unable to finish the sentence. Gaveston sat with the palms of his hands flat against the tabletop; a slight sweat laced his face. Edward pushed back his chair, head to one side as if listening to the various sounds of the palace. 'Lincoln and the earls are well provisioned, but they are also well advised.' He stared tearfully down at his favourite.

'A traitor?' Isabella asked. 'Here in your midst?'

'What could he or she betray?' Edward mocked. 'What secret plans do we have? Whom could we plot with? No, it is more subtle than that.' He turned to me, right eye drooping, a cold, hard glance. 'Mathilde, you are a physician, or you say you are.' He let the spiteful words hang like a noose as he studied me, then his face relaxed. He took off a silver ring from his little finger and pushed it across the table towards me.

'I am sorry!'

Isabella was glaring at her husband. Gaveston had his head down. I stretched, took the ring and sent it rolling back.

'Your grace, I am very grateful for the gift, but in the circumstances, I think you need all the treasure you have. Moreover, if you go down, what need will I have for silver?'

Edward stared in astonishment. He opened his mouth to object, but Gaveston laughed merrily, clapping his hands.

'Your grace,' he quipped, 'a physician tells the truth. A rare event!'

The king roared with laughter; the tension disappeared. Edward, hands joined, leaned across the table.

'Mathilde, my dear, you study the symptoms of an ailment, then search for its cause, yes?'

'Of course, sire.'

'So it is here,' the king continued. 'The Lords are united, well provisioned and advised. They treat my demands with impunity. They mockingly reject the mediation of my good stepmother, the Queen Dowager Margaret. One of them even hinted that she should go on pilgrimage, the longest she can find.'

Isabella laughed sharply at that.

'Something or someone is uniting them; that is the cause of our present troubles.' Edward shrugged. 'Who, what, why, we don't know. Is it the Poison Maiden?' He pointed at Isabella. 'You told me that you once heard your father, in secret council with his coven in the gardens of the Louvre, talk of La Demoiselle Venimeuse, the Ancilla Venenata.'

'Just words,' Isabella warned. 'I also listened to the chatter of the clerks of my father's secret chancery; even they wondered who this Demoiselle Venimeuse really could be.'

'As did my father,' Edward added bitterly. 'About seven or eight years ago he was here at Westminster. One night I came to his chambers.

95

My father's rages were famous. On that occasion, he was furious. He tore at the servants' hair, beat them and threw them against the walls. He was ranting and screaming. I dared not enter the chamber. Later, a retainer told me how the cause of this rage was someone called the Poison Maiden. My father said that great damage had been done by her, but what he meant, no one understood. On my accession, I asked the clerks if they knew, even men like Drokensford of the secret chancery. They replied how they'd heard passing reference to the Poison Maiden, but nothing more.'

'Your grace?'

'Mathilde, *ma cherie*?'

'Would Langton know?'

'Perhaps.' Edward's smile faded. 'But we will come to our perfidious bishop and your visit to him in my own good time.' He left the threat hanging in the air. I recalled my words to Demontaigu, how Chapeleys had died in our care.

'We believe,' Gaveston said brusquely, 'that the Demoiselle Venimeuse meddles in our present troubles, but that is suspicion only; we have no firm evidence.'

'Perhaps you are just casting about.'

'My lady,' Edward wagged a finger at Isabella, 'I wish to God that was true. Pax-Bread,' he smiled thinly, 'has assured me I am not.' The king chewed the corner of his lip, staring at me as if challenging me to ask who Pax-Bread was. I kept silent. Edward was fickle. He could sit and argue with a groom about a brass buckle as if the man was his born brother, only to change abruptly, demanding all the rights and appurtenances of kingship. I stared past him at the weak sunlight pouring through the lattice window, and prayed quietly that I would be able to meet Demontaigu later that day.

'Pax-Bread?' Isabelle asked softly.

'If Philip has his spies, so do we,' Gaveston explained. He eased the folds of his cotehardie, undoing the clasp of the cambric shirt beneath. 'Pax-Bread's true name is Edmund Lascelles, a Gascon, a close friend of my family. One of the finest pastry cooks under God's heaven. He is also the most subtle of spies. He hates Philip and did good work for the old king exploiting one of Philip's few weaknesses.' Gaveston paused at Isabella's sharp gasp.

'Your father, my lady, is well known for his sweet tooth: he relishes tarts, blancmanges, pastries, jellies, creams and sugars. Pax-Bread soon rose to prominence in Philip's kitchens as a man who would serve delectable dishes when the claret and osier had been drunk. Tongues eventually turn loose, even in the French king's private chambers, especially when Philip dines with Marigny and others of his ilk. Of course, no bird flies free for ever. Pax-Bread . . .' Gaveston smiled. 'An appropriate name, is it not? The bread passed between friends at the *osculum pacis*, the kiss of peace during the mass. Anyway, Pax-Bread fell under suspicion and was forced to flee to our garrison at Boulogne; that was at the end of February. He spent a great deal of time trying to cast off his pursuers. In case he never reached London, he sent us a letter.' Gaveston dipped into his cotehardie and drew out a parchment. He gave this to Isabella, who undid it, read it, pulled a face and, when Gaveston nodded, passed it to me.

The letter was well written. It began: *Monsieur Pierre s'avisera* – 'Monsieur Pierre, be well advised.' It then delivered a list of pastry, herbal and other items. These were written in sentences of eight words, every third word now underlined in green ink. The words thus scored were: *s'avisera, demoiselle, venimeuse, ageant, grande, damage, parmi, seigneurs', employa, ombres, Jean, Haute, Mont, 'a', verité, Secrète, Solomon, Annonciation.*

'The emphasis is mine,' Gaveston explained, 'a code Pax-Bread and I often used. Put these words together and Pax-Bread is advising us to be aware that the Poison Maiden will do great damage amongst the Lords.'

'*Les ombres*, the shadows?' I asked.

'More precisely,' Edward intervened, 'they like to be called Tenebrae – the Darkness: that's the Latin translation. They are professional assassins skulking in London, one of the more vicious gangs that can be hired by the city fathers to settle grudges with each other.'

'And Pax-Bread is claiming the Poison Maiden will use these?'

98

'Of course.'

'Against whom?'

Gaveston coughed and stared full at me.

'You, my lord,' I breathed. 'Yes, that would be logical. If your opponents took up arms, they could be called traitors, but an attempt on you by some secret, silent assassin couldn't be laid at their door.'

'We should move,' Isabella declared, 'not stay here.'

'Not yet.' Gaveston held up a hand. 'The palace is secure, Burgundy Hall even more so. This game has to be played out. You understand that? The problem is to be dealt with immediately. To retreat now would mean defeat. The king must show he is master in his own home.' Gaveston spread his hands. 'Westminster is the royal palace, its abbey the royal mausoleum. If he cannot rule here, where else?'

'And the other references, such as Solomon and the Annunciation?'

'The Secret of Solomon is a tavern in an alleyway off Cheapside. Pax-Bread is saying he'll be there today, the Feast of the Annunciation. Mathilde,' Gaveston breathed out noisily, 'royal messengers are watched; Isabella's household not so closely. After all, her grace,' he pulled a face, 'is supposed to detest me as much as Winchelsea does. You, Mathilde, can be trusted. We want you to meet Pax-Bread at the Secret of Solomon.' He smiled lazily. 'Demontaigu, the queen's clerk, can go with you. He is acceptable, yes?'

I stared back, determined not to blush or be disconcerted.

'Anyway,' Gaveston plucked a sweetmeat from the dish, 'you can go and discover what Pax-Bread really knows.' He fished in his wallet and slipped across an impression of his seal. 'Show him that; he will trust you.'

'When, my lord?'

'When I am finished.'

'My lord,' I was determined to question those other items mentioned in Pax-Bread's letter, '*Jean Haute Mont à la verité* – John High Mountain has the truth. What does that mean?'

Gaveston shook his head. 'I cannot tell you, Mathilde; Pax-Bread will. Now Chapeleys? Her grace has told us already, but you must relate everything that happened.'

I did so. Edward and Gaveston heard me out. The favourite kept still, now and again staring up at the rafters as if weighing the worth of what I said. I also described the murder of Rebecca Atte-Stowe and my faint suspicion that her death was part of the mystery surrounding Chapeleys' murder. At the mention of Robert's attack on Ingleram Berenger and my plea that the king should show mercy, Edward raised a hand.

'Undoubtedly Chapeleys' death is most regrettable. He apparently had something to say. However, unbeknown to you, Mathilde, he had already written to me, asking to be relieved of his duties at the Tower. He declared that he was innocent of any charges and asked why he had been punished along with Langton. He then made the most surprising confession: that Langton had hinted at the true identity of the Poison Maiden.' Edward paused for effect.

'Who, my lord?'

'Me,' declared Gaveston, his face hard and humourless. 'According to Langton, I am Philip's creature, planted at the heart of my lord's affections to wreak hideous damage.' He forced his voice to remain calm. 'I created chaos and division between my lord and his late father; the same between the king and his barons, not to mention his grace and his bride as well as between Edward and Philip of France.'

I stared across at Isabella. She looked startled by the logic of the revelation. According to all the evidence, Langton was correct. Gaveston had caused deep, rancorous division at the English court.

'It's true, isn't it?' Gaveston whispered. 'In more senses than one it's true.'

'Yet it's not!' Edward countered. 'Relations between my late father and myself were never cordial, God rest his bones. As for the barons, my good father fought them as I do now. I should have ripped Chapeleys' tongue out, but what was the use? He was simply repeating what Langton had said. His trial for treason would only have proclaimed the matter to the world. In the end I decided to let him rot in the Tower . . .'

'Is that why you sent Mathilde to treat Langton's ulcer?' Isabella asked. 'To find out more?'

'Ah, *ma coeur*.' Edward smiled at Isabella. 'You are right. I wondered if Chapeleys had anything more to say. I doubted it; just a repetition of his foul lies. However, I do wonder, and always will, what that circle surmounted by a cross with the letter P inside signifies? As for the words "basil" and *sub pede* . . .' Edward shrugged. 'Chapeleys may have been murdered. More probable is that overcome with fear, he decided to take his own life. Now, as for Robert Atte-Gate . . .' He pushed back his chair, rose, strolled to the door and opened it.

'Ap Ythel,' he shouted. The captain of the King's Welsh archers, small, dark-faced and wiry, swaggered into the room and went to sink to one knee.

'No need for that.' Edward clapped the Welshman on the shoulder. 'Take some of your lovely boys and go to the dungeons in the Old Palace gatehouse. Drag Robert Atte-Stowe out to the gallows, put a noose around his neck—'

'Your grace,' I begged.

'Put a noose,' Edward insisted, 'round his neck and turn him off the ladder,' he held up a hand, 'for no more than a few heartbeats, then cut him down. Proclaim that the king will not allow weapons to be drawn in his palace against his servants.' Edward dug into his purse and tossed a silver coin, which Ap Ythel caught. 'Give Robert that. Take him back to the stables, and tell the *avener*, the keeper,' he translated for Ap Ythel, 'to give him preferment. Finally, instruct that hapless groom to present himself at the office of the Chancery of the Red Wax. A full pardon for his crimes will be issued to him. Should he ever do it again, however, I will hang him myself!'

Ap Ythel bowed and left. Edward closed the door and leaned against it. I remember that day so clearly, even the insignia on Gaveston's rings as he clenched his hands open and shut. He had scarcely heeded the king's judgement on Robert Atte-Gate, still absorbed with Chapeleys' allegation against him. Edward, too, seethed with rage, hence his treatment of the groom, a mixture of savagery and mercy that made the king so unpredictable: on one breath cruel ruthlessness, on the next unexpected generosity.

'Kill him!'

Gaveston threw himself back in the chair so violently I heard its padded frame creak. Both Isabella and I started. The favourite had swiftly changed from the charming courtier; his face was now tight with anger. Isabella warned me with her eyes to be careful.

'Kill? Kill who, my lord?' she asked gently.

'Langton!' Gaveston jabbed a finger at me. 'Mathilde, do that for us. Go back to the Tower and dress that fat old prelate's weeping leg, rub in a poison, give him some deadly potion, watch him gargle and choke on it.'

'And then what, my lord?' Isabella gently insisted.

'Give Winchelsea and Lincoln their martyr? Allow Philip of France to crow like a cock to the world about what you have done? Permit Clement to issue bulls of excommunication against Langton's murderers? Raise all hands against you?'

There was silence in the chamber. Edward pushed himself away from the door and walked round to Isabella. He placed his hands on her shoulders and gently kissed the top of her head.

'*Ma douceur,*' he whispered, 'is correct.' He returned to his chair and wrinkled his nose. 'The foul odours of the galleries and passageways can be smelled even here.'

'The sewers are blocked or choked.' Gaveston swiftly broke from his tantrum, 'They must be cleaned. Ap Ythel, when he returns, will bring in scavengers and rakers.' He pulled himself up in the chair. 'We have our own sewers and runnels to clear. Listen now.' He rubbed his hands. 'Margaret, the queen dowager, is busy on our behalf. She mediates with the Lords. She may not achieve much.' He grinned. 'She and my good lady wife are more interested in Glastonbury and Arthur than Westminster and Edward. Perhaps she chatters in the wind, but Winchelsea and the rest cannot refuse her. To do so would offer great insult. The queen dowager is delaying matters yet at the same time giving his grace the appearance of negotiating with his adversaries. No one can object to that.'

'We know,' Edward intervened, 'that Queen

Margaret tires of this, eager now that spring has come to go on pilgrimage. More importantly, Philip of France is urging his beloved sister to mind her own business and go back to her prayers; even better, to throw in her lot with Winchelsea and Lincoln. My dear stepmother, of course, has refused. She has no love for Winchelsea or Lincoln.'

'My lord,' Isabella interrupted, 'how do you know that?'

'Because my beloved stepmother tells me.'

'And?'

'As does her minstrel-leech Guido the Psalter, not to mention Agnes d'Albret.' Edward laughed softly at our surprise.

'Guido has no love for Philip of France. He does not wish to return there and he is dependent on our favour. Agnes d'Albret is no different. She was sent by Philip to keep an eye on his pious sister, your holy aunt. Agnes does that, but she divulges all to us.' Edward pulled a face. 'She does not want to return to Paris and marry an elderly *seigneur*. Not only are they informants, but at our instruction, they encourage the queen dowager to plead on our behalf.' Edward bowed to Isabella. 'My lady, I would be grateful if you would continue your good offices in this matter. On Sunday next, the twenty-seventh of March, the queen dowager will meet Winchelsea and the rest in the Abbot of Westminster's gardens. Mathilde must join her. You must also encourage our beloved stepmother not to withdraw but to remain

105

here at Westminster. Point out,' Edward added, 'that soon it will Easter. How his grace the king is so pleased with her efforts that she will be allowed to hold the Virgin's cincture, the great reliquary housed in the Lady Chapel of the abbey. Now, as there is no more . . .' Edward stared at Gaveston. Both king and favourite were eager to go. They rose abruptly. Isabella and I hastened to follow. Edward and Gaveston bowed as we curtsied. The favourite pointed to Pax-Bread's letter still lying on the table.

'Make a fair copy, Mathilde. Her grace can hold it secure for me.' Then they were gone, changeable as ever, shouting and laughing along the gallery, Edward insisting on a hunt, a wild ride through the moorlands to the north of the abbey. Isabella sat listening intently, head down, staring at a ring on her finger. She let her hand fall away, stretched and picked up her wine cup.

'My lady?'

'My lady is wondering, Mathilde.'

'About Guido and Agnes?'

Isabella shrugged. 'At court, everyone watches everyone else. Who blames Guido and Agnes? They have to walk their own path. If my husband and Gaveston didn't know better, they would certainly ask you about me.'

'And Pax-Bread?'

'Yes.' Isabella nodded. 'Gaveston did not bring him here to Westminster, which means Pax-Bread is still being pursued. It shows how dangerous it is. Someone is watching what is happening. Then there is the Poison Maiden. Interesting that Langton alleged it might be Gaveston. Little wonder my husband wondered if it was me. What is the Poison Maiden, Mathilde? Who is she? Or is it a he? Or a group of people? *Dominus benedicit nos*,' she added. 'Mathilde, we shall, perhaps, talk later. Now you must go. Pax-Bread will be waiting.' She straightened in her chair and smiled dazzlingly at me. 'And tomorrow I want you to teach me that Goliard dance.'

CHAPTER 5

Because of these and other incidents, rancour deepened every day.

Vita Edwardi Secundi

Shortly before the Angelus, Demontaigu and I made our way down to King's Steps, fighting through the throng, searching for a barge. The abbot's bailiffs were out in force, placing a liar in the stocks with a whetstone around his neck and burning another through the gristle of his left ear for some petty theft. They became distracted, and yelled at two butter-women involved in a shouting match over who should sell their goods where. Next to these, mourners hoisted up a parish coffin draped in a black and gold pall on which the absolution was pinned. They sang the 'Dirige' as they waited for a funeral barge to take them further downriver to Timberhithe. Grooms and ostlers revelled in spreading the chaos as they brought horses of every description down to water. Traders bawled, 'Ten finches for a penny', or 'A slice of roast pork for eightpence'. The greatest crush was around the palace stewards, who, helped by the Widows of Christ in their tawny mantles, were distributing lady loaves and lady meat, the remains of the previous evening's banquet. I recalled my promise to the Keeper of the Dead at St Margaret's, and shouldered my way through, showing Isabella's seal and that of Gaveston to the chief steward. I told him what I wanted done, then rejoined a bewildered-looking Demontaigu at the top of King's Steps.

No royal barge was available, so we shared one with a garrulous parson taking a portable altar fashioned out of jasper and set in a wooden frame to All Harrows by the Tower. We were joined by a relic seller cradling a fosser of blue and black velvet which, he breathlessly informed us, contained the relics of St John Chrysostom and other Eastern fathers. He was shouted to silence by a merchant dressed in a splendid coat of blue and white damask edged with velvet and lined with green buckram, who boarded the barge as if he owned it. Conversation with Demontaigu was impossible. I sat in the bobbing barge watching a group of beggars at the top of the steps with their long T-shaped crutches chanting the 'Salve Regina', the words floating melodiously across the water. At the time, little did I know how that hymn had been used to conceal a great secret. Gusts of fiery smoke belched from a nearby forge. In front of us rocked a pardon barge fastened securely to a hook in the quayside wall. On board a zealous friar waited to hear the confessions of all comers beneath a crucifix on a pole, whilst in the stern a blessed candle glowed in a lantern horn to drive away the demons.

At last our barge pulled off. The day, if I recall correctly, was fair, the clouds breaking, the sun strengthening. The river ran full and fast, busy with craft of every description; after all, winter was spent, spring was here, and soon it would be the great feast of the Resurrection. Demontaigu sat shrouded in a military cloak. He was well armed in a light mailed hauberk and a war belt from which hung sword, dagger and small arbalest with a pouch of bolts. He had insisted that I change into a smock that hung down just above my stout low-heeled leather boots. I understood that his meeting at the Chapel of the Hanged might be dangerous.

The noise and chatter on board the barge was stilled by the booming Angelus bells from the city. The parson obligingly recited: 'The Angel of the Lord declared unto Mary . . .' whilst the merchant and the relic seller kept up their argument about sacred bones in a harsh whisper. I was more concerned with a thin-faced, scrawny-haired man who had joined the barge just before it left. I wondered if he was a spy. I did not like the insolent look in his close-set eyes as he scrutinised me. I whispered to Demontaigu where we were going. He nodded, more preoccupied with his own meeting later that day.

We disembarked at Queenshithe and were immediately swamped by a sea of colour, noise and smells as we fought our way through the crowds up towards Thames Street and into Fish Lane. On the quayside and along the alleyways leading to it, hawkers, hucksters, chapmen, free fruiterers and pedlars sold tarts, fresh skinned eels, meat pies of every description, mousetraps, bird cages, shoe-horns and lanterns. Tipplers with their upturned casks offered stoups of beer to passers-by. Water bearers staggered along with ladles and buckets of 'pure spring water'. Stalls in crooked lanes, built for wheelbarrows rather than carts, forced the crowds to pause. These were entertained by the apprentice boys from the nearby clothiers who imported fabrics from Paris, Hainault, and Cambrai. These envoys shouted how their masters had hangings, coverlets, canopies and testers for sale as well as precious canvas from Ostia. Other enterprising traders held up boards advertising linen thread, amber and bone beads, silk garters, brass rings and beaver hats, paxes, kissing boxes, pepper mills and girdles of every kind. One taverner had organised a six-boy choir to advertise the fresh oysters available in his comfortable oyster room. The song they chanted was well known:

'They are all alive and very fine
So if you like them come and dine
I'll find you bread and butter too
And you can have them open for a stew.'

111

Bells clanged. People shouted. Carts creaked. Dogs barked. People fought and swore. Shops and tavern signs, all garish in their colours, creaked dangerously above our heads, proclaiming: 'The Hare', 'The Honey Pot', 'The Saracen', 'The Bell at Night'. The air reeked of every stench, perfume and odour possible: sweaty clothes, smoke, dung, pitch, oil, cooking smells, as well as the sweet soapy perfumes of the rich in their satins and furs. Great lords and their retainers, in half-armour or costly clothes, rode by on powerful destriers, while beggars, almost as bare as when they were born, crouched in every cranny available and whined for alms. Bailiffs and beadles eager for trouble swaggered about looking for custom; their chosen prey, the foists, pickpockets, rogues and vagabonds, moved swiftly away like a shoal of fish from hunting pike. No one dared accost us. Demontaigu had thrown back his cloak; the sight of his sword and dagger were protection enough. At All Hallows Bread Street, we had to pause for a while. A red-faced, perspiring beadle informed us how two outlaws had been seen and put to the horn. They had apparently taken sanctuary in the tower of a nearby church and were loosing arrows whenever they wished. One man had already been killed. The delay wasn't for long. A group of city bailiffs, wearing the blue and mustard livery of the Corporation, stormed the tower. As we passed the church's great preaching cross in God's Acre, both outlaws were being summarily hanged from the beams of the lychgate. They were still gasping and struggling against the ropes as we went by.

At last we entered the trading thoroughfare of Cheapside with its great water conduit, the Tun, which was, and still is, used as a prison, with huge cages placed on its roof. On that particular day, a group of screaming doxies and their pimps caught touting for business beyond Cock Lane were being forced up into the cages for the rest of the day. In the stocks beneath, ale-conners and beadles were locking up a number of ale-masters who'd sold their drink in measures shortened by a thick coating of tar at the bottom of the jug. A beadle busily proclaimed their crimes and invited all passers-by to empty brimming buckets of horse urine over the miscreants' heads. For the rest along that great thoroughfare it was trade as usual, in everything from silver jugs to green wax, rabbits from Hampshire to precious stuff brought across the mountains of Tartary. The broad stalls under their rippling striped awnings stood in front of the lofty mansions and stately houses of merchants with their pink and white plaster, gleaming black timbers and ornately gilded gables. I paused and stared round in wonderment. Ignoring Demontaigu's puzzled look, I turned as if fascinated by two jongleurs and a tumbler practising their arts to a group of gawping boys. I quickly surveyed the crowds, searching for 'Close Eyes', the man who'd been on the barge with us, yet I could glimpse no one. We went up Milk Street towards St Andrew's Jewry and along a needle-thin alleyway, the houses jutting out above us. On a corner of this lay the Secret of Solomon.

The tavern stood in its grounds behind a grey ragstone wall entered by an ornamental wooden gatehouse with a chamber above boasting mullioned glass; this gave the hostelry the impression of being a wealthy manor house. The old porter waved us into a slightly sloping, broad cobbled bailey. Stables stretched along three sides; on the fourth, facing us, was the magnificent tavern. In honey-coloured Cotswold stone, it rose three storeys high with a black-and-white-painted wooden gallery around the top one. The roof was of gleaming red tile, whilst the front of the building boasted windows of coloured glass above wide steps sweeping up to a grandiose front door. On either side of this hung broad painted signs showing the great King Solomon seated at table pondering some mystery. You can still go there today. The tavern is not as magnificent as it used to be, but any who have survived my tale will tell you about the great mystery from the spring of 1308. Inside, the taproom was as spacious as a lord's hall, with its raftered ceiling. Yawning hearths were built into the side walls, each with a flue and stack. The floor was of polished dark planks coated with crushed herbs; none of the foul, soggy rushes of dirty alehouses. Tables stood in the window embrasures overlooking the herb and flower gardens, whilst the great common table stretched at least five yards across the centre of the room. A welcoming place. The whitewashed walls were covered with crude yet vivid paintings on stretched linen over wooden backing, all depicting scenes from the life of Solomon. Other notices proclaimed the price of food:

Loin of beef = 5 pence

Ham = 1 shilling

Rabbit = 4 pence

4 Larks = 1 penny

A man came out of the kitchen, from which white steam curled, wafting the most delicious smells. He wiped his hands on his leather apron and waved us to a window seat, offering 'hot sheep's feet, enriched with pepper and saffron sauce' as the delicacy of the day.

'Edmund Lascelles?' I demanded.

The man babbled the rest of the day's menu, scratched his balding head and pointed to a narrow staircase in the far corner.

'Second gallery, fourth chamber, under the sign of the ram. He is probably still asleep. The maid couldn't wake him.'

We thanked the taverner and went up the staircase on to the dark gallery. Five chambers stood there; above each of the oaken doors was a carved astrological sign. We stopped beneath that of the ram and knocked hard, pushing down on the handle.

No answer, no sound, nothing but the creak of wood and the faint noises of the tavern. Mystery has its own perfume or smell; perhaps it's the passing of the years: that juddering of the belly, the slight quickening of the heart. Pax-Bread wouldn't answer. Why? Demontaigu, who'd acted almost like a dream-walker since we'd left Westminster, now stirred himself, hammering at the door and rattling the handle. I felt the wood; the door hung solid. I crouched down and ran my hand along the gap between wood and floor; the door was at least three inches thick. We returned to the taproom. Mine Host was not alarmed by my news, more eager to return to his smoke-filled kitchen. I produced Isabella's seal. The tavern master smiled as if he was a mainour: a thief caught red-handed. He stood staring around at his few customers: a lick-penny trader with his tray of cheap laces, caps, pin cases, rosaries and chains; a limner man and his white-muzzled greyhound; two carters and an old woman with her pet duck. I remember them all quite vividly. I was still most vigilant for Close Eyes from the barge.

'There won't be many customers yet,' mine host muttered.

'Do you have another key?' Demontaigu asked.

'Yes, yes.' Mine Host hurried away. He went into the kitchen, came out and, ignoring us, went straight up the stairs by himself. We heard a crashing, faint oaths, then he returned.

'I cannot!' He shook his head. 'Master Lascelles must have drawn across the bolts, but come . . .'

He led us through the kitchen, past tables swimming in blood, chopped vegetables, pieces of gristle and meat, and out into the broad gardens. Few flowers yet blossomed there. The air was rich from the compost that coated the soil. The garden could be entered by a wicket gate at either side. Mine Host hurried to one of these, put his fingers to his lips and whistled. He was joined by three of his ostlers. A brief conversation ensued, then one of them crossed the garden and returned with a long siege ladder, a pole with rungs on either side. This was laid securely against the brickwork under the fourth window and one of the ostlers, encouraged by my promise of a reward, climbed gingerly up. He pulled at the shutter; it wouldn't open, so he shouted down for further guidance. Mine Host breathed in deeply and closed his eyes.

'May Michael and all his angels help us,' he whispered. 'You see, mistress, the door is locked and bolted – it would take a battering ram to clear it of its hinges. Sometimes this does happen. We have had travellers, particularly pilgrims, die on us and we have to gain entry from outside. The shutters cover a window that is broad, beyond it a leather curtain to keep out draughts.' He shouted at the ostler to come down. He did so, nimble as a squirrel. Mine Host returned to the kitchens and brought back a long, thin cutting knife. He gave careful instructions to the ostler, who went back up the ladder, wedged the knife between the shutters, prised open the bar beyond and, with a yell of triumph, pulled back the wooden slats and climbed in.

A short while later he leaned his head out.

'Nothing!' he yelled. 'Nothing at all, come and see.'

We hurried back inside and up the staircase. By the time we reached the chamber, the door was flung open. We went in. The chamber looked unoccupied; the key still hung in the inside lock. I glanced around. A large room, neatly furnished, with a bed, chests, coffers, an aumbry, table and stool. I walked across to the lavarium. The water looked clean, the napkin unruffled. I sat on the bed and studied every inch of that room: the polished wooden floor with its thin turkey rugs of dark blue, the clothes pegs on the wall either side of the door. Mine Host was equally bemused. He sat down on the stool and stared around.

'It is as if he was never here,' he whispered. 'And yet . . .'

'And yet what?' I asked

'Master Lascelles arrived late yesterday afternoon. He stabled his horse in a yard not far from here. He left his saddle there but brought his saddlebags, belt and cloak. He seemed personable enough. He paid half a mark, hired this chamber and went upstairs. A little later he came down, sat at the common table, broke his hunger on bread, cheese and ham with a pot of ale, then returned to his room.' He lifted a hand, walked to the door and shouted a name.

I heard a pattering on the gallery outside. A tousle-haired boy clad in smoke-stained rags, his coal-spotted face shining with oil, came hurtling into the chamber. He stopped abruptly and gazed around.

'This is Spit Boy,' Mine Host announced, 'also our messenger.' He winked at me. 'Spit Boy knows every corner and runnel in the ward, aye and beyond!' He chattered at the boy in the patois of the slums. Spit Boy, arms rigid either side of him, replied in a sing-song voice.

Demontaigu, who had been studying the door, moved silently across to inspect the window embrasure deep in the wall and the shutters now flung wide open. He hoisted himself up and looked out. Mine Host gestured at Spit Boy to remain quiet and turned back to me.

'Master Lascelles came here,' he declared. 'He hired this chamber and brought in his saddlebags and war belt. He came down to eat but also hired Spit Boy to deliver a message to Sister Alvena.' Mine Host now mumbled so quickly that I had to ask him to repeat it.

'The Domus Iucundarum – the House of Pleasures,' he whispered as if everyone in the neighbourhood were eavesdropping. 'It is a brothel, a rather exclusive one, to the north of Lothbury not far from All Hallows in the Walls, between Walbrook stream and the Austin Friars.'

'And?' I asked.

'Spit Boy simply took a message to Sister Alvena

and returned. He informed Master Lascelles that Sister Alvena would meet him after the Compline bell.' Mine Host touched his lips. 'I saw him leave all hooded and gowned like a friar, a very expensive gown if I remember, lined with costly ermine. His cloak was open, he was armed with sword and dagger and he carried his saddlebags. He said very little to me or Spit Boy. About three hours later he returned. I certainly remember that cowl and hood. By then the taproom was very busy. He shouted greetings and went up the stairs.' Mine Host shook his head in wonderment. 'He couldn't have fled.' He waved towards the window. 'That's broad enough but it's a long jump to the garden below. The shutters were closed, the door locked and bolted from the inside. Nevertheless, he is gone and taken everything with him.'

'Do you know where he stabled his horse?'

'No.'

'Do you know where he came from?'

Mine Host shook his head. 'Or where he was going,' he added mournfully.

'And the chambers either side?'

'Empty, mistress! Once Lent is finished, business will grow brisk.'

'Did you notice anything? Untoward strangers, unexplained mishaps?'

Again the shake of the head. 'Mistress, I saw him arrive back from his pleasures.' The taverner got to his feet. 'After that, nothing, a true mystery. Perhaps a ghost, a visitation from some demon?'

I could already see the story forming, one he'd sell to his many customers.

'I have business to attend to.' He snapped his fingers at Spit Boy and both strode out of the chamber. He came hurrying back.

'If you wish to eat, I can serve a delicious beef broth with freshly baked maslin bread.'

I accepted, and Mine Host left, closing the door gently behind him. Demontaigu and I inspected every inch of that room. To all intents and purposes no one had stayed there. The squat candle had burnt, but everything else was undisturbed: the bed, the lavarium, the chests and coffers. The door, as I thought, was thick and heavy, its lock and bolts undisturbed. The window deep in the wall, about two feet across and the same in length, was shielded by a leather draught-catcher. The shutters beyond were fixed in a wooden frame, their hinges of the stoutest leather. The shutter on the right held a bar; this would swing down to rest in an iron clasp on the left one. A small gap peeped between the shutters, broad enough to insert a blade. I recalled Mine Host's words about gaining access to a chamber where a guest had died. I peered through the window; there was no ledge below or on either side. The drop was sheer, precipitous, whilst the windows to the chambers on the right and left were a considerable distance away. No one could have gained access by any ledge or foothold. So what had happened to Pax-Bread and his belongings? I sat on the edge of the bed, Demontaigu on a stool. He questioned me about Pax-Bread and why he was so important.

I told him succinctly what the king and Gaveston had said earlier that day. Demontaigu heard me out. He asked me to repeat precisely Edward's words about the Templars and the possibility that the French were bartering for their total destruction. He was deeply disturbed. He'd been quiet ever since we left Westminster. I held my peace as a servant brought the food and ale, but once she'd gone, I gently teased him about why he looked so worried. He explained how we were to meet the Templars, at least those who still remained in London, later that day and how Alexander of Lisbon and his Noctales, because the king was besieged in Westminster, were free to cast their net far and wide.

'As for the possibility that Edward might agree to the destruction of the Temple in return for Philip's support of Gaveston . . .' Demontaigu, visibly agitated, put down the lump of bread he was eating. He looked so woebegone, I regretted telling him.

'Friend?' I knelt beside him. 'You are deeply worried?'

Demontaigu opened his mouth to speak, but shook his head and took a mouthful of ale.

'I am,' he confessed wearily, 'cut to the heart. Mathilde, you've simply described how dangerous it has all become. I also received bad news this morning. Five of our brothers have been taken up and placed in Newgate. One is an old man well past his sixtieth summer. There is talk amongst the brethren,' he mused, 'that we should withdraw into the northern shires, even seek sanctuary with Bruce in Scotland.'

I caught my breath. He stroked my hair gently.

'I will stay here, Mathilde. Tonight I might advise the rest that they should go, but this business: Pax-Bread, or Lascelles . . . He comes here, then disappears out of a locked room, a man with his baggage, no trace of him!' Demontaigu sighed and got to his feet. 'Mathilde, we've spent enough time here. Let me surprise you.' He smiled. 'Have you ever visited a brothel?'

'Just Philip of France's court,' I retorted.

'Ah well.' Demontaigu walked to the door. 'This will not be so wicked.'

We left the chamber and went down to the taproom. I instructed Mine Host that if he discovered anything new he should let me, Mathilde de Clairebon, know as soon as possible. I would lavishly reward both him and Spit Boy for any information sent to the Palace of Westminster. He assured me he would and we left.

A strange journey. I was still intrigued about what had happened to Pax-Bread, as well as concerned about what Demontaigu had told me. In many ways the conclusion he and his colleagues had reached was logical. If Alexander of Lisbon and his Noctales were given a free hand in London and elsewhere, the only place of refuge was amongst Edward's enemies in Scotland. Yet I had to steel myself to the present dangers. The day was drawing on. Most people had retired to the alehouses and cook shops for a potage of vegetables, peas and cabbage washed down with cheap ale. Because of the terrors that were to occur later that day, I remember certain glimpses, vivid memories: the various colours of people's clothes, black and white, blue and white, red and mustard; a fop wearing a quilted jacket and hose with a strange contrast of tint throughout like something glimpsed in a dream. I was on guard for danger, the sudden movement, a dagger in a hand. I kept my eyes on clothes rather than faces and I realised how people's wealth and status were determined by the girdle around their waist, be it wool, leather, linen, garnished with copper, iron, steel or, in the case of the very rich, gold or silver. Other memories come floating back. A butcher was slaughtering a pig because it had been found wandering where it shouldn't have been. Two dogs darted in, eager to lap the blood, only to be driven off with kicks and blows. On the corner of Wood Street, bailiffs were putting five bakers into the stocks for selling underweight loaves; across the lane, a prostitute lifted her skirt and called raucously at a group of gallants swaggering by. A friar was also trying to seek the young men's attention by attacking the way they dressed.

'Ye proud gallants, cold and heartless,' he thundered, 'with your high caps witless, and your short gowns frithless, are bringing this land to great heaviness.'

He kept repeating the refrain so the words, like the tune of a carol, dinned in my own memory, as did the friar's sombre warning how in hell, 'those who dress lavishly will be tormented by demons dressed in the same apparel they flaunted during life'.

On occasion Demontaigu would stop. We were not taking the direct route to Lothbury but going along those narrow lanes towards Cripplegate. Demontaigu would pause and enter the taprooms of various taverns – the Roebuck, the Spread Eagle, the Whirl, the Jackanapes – where comrades of his order were sheltering, disguised as beggars, tinkers, chapmen or, on occasion, even as lepers or Bedlamites. Outside the Glowing Worm, I was approached by a herb wife who offered me some parsley and thyme. I shook my head and smiled, but she drew closer. She was not so much interested in selling herbs as in seeking my attention for a narrow-faced man sheltering in a doorway further down the street: in truth a pimp and his whore seeking fresh flesh for their trade. Demontaigu came out of the tavern, took one look at the woman, glanced down the street and drove both off with curses.

'I am sorry,' he apologised. 'But that was my last visit. Come.'

We went up Gutter Lane, past Bakewell Hall into Lothbury and across the Great Common dotted here and there with stately houses, their towered roofs and occasional glass-filled windows glinting above high stone curtain-walls. Demontaigu took direction from a chapman who smiled at his enquiry but pointed to a track-way winding through a thick copse of trees.

'The path to pleasure,' he joked, then pointed at me. 'But why go there with a merry handful so close?'

Demontaigu laughed. I blushed. We made our way down across the wasteland, the soil and grass slippery underfoot. A group of boys with their lurchers appeared, eager to raise a hare; the shouting and barking dinned our ears as we entered the silent copse, to be greeted by strange cooking smells. A group of Moon People sheltered in the trees; they were busy baking in hot ash small birds, skinned hedgehog and squirrel, which a dark-faced woman offered us for a penny a piece. The smell was foul. I gave her a coin but refused the food, pinching my nostrils even as Demontaigu teased me how he'd eaten such fare when fighting in France. The woman, apparently a bawdy basket, followed us along the path shouting in a language I could not understand. A man slipped out of the trees carrying a club, approaching us as if we'd insulted the woman. Demontaigu half drew his sword and both the bawdy basket and her protector promptly disappeared. At last the trees thinned. The track-way branched on to a lane leading up to a red-brick wall with a smartly painted blue gate boasting a black cross above the grille high in the wood. Demontaigu asked for Isabella and Gaveston's seals. He approached the gate and pulled hard on the chain hanging from the bell-cote. The grille opened. Demontaigu held up the seals.

'The king's business,' he shouted as loud as any herald, and the bolts were drawn. Demontaigu beckoned me closer as the gates swung open. A young woman dressed like a novice nun in black from head to toe, an ivory-coloured wimple framing her lovely face, gestured at us to come in. I noticed how the white ruffs at her neck and wrists offset the bleakness; I also glimpsed the carmine-coloured nails as well as the bright red pointed shoes peeping out from beneath the black kirtle. She smiled gracefully, sketched a curtsy and led us up the well-swept path. Only then did I notice the two men, pug-nosed and aggressive, sheltering behind the gate, which they now swung shut.

A flowery arbour trellis shrouded the path with plants climbing up across the top; on either side of this lawns, herb banks and flowerbeds budded under the spring sun. At the end of the path, steps led up to a metal-studded black door with grilles and eyelets, like that of a convent. Our guide pulled at the brightly polished copper bell. The door swung open and she invited us into a rather stark parlour with cushioned stools, benches and tables. The walls were a brilliant white, with linen paintings stretched over wooden board fastened to the plaster, each showed a young woman busy about some household task. Demontaigu studied one of these, grinned and sat down on the bench beside me. The Novice, as I now thought of her, stood smiling demurely down at us. She moved from the door as a more mature woman, harsh-faced, dressed in a similar fashion to the Novice, swept into the room. She glanced in surprise at me, but shrugged and, rounding on Demontaigu, spoke quickly in Norman French, demanding to examine the seals. She did so carefully before sweeping out of the chamber, beckoning the Novice to join her. Demontaigu whispered, lips almost touching my ear, '*In hoc loco muri oculos auresque habent* – in this place the walls have eyes as well as ears'. He rose, tapped one of the paintings and came and stood over me. 'Alvena is here,' he whispered.

A short while later there was a knock on the door and a young lady entered. She was dressed like the Novice, though her gown was dark green, the wimple blood red. She had skin as white as a water lily, brows as black as jet, an impish face with laughing eyes, snub nose and full lips. She offered us Leche Lumbard and dates in spiced wine, but we refused.

'Then what can I do for you?' she asked mischievously. 'The hour is early. We sisters usually rest and begin our service after Vespers.' She looked questioningly at me.

'Not here,' I murmured, moving to the door.

The young woman shrugged, pulled a face and brushed past me, going back down the passageway. I heard the mutter of conversation. Alvena started to come back. A voice called. She returned; more conversation, then she appeared out of the gloom, slightly flushed, eyes more wary.

'Mother Superior says we may sit in the garden.'

We made ourselves comfortable on a stone bench outside. For a short while Alvena chattered about the flowers, how she looked forward to summer and how lovely it was to sit here especially in the evening and watch the sunset.

'Pax-Bread?' I declared. 'Edmund Lascelles? He came here last night, didn't he? He visited you?'

'I don't know,' she replied, eyes rounding in surprise. 'I don't know if I can help.'

'Mistress,' I retorted, turning to face her squarely, 'you can answer our questions either here or in the gatehouse at Westminster. We know Edmund Lascelles sent Spit Boy here to arrange an assignment with you after Vespers. He came here?'

'Yes, yes, he did.'

'Tell me – and please, mistress, the truth, or it's the gatehouse and much rougher questioning. We mean you no harm,' I insisted. I took two silver coins from my purse. 'These are yours. I assure you, we mean no harm.'

Alvena's demeanour changed, her face hard, no more pretence. She pocketed the coins and stared across the grass as if fascinated by a thrush jabbing at the soil.

'I am originally from Poitou,' she declared. 'I came here four years ago. Master Lascelles met me in Cock Lane where I was doing service in a boarding house. He offered better: this place under the care and protection of Mother Superior. Our guests are, how can I put it, carefully selected? Not everyone is allowed through that gate. Edmund is kind and gentle. He is also a superb pastry cook. He often delighted us as much as we delighted him.' She laughed softly. 'Then he had to return to France. Occasionally he returned to London. He would always visit me, bring me some present. Last night he did the same but this time there was no present. Edmund was usually cheerful, a merry soul, but yesterday he was silent and withdrawn. It took some time for him to relax, a few cups of wine, some soft music. I asked him what the matter was. He just shook his head and said he was on king's business and that he was frightened. I must admit, mistress,' she glanced sharply at me, 'he was so fearful that even I became cautious, especially when he said he felt as if he was followed to this house. I asked him by whom. He just shook his head and we fell to our games. Afterwards I pressed him: what was his business? Why was he so frightened? He told me he was staying at the Secret of Solomon and that he would return this evening.' She glanced at me. 'He won't, will he?'

'No, mistress, he will not, because he cannot. He seems to have disappeared.' I quickly told her what we'd found at the tavern.

Alvena swallowed hard. 'This is not my business.' She made to rise but I pressed her back. 'Did he say anything,' I insisted, 'anything at all?' Alvena stared down at her hands, soft and white, the nails neatly pared and painted. She moved in a gust of fragrant perfume, her hand pushing back the ruffle at her neck to scratch the sweat. The woman was fearful, wondering whether to speak or not.

'What danger could you be in, mistress?' I asked.

'Danger?' She laughed sharply. 'No danger, not for me anyway!' She murmured, 'Edmund said something rather strange. After I pressed him about his worry, he declared that great danger lurked at Westminster. How old Jean might be as mad as a March hare but he had the truth of it and he sang the right hymn. I asked him what he meant. By then Edmund was deep in his cups, more interested in his pleasures. Of course,' she shrugged, 'I encouraged him in that.' She rose to her feet and turned to face us. 'I owe a great deal to Edmund. If something has happened to him, then I shall weep. I shall be sorry. I shall light a candle. Remember him in my prayers.' She stood swaying gently, studying our faces carefully. 'Do you think ill of me, mistress?'

I shook my head. 'Each soul has its path,' I replied. 'Only God knows the truth.'

'You have kind eyes, and you, sir,' she looked at Demontaigu, 'are you a priest?'

I realised how sharp this young woman was.

'What I am,' Demontaigu smiled, 'only God knows. Do you have anything else to tell us, mistress?'

She shook her head, made to go, but came back and crouched before us, one hand resting on Demontaigu's knee. 'Go with God,' she whispered. 'You have been kind, so I shall give you clear warning. You talk of danger. There is no danger for me here, but,' she gestured with her head, 'beyond that gate our porters have seen three men sheltering in the trees.'

'Moon People?' Demontaigu asked.

'No, no.' She shook her head again. 'Not Moon People. These are well armed, hooded and visored. Monsieur,' Alvena rose, smiled at Demontaigu and touched me gently on the cheek, 'mademoiselle, take care.'

CHAPTER 6

He has convened a council . . . and disposed of the Templars.

Alvena left in a rustle of skirts. Demontaigu rose to his feet. I tried to control the shivering, the fear curdling my belly.

'Bertrand, shall we leave by another way?'

He shook his head grimly. 'They'll have the entire house watched. It's best if we leave by the gate. Walk quickly, yet act as if we suspect nothing. Above all, move swiftly but keep with me.' He unhitched the arbalest from the hook on his war belt, plucked a bolt from the small pouch, wound the cord back and placed it in the groove, taking great care that the catch was primed. 'Hide this beneath your cloak. Do not loose until I give the order.'

I took the arbalest, though first I had to dry my hands on my cloak. Demontaigu noticed this and cupped my face in his hands. He kissed me gently on the brow and on the lips, holding me tenderly, staring into my eyes.

'I feel the same as you, Mathilde, the guttering in the belly, the clammy sweat, your breath coming hard. Forget that. Once we leave this house, we are going to meet three men who will try to kill us.'

'What if they do so from afar?'

'I doubt it.' Demontaigu shook his head. 'There is more to it than that. I suspect they want us alive, to question, to interrogate to discover what we know. Now come.'

The two ruffians opened the gate. Once we were through, Demontaigu walked so briskly I almost ran to keep up with him.

'Did I tell you that story, Mathilde,' Demontaigu's voice rose, 'about the disreputable clerk who visited the Cistercians at Clairvaux to see what he could rob? He stayed a year hoping to steal their precious candlesticks from the altar but found it difficult to plan . . . In the trees to the left,' he whispered. 'However, this man,' he continued loudly, 'because he spent a year in such a holy place found that he was converting to needing the grace of God more than the candlesticks, so he confessed his sins and entered the order.'

Demontaigu threw back his cloak.

'And there's the other story. Once, in the monastery of St Benigny, I saw a devil: it was just after dawn, a little thin man, black-eyed, with sunken cheeks and receding hair. He was hunchbacked and dirty, dressed in garish rags. They are here,' he added in a whisper.

I glanced up. We were well away from the gate, almost approaching the trees when the three emerged, cowled and visored, long cloaks hanging to their ankles, faces masked, with only slits for their eyes and mouth.

'Good brothers three,' Demontaigu shouted, 'how are you?'

Closer and closer we drew. The men, taken by surprise, didn't know what to do.

'The one in the centre,' Demontaigu murmured, 'he is the leader.'

The gap between us closed. The three recovered, cloaks were thrown back, swords and daggers drawn. They hastened towards us.

'Now, Mathilde, now!'

I paused, pushed back my own cloak and brought up the arbalest. Our opponents were running towards us. I took aim, released the catch and the bolt flew sure and fast, powerful testimony to the training Uncle Reginald had given me in Paris. The quarrel struck the leader deep in the chest. He screamed as he was flung back. The other two, disconcerted, separated from each other and paused. Demontaigu rushed in, sword and dagger whirling as he attacked the man on his right. The other looked at me. I was already putting a second bolt into the groove. He hesitated, made for Demontaigu, then turned back to me. I fumbled with the catch, then released it. The bolt whirred out. At such close range it had a deadly impact, piercing the man in the face just beneath the left eye, shattering skin, bone and muscle. Blood spurted out through nose and mouth as he staggered back crying and shrieking, a horrid sound. Demontaigu was a knight, a trained swordsman. The third ruffian was no match. He almost fell upon Demontaigu's sword; it sliced up into his belly as Demontaigu plunged his dagger deep into the side of his assailant's neck. So quickly! Isn't it strange how swiftly Death comes? There on the heathland, the trees moving gently, the distant sounds of a dog barking, children shouting. Three men killed, blood spurting out of ear, nose and mouth. The one Demontaigu had attacked died quickly, as did the first whom I'd loosed at: the quarrel had cut deep, straight into his heart. The man who had taken the bolt in the face lay screaming and moaning on the ground. Demontaigu went over. Dropping his sword and moving his dagger to his right hand, he knelt, cupping the man's chin between his fingers, forcing him to look up.

'You are dying,' he murmured. 'I am a priest. No physician under the sun can save you. Tell me now and I will shrive you. Lascelles, Pax-Bread?'

'Gone!' muttered the man, gargling on his own blood. 'Taken.' Then his head fell slack.

Demontaigu whispered the words of absolution, sketched a blessing in the air and came back to me. I stood clutching the crossbow, shivering at the cold.

'Mathilde.' Demontaigu prised the crossbow from my fingers and placed it gently on the grass beside me. He took my hands, cupping them in his, rubbing hard so I could feel the warmth.

'So swift?' I murmured. 'So swift.'

Demontaigu embraced me, putting his hand behind my head, pushing my face into the side of his neck. 'Mathilde, they didn't expect it. They hoped we would be terrified, stand still, perhaps turn to flee, not advance towards them, attack vigorously and deadly as any knight on horseback. Now their souls have gone to God, and if one of them spoke the truth, so has Lascelles.' He let me go.

Staring back down the track-way, I saw the gates of the House of Pleasure open and shut quickly.

'God bless Alvena,' Demontaigu murmured. 'We owe her a debt.' He knelt beside the three ruffians, searching their clothes and wallets, but apart from a few coins, there was nothing else. 'Professionals,' he declared, getting to his feet. 'Leave them to the Moon People.'

'The Tenebrae?' I asked. '*Les ombres?*'

'Possibly.' Demontaigu tapped one of the corpses with his boot. 'Former soldiers, I suppose, ruffians: they can be hired a dozen a penny in the city.' He glanced up the sky. 'There is nothing like swordplay and blood to whet the appetite, eh, Mathilde?' He beckoned me forward. 'We still have business to do.'

We left Lothbury, entering the tangle of alleys and

lanes stretching down to Aldersgate. The Chapel of the Hanged lay between St Bartholomew's and St John's Clerkenwell. The light was greying, darkening those reeking, shabby runnels. On either side the houses, old and crumbling, blocked out the sky. The sense of watching malevolence deepened. The shabby scrawled signs creaked in the wind. Shadows jumped and fluttered in the glow of the occasional lantern horn. Faces leered at us through the poor light, grotesques with their wrinkled skin, furred brows, hairy lips, squinted eyes and gabbling mouths, their gums all sore with blackened teeth. In my fevered state they looked like demons massing against us. Only Demontaigu's calm demeanour stilled my qualms. We skirted the Shambles stinking of the guts and innards of animals slaughtered in the fleshing yards near Newgate. As I've written, I was still recovering from the swift savagery of that hideous mêlée. Demontaigu, however, seemed more comforted and assured, as if the violence had drawn the tension from him. He paused when he glimpsed the tops of Newgate's turreted towers and pattered a Pater, Ave and Gloria for his comrades imprisoned in that hideous hole. We continued on, vigilant against the rogues, vagabonds and petty thieves slyly emerging as the light faded and the bells of St Martin le Grand tolled the curfew, warning of the approaching dark. On the crumbling steps of a church porch, a wandering preacher proclaimed disasters in the heavens: how Death, a grinning Antic, postured in the shadows waiting for the Day of Doom, and Satan, all-horned, readied his fiery sickle to reap his harvest. I wondered if the man was one of Demontaigu's brothers hiding in this den of thieves and easy livers. But there again, anyone could be anything in those dark, evil alleyways. I even wondered about the rat catcher, trailed by his ferocious dogs, who beat a drum and rattled his traps as he sang:

'Rats or mice,
Have ye any rats, mice, polecats or weasels?
Or even an old sow sick with the measles . . . ?'

I was relieved to reach Aldersgate, to go beyond the bar, along open lanes and into the inviting warmth of the Paltock Tavern. Demontaigu had been watching me closely. He insisted that we eat and I would feel better. We hired a special table close to the inglehook and ordered venison stewed in ginger, chicken boiled and stuffed with grapes with freshly baked rastons and goblets of claret. We ate hurriedly in silence, then continued into the darkening day along rib-thin track-ways. At last we reached the 'corpse road', as Demontaigu described it, leading to the derelict Chapel of the Hanged. In truth it was an eerie, ghost-haunted place. Its cemetery was a tangle of undergrowth that covered and smothered the battered headstones and decaying wooden crosses. A place of desolation. Bats, like dark sprites, swooped and swirled over the gorse bending under a sharp evening breeze.

'It's owl time,' Demontaigu murmured. 'Vespers will soon be finished.'

He pushed back the creaking lychgate and we went up the weed-strewn path. The main door of the chapel was bolted with wooden bars nailed across. Demontaigu ignored this and led me round the church to the other side, an equally desolate place. He paused before the narrow corpse-door, inserted his dagger, expertly lifted the latch and ushered me into the chapel, a long, barn-like structure. He knew where to go and quickly lit the sconce torches fastened into clasps on the squat round pillars. The light flared, revealing a gloomy nave of table tombs, a derelict rood screen, mildewed paving stones and faded wall paintings. If I ever visited a hall of ghosts, the Chapel of the Hanged was certainly one. Demontaigu gestured me across into a far corner. He took a sconce torch from its clasp, opened a coffin-shaped door and led me down into the crypt, a barrel-vaulted chapel with rounded pillars stretching along each side. A stark stone altar stood on a slightly raised sanctuary plinth at the far end. I have been in many eerie places, but that crypt was surely one where the veil between the visible and the invisible became extremely thin.

Demontaigu led me across to the far wall. He took off his cloak and laid it on the ground for me. He then made sure the coffin door leading down to the crypt was bolted and secure. He ignored my questions, more concerned with lighting the sconce torches. Their orange tongues of flame licked out, bringing that macabre place to life. The wall paintings were stark and vivid. One I remember distinctly depicted a confrontation between the living and the dead on a hunting field. The living were all intent on pursuing some quarry. They were well dressed, cloaked and spurred astride fat, sleek destriers. The dead were skeletons garbed in funeral cloths and tattered shrouds, their horses ghastly-ribbed mounts from the meadows of hell. On either side of this horrid vision other paintings emphasised the dissolution of all things, the imminence of death, the terrors of hell and the pains of purgatory.

'What is this place?' I repeated. My voice echoed through that cavern of atonement like that of a disembodied soul. 'It reeks of the smell of death and the anguish of the tomb.'

'This,' Demontaigu explained, squatting down in front of me, 'is an ancient church built over a Saxon crypt. About two hundred years ago, Pope Urban II proclaimed the Great Crusade at Clermont. The founders of our order, the Templars, Hugh de Payne and Geoffrey of St Omer, immediately took the cross and journeyed across the world to storm the walls of Jerusalem. They later instituted our order. An Englishman – we do not know his full name; legend calls him Fitzdamory – also took the oath, vowing solemnly to join Hugh and Geoffrey on their holy pilgrimage. Fitzdamory's wife, however, distraught at the prospect of losing her husband, persuaded him not to join them at the

141

mustering place near Vezelay in France. The Crusaders left for Outremer. Fitzdamory's wife died soon afterwards; Fitzdamory saw it as God's judgement on his broken vow. He became a hermit beyond the city walls and used his wealth to build the Chapel of the Hanged above this crypt.' Demontaigu touched my cheek. 'A cavern of lost souls. Perhaps it is! Fitzdamory, as an act of penance, vowed this church as a place to receive the corpses of those hanged in London. The cadavers of condemned men and women, too poor or too wicked by reputation to secure a lasting resting place in God's Acre elsewhere.' He gestured at a trapdoor hidden in the shadows of the ceiling, its bolts all rusted. 'The corpses of the hanged were lowered down here, dressed for burial, then taken out, hence the name of the chapel.'

'But now it's derelict?'

'It lies beyond the city walls. Many regard it as a haunted, ill-cursed place. Our order took it over. They did not know what to do with it . . .' Demontaigu paused at a knock on the crypt door, dull but threatening, echoing through the crypt like a drum beat. He held his hand up, listening intently. Again the knock. He hastened up the steps. I followed.

'As ye are,' he called.

'So shall ye be,' came the reply.

Demontaigu drew back the bolts. Dark shapes slipped through the doorway, tripping down the steps. In the light, most of them looked grotesque, hair and beards thick and bushy. Beneath the cloaks and hoods, the arrivals were dressed in a variety of attire, cotehardies, jupons and jerkins, some costly, others stained and ragged. I caught the tension, the rank smell of fear, the sweaty haste of men who lurked in the shadows, now relieved to reach this sanctuary of peace. All were well armed. They gathered in the pool of light below, about fourteen or fifteen people. I glimpsed the preacher from the Tower quayside; his eyes, no longer gleaming in passion, were gentle and mocking. Demontaigu introduced him as Jean de Ausel, and he grasped my hand and kissed me full on each cheek in a gust of wine, sweat and leather. He then introduced Padraig, the cripple who had crouched on those wooden slats, now nimble enough to make everyone laugh by tumbling and somersaulting along the floor of that gloomy crypt. Ausel truly surprised me. He was no longer the fanatic; even his voice had changed, becoming soft and lilting. I tried to trace the accent. Ausel explained how he was of Norman family from the Pale around Dublin, with a hunger to return to the mist-strewn glens of what he called 'the Blessed Isle'. More Templars arrived, knights, serjeants, servants of the order. Some were calm, well fed and equitable, others haunted, harassed and careworn. A few, particularly the old, objected to my presence, muttering that no woman should be allowed into their mysteries. Demontaigu, without giving my name or status, voiced that he would vouch for me, as did Ausel and Padraig.

'Our order is no more,' Ausel declared. 'We need every friend we have.' The protests faded away.

Simon Destivet, their leader, called what he termed their 'parliament' to order. He knelt on the dais before the crumbling altar, and made the sign of the cross as we gathered behind him and intoned the 'Veni Creator Spiritus'. The refrain was taken up, powerful voices calling through the dark. Once it was finished, Demontaigu nipped my wrist as a warning to remain silent. Two candles were lit, the iron spigots being brought from a chest concealed in a corner; these were placed on the altar. A coffer, ironbound and secured by three locks, was put between them; Destivet, Demontaigu and Ausel each produced a key. The coffer was opened. Meanwhile lanterns, thick coloured candles gleaming behind the horn covers, were also positioned along the altar. A roll of linen was taken out of the coffer and stretched between two wooden frames. The cloth must have been a yard long and the same across, ancient but very well preserved. The lantern horns behind it were moved closer. I gasped in amazement. The more I stared, the better I could distinguish the face of a man. I could make out his tangled hair and beard, the half-closed eyes, a disfigured, bruised face, yet also gentle, a soul-searing vision of deep suffering. The Templars immediately bowed, foreheads touching the ground as they intoned a prayer: 'Ah my Jesus, turn your face towards each of us as you did to Veronica. Not that we may see it with our bodily

144

eyes, for this we do not deserve, but turn it towards our hearts so that, remembering You, we may ever draw from this power and strength the vigour necessary to sustain the combats of life. Amen.'

I bowed with them, realising this must be the Mandylion, the cloth that had covered the face of the crucified Christ. My uncle, Sir Reginald, had often obliquely referred to this, whilst in their hideous allegations against the Templars, Philip's lawyers had accused them of worshipping a disembodied head. Now I saw the truth! We all knelt back on our heels, and Destivet began a mournful prayer, a quotation from scripture: 'It is close, the day of their ruin, their doom comes at speed.'

'No, no.' Ausel's voice rang clear. 'No, no, let us not be dismayed or downcast, brothers. Let us not seek vengeance on our enemies but leave that to God. Let us be triumphant.'

Destivet nodded, even though, kneeling behind him, I sensed he was crying. Ausel was determined to lift the pall of gloom. In his lilting Irish voice he chanted a beautiful Celtic prayer. I later asked Demontaigu to copy it down for me:

'I offer you, Lord,
Every flower that ever grew,
Every bird that ever flew,
Every wind that ever blew.
Good God, every thunder rolling,
Every church bell tolling,

Every leaf and every bud.
Multiply each and every one.
Make them into glories, millions of glories.'

Others took up the prayer. I felt a slight chill, not of fear but of awe at those men, hunted and harassed to death, still determined to pray, to fight, to proclaim their message. Afterwards, they all joined Ausel in a Celtic hymn:

'Be thou our vision, Oh Lord of our hearts . . .
Be thou our first thought in the day and the
   night,
Waking or sleeping your presence our light,
Be thou our shield, our sword for the fight . . .'

The chant finally finished, and Destivet made the sign of the cross. The candles were doused, the sacred roll relocked in its coffer. Destivet turned and sat on the edge of the dais. The rest of us grouped around him in a circle. Each reported what had happened. One tale of gloom after another. In France, the Templars were being accused of the most heinous crimes: intercourse with demons, spitting on Christ's image, urinating on the cross, administering the kiss of shame to the penis, buttocks and lips of superiors, or engaging in other homosexual acts.

'According to one of Philip's lawyers,' a Templar spoke up, 'the allegations against us are "a bitter thing, lamentable, horrible to contemplate, terrible to bear, almost inhuman, indeed set apart from all humanity".'

'But are they believed?' Destivet asked.

The speaker shrugged. 'A very few of our comrades escaped, but most of them were tortured: weights hung on their genitals. They were strapped to the rack, ankles and wrists, dislocated through winches, wrenched from their sockets. Others were pulled up to the ceiling by ropes which would suddenly go slack, their fall broken by a violent jerk. Burnings and scaldings are commonplace. The brothers are confessing; they have to for a moment's peace.'

The Templars prayed for these unfortunates, then moved swiftly on to other business, including King Edward's reluctance to allow papal inquisitors into the realm. Some of the Templars knew about the troubles at Westminster and the presence of French envoys. Destivet raised the possibility of attacking these, arguing how the assassination of Marigny and his coven would be 'a righteous act'. Demontaigu disagreed, pointing out how the French were well protected, whilst such an attack might alienate Edward. Moreover, the Noctales were a malevolent, ever-present menace. They would continue the hunt whatever happened. Demontaigu's argument was accepted. Various Templars related how the Noctales, armed with descriptions and information about hiding places supplied by spies and informers, had already captured and imprisoned a number of their brethren. The whereabouts of Templar treasure was discussed, its hiding places and worth. I was particularly intrigued by the references to gold and silver held by Langton, secretly hidden away before his fall. Destivet was of the mind that they should gather all such treasure, memoranda and relics, move swiftly into the northern shires and open secret negotiations with the Scottish rebel Bruce. This was being hotly discussed when the wail of a hunting horn immediately created silence. Candles were doused, war belts strapped on, arbalests winched back, bows and arrows seized.

'Our lookouts!' Demontaigu hissed.

A second horn echoed through the darkness, followed by the sound of running feet along the hollow nave above and a furious pounding on the crypt door. Demontaigu hastened up the steps. He asked the password and was given it. He drew back the bolts. Two men almost threw themselves down the steps, tumbling and tripping over each other.

'Noctales!' one of them declared. 'Not just a few; perhaps all of them. They are in the cemetery, guarding every entrance.'

Demontaigu immediately re-bolted the door and stood on the top of the steps banging his sword against the wall for silence.

'They know we are here!' he declared. 'We could break out through the church and take whatever opportunity exists in the open fields around, but they are on horseback. God knows how many there are and what other rogues they've hired for tonight's work. They think they have us trapped; we will prove them wrong. Crossbowmen and archers, you stay.'

About a dozen men stepped forward. Demontaigu hurried down the steps and had a word with Destivet and Ausel. They quickly agreed that the aged should leave first carrying the treasures, relics, documents and whatever else the Noctales wished to seize. I was going ask how they were going to get out when Demontaigu led me over into a corner. He and two others grasped the rusting key in a flagstone and lifted it up. A gush of cold foul air swept through the crypt.

'You don't think,' Demontaigu whispered, 'that we'd shelter here with no way out? This is an old church. The passage beneath runs close to St Bartholomew's near Smithfield. Mathilde, I ask you to stay with me. We will be the last to leave, but if you are captured . . .' he grasped my hands, 'stand on ceremony. Declare who you are. Demand that you be taken immediately back to the palace. But if God is good, that won't happen.'

The crypt began to empty, the old ones first, with a small escort; some carried sacks, others coffers and chests. The steps leading down into the pit were crumbling and steep. Curses rang through the darkness. Cresset torches were hastily relit and handed down, Demontaigu shouting that some must be fixed into wall niches. By now I was aware that the nave above us was filling with men; it echoed with shouts, mailed footsteps and the clash of armour. Eventually the Noctales reached the crypt door. It was tried and pushed, followed by silence, then I heard the sound of running feet and a hideous crashing. The Noctales had found a fallen log or an old bench and were using it as a battering ram. The door however was thick and stout, its hinges almost welded into the wood. Meanwhile the crypt emptied further. Archers and crossbowmen prepared, arrows lying on the ground beside each man's right foot, one notched to the bow. Demontaigu took a small sack of oil, with which he doused the steps; then he piled whatever rubbish he could find against the crypt door.

I watched sweat-soaked, heart pounding, feeling at the same time hot and cold. The battering ram was now having an effect. The wood buckled. The door shivered. There was a great crash and the bottom half gave way. A figure slipped through, sword glinting. An arrow was loosed. The man screamed and slithered down the steps. Demontaigu threw a torch. The steps and rubbish piled against the door were engulfed in a sheet of flame. The Noctales were foolish. Some tried to jump through; those who did, slipped on the oil and were easy targets against the light for our crossbowmen and archers. The air now sang with the twang of bows and the whistle of arrows, followed by heart-jolting screams as each shaft found its target. Demontaigu, sword drawn, directed the bowmen as the Noctales, with cloaks and whatever else they could find, tried to douse the flames. Demontaigu ordered his men to withdraw; crossbowmen first, then the archers.

The fire began to die down. Demontaigu urged some of the crossbowmen out down the secret passageway, followed by men-at-arms. The Noctales, however, were desperate, furious at being thwarted, eager to seize their prey. Three of them reached the bottom of the steps unscathed and rushed towards our remaining crossbowmen. One leapt, bringing his sword down with two hands, and cut through the arm of an archer as he fumbled for another shaft. The man collapsed screaming. The Noctales showed no mercy and immediately drove his sword straight into the archer's throat before one of the Templars loosed a quarrel that took the attacker full in the side of the face. Pandemonium and chaos ensued. Shouts and screams, the clash of swords. Demontaigu's line held firm. I was now in the centre of a V, which was retreating back to that life-giving tunnel. Demontaigu had first used whatever crossbowmen had remained. The archers were now told to mass and loose at the same time; their shower of arrows drove the Noctales back.

'Enough!' Demontaigu shouted. 'Enough!'

Four or five master bowmen stayed, loosing shaft after shaft as the rest hurried down the steps. Demontaigu pushed me into the arms of one of his companions; looking up, I stared into the smiling face of Ausel.

'What a fortunate night,' he said. 'A fight with the Noctales and the embrace of a beautiful woman.' He laughed at his own mock chivalry and

151

pushed me further down towards the steps. I was half carried into the darkness below. The tunnel was narrow, no more than two yards across, and about the same high. Ausel told me to watch my head and follow him. Behind me, the last men hurried through. In the glow of a torch I glimpsed Demontaigu pull the paving stone back into place. He poured oil on the steps and dropped the torch, fleeing after us as the flames leapt up. We stumbled and ran, gasping for breath, bodies sweat-soaked. I tried not to think as rats scurried by, squeaking stridently at being disturbed. At one point the tunnel branched to the left and right. Ausel paused, waiting for Demontaigu to catch up. He stared at certain markings on the wall and indicated we should take the left fork. No sounds echoed behind us. Demontaigu gaspingly informed us that the paving stone was intricately placed and not easily raised, whilst the fire would be deterrent enough, not to mention the prospect of arrows being loosed through the darkness.

At last the tunnel sloped upwards. I felt a flurry of cold night air and we were out into an old derelict cemetery lying to the north of Smithfield, bordering its great open meadows. In the distance I could see the gibbets and scaffolds of the execution ground lit by torches as carpenters worked late into the night for some execution the following morning. A grim, macabre scene. By then most of the Templars had escaped, scattering in every direction. Demontaigu explained that there would be little time for farewells but that they all knew how and when they would meet again. Dragging me by the arm, he skirted the common on to a track-way down to the lanes leading into the city. Only then did I became aware of how deep the darkness was. The rasping night air bit at me even as lantern horns at windows or slung on hooks outside doors glowed comfortingly. The final curfew had not yet tolled. The watch were not out. The streets were busy, especially near the fleshing yards where the taverns and alehouses still provided welcoming light and warmth. Demontaigu took me into one of these, hiring a table deep in the shadows. He ordered water and napkins, and we roughly cleaned ourselves whilst sharing a goblet of wine and a platter of bread. Demontaigu then leaned back, head against the wall, peering at me through half-opened eyes.

'We never expected that,' he murmured. 'Those poor unfortunates at Newgate? Perhaps one of them was interrogated? They could only have discovered the Chapel of the Hanged from a Templar . . . But come, mistress,' he smiled, 'let's go hand in hand back to the palace and pretend that whatever happened today did not.'

CHAPTER 7

Even when such things had been carried out,
neither true charity or peace remained.

Vita Edwardi Secundi

S uch advice was easily given yet hard to act
upon. By the time we reached the main gate
of Burgundy Hall and the welcoming faces
of Ap Ythel and his archers, I felt exhausted. My
legs were weak, my stomach queasy, eager to retch.
Demontaigu gently kissed me good night and
slipped away. Ap Ythel took me into the royal quarters, up the stairs, past chamberlains and servants
hurrying here and there on various tasks. The
smell was still fetid and rank. I commented on
this. Ap Ythel shrugged apologetically.

'Tomorrow,' he said, 'the drains and sewers, the
latrines and garderobes will be cleaned.' He
gestured at servants laying out pots of crushed
herbs. Sweet smoke curled from incense boats
whilst the brazier coals had been heavily coated
with aromatic powder. I knew Isabella was going

to be busy that day meeting representatives of the French envoys, so I was surprised when a chamberlain insisted on taking me to the king's chamber. Edward, Gaveston and Isabella were sitting before the fire, heating chestnuts on the coals and ladling out hot posset from a deep silver-engraved wassail bowl. All three turned as I came in, the chamberlain announcing in a carrying voice that I had just arrived. Edward and Gaveston were dressed as they had been early that day, the boots they'd kicked off thickly caked with mud. The king rose and came towards me. I would like to think that was courtesy, but I suspect he could tell from my face and the smuts of dirt on my cloak and kirtle that something had happened. He grasped my hands and gently kissed the fingertips, his eyes studying mine closely.

'You are late.' Isabella's voice was soft and languorous. She and Gaveston were sitting so close I felt a pang of jealousy. These Great Ones also had their own secrets, part of their lives hidden from me.

'All went well?' Edward asked.

'No, my lord,' I replied wearily. I took off my cloak, curtsied towards my mistress and the king and almost stumbled towards the stool Gaveston pushed between himself and the queen. 'No, my lord, all did not go well. Nor do I feel well.' I slumped down before the fire and told them everything that had happened at the Secret of Solomon, our visit to the Domus Iucundarum, and the possibility that

155

Pax-Bread was dead. All merriment faded. The king gnawed angrily on his thumb. Gaveston put his face in his hands. Isabella stared down at her lap, playing with the ring she had taken off, moving it round as if it was something living. I informed them about the attack on us, how I had been so shaken Demontaigu had taken me into a tavern to allow my tremors to pass, hence my agitation. Isabella looked sharply at me as if she did not believe that. The king, however, cursed quietly under his breath.

For a while they discussed the possibilities between themselves. I stared around, becoming aware of the rich blue, red and gold tapestries hanging on the wall; the gleaming polished furniture: the comfortable turkey rugs; the pewter, silver and gold jewel-encrusted pots, cups and jugs on an open shelved aumbry. The wealth and power of these two men were such a sharp contrast to the desperation and fear of that ghostly crypt and my fearful, frenetic departure from it. Memories remained. The door burning. The Noctales breaking in. Dark figures against the light. The whirr of arrows. The cries and shrieks of wounded men. Such a contrast! Edward and Gaveston now wished to be alone. Isabella and I returned to the queen's quarters where, half-asleep, I almost limped to a settle in front of the fire.

'Mathilde? Mathilde?' Isabella shook me from my reverie. 'Are you tired? You look very pale.' She touched the sleeve of my kirtle, picking at a charred fragment then moving her finger to a stain of oil on the white cuff of one of my sleeves. She touched me lightly on the face. 'Mathilde, your friends are mine, your enemies mine. I have left France. My father is my enemy; so are his envoys, his mercenaries. Yes,' she plucked at the sleeveless gown over her tawny kirtle and spread her hands, 'even my father's sons, my own brothers. What Demontaigu was, what he is, poses no threat to me or mine.' She sat down on a chair next to me. 'Mathilde,' she whispered hoarsely, and I glimpsed the fear in her light blue eyes. 'Mathilde,' she insisted, 'we are pressed close here: either Edward concedes or we face great troubles. Have you heard the whispers? Some assert that not only Gaveston should go but the king also.' She paused, breathing noisily. 'If that comes about, Mathilde, what happens to us, to me, to you? My lord requires time. We have to play the great game, and play it well. Publicly I oppose my husband. Everyone, including my beloved aunt, continues to believe that. So tomorrow you must dine with her, provide some excuse, say I am not well, but,' her hand fell to caress mine, 'win time for my lord. Say whatever you have to to encourage the queen dowager to continue her negotiations with Winchelsea and the rest.' She narrowed her eyes. 'Yes, whatever you have to! Now, come.' She kicked off her slippers. 'It is time we slept. My lord will not visit me tonight or invite me to share his bed. So stay with me, Mathilde, like the young women we could have been. We shall lie next to each other and whisper against the world . . .'

The following morning, dressed in a snow-white wimple, a kirtle and a sleeveless gown of heaven blue, one of Isabella's ermine-fringed cloaks wrapped about my shoulders, I presented myself to the queen dowager's chamberlains in the King's House, that ancient part of Westminster Palace overlooking the Old Yard. I arrived early, so confusion ensued as pages and servants gathered up the two young princes named after the places of their birth, Edmund of Woodstock and Thomas of Brotherton. Guido the Psalter and Agnes d'Albert supervised the infants' departure with their nurses to the children's chambers further down the gallery. Once the infants and their entourage had disappeared, Guido and Agnes returned and escorted me into the inner sanctum, where the queen dowager and Countess Margaret presided. They were dressed like peas from the same pod in red and gold cotehardies, dark fur mantles with costly linings about their shoulders loosely tied with silver-tasselled cords and clasped with precious brooches. Both wore ridiculous-looking gold-coloured barbettes and fillets to hide their hair as if they were nuns in some convent rather than princesses of the blood. They were sitting close together, poring over a manuscript stretched out across a wooden frame. According to the queen dowager's excited murmur, this was a monkish account of the discovery of Arthur and Guinevere at Glastonbury.

'Their bodies,' she thrilled, 'were wonderfully preserved. Mathilde, is that not miraculous?'

I said it was, a God-given sign. I tried not to catch Guido's eye as he stood next to the queen dowager. One look from him showed me how both he and Agnes were bored to yawning with this constant description of relics. The queen dowager gathered us around the hearth. Madeira sack was served with sugared biscuits, and without any bidding, Margaret continued her description of holy relics, adding how she hoped one day to return to France to worship the Crown of Thorns that her saintly ancestor Louis had bought from Baldwin of Constantinople. Her babbled list also included the baby linen of the Son of God; the lance, sponge and chain of His Passion, a portion of a true cross, Moses' rod, the skull of St John the Baptist, not to mention the platter Abraham used to feast the angels before they visited Sodom and Gomorrah. Guido intervened, wondering about whether the true cross had really been discovered.

'No, no.' The queen dowager waved a finger like a magister in the schools. 'According to what I have read, St Helena, mother of the Emperor Constantine, found three crosses in a cellar forty-two feet in depth dug under Mount Calvary. These were the crosses on which Our Lord and the two thieves were crucified, but there was nothing to show which of the three was the true cross. So a dead body was laid on each. In two cases nothing happened, but when the corpse was placed on the third, it was immediately restored to life, and that's how Helena knew she had found the true cross. It was made out of four trees,' she continued breathlessly. 'The portion from the earth to the cross is cypress, so the sweet smell might counteract the smell of a decaying body. The crosspiece is of palm, indicating the victory of Christ. The foot of the cross is fashioned from cedar, which is well preserved when in the earth, whilst the wooden inscription was of olive, signifying peace.' Margaret paused. 'Mathilde, where is her grace?'

I'd been sitting in front of the fire, my eyes growing heavy, still tired from the previous day's excursions. As soon as Margaret asked her question I leaned forward and replied, God knows why, 'Madam, I bring you good news. My lady does not feel well; she is suffering from sickness in the morning. In a word, my lady, the queen might be pregnant.'

Mirabile dictu! The effect of my words was startling. Margaret drew back, her face lost that sanctimonious look; no more pious, elegant gestures. She looked abruptly younger, her face harder, those eyes questioning. I could see the beauty there as well as a close resemblance to her brother. Beside her the Countess Margaret just gaped like a landed fish. Agnes clapped her hands excitedly. Guido immediately demanded symptoms and signs. How was the morning sickness, high in the queen's stomach or low? Would it last the morning or was it assuaged by food? Had she

160

taken dried bread? That could help. I just simpered back how I might be mistaken. I regretted my impetuosity, yet as I've said, God knows why I spoke as I did. Perhaps the idea had taken root the previous evening, a symptom of my own desperation or watching Isabella turn like a bird trapped in a house. The king's opponents had to be distracted, even if it was for a short while, from their relentless pursuit of him. The prospect of an heir might cool their malevolent hostility, lessen the rancour of the Great Lords.

The queen dowager soon recovered from her surprise and said she would light a taper before the Confessor's tomb. I swore all to secrecy, even though everyone knew such a secret would never remain so at court.

'*Ma belle fille*,' Margaret breathed. 'No better place for her than here at Westminster, the House of Kings.'

'And the Virgin's shrine,' Countess Margaret breathlessly intervened, 'its precious relic.'

'Yes, yes, her grace must wear that, the Virgin's girdle,' the queen dowager claimed triumphantly.

Once again we were back to relics. My mind, nimble as a clerk's pen, skipped and jumped at the implications of what I'd said. The queen dowager and the countess heatedly discussed whether Canterbury on St Swithun's was the appropriate shrine for Isabella to visit. They were still debating this when we gathered to dine in the queen dowager's wood-panelled parlour on aloese of beef, pike in gelatine sauce, dishes of peas and onions with sippets. After the platters and tranchers were cleared, Agnes d'Albret excused herself. I did likewise, saying I must wait on the queen to see if all was well, though I would return soon enough. In truth, I wanted to hasten away and warn my mistress. To my horror, Guido the Psalter offered to accompany me whilst the queen's servants prepared the pears in wine syrup. I had no choice but to smilingly agree. We took our leave. However, once we were in the gallery with its wall paintings depicting the glorious exploits of the Confessor, Guido plucked at my sleeve and took me into a window embrasure overlooking Old Palace Yard. I leaned against the cold plaster while that devilish-eyed, nimble-witted teller of tales once again expressed his joy at the news about the queen. He peered down the gallery to ensure no eavesdropper lurked.

'Chapeleys,' he leaned closer, 'the clerk who was found hanging?'

'What about him?'

'Langton's clerk?'

'Yes.'

'I returned early this morning to the Tower. I wanted to ensure Langton's leg was healing. The king instructed me to do so as well as inform our noble bishop that Chapeleys had committed suicide,' he shrugged, 'or been murdered.' Guido wiped his mouth on the back of his hand. 'Langton talked briefly about Chapeleys. Our fat bishop called him thriftless and unreliable, even hinting that he might have been my lord Gaveston's spy on him.'

'And?' I was impatient to meet my mistress.

'A fabulist, Langton claimed, Chapeleys was a pickle-brain, a man whose ambition outstripped his talents. An outrageous liar whose tongue must be blistered with his many falsehoods. Langton also told me an incredible story about a French spy or agent called the Poison Maiden, maliciously opposed to the English Crown. He claimed he'd heard similar tales but openly mocked them. Apparently rumours about this Poison Maiden were known to the old king's chancery clerks, one of whom was Chapeleys. Anyway, Chapeleys informed Langton how he believed that the Poison Maiden, 'La Demoiselle Venimeuse', was not a person but a canker at the heart of the kingdom.'

'Pardon?' I shook my head, genuinely mystified.

'Edward's marriage to Isabella,' Guido murmured, 'the alliance between England and France. Chapeleys maintains it provided Philip with a road into the affairs of this kingdom. According to Langton, Chapeleys had chattered about how the old king had agreed to such an alliance under duress, as had our present sovereign. Apparently Chapeleys was a scripture scholar who also specialised in canon law, and he argued that such a marriage, arranged by force and pressure, was invalid. According to him, our present king could have his marriage vows annulled, repudiate Queen Isabella and marry another.'

I stared down into the yard. The day was brightening, yet I was aware of the cold, seeping draughts, of how the trees clustered near the far wall were still black and stark. Winter was not just a season but a state of mind. I hid my disquiet. I'd certainly heard similar gossip. How Isabella's marriage was forced on the English Crown by the Papacy and the French king through solemn treaty and holy vows. If the English had repudiated it, Gascony, England's last possession in France, would have been occupied by Philip's troops. Edward himself had been reluctant to honour such a treaty. He had only agreed because Bruce threatened his northern shires. His Great Lords were bitterly opposed to Gaveston, and Edward could not afford to send ships, men and money to defend the wine-rich province of Gascony, its prosperous port of Bordeaux and the fertile fields and vineyards that stretched beyond.

'Some of the Lords,' Guido added, 'would certainly support the king's repudiation of the French marriage. Langton also referred to this. I suspect our good bishop was shocked by Chapeleys' sudden desertion and violent death, hence his garrulousness. According to him, the Lords want to see the back of Gaveston but they might also wish to see Isabella and her dowry returned. They argue how the king could start again, marry a different princess from Hainault, Brabant or even Spain.' Guido shook his head. 'I have discussed this with the queen dowager; she believes it is only chaff in the wind.'

'And Chapeleys?'

'Apparently he tried to urge Langton to take this matter up with the king, win his freedom, forsake his fellow bishops and, on the king's behalf, petition the Holy Father for an annulment to his marriage with Isabella.'

'And would Clement have agreed to that?'

'According to Chapeleys, Clement might agree if the Templars were suppressed and Edward supported the papacy against Philip. Langton told me this as I tended him. In the end, however, Langton, like the queen dowager, dismissed Chapeleys as a tickle-wit, a malt-worm. At the time, mistress, I thought it was one strand of gossip amongst others until I heard your news: the Queen's pregnancy would certainly end any talk of an annulment.'

'Could Chapeleys have been murdered?' I asked. 'For what he said?'

Guido pulled a face. 'Chapeleys was apparently a clack-tongue, eager to escape the Tower. He may have been ready to tell any lie.'

'So he could have been silenced for what he said? Or perhaps he realised what he was doing, what might happen to him, and turned to despair.'

A door opened further down the gallery; Guido put a finger to his lips. 'We shall speak later.' Then he was gone.

I continued on my way. The guards allowed me back into Burgundy Hall. I was halfway along the path when I heard my name called. Ap Ythel came out of a side chamber of the gatehouse and, clutching his sword, hurried up the path. He informed me how Robert the groom, apart from a sore neck – the Welshman grinned at that – was most grateful for my intervention. Robert had asked, if I graciously agreed, could he thank me himself sometime? I absent-mindedly agreed and hurried on to my mistress' chambers. I found these busy. Maids of the household and other servants were bringing up costly cloths from London merchants eager to gain the queen's favour. Their precious fabrics were being laid out over chests, coffers, stools and tables. Isabella, golden hair hanging loose, and dressed in a simple russet gown, was assessing the cloth with her household steward, Walter de Boudon. She expressed surprise at my sudden return, but caught my glance and we withdrew into her bedchamber, its coverlets and sheets still in disarray. She grasped a bolster and sat on the edge of the bed like a little girl, legs swinging, looking up at me all expectant.

'My dearest aunt wishes to send me Goliath's tooth, which, I suppose, is ten pounds in weight, or has she discovered Veronica's finger or the Magdalene's toe?'

'Your beloved aunt,' I retorted, 'now believes you are pregnant.'

Isabella dropped the bolster as I told her what had happened. I half apologised but explained my reasons, especially how such news might gain more time, perhaps startle the king's opponents into silence. Isabella sat fascinated, head slightly to one side, assessing what I'd said. Her lovely face changed, eyes half closed, skin tight, lips slightly parted as she clicked her tongue. She picked up the fallen bolster and cradled it as if holding a child.

'Oh Mathilde, you've not only released a fox into the hen-coop but locked it in. No, no,' she laughed, 'sometimes it's necessary to lead others by the nose as you would a donkey. I'll reflect on what you said. In a sense it is mere prattle, but it will be interesting to sow the seed and watch it grow. After all,' she smiled, 'that is why I'm here, is it not, to conceive a son?'

'Or not,' I replied and told her about my meeting with Guido and what he'd said.

'Now there's a flaunting jack,' Isabella murmured, 'but what he said could be true. Does Edward wish to get rid of me so as to be alone with Gaveston, or vice-versa?' She shrugged. 'Do some of the Lords, those petulant hunchbacked toads, wish me gone because I'm French?' She smiled thinly. 'Or there's himself, a man unfit for any place but hell, and speaking of toads, never hung poison on a fouler one!'

'My lady?'

'My father!' Isabella quipped. 'Has he sent that unholy trinity Marigny and the rest, treacherous as Judas' kisses, simply to undo it all?' She picked up the bolster and threw it down. 'Think, Mathilde! Philip bitterly opposes Gaveston, so Philip meddles.

Edward, besieged in his own kingdom, locked up in his own palace, retaliates. He spurns me, baggage and all. I'm dispatched along the Dover road to a cog ready to take me back to Calais or Boulogne.' Isabella spread her hands. 'Philip's heart is stuffed with deceits; lies lie thick on his tongue. If that happened, Mathilde, my father would have reason for war. He'd appeal to the pope, to the princes of Europe, yes, even to Edward's disaffected lords. Philip's troops would overrun Gascony whilst another army landed at Dover. If that happened, my blessed father would be one step closer to being the new Charlemagne of Europe.'

'Is that possible?' I asked.

'A year ago,' Isabella rose to her feet, 'did you think the Templars could be so quickly destroyed? Oh yes, I fully understand how the old king, Chapeleys, perhaps even Langton, regarded me as the Poison Maiden, a threat hanging over the English Crown for the last twelve years. Ah well, sorrows never walk alone, but bring a host of others.' Isabella studied me closely, almost standing on tiptoe as if searching my eyes. 'I, we, cannot leave here, Mathilde, not to France, certainly not to Philip.' She patted me on the arm. 'God save me if I was pregnant; perhaps my sorrows would be halved.' She walked to the door and turned swiftly. 'Langton,' she exclaimed, 'you must visit Langton again, Mathilde. He is playing the devil's own game here. God knows if he told Guido the truth. My father always thought the English bishops were idle baits, but not Langton. A true serpent, Mathilde! I'm sure there is more than one clasp of the chain linking our beloved bishop to those disaffected lords. Anyhow, you must return to my blessed aunt. I'm sure she has much more to say. Please reassure her that the workmen are clearing the foul smells of Burgundy Hall, so perhaps she could visit me?'

I made my farewells. As I approached the gatehouse, the sounds of carpenters and masons echoed raucously. Now the Angelus rest was finished, the labourers were returning to their work. Ap Ythel, busy tying the points of his hose, came striding up the path.

'Mathilde, the queen dowager's man Guido, that lord of the latrines, has been looking for you. I told him you were still closeted with the queen.' Ap Ythel smiled. 'He asked if the new perfume in Burgundy Hall was a Welsh fragrance. I told him it was probably Gascon, but,' he nodded to the main door of the hall, 'the workmen have solved the problem. The latrines and gulleys need to be cleansed. It will take a few more days until the stench has gone. Tell our pert Gascon that.'

I promised to do so, my mind on other matters. I reached the upper gallery of the Old Palace and hastened along to the queen dowager's chamber. I passed a window and glimpsed movement in the yard below. Agnes d'Albret, her cowl half hiding her head and face, slipped out of the line of trees and paused. Another figure followed, a man. He glanced up at the sky, and just for a few heartbeats

I recognised Gaveston's handsome face. Agnes turned and stroked his arm. The favourite grasped her hand, and drawing her closer, kissed her full on the brow and lips before slipping back into the trees. I stood dumbfounded. Agnes might be informing the favourite of what was happening, but was there something else? The way they'd parted seemed more like lovers after a secret assignation. I hurried on. By the time I reached the queen dowager's apartments, Guido was entertaining her and the countess with stories in the patois of the scholars of the left bank of the Seine, explaining how *mariage* was slang for hanging; *arques petits* were little dice, and *empz* corpses. At the same time he was showing how a dice could be cogged and loaded so it fell the way the thrower wanted, translating it as *frouer des gours arques* and explaining how such counterfeits must always have an accomplice, a lookout against the Angelz, the archers of the Provost of Paris. Agnes interrupted this, bursting in all hot and flustered. Countess Margaret, however, for reasons best known to herself, suddenly began listing her favourite months of the year. She declared how January was one of these because the last of the Yuletide feasts, the 'Day of the Boy Bishop', was celebrated then, and how, in her father's manor at Oswestry, sausage, meat and game bird were, after the Feast of the Epiphany, hung from the kitchen's rafters to be smoked and dried.

'And that smell,' she declared smilingly. (God

knows she could act as witless as a butterfly!) 'It always makes me feel homely and comfortable.'

The queen dowager took up the point, declaring that June was her favourite month because she could remember the royal gardeners culling the red roses of Provence to be crushed so as to obtain their perfumed, soothing oil whilst their petals were woven into sweet-scented garlands. The conversation moved on to gardens in general: the classic arrangement of sixteen beds, one for each variety of herb, whilst the larger kitchen garden, or *hortus*, had eighteen, divided by a path into neat rows sheltered from the sun. The queen dowager asked me about the peony. I explained how the plant was named after Paeon, physician to the ancient gods, and was to be regarded as the plant of the moon. Guido mockingly quoted Pliny on the subject; how the peony could be both male and female and should only be garnered at night, whilst a string of dried peony beads were a sure protection against evil.

During the conversation, I watched Agnes closely. She was undoubtedly agitated, refusing to meet my eye, casting about, acting very disconcerted. If she talked, she chattered aimlessly then lapsed into silence. Under my direction, the conversation moved from flowers to the meeting arranged for the morrow after solemn high mass in the abbot's garden. The queen dowager, after making pleasantries, conceded there was little more she could do. Winchelsea and Lincoln, leaders of the disaffected lords, were demanding the immediate convocation of a parliament to publish their *gravimina* – their grievances against Gaveston. I intimated how my mistress' possible pregnancy must not be overlooked. The queen dowager accepted this, but replied that the king would have to concede something to the Lords. Nevertheless, Margaret promised to reflect on what I had told her; she declared that she hoped for the best but planned for the worst.

The queen dowager was undoubtedly uncertain and unsure. She'd lost her usual calm poise, and as if to distract us all, announced that we should play Hoodman's Blind, Guido being the Hoodman. Countess Margaret, God bless her simple soul, rapturously agreed. I reluctantly joined in, helping to pull the hood over Guido's head then scattering with the rest as he began to play about, trying to catch us. I moved and turned. I wished to be away when Agnes abruptly caught me by the arm.

'Is it safe?' she whispered.

'Is it safe what?' I answered.

'To cross over,' she replied. 'Mathilde, you tell your news, but how will this end? Are you not suspicious?' Then she hastened away as Guido came blundering towards us.

Eventually Guido caught the countess Margaret and the game stopped. The hood was taken off and passed to her, and all was about to begin again when there was a knock on the door. Ap Ythel came in, bowed and beckoned towards me. I made my excuses to the queen dowager and joined him in the gallery outside.

'*Deo gratias*,' I murmured.

Ap Ythel looked at me strangely.

'*Deo gratias*,' I repeated. 'I could not play another second.'

The Welshman grinned.

'You have another game waiting for you, mistress, down at the gate. The clerk Demontaigu, he is there with a lad called Spit Boy, come from the Secret of Solomon tavern. He says he must have urgent words with you . . .'

I hastened down. Demontaigu stood solemn-faced. Spit Boy, sweat-soaked, thrust his hand out, eager for the coin I pressed into his palm.

'You must come, my master is most insistent.' He beckoned at me. 'He has something to show you.'

'What?' I asked, pulling my cloak about me. I thanked Ap Ythel and led them away from the gate.

'There's a corpse,' Spit Boy whispered hoarsely, 'stiff and cold as a poker. He's lying in the tavern, the man you were asking about, Pax-Bread? He's been murdered, mistress.' Spit Boy dragged a finger across his throat. 'A piece of rope around here, tied tight, eyes bulging, mouth gaping, tongue sticking out! A horrible sight. Mistress, you must come and see for yourself.'

CHAPTER 8

This treacherous quarrel between the king and his lords now spread far and wide.

Vita Edwardi Secundi

I grasped Demontaigu's arm. He was pale, unshaven and unwashed, like a man who'd suffered a bad night's sleep and a day equally as troublesome. I was not able to converse with him, but followed Spit Boy as he led us through the palace grounds down to King's Steps. It was early evening. A waiting barge took us quickly towards Queenshithe, where we disembarked. Spit Boy, who regarded it all as a great game, scampered before us like a puppy leading us through the streets. The day was dying, the city emptying. I suffered what I call the horrors, an eerie blood-chilling experience that has never waned over the years: it is provoked by moving swiftly from one extreme to another. I've sheltered in comfortable courts, in luxurious palaces, in chambers lined with tapestries, only to step into a world

174

completely different. I have often reflected on this. How the times I've lived in are not moderate, but intense in every way. I have worshipped in cathedrals where the stone arches like a hymn and the light pours through beautiful multicoloured glass to bathe the nave in all the glory of heaven. And yet I've passed through those same cathedral doors on to its steps where beggars, with wounds turning green, plead for alms; madcaps and malaperts perform strange dances; and hermits, maddened by their own vision of God, preach the horrors of hell and the wickedness of the world. In the square below, bodies dangle from scaffolds, the breath choking out through their twisted throats even as the last beautiful notes of the cathedral choir echo in my ear.

So it was that evening as we hastened through the emptying streets. Traders were taking down stalls, whilst half-naked men, women and children fought over scraps scattered on the cobbles. A beggar, drunk on cheap ale, tried to kiss an ancient whore clasped in the stocks. Dogs tore the corpse of a bloated cat. A friar crouched over a fallen man, hissing the words of a penitential psalm. A madman prayed before the statue of a saint high in its stone niche, whilst beside him, a gallant undid the bodice of a whore and greedily felt her full breasts. Bailiffs were beating a drunk. The cage on the Tun in Cheapside was full of dark figures scampering and leaping about shouting obscenities, whilst further down the thoroughfare, a group of bedesmen moved from house to house singing the Salve Regina. A knight in half-armour returning from a tourney passed by on his black destrier like the figure of death. A tousle-headed bearded giant, dressed in the fraying skin of a horse, stood on the steps of a church. He shook the great cudgel he carried and shouted how he had been sent by the Baptist to search out Herod and smash his skull. Images, memories, a mix of fears and terrors at all I saw and heard. Spit Boy raced ahead of us, leaping like a March hare. Demontaigu, head down, cowl pulled over his face quietly mouthed a prayer. I felt like stopping and screaming at the tensions that surrounded me. I swiftly turned, eyes searching for any pursuer, but the dark twisting lanes were empty. Shadows drifted across. I could not tell if they were part of my world or some strange other. We continued on, and at last reached the Secret of Solomon.

Mine Host met us in the noisy taproom, eager to keep the matter, as he put it, tapping his swollen fleshy nose, '*sub rosa*'. He led us into the garden and across to an outhouse. Spit Boy went ahead of us, hopping like a flea on a hot plate, screeching at the top of his voice how it was all horrid murder and the victim was terrible to see with his popping eyes and swollen tongue. Mine Host roared at him to be quiet and led us into the outhouse. He took a lantern horn off its hook and brought it closer so we could view the corpse more clearly. Spit Boy had spoken the truth. Pax-Bread in life had been comely; death had turned him ugly, his face all puffy and livid because of the red-purple weal from the garrotte string around his neck.

'He was found early this morning,' Mine Host declared, 'by scavengers clearing a nearby brook. He was brought here, the nearest tavern. A coroner came and declared that it was a "death other than his natural one". The knave demanded his fee, drank a pot of ale, gobbled a platter of diced pork and left. I'm supposed to pay the full cost of burial.'

I opened my purse and thrust a silver coin in to his hand. 'That should cover everything; if not, Spit Boy knows where to come.'

'Very good.' Mine Host mopped his brow with his dirty apron. 'Get Hawisa,' he breathed. Spit Boy scampered off.

'Who is she?' Demontaigu asked.

Again Mine Host tapped his nose. Spit Boy came hurtling back, eager for another coin. I gave one to him and his companion, a young scullery maid, red-faced, desperate to keep the flimsy hat firmly over her thick hair. She yelped as she caught sight of Pax-Bread's corpse and stared round-eyed at me.

'Dead!' she screeched. 'Mistress, he wasn't when I saw him!'

I grasped her hands. 'Hawisa, stay calm, just tell me what happened.'

'I didn't know about this,' Mine Host blustered, 'not until the corpse was found. She took the message up. She should have told me, but there again, the taproom was busy.'

177

'Hush now. Please.' I gestured at the corpse. 'Cover that.'

Spit Boy, disappointed at not being able to view the macabre sight more closely, came and stood by Hawisa.

'Tell her,' he hissed, 'what you know. You'll get another coin!'

'He,' Hawisa pointed at the sheeted corpse, 'was in the tavern. I was in the kitchen. I was hot, so I came out into the yard, you know, towards the rear gate. This woman came out of the dark. At first I thought she was some apple squire, a pimp or a whore.'

'Describe her.'

'Mistress, I've told you it was very dark. She looked like a nun.'

'A nun?'

'Yes, there was a wimple round her face. In the faint light her skin looked smooth; her voice was soft. I said, "Mistress how fare ye?" and she replied, "I have a message for him."' Hawisa pointed at the corpse. 'She gave me his name. I replied, "How will he know, what are you called?" "Agnes," she replied. "Give him this." She handed me a coin and thrust a leather pouch into my hand. I ran back into the tavern, went into a corner and opened the pouch. I thought it might be coins, but it was a roll of parchment. Very thin, with some letters on it.' She shrugged. 'I cannot read. The pouch also contained two waxen seals.'

'What mark did they carry?'

'A large bird: a hawk, maybe an eagle. Anyway, she said that I would be rewarded by him, he'd give me another coin. So I ran up the stairs; the taproom was very busy. I knocked on the door. Master Pax-Bread was lying on his bed, boots all off. I think he'd been drinking. I told him what had happened and gave him the pouch. He read the parchment, took the seals, examined them carefully, then nodded, saying he would be down shortly. I stayed until he tossed me a coin, then I left. I returned to the kitchen, and that was the last I saw or heard of him.'

I thanked both Hawisa and Spit Boy, and they disappeared.

'So,' I grasped Mine Host's arm and walked him over to the sheeted corpse, 'I have given you money for his burial, sir. You claim he came in from his pleasures and went up the stairs to his room. A short while later that kitchen wench brought Pax-Bread a message asking him to meet a stranger, a woman, outside the rear gate. But after that, nothing?'

'Nothing,' Mine Host agreed, wiping his hands on his jerkin. 'Mistress, it wasn't until his corpse was brought in and the coroner made his judgement that Hawisa told me . . .'

Demontaigu and I left the tavern. Out in the street it was quieter now. Somewhere a night bird screeched. Doors opened and shut. Shutters banged and clattered. A dog barked up an alleyway. Shadows flittered across the pools of light. Demontaigu grasped me by the arm and led me down the street, then into the comfortable warmth of a small alehouse. The taproom was noisy, with two men shouting at each other about an impending cock-fight. The ale master looked us up and down and led us into a small chamber beyond smelling sweetly of apples. He waved us to a table in the far corner. Demontaigu ordered stoups of ale, some bread freshly baked and a pot of butter. We ate and drank in silence. Demontaigu was obviously despondent. For a while he kept his head down, more intent on his food and drink. Now and again his lips moved as if he was having a quiet conversation with himself, then he began to speculate on Pax-Bread's murder.

'Undoubtedly the wench Agnes!' he murmured, biting into the bread, then gestured at the eerie painting hanging against the far wall. It showed a cat dressed as a bishop shepherding a flock of sparrows clothed in the red garb of whores.

'Agnes d'Albret?' I mocked. 'Slipping along the dark alleyways of London to a common tavern, enticing Pax-Bread into the shadows, then garrotting him? I don't think so. Bertrand, you are tired!'

'Whoever it was,' he retorted heatedly, 'carried Gaveston's seals.' He shrugged. 'I suppose the favourite could disguise himself, even though he is a warrior. There is talk of him having a woman's heart in a man's body. Gossip and chatter cast him as a king's catamite, his lover a male bawdy-basket.'

'The malicious clacking of tongues,' I retorted,

'chaff in the wind!' I paused. Isabella and I often reflected on the true relationship between Edward and Gaveston. They undoubtedly loved each other, but as Isabella had whispered in my ear, had they ever lain together like man and wife? I always viewed it as a matter of no concern to myself.

'Anyway . . .' I spoke up, then remembered where I was, and drew closer and whispered in Demontaigu's ear. 'Why should Gaveston kill his own man?'

'To silence him on other matters. Think, Mathilde! Pax-Bread arrives at the Secret of Solomon, he rests and relaxes. He expects a meeting with Gaveston or someone the favourite will send. He visits Alvena at the Domus Iucundarum; he returns only to be lured out by that woman and murdered.'

'True, according to Alvena, Pax-Bread was very wary. He would only meet someone he could utterly trust, and that's not the end of the mystery,' I continued. 'Whoever murdered Pax-Bread somehow walked into the Secret of Solomon, slipped into his chamber and removed all Pax-Bread's possessions, though how he, she or they came and left without being noticed is a mystery. The room was locked and bolted from the inside. Why? Of course,' I whispered, 'they wanted to seize anything Pax-Bread had brought; they were also determined to create the impression that he had fled. But why all this mystery? Pax-Bread told

Hawisa to go and that he'd be down shortly, yet no one saw him leave.' I shook my head. 'We do not know what was written in that parchment note, and those seals? Only Gaveston, or someone close to him, would be able to produce them.'

'Shadows,' Demontaigu breathed. '*Parvae substantiae* – of little substance.' His voice turned bitter. 'What is it to me? What do I care about pompous princes who fight other pampered lords so they can do what they want for themselves without any thought for others? For the likes of my brethren, the Templars, rotting in dungeons, facing scandalous allegations, denied even a fair trial—'

'And why should I care,' I interrupted angrily, 'for men who once lorded it over others?'

'Does that include your uncle?'

'He was my uncle,' I retorted. 'Whatever else he was is, as you say, *parvae substantiae*. I mourn my uncle, Bertrand, because he was my uncle, because he loved me. I loved him, yet he was murdered in a barbaric, ignominious fashion.'

Demontaigu sighed and put his face into his hands. He took a deep breath and let his hands fall away.

'Pax-Bread was murdered,' he declared. 'This business of the Poison Maiden, all I'm saying . . .' He shook his head. 'I want to break free of it, look after my own.'

'Bertrand,' I seized his hands between mine, 'there is a right and wrong here. Philip of France is truly wicked. He made his daughter what she is and, to a certain extent, what you and I now are. We are here because of what he did. I agree Edward and Gaveston are no saints. I do not wear their colours and neither do you. Both are fickle-hearts and would betray us if it so suited them.' I paused. 'Bertrand, I study the world of herbs. Some, like belladonna, are pure poison; others, such as broom, contain some good if used correctly. So it is with us. I agree with the psalmist: all men are liars. I also accept his advice: put not your trust in princes. However, in this vale of wickedness, Edward and Gaveston are our best protection against the malice of Philip. My world has come down to this: to care for and protect my mistress, you and myself; to me that's all. The rest?' I shrugged. 'God knows I did not want it this way, yet God only knows why that's the way it is. Philip is a noxious plant. He has poisoned my life and those I care deeply for. If I can, I will do all in my power to uproot him and his. True, what I say is nothing to do with the love of Christ or the virtue of religion. Yet I do take comfort in the fact that God may wish to use me to achieve his own mysterious purposes.' I punched Demontaigu playfully in the arm. 'I believe the Poison Maiden, whoever he, she or they may be, is of Philip's making. They threaten us so I will threaten back. We have to be prudent and cunning. Put on our masks to face their masks.'

'Fierce, little spear-maiden.' Bertrand kissed me full and sweet on the lips. So swiftly, my spate of words dried up. I went to kiss him back but he brushed my lips with his fingers.

'Mathilde, Mathilde, listen to my confession. I am a priest; I consecrate the bread and wine, turning them into Christ's body and blood. Yet here I am in the fleshy sinews of life,' he smiled thinly, 'fighting all kinds of demons.'

'My uncle,' I retorted, 'once discussed the same with me. He said a Templar is dedicated to the love of God and his neighbour. He not only struggles against flesh and blood, but also wages a spiritual war against the Lords of the Air. Uncle Reginald talked of a clash of realities; of how life should be and how it really is. How we would like to do good but often simply do what we have to.'

'And the Eucharist, Christ's body and blood? Did your uncle Reginald talk about that? Would he explain why I celebrate mass in the morning and fight for my life in the evening?'

'Yes, I think he would. Whether you found his answer acceptable or not would be a matter for you. He claimed that Christ became man to become involved in the petty but vicious politics of Nazareth, of Galilee, so why should we now reject those of the Louvre, Westminster or Cheapside?'

Demontaigu sat staring at the hanging on the wall. Abruptly, from the taproom, as if some invisible being had been listening to what we'd said, a beautiful voice carolled. I do not know if it was a boy or a girl, but the song was haunting and heart-tingling. It was about ruined dreams, yet the second verse described how those same dreams, although never realised, made it all worthwhile. Tears stung my eyes. I watched the moths, small and golden, hover dangerously round the candle flame. Demontaigu's hand covered mine.

'Mathilde, let's move to the point of the arrow.'

'What do you mean?'

'I met Ausel today. We Templars house a traitor close to our heart. No, no, listen. The only people who knew about when and where we were to meet last night were Ausel, myself and Padraig. Ausel and I are responsible for organising such convent-icles, and as far as the time and place are concerned, only as few as possible are informed, including our leaders. The rest were only told to meet at a certain point at a certain time. They were then brought to the Chapel of the Hanged. None was given the time to inform Alexander of Lisbon so he could bring so many men to that place. The Noctales were prepared, Mathilde; they let us go in and thought they had us trapped.' He paused. 'At first I blamed those taken up and imprisoned in Newgate, but they wouldn't have known.'

I pushed away my platter and tankard. In the corner a spider clambered down into the heart of its web to feed on an imprisoned fly. A cat moved out into the shadows. A mouse screeched in the corner, whilst cold air seeped through the ale chamber, ruffling the smelly rushes and dousing a candle. I wanted to leave. We had discussed the harsh realities of life; Demontaigu had just told me one of these. His news was chilling.

'You have suspicions?'

'No one, Mathilde, but any Templar caught last night would have expected little mercy. That is the problem we always face: betrayal. This is the first time, in England, that we have suspected a traitor amongst us.' Demontaigu turned to face me. 'What we need is protection, pardons so that we can move freely. At this moment in time we live in the murky twilight between the law and being declared *utlegatum* – beyond it. Alexander of Lisbon, or any reward hunter, can trap, imprison, even kill us. We have lost the favour of both God and man. The king has ordered our arrest, the pope has declared us excommunicate. In truth, I should not even be celebrating mass. Mathilde, this cannot go on. I am a realist. The Templar order has been destroyed, and will never reconvene. We need protection. If we cannot get it here, then we will move into Scotland.' He gazed expectantly at me.

I knew what he was asking. Isabella often petitioned the chancery to issue pardons under the privy seal, but for that, she would need royal approval.

'You'd have to name yourself,' I murmured, 'confess who you really are. Bertrand, King Edward is fickle. He could hang you from a beam, embrace you as a brother, or dismiss it as a matter of petty importance.'

'Either way,' Demontaigu conceded, 'this must

be brought to an end.' He patted my hand. 'Think about it, but the hour is growing late; we must return.'

We did so without incident. Demontaigu left me at the gatehouse of Burgundy Hall. Ap Ythel was dicing with a group of archers in the guardhouse. He grinned and gestured with his head towards the main door of the hall.

'It smells a little sweeter now, mistress. The masons and carpenters have been very busy.' His voice took a wry tone. 'Even his grace helped to clean one of the refuse ditches.'

This provoked muted laughter from his companions. The king's fascination for physical labour, be it thatching a roof or digging a ditch, was common knowledge at the court. Some mocked it. Others claimed it was a legacy of the prince being left to his own devices by his warlike father. The old king had relegated his son to the care of servants and labourers at the palace of King's Langley, where the young prince had spent his youth consulting and consorting with companions such as Absalom the boatman. I thanked Ap Ythel and passed into the hall. My mind was a jumble of mosaic pieces. Yes, that was what is was like: those miniature paintings you find in a Book of Hours, so small, yet so complex, full of detail and observation. Pax-Bread's naked corpse, that horrible blue-red mark around his throat; Agnes and Gaveston touching each other; Hawisa staring at me wide-eyed – had she been lying? Demontaigu's tight face in that

187

alehouse. Ap Ythel staring slyly up at me as I passed.

The galleries and staircases were a blaze of light. The workmen were still busy, surly faces peeping out of heads and capuchons. Carpenters planed wood for new shafts for the garderobes. Masons studied charts and plans. Even then, albeit distracted, I noticed how many were milling about at such a late hour. Yet that was Edward: he showed greater tolerance for labourers and artisans than his fellow princes or lords. The queen's chamber was equally busy. Isabella was choosing gowns for the solemn high mass the next morning. We had little time to talk. I told her about my visit to The Secret of Solomon. She heard me out, nodded, and promised to tell Edward and Gaveston, adding that tomorrow's meeting between the queen dowager and the earls was of more importance. She teased me about how the news of her so-called pregnancy had now swept the palace. I asked her if she had told the truth to the king. She winked at me.

'Perhaps.' She smiled. 'Perhaps not, we will see.'

The rest I cannot recall, a swirl of events. The mass the next morning celebrated the solemn liturgy of Lent. The abbot, prior and sub-prior, clothed in glorious purple and gold, almost hidden by the rich gusts of incense, offered the holy sacrifice. A magnificent occasion. The choir intoned the introit, kyrie and other verses in the majestic tones of plainchant. The candles clustered on the high altar and elsewhere blazed. Sunlight poured through the glazed coloured glass to shimmer on the gilded cornices and precious chalices, patens and pyxes along the ivory, white and red-embroidered altar cloths.

Edward and Isabella knelt at their own prie-dieu. Gaveston and others of the royal party gathered in a special enclosure to their right. At the top of the sanctuary steps stood Lincoln, Pembroke and their entourage. I was relegated to standing in the hallowed precincts of the Lady Chapel with its statue of the Madonna clothed as Queen of Heaven, the Divine Infant resting on her lap, little hands raised in blessing. Beneath the statue, protected by an exquisite glass case framed in gold and studded with precious gems, lay the abbey's greatest relic, the Cincture Cord once worn by the Virgin. My eyes drifted to that as they did to the various tombs in the royal mausoleum: Edward the Confessor's in magnificent red and gold; Edward I's sombre black purbeck marble; close to it the gracefully carved tomb of his beloved first queen, Eleanor of Castile. I remembered how the old king had supposedly wept himself to sleep at her death and marked the stages of her funeral cortège south with gloriously sculpted soaring stone crosses. A thought occurred to me, but I let it go. Perhaps, on reflection, I should have seen it as a prayer brought by the invisible hands of some angel. However, on that particular Sunday, angels scarce moved in the harsh, tense atmosphere of the abbey sanctuary. The previous evening members of the Lords' retinues had met those of Gaveston as both groups took horses down to the river to water. The Lords' retainers had accused Gaveston of being *quasi rex* – almost a king – as well as being a coward, hiding behind his royal master and refusing to meet his accusers. Gaveston's retainers had replied with a spurt of invective, calling the Lords nicknames. According to Isabella's hushed, hasty whisper when I met her before the mass, these insults, the creation of Gaveston's nimble wit, had apparently struck home. Gloucester was a whoreson; Lincoln Burst Belly; Warwick the Black Dog of Arden; Pembroke Joseph the Jew; Lancaster the Churl. I turned my head and looked around the great drum pillars of the abbey. The Lords stood stone-faced and hard-eyed, muttering amongst themselves. Now and again they would turn towards Gaveston and his coterie, fingers touching the scabbards on their brocaded belts. *Deo gratias*, all weapons had wisely been left with the lay brothers in the Galilee Porch of the abbey.

The mass continued. At the kiss of peace, the *osculum Pacis*, Edward immediately left his prie-dieu to greet Gaveston. They embraced warmly, kissing each other on the cheek. The king then strolled over to Lincoln and, without pausing, shook his hand before returning to clasp his wife and kiss her gently. A growl of protest at such a hasty insult to their leader rose from the Great

Lords and their retinues clustered on the sanctuary steps. Abbot Kedyngton, sensing what was happening, moved swiftly on to acclaim: '*Agnus Dei, qui tollit peccata mundi*' – 'Lamb of God, who takes away the sins of the world'. At last the mass ended, with the sub-prior's powerful voice singing, '*Ite missa est*' – 'the mass is now finished' – to be greeted by the thundering response of the choir, '*Deo Gratias*' – 'thanks be to God'.

'And thanks be true!' whispered a voice behind me. I turned. Guido was smiling at me. Agnes, whey-faced, eyes all tearful, stood beside him.

'If we can leave here,' Guido hissed, 'without sword or dagger play, then the age of miracles truly hasn't past.' His words were almost drowned by the shrill call of the trumpets. Edward and his queen left their prie-dieus in solemn procession. Isabella looked magnificent in sky blue and gold, a white gauze veil hanging down either side of her face, a jewelled chaplet around her forehead. Edward and Gaveston were dressed alike as if they really were brothers, two princes of the blood, in red and gold cotehardies of stiffened brocade embroidered with silver thread, ermine-lined mantles warming their shoulders, on their feet beautifully decorated blood-red ankle shoes. Gaveston walked slightly behind the king and queen. They first visited the Lady Chapel, then the Tomb of the Confessor, and at each Edward and Isabella offered pure wax candles in silver holders. Afterwards they returned to the sanctuary. They had hardly reached the top of the steps when Ap Ythel and a host of armed Welsh archers emerged from the shadowy transepts to seal the royal party in a phalanx of steel. The king and queen went down the steps along the nave to the south door, which would lead them through the abbey grounds and into the palace. Guido, Agnes and I followed. I glimpsed Demontaigu, who raised a hand in greeting.

Outside, the sunshine was brilliant; a beautiful spring day was promised. Crowds pressed against the three-deep line of men-at-arms. Behind me I heard shouts from the Lords and their retainers. How Gaveston was a coward, a minion, a catamite! The insults were drowned by further trumpet blasts and the choir intoning the 'Christus Vincit'. Edward seemed determined to accept the applause of the crowds, who appeared captivated by his queen. She and her husband were greeted with showers of flower petals and cries of '*Vivat regina*' or the coarse bellowing of 'God save ye' and 'Praise and honour to ye'.

Once back in the enclosed garden of Burgundy Hall, the gates firmly sealed behind us, the royal party relaxed. Edward's shoulders slumped as he took off the jewelled chaplet around his head. Gaveston, however, was livid with fury at the accusations of cowardice hurled at him. He undid his furred mantle, calling for sword and dagger, intent on going back to confront his tormentors. Gaveston might have been many things, but he was no coward. Edward plucked him by the arm; Gaveston shrugged this off. Eventually, both Isabella and the queen dowager blocked his path. The king hastily called for a tray of sweet wines and silver platters of honey toast with pine nuts. He undid his own furred mantle and led Gaveston along to a flower-covered arbour with cushioned turf seats. They sat there like two boys, heads together, talking softly. Ap Ythel took up guard on the black-and-white chequerboard stone path leading down to it: a sign that the king and his favourite were not to be disturbed.

We all broke up, drifting to different parts of the garden. Strange, on that particular morning I glimpsed Mortimer of Wigmore for the first time. Handsome as the devil, of athletic build, sharp-faced and keen-eyed, he wore his black hair long, his face completely shaven. He was dressed sombrely in dark fustian with blood-red boots on which silver spurs clinked. He had recently been in Ireland strengthening English defences against possible Scottish invasion. He was with his uncle, that old reprobate and pot of wickedness Mortimer of Chirk, a man of evil reputation, with his prematurely white hair framing a face as cruel as that of a bird of prey.

'Now there's night and day,' Guido whispered in my ear. 'The younger Mortimer is a knight but his uncle is a killer, given custody of two Welsh princes he was! Poor boys were later found floating in a river. Mortimer of Chirk then had the impudence to claim their lands.'

'Not all plants and herbs,' I retorted, 'are what they appear.'

'Ah.' Guido gently pushed me with his shoulder. 'How does it go, Mathilde? "This painted rose is not the whole. Who paints the flower paints not its fragrant soul"?'

'Guido!' The queen dowager, dressed like a mother abbess, with the countess Margaret garbed like her novice, swept towards us. 'Are you trying to seduce Mathilde with poetry?'

'No, madam, with herbs,' I teased back, 'and with little success.'

Isabella walked over. We all moved towards the shade of some willows planted against a reed-fringed carp pond. Everyone felt slightly embarrassed that the king and Gaveston were still deep in conversation in the arbour. The queen dowager, to cover this, explained how the previous evening she and Guido had been discussing herbs and their potency – she glanced sideways at Isabella – especially in childbirth.

'And what is your opinion, Mathilde?'

'None, madam.'

Margaret's finely plucked eyebrows arched. Just for a heartbeat I realised how mask-like her face was, how the austere veil and wimple also served as a disguise.

'None,' I repeated. 'A woman in pregnancy should avoid all medicines and herbs where possible.'

'And your authority for that?' The queen dowager was now clearly interested.

'My uncle . . .' I paused at Isabella's warning glance. 'He served as a physician in Outremer. He conversed with the wise amongst the Arabs, whose theories were similar to those of the ancients, Galen and Hippocrates: *natura fiat natura* – that nature should be nature, or, more precisely, leave nature alone. My uncle observed native women. How in pregnancy they avoided drinking or eating anything out of the ordinary. In the main, their pregnancies were untroubled, their childbirth straightforward and the infants themselves healthy. He compared this with certain court ladies of the West who eat and drink all sorts of concoctions with harmful results. Let me give you one example,' I continued. 'Broom has silvery-blue leaves which, when crushed, exude a pale yellowish oil. Now as you may know, madam, this is often used to rub on the skin to repel flies and other irritants. However, it also affects the muscles, and in a pregnant woman may induce early contractions and bring about a miscarriage.'

'Very, very good. You see, Marguerite,' the queen dowager turned to the countess, using the French version of her name as she often did, 'you too must consult with Mathilde when you become pregnant.'

The countess blushed with embarrassment. The queen dowager was about to return to her questioning when Edward and Gaveston came strolling over arm in arm. The king's face was wreathed in smiles; Gaveston was still tight-lipped, his handsome face, so ivory pale and smooth, reflecting the fury seething within him: eyes glittering, high cheekbones more pronounced, the usually generous lips now a thin, bloodless line.

'Come, come.' Edward freed his arm and clapped his hands. 'Let us celebrate.' He gestured round. 'This beautiful morning pales in significance beside the beautiful women who now grace it. Guido, tell us that amusing tale about the old knight, his young wife and the chastity belt with two keys.'

This provoked laughter, and the guests drew closer. Guidio, a born mimic, played out the tale to the assembled company. Edward bawled in merriment at its conclusion, beating a gloved hand against his thigh. The bells of the abbey abruptly tolled, marking the passing hours. Midday would soon be here and gone. Edward whispered to Gaveston, who drifted over towards me. He placed a hand gently on my shoulder and steered me away from the rest, back towards the vaulted entrance to the garden. He paused as if staring at the corbels on either side of the gateway; babewyns and gargoyles glared stonily back, horrid faces with bulging eyes and gaping mouths. From the abbey floated the faint sounds of singing, a hymn to the Virgin Mary – 'Alma Mater Dulcis'.

'Poor Pax-Bread is dead,' Gaveston tapped my shoulder, 'and all he brought gone, yes, Mathilde?'

I told him exactly what we had learnt. Gaveston gently stroked my shoulder, then squeezed it hard.

I stared into that lovely face, those half-open eyes with their lazy, slightly mocking gaze. He leaned down and kissed me full on the lips, then turned back, arm around my shoulder as if we were to enter the gateway.

'Pax-Bread is dead; he cannot help me any more.' He glanced down at me. 'The Poison Maiden has seen to that. I will light a taper to guide him on his way and have a chantry mass sung to help him meet his God. As for his murderer . . .' Gaveston chewed the corner of his lip. 'Agnes – that was the assassin's name?' He shook his head. 'Not our Agnes! She isn't the killing sort; too gentle, more used to damask than a dagger. I doubt if she could crush a flea, let alone garrotte a man. Yet . . .' He moved his head from side to side, like a merchant assessing the value of some goods. I recalled Demontaigu's words from the night before. Gaveston was cold; no mourning for poor Pax-Bread who'd been cruelly murdered for his loyalty to this royal minion.

'Yet what, my lord?'

'The seals. Someone close to me must have given them to the murderer.'

'Or you, my lord?'

Gaveston turned, hands on his hips, and smiled chillingly down at me, so beautiful, so graceful! I could smell the rich perfume, almost feel the warmth of his splendid body through the brocade and taffeta; such an elegant man, with no mark or blemish. Yet there was a darkness there. The favourite bowed mockingly, waggled his fingers at me and swaggered off.

The royal party now made to leave. Edward and Gaveston moved amongst their household retainers distributing small gifts. Isabella, deep in conversation with Mortimer of Wigmore, laughed heartily at some story he was telling. Nearby hovered some of the ladies of her chamber, eager for Isabella to leave so she could change her robes of state. The queen dowager and her novice were paying their respects to burly-faced Abbot Kedyngton, who had joined us late. Guido waved at me and mouthed the word 'relic'. I grinned back and turned at the touch on my elbow. Agnes, her hood pulled up against the sun, gestured with her hand. I followed her into the shade of a trellis walk. She appeared anxious; she had certainly lost her air of impudent mischievousness.

'Mistress Mathilde, I ask a favour. Would it be possible to be given a place in the queen's household? Not her private chamber, but any of her departments, the spicery or the chapel?'

'You are not happy serving the queen dowager?'

She paused, gently brushing my arm, eyes brimming with tears, lower lip quivering. 'They are not happy with me. The queen dowager hints that I am too friendly with the French envoys, particularly Seigneur Marigny.'

'Are you?'

'Mistress, I have to please so many people, which

makes it tiresome. Guido has even questioned whether I spy for them. He has no love for the French envoys and none for their master.'

'And do you?'

'Mistress, when the queen dowager meets the envoys, I have to chat and gossip. They single me out, they question me.' Agnes flailed a hand. 'I cannot offend them. Mathilde, I do not wish to return to France to some loveless marriage. I like it here, there a freedom . . .'

The queen dowager called her name. I hastily assured her that I would do what I could. I asked if she knew of Pax-Bread or a tavern known as the Secret of Solomon. She shook her head, looked at me quizzically and hastened away.

CHAPTER 9

*Sire, if the Lords have done you wrong, it must
be put right.*

Vita Edwardi Secundi

We met the Lords mid-afternoon, deep in
the enclosure of the abbey precincts.
The garden was ringed on three sides
by buildings that soared above us, brooding
buttresses, carved cornices, glorious stonework
and the occasional stained-glass window that
caught the sun and dazzled in brilliant colours.
The fourth wall was ornamentally crenellated; it
even had a small military gatehouse above its
double-door entrance. The abbot's garden was
what a poet might call a subtle conceit. Carefully
positioned to catch the sun, it possessed all the
elaborate ostentation of a planned garden, with
sunken pavements, smoothed lawns, garden plots,
herb banks, benches of limestone, turf seats and
tunnelled arbours with copper poles tied with
willow cord over which rose plants and vine shoots

200

climbed. Small stew ponds glittered. Lead-lined pools splashed and gurgled under water gushing out from fountains carved in the shape of bronze falcons. On either side of the gatehouse four luxurious yew trees blossomed, representing, so the abbot told us, the Blessed Trinity and the Virgin Mary. The central lawn had been prepared for the *concilium*. An eye-catching pavilion displaying the abbey arms, three doves on a green background, had been erected. Inside stretched a long trestle table covered with waxen cloth; along this, cups, goblets, tranchers and bowls glittered in the light pouring through the vents in the top and sides of the pavilion. The sweet scent of herbs mixed with the fragrance from the bowls of freshly cut flowers and the perfumed smoke from gilt-edged incense boats filled to the brim with burning grains. Chairs and a cluster of stools stood at each end for the Lords and the queen dowager's party. In the centre, on each side, were throne-like chairs for Robert Winchelsea and Abbot Kedyngton, who would act as mediators and arbitrators.

We were all ushered in. The queen dowager took her seat, as did the leading earls, Lincoln, Pembroke and Warwick. Lincoln was soft-faced, with a mop of white hair. He smiled genially and sat clasping his pot belly. On his left was Aymer de Valence, Earl of Pembroke, tall and angular with a sallow, pinched face; his raven-black moustache and beard, neatly clipped, emphasised a thin-lipped, womanish mouth. He sat narrowing his eyes and pursing his lips as if wondering whether he should really be present. On Lincoln's right sat the Earl of Warwick. He was cold and distant, a hard face made even more so by the small, unblinking eyes and broken nose, his protuberant mouth like that of an angry mastiff. Dishes were served. A light collation if I remember well: venison pastries followed by dishes of marchpayne, and red, white and sweet wines. I singled one of these out, Maumeneye, tasting of pine nuts, cinnamon and other spices. Sitting on a stool behind the queen dowager, I loudly whispered that such a wine should not be served to my mistress in her present condition. A reminder about Isabella's possible good news.

Abbot Kedyngton said the grace. Winchelsea bestowed his blessing and reminded everyone that each meal was a reflection of the Eucharist, so it should be conducted in peace and harmony. We had little choice. They all sat and ate as we did. The queen dowager sent her cup to the three lords, a sign of great trust, but any further dialogue was impossible. Abbot Kedyngton had been cunning. Any real conversation between the two parties, or among themselves, was cleverly obstructed. The flaps of the pavilion had been folded back and a choir of novice monks chanted romantic songs, including a favourite of mine. I recall the opening words:

'Sweet lady, innocent and pleasing,
I must take my leave of you.

I do so with heavier heart
Than any man could ever imagine.'

I watched Winchelsea. He sat in his throne-like chair garbed in the brown robe of a friar. He was red-faced, his high cheekbones and sunken eyes portraying his anger, bony fingers brusquely tapping the table showing he wished to proceed. Eventually Kedyngton left the pavilion. The choir fell silent. Once the abbot had returned, Winchelsea, with little ceremony apart from a nod in the direction of the queen dowager, turned to Lincoln.

'My lord, you have certain matters to lay before us.'

Warwick fished beneath the table and handed Lincoln a scroll tied with a green ribbon. The earl undid this, laying it out flat. First he respectfully saluted Winchelsea and Kedyngton and thanked the latter for his hospitality. Lifting his head, he complimented the queen with sweet words, ignoring the table-rapping of Pembroke and Winchelsea. He then listed the *gravamina* – the grievances – of the earls, followed by the *articuli*, or articles that would bring about redress. I listened carefully. Mere words then, dusty words now, but they reflected the earls' hatred for Gaveston. The document, prepared by some clever lawyer or chancery clerk, soon touched on the heart of the problem. It wasn't that Edward loved Gaveston or showered favours on him, but that he had ignored those who, by birth, were his natural advisers and councillors, entrusting both the realm and the council to an upstart. In a word, they wanted Gaveston dead, but they disguised this in smooth words and clever phrases. They insisted a parliament be called to redress a whole series of grievances, and demanded a commitment by Edward that he would rule justly; that he would seek the advice of those qualified by birth and God's good grace to give it. Above all, Gaveston must go. The earls wanted him arrested and imprisoned to answer the charges levelled against him: abusing the royal favour, stealing royal treasure, violating the peace of the kingdom. I could list more, but go to any chronicle or the chancery archives and you will find it there, the same indictment Lincoln published on that clear March day so many, many years ago.

The earls were not in the mood for conciliation. Lincoln rapped the table with his knuckles, insisting that what they demanded must be completed before Easter without any let or hindrance. Once he had finished, Winchelsea turned to the queen dowager. The archbishop was a born fighter, a man used to the move and counter-move of debate and hot words. He had no love for the young king, or his father, and now all his venom and hatred spilled out. He warned the king, through the queen dowager, how he was violating his coronation oath, whilst his imprisonment of Langton was a direct attack on the

Church. Edward risked the horrid sentence of excommunication that Winchelsea would certainly pass against Gaveston. Winchelsea then moved on to other matters. He conveyed to the queen dowager how deeply distraught the Holy Father was about the treatment of the Church in England, as well as Edward's obstinate refusal to take effective measures against the Templars. Those words chilled my heart. I glanced at the queen dowager. She sat, her beautiful face all masked, eyes slightly closed, head turned as if listening very carefully to what was being said.

Once Winchelsea was finished, Abbot Kedyngton invited the queen dowager to reply. Margaret simply sat staring down at the tabletop. She turned to her left as if going to speak to me, then to the right where Margaret of Cornwall, Agnes and Guido sat. Finally she put her face in her hands and began to weep; quiet, subdued, shoulders shaking. She wiped her eyes on the back of her hands and, lifting her head, solemnly made the sign of the cross. Then she began to speak, first rather faintly, so the earls at the end of the table had to strain to catch her words. Nevertheless, she had prepared well. She talked of the glories of her late husband's reign, of the community of the realm; of Bracton's principle, 'what affects all must be approved by all'; of her stepson's tender years; of his need for good advice; of his love for his realm, his natural affection for the Great Lords, and how Gaveston enjoyed a unique position in the king's heart and life. She then moved to my mistress. At first she hinted, then she became clearer. The queen might be pregnant, expecting an heir; this was not a time for conflict or dissension. The community of the realm must unite. The king must be given time to reflect on the grievances and demands of his earls. She would do her utmost to advance their cause but there was no need for haste. It was apparent from her words that she had negotiated and met individually with each of the Great Lords; Lincoln, Warwick and Pembroke were clearly moved by what she said. Winchelsea was more obdurate.

'There are other issues,' he trumpeted, his beaked nose cutting the air, red spots of anger blooming high on his sunken cheeks. 'The Holy Father is most insistent, the Templar order must be crushed.'

'Hush, my lord,' the queen dowager intervened. 'Matters are still *sub judice* – I understand that King James of Aragon is equally determined to discover the truth behind the allegations against the Templars and has delayed proceedings.'

Winchelsea nodded angrily. 'But there is the question of New Temple Church,' he riposted, 'which lies within my archdiocese. It is the heart and centre of the Templar order in this kingdom. I am, my lady, more than prepared to accept what you say on condition that New Temple Church and its environs be handed over to the

See of Canterbury. After all,' he pointed at dark-faced Pembroke, 'it is not just a Templar church, is it? It also holds the remains of your revered ancestors.'

Pembroke nodded vigorously. Margaret replied that she understood and would place such a petition before the king. The earls appeared to be mollified. Nevertheless, I felt a deep unease. The *magistri scholae* – the masters of the schools – will pose the question: *Quod erat demonstrandum* – what must be proved? They argue that all matters must be brought under the rigour of the intellect. Yet surely we are more than this? One of the great attractions of herbs is that they are more than the sum total of their parts, root, stalk and flower. They may also contain a benevolence or a malignancy hidden to the eye. If that is true of simple plants, how much more of us, body, mind and soul? I listened to that debate. Oh, it was logical, but it contained something else, hidden and dangerous. Hindsight makes philosophers of us all, yet at the time, I smelled treachery. I sensed all this must end in violence. Gaveston was certainly marked down by the Angel of Death. The fury seething within these Great Lords was obvious. Little did I realise the full malice of Edward's opponents.

At last an accord was reached. The earls expressed their delight and hopes that Isabella was truly enceinte. They sent her their loyal felicit-ations, and as for the matter in hand, they would postpone their demands for Parliament to be reconvened. They understood how the king would be absorbed with his young wife so the business of council would have to wait. On her part, the queen dowager promised to bring their grievances before the king, as well as Winchelsea's specific request regarding New Temple Church. Other minor matters were swiftly dealt with and the meeting ended.

The queen dowager, hand in hand with Lincoln, led the way out of the pavilion into the garden. I heard Agnes' hissed exclamation and glanced to my right. Marigny, Nogaret and Plaisans had appeared. They were just within the gateway, with two other men standing in the shadows behind them. These followed Marigny as he walked across the grass towards the queen dowager. I recognised Alexander of Lisbon and one of his lieutenants. The French envoys were all dressed in sombre clothes with the odd flurry of white at collar and cuff. They walked with power, their arrogance obvious; they didn't even bother to bring along the Abbot of St Germain, who was only a figure-head. They all wore knee-high boots coated in mud, spurs clinking ominously. They'd apparently come from the hunt and were now eager to join a fresh one.

I abruptly recalled being in a beautiful meadow with my father many years previously, a warm summer's day, the grass ruffling under a gentle breeze. We were watching hares, golden skins glowing as they danced in the freshness of the morning. Abruptly floating shadows darkened the meadow as buzzards swooped in to hover threateningly. So it was on that day. Marigny and his coven were a cluster of hawks come to seek fresh quarry. They grouped around Lincoln and the queen dowager whilst abbey lay brothers scurried up to serve pewter cups brimming with chilled Rhenish wine.

'How low the king has fallen,' Guido murmured. 'The envoys of France gather like carrion crows on a carcass. In the old king's day they'd have had their backsides kicked and been sent packing.'

'They claim,' Agnes murmured, 'that their main concern is her grace the queen, how Gaveston has usurped her position.'

'Nonsense!' Guido hissed. 'Philip meddles for Philip and for no one else. Be not tender towards Marigny, Agnes.'

I could sense a quarrel was brewing. I felt tired, uneasy. I wanted to be alone. I walked across the lawn to a barrel chair facing the herb beds, placed, I suppose, so the abbot could sit and savour their sweetness. I sat down, sipping at the wine a servant handed to me. I was determined to make sense of all I'd seen and heard. Memories and images danced through my mind like sparks above the coals. So absorbed was I, I jumped as the shadows grouped around me. I glanced up, shading my eyes. Marigny, Nogaret and Plaisans, with Alexander of Lisbon standing behind like a grim black crow, were grouped around me. Marigny cradled his cup against his chest. He smiled like old Renard studying a capon he'd trapped.

'Why, Mathilde de Clairebon.' He leaned down. 'So far from home, so lonely.'

'And yet so happy!' I retorted. 'Well, I was until a few heartbeats ago.'

Plaisans sniggered. Nogaret slurped at his wine. Alexander of Lisbon studied me as if trying to place me. I wondered then if he knew the full truth about Demontaigu and myself. Marigny toasted me with his cup.

'We've discovered a great deal about you, Mathilde de Clairebon, niece of Sir Reginald de Deynecourt, physician general no less in the now disgraced Templar order.'

'You murdered him!'

Marigny waved a hand like a master correcting a particularly recalcitrant scholar. 'No, no, Mathilde, you don't know the truth.'

'Something we must have in common.'

'We could have a great deal more . . .'

'Oh, we do, my lord. I hate you! If I can, I will kill you.' I sprang to my feet. 'You do not frighten me, you and your fellow crow-souls,' I hissed, 'toad-spawn, killers, liars, perjurers, blood-soaked assassins.'

Marigny stepped back, and for a moment I glimpsed his confusion at such a retort.

'We could ask for your return to France. We could demand it.'

'You could also ask the sun not to set.'

'Your mother, Mathilde?'

'Don't talk of her!' My hand felt for the dagger concealed in its hidden sheath in my belt.

'Oh, I . . .' Marigny paused, shaking his head. 'Perhaps . . .'

'Mathilde, are you well?'

I whirled round. Guido was striding across.

'Mathilde, come.' He gestured. 'You must meet my lord Abbot.' He glanced anxiously at me, then at my group of taunters.

'We are talking,' Marigny demanded. 'I do not need your presence Master Guido, better known as Pierre Bernard. The Provost of Paris would certainly like to meet you. As for Mathilde—' His words were cut short, their dagger-like message never delivered. A trumpet shrilled three times from beyond the gate, followed by a pounding that shook both doors. Lay brothers hastened to open them. Gaveston, dressed completely in chainmail beneath a livery of scarlet and gold, silver-rolled spurs clasped about his mailed ankles, coif pulled over his head, ornate helmet swinging from the cantle of his saddle, rode slowly through the gate like the Bringer of Battles. Behind him walked three squires, two of them carrying banners, the third a trumpet. On Gaveston's left arm was a triangular shield emblazoned with the eagle arms of his house, in his right hand a mailed leather gauntlet. All conversation died. Marigny hurried away. Gaveston remained motionless; his superb

211

dark destrier, in full battle armour, pawed the ground as if eager for the charge. The favourite stood high in his stirrups.

'I have been called a coward!' Gaveston's voice thrilled with passion. 'I am no coward.' He flung the gauntlet down. 'I challenge any man here to meet me.'

The assembled company simply stood and gaped. The destrier snorted, shaking its head. Pembroke moved to go forward, but Lincoln gripped his arm. Marigny, one hand raised in peace, walked forward.

'My lord . . .'

'Either pick up the gauntlet,' Gaveston jibed, 'or stand aside, sir.'

Alexander of Lisbon pushed his way through and picked up the gauntlet, beating it against his thigh to clear the dust. Then he threw it back at Gaveston, who caught it deftly.

'I am Alexander of Lisbon, a knight.' The Portuguese voice was harsh as it echoed round the garden. 'I accept your challenge.'

The favourite leaned down, gently stroking the neck of his warhorse. 'I recognise you, Alexander of Lisbon. You are a knight, and if it is to be done, then it is best if we finish this business quickly. The tourney ground behind the Old Palace within the hour?'

The Portuguese nodded. Gaveston turned his horse and, followed by his squires, slowly left, the gates slamming shut behind him. Immediately the festivities were forgotten. Household retainers, squires, pageboys and servants were sent scurrying through the abbey and palace announcing the news. Winchelsea openly protested that the challenge was against the Truce of God, an agreement demanded by the Church that tournaments be banned between Thursday evening and Monday morning so as to avoid the holy days of Friday and Sunday. His words went unheeded. I slipped out, hurrying back across the abbey grounds into the palace and through the gatehouse into Burgundy Hall. Of course, my mistress already knew. Edward and Gaveston had planned this carefully. Isabella was ready, cloaked and hooded.

'Good, good,' she whispered, grasping my arm, eyes bright with excitement. 'Men's fury, like their seed, must spurt out, then we'll have a time of peace. Come, Mathilde.'

When we reached the tourney park, the stands were already filling. The old tournament ground or lists have now gone, replaced by a more splendid affair. In my day it comprised a long barrier covered with coloured canvas. The fighting ground itself was ringed by a palisade two yards high; this in turn was encircled by a fence about fourteen feet tall. In between the two were the stands, and in the centre, with a clear view of the lists, the royal box draped in blue and gold, all being busily prepared by liveried servants. We waited for the king. Edward arrived jubilant as a boy. He swung a richly brocaded cloak about his shoulders, shouting that he was prepared to wager on Gaveston's victory. Everything was frenetic. Heralds, trumpeters and grooms were running around. The list was scrutinised, straw scattered around to break any fall. Sunday or not, the stands filled: monks, clerks, servants, not to mention the retinues of the Great Lords, all eager to gain entry. Edward and Isabella, escorted by those members of the household nimble enough on their feet, pressed into the royal box and sat on their throne-like chairs. Ap Ythel, sweat-faced and cursing, tried to impose order, pushing back the throng to allow a breathless queen dowager to sit alongside Isabella. Around the tourney ground, the stands filled. Gilbert de Clare, Earl of Gloucester, emerged as master of ceremonies, riding into the list emblazoned in the glorious colours of his house. Pennants and banners were flown. The lists cleared. Gaveston, fully armoured, face and head hidden beneath an ornate helmet with a leaping fox on top, entered the far side of the tilting yard. Alexander of Lisbon, garbed in black, an old-fashioned helmet over his head, cantered in escorted by two of his coven. Both combatants were called to the centre of the list, and de Clare had quiet words with them. The herald announced that the course would be run with blunted lances. After three turns, swords would be used.

I cannot remember all the details. A beautiful spring day slowly dying; the tourney ground bathed in sunlight and shadow; the royal box packed to overflowing; the excited crowds, puffs of dust rising; traders trying to earn a quick profit with jugs and buckets of wine as well as 'the clearest spring water'. Then silence, an ominous quiet. Once the two combatants rode back to either end of the lists, trumpets blared. Banners and pennants were raised and lowered. Gaveston, astride his destrier, sat motionless as if carved out of stone. Alexander of Lisbon raised his shield and couched his lance, bringing it up and down as if testing the weight and poise. De Clare rode out to face the king across the lists. Edward lifted a hand. De Clare followed suit. Edward's hand fell. Trumpets shrilled. De Clare's hand opened. The red silk pennant floated like a leaf falling to the ground. Both fighters, as if possessed by some invisible fury, urged their horses forward. Both were skilled riders. Their destriers broke from a trot into a gallop, faster and faster, hooves churning the earth. They met in a shatter of lances. Gaveston swayed in the saddle. The crowd leapt to its feet but the favourite regained his poise. Again they faced each other. Fresh lances were brought. Squires gathered round checking girth and harness. De Clare rode forward. Edward raised his hand again. I sat beside my mistress on a faldstool, peering over the rim of the decorated rail. The red silk fell. The charge began. The hammering hooves, the creak of leather and the resounding clash as both combatants splintered their lances on each other's shields. I studied the

215

crowd and wondered if Demontaigu was there. I glanced over the rail. Gaveston had taken off his helmet, splashing water across his face. Alexander of Lisbon was doing likewise. Squires and pages went under the horses' withers, testing saddle straps and stirrups. Alexander of Lisbon asked for a new shield. Once again de Clare rode towards the king. Alexander of Lisbon came forward, shield slightly up, lance couched. Gaveston put on his helmet and grasped the lance from a squire, but then surprised his retainers by refusing the shield.

'Foolish boy! Foolish boy!' the king breathed.

Gaveston had decided to show his courage by riding the third course without a shield. Alexander of Lisbon appeared perplexed. His horse turned from side to side, and the Portuguese expertly brought it back under control. I recalled what Demontaigu had said about Alexander: how he had served in campaigns against the Moors both in Spain and along the River Tagus in his native Portugal. Gaveston seemed rather shocked, shoulders hunched, head forward as if something terrible had happened. De Clare, however, was watching the king, whose hand rose and fell. The red silk pennant floated down. Alexander broke into a charge. Gaveston waited for a few heartbeats, then he too came on. I watched intently. The saints be my witness! I have never seen anything so daring or courageous. Alexander of Lisbon's lance was now pointed directly at

Gaveston's unprotected chest. Even though the favourite was wearing mail, one thrust could be fatal, yet just before they met, Gaveston displayed his incredible skill. He actually swayed in the saddle but at the same time kept his lance directly on Alexander of Lisbon's shield. The Portuguese missed. Gaveston's lance hit him full on. The Portuguese rocked in the saddle. He dropped his shield in an attempt to gather his reins but he was lost. His horse was at full charge. Alexander tipped from the saddle and, with a resounding crash, sprawled flat on the ground. For a few heartbeats there was silence, and then the entire crowd, led by the king, jumped to its feet clapping and shouting, praising the Gascon's courage. Trumpets blared. Heralds and squires thronged into the lists. Alexander of Lisbon's Noctales ran across; two carried a stretcher, though their leader seemed stunned rather than hurt. He staggered to his feet, took off his helmet and threw it to the ground. At least he had the courtesy to turn and raise his hand in salute to Gaveston, who was now riding round the tourney list, lance raised, to receive the acclaim and plaudits of the crowd. He stopped before the king, lowering the tip of his lance to a few inches before Edward's face. The king was smiling. Gaveston took off his helmet and handed it to a squire who came running up. Edward undid a rich bejewelled bracelet from his wrist, clasped it shut and placed it on the tip of the lance.

'Well run, my lord, you are the victor!'

Gaveston bowed, his lance came up, and the glittering bracelet slipped down the pole. He saluted the queen and, turning his horse, rode in triumph from the tourney ground.

I sprang to my feet and went behind the king and queen. To the right of the royal box clustered the Lords with Marigny and his companions. The look of fury on their faces told me everything.

Despite Gaveston's victory, the murderous darkness, unbeknown to me, was gathering thick and fast. The king and his favourite were jubilant at the victory and immediately withdrew into the fastness of Burgundy Hall to celebrate. I recall passageways lit with torches. Servants hurried around. Edward had already arranged for the beautiful Grande Chambre at the heart of his palace to be prepared. The hearth was ablaze, the flames curling up and cracking the scented dried logs. On pillars either side of this, a grinning wodwose gaped out with other mantle-faces. Ceremonial shields, vividly proclaiming the royal arms of England, France, Castile, Gascony and Scotland in a variety of brilliant colours, ranged along each wall. Beneath these were arrayed eye-catching murals and hangings. In one darkened corner stood a camel embalmed and stuffed after death, in the other a fully grown lion, apparently pets of the king when he was a boy. These grotesque beasts, dead yet looking so alive, peered out on to a splendid scene. A great trestle table, covered in cere-white cloth, was laid out. The most exquisite goblets, cups, jugs, platters and bowls of gold and silver, along with cups of pure Venetian glass, glittered like lights in the glow from the fire and candles. The king, clapping his hands, strode about proclaiming loudly that he had no doubt about the outcome of the tourney. I recalled stories I'd heard: how Gaveston was a superb jouster, a warrior despite his foppish ways. Both he and his royal master now wished to celebrate their victory and the humiliation of their enemies. The king sat on a throne at one end of the table, Gaveston on a similar chair at the other. The queen dowager and Isabella sat on the king's left and right. Margaret was intent on telling Edward about the details of the *concilium* in the abbot's gardens. The Countess of Cornwall sat on Gaveston's right with myself on her left. Guido and Agnes were also included.

I shall describe the scene as memories, pricked by danger, return like whirling snowflakes in a flurried storm. A triumphant, gorgeous occasion! Gaveston looked resplendent in green and white silk, full of his own prowess. Edward sat laughing, slapping the table in glee. Ap Ythel, dark-faced, deployed his archers around the chamber and in the galleries and rooms beyond. The Welsh captain assured Gaveston that the cause of the foul odours had now been removed. Gaveston shouted back that he wished other, more fetid smells could be as easily expunged. The food was served by a myriad of servants. A stream of dishes came from the royal kitchens along a passageway under the choir loft at the far end of the hall. Musicians grouped in the loft above tried to play but eventually gave up due to the shouts and laughter from the king and his favourite.

I remember certain dishes: juschelle stuffed with egg and herbs; Carmeline beef; boiled and spiced veal; oat-stuffed pike. Isabella was watchful and tense, as she always was when her husband was in his cups. The king could be generous but he was also fickle-tempered. He could move swiftly from bonhomie to heart-breaking cruelty. When he announced loudly how he hoped she was enceinte, Isabella grimaced with annoyance. Nevertheless, there was no stopping the queen dowager; she eventually persuaded Edward to listen to her. She asked Gaveston and Guido to exchange seats so that the favourite could also learn what had been discussed and agreed. Gaveston playfully teased that he was Lord of Misrule and now was not the time for advice. Eventually, persuaded by Margaret and Isabella, and slurping noisily from his wine cup, the favourite staggered to his feet and waved Guido to his vacant throne-chair. I was distracted between Agnes and trying to listen to the queen dowager. What I remember at the time is what I recall now. Guido had taken his wine cup, though he had drunk sparsely during the meal. I definitely remember him sipping at the Venetian glass of water Gaveston had left behind. The banquet continued. Edward and Gaveston were laughing at Winchelsea's petulance, only to sober at the queen dowager's mention of New Temple Church.

The king pulled a face but nodded. He patted Gaveston on the arm and remarked how such a concession was perhaps worth it to keep a Great Lord. The candles burnt low. Fat blobs of wax formed on the gilt-edged spigots. The king's hounds were allowed in to feed on the scraps. The musicians tried again. Servants hurried in and out, clearing the table. I was becoming impatient to leave. Isabella looked tired and heavy-eyed. The banqueting chamber filled with flickering shadows. I noticed Guido had left his seat. I was about to fill my mistress' water glass when Ap Ythel came hurrying into the chamber.

'Sire,' he announced, bowing low. He raised himself, trying to control his breathing, and clapped noisily. The sound of the harp and lute died. Edward and Gaveston glanced up. 'Sire.' Something about Ap Ythel's face and tone made my stomach clench. 'Mistress Mathilde,' he gestured at me, 'you'd best come.'

'What is it, man?' Edward bellowed.

'Master Guido has collapsed in the garderobe!'

'No, no!' The queen dowager's fingers flew to her lips.

'Drunk!' Gaveston scoffed.

'I think not, my lord. He is ill. He claims he might have been poisoned.'

'How?' demanded Agnes, pushing away her wine

goblet. 'We drank from the same jugs . . .' Her voice trailed off as she stared to where Guido had been sitting. 'The water . . .'

'Sire, my lords,' I pushed back my chair, 'Master Guido needs my help. I beg you not to drink or eat any more.'

Isabella nodded in agreement. Edward sprang to his feet, shouting that the hall should be secured. I followed Ap Ythel out along the dark, draught-filled galleries to a garderobe at the far end; a small vaulted chamber built into the wall under a narrow window. The door to this was flung open, and a lantern horn on a hook just inside shed a pool of light. Servants carrying torches and candles were grouped around a man kneeling in the garderobe, head over the wooden bench with a hole in the middle leading down to a gulley that fed into an iron-bound barrel. Guido was vomiting; every so often he would kneel back on his heels as if to rise, only to lurch forward again to retch noisily. I pushed my way through. Using my authority and Ap Ythel's presence, I dispatched a servant for bowls and napkins. Guido, as God is my witness, was, at that moment, very sick.

Ap Ythel and I managed to get him to stand. He was pallid-faced, sweat-laced and retching, complaining of pains in his belly, weakness in his legs and tightness in his chest. Ap Ythel said he should be taken to the royal infirmary, a sheltered room on the top floor of the palace above the royal quarters. I agreed, and followed them up to the spacious chamber. The walls of lime-coloured plaster were scrubbed clean, the floorboards polished to a shine. It was well aired by two casement windows. In between these stood a broad four-poster bed with a canopy of dark blue, its sheets, bolsters and coverlets clean and crisp to the touch. On the wall opposite hung a huge crucifix with paintings either side showing a blond-haired, freshly shaved Christ in gorgeous robes healing the sick and raising the dead. We managed to put Guido into bed, half propping him up with bowls on either side of him. I hastily scrutinised him – he was clammy, and a red rash had appeared on his arm and the top part of his stomach. I ordered Ap Ythel to bring fresh water and forced Guido to drink. He was encouraged to retch and vomit; closet stools were also brought.

'For a while,' I declared, 'the contagion will press down on his bowels. We must try and purge the poison from him.'

I sniffed at the sick man's mouth. The wine and food odours were obvious, but there was something else, the bittersweet fragrance of a flower I could not place. I hastened back to the Grande Chambre, where the king and Gaveston had set up a summary court of oyer and terminer. Cooks, scullions, servants and maids, terrified out of their wits, were being roughly questioned in the presence of Ap Ythel's archers. These were no longer the laughing, singing yeomen who lounged in gardens and yards, teasing and joking with the maids. Their dark faces were now sombre, hoods pulled up, packed quivers slapping on their backs, bows over their shoulders, long stabbing dirks in sheaths or rings on their belts. These men were devoted to Edward and an attack upon him was an attack upon them. The mood in the hall was oppressive, chilling and threatening. The archers pushed and prodded the servants forward to kneel before Edward and Gaveston; who sat behind the trestle table like justices intent on a hanging. Isabella was stone-faced. The countess sobbed prettily, whilst the queen dowager immediately jumped to her feet when she saw me, almost hysterical about her 'dear Guido'. I hastily assured her and hurried to whisper in Isabella's ear. She nodded.

'This is mummery,' she agreed, 'nothing to the good. My lord?' Her voice rang out strong and carrying, echoing around the banqueting chamber.

Edward, surprised, turned.

'My lady?'

'This is not justice.' Isabella waved at the terrified servants. 'You have no proof or evidence they were involved. Why should they wish to harm anyone in this hall?' Her words were greeted by a murmur of assent from the servants. 'My lord,' she gestured at me, 'this mystery is to be prised open with a dagger rather than a mallet.'

Edward glanced at Gaveston. The favourite sat hunched in his chair, red spots of anger high in his cheeks. He clicked his tongue and stared at the huddle of servants as if he wished to behead them all with his sword. Then he took a deep breath and closed his eyes. He muttered something to himself, glanced at the king and nodded. The hall was cleared; only members of the royal party remained. Edward imperiously beckoned me forward to the far side of the table. I went to kneel.

'My lord!' Isabella hissed.

Gaveston placed a hand on Edward's arm. The king, fickle as the moon, smiled and waved me to a chair next to his wife. The atmosphere changed. Edward flicked his hand at the table crowded with cups, platters and mazers.

'Mathilde, *ma petite*, we are listening.'

I swiftly told him about Guido's ailments and symptoms. Edward heard me out, then ordered me to move round the table and scrutinise the various cups and bowls. In the end I could find nothing amiss except for the beautifully fluted Venetian water glass set for Gaveston but drunk by Guido – empty except for a few dregs. I caught the same strange flowery smell I had detected from Guido and the garderobe, which I had inspected on my return to the banqueting chamber. A sharp, brief discussion took place as to how the water could have been poisoned. Matters were complicated by the possibility that Guido may have been the intended victim rather than Gaveston. The queen dowager described the French envoys' open hostility to her squire, a malice I had also witnessed earlier in the day. Yet again, what are words and looks? Perhaps they should have been more closely scrutinised at the time. The queen dowager added that such an attempt was likely following Guido's open delight at the Lord Gaveston's victory. Edward sat nodding, speaking quietly to himself in Castilian, the tongue of his beloved mother, a strange habit that manifested itself whenever he was deeply agitated. Questions were asked about how the poison was introduced. Everyone realised the futility of pursuing any logical answer. Servants had clustered around the table, household retainers had come and gone, even members of the royal party had left their seats to approach Gaveston to offer their congratulations at his victory. This was the only allusion, veiled though it was, that the assassin might have been one of our company.

CHAPTER 10

Every kingdom divided against itself shall be brought to desolation.

Vita Edwardi Secundi

S trange, I sit and reflect on this page of my chronicle. How the events of that long-lost Sunday opened a path to so much. The loose thread in a tapestry of lies and deceits. Truly our words and actions are seeds for the sowing. They quicken and thrust up, all ripe for the harvesting. Nevertheless, at the time, the sinister threading of that sombre tapestry continued to be woven. Guido was now in the royal infirmary, visited by court physicians. Queen Margaret, all tearful and piteous, like a damsel from some Chapel Perilous, entreated me to take special care of him. I did so.

At first Guido vomited and retched, and his bowels became loose. Red rashes appeared on his skin. He continued to have some difficulty breathing. I purged him with fresh water and fed him on broths thickened and rich. The danger passed. The queen dowager with her children, the countess, Agnes and a few other chosen retainers moved into Burgundy Hall to personally supervise Guido's recovery. Where possible, I slipped out of the palace, away from my care of Guido and other duties, to meet Demontaigu. He was still absorbed with his own troubles and the possibility of a traitor, a Judas man, amongst his brethren. He told me how many of his comrades had now scattered into hiding. I told him about Guido. Demontaigu believed the intended victim must have been Gaveston. According to him, the Great Lords were seething at the favourite's victory over Alexander of Lisbon, who, Demontaigu ruefully reflected, had suffered little more than a few knocks and bruises, the blow to his pride being the worst. Demontaigu also confirmed what Isabella had secretly confided in me. The Great Lords gathered at Westminster were becoming restless. They had brought their retinues into the city and the daily cost of maintaining their men under arms was biting deep. Edward and Gaveston's strategy began to emerge. They might be under siege at Burgundy Hall, protected only by the power and sacredness of the Crown, but the Great Lords were spending their revenues on this costly exercise. Some of them were already negotiating with the Bardi, the Italian bankers in Lombard Street, for fresh loans. Winchelsea was drawing heavily on the revenues of Canterbury as well as daily reminding the king about the transfer of New Temple Church.

Demontaigu was deeply intrigued by Winchelsea's interest in a Temple church. On the Wednesday following the *concilium*, he invited me to the private celebration of mass in his locked chamber. Despite the surroundings, the makeshift altar and pewter vessels, it was, as always, a solemn, sacred occasion. I found it deeply intriguing. Demontaigu often quoted the bishop's oath from the ritual when a priest was ordained: 'The Lord has sworn a great oath. He will not repent of that oath. You are a priest for ever according to the order of Melchisedech.'

'I will always celebrate my daily mass,' Demontaigu confided in me. 'Whatever the cost!'

I watched him that morning breathing the sacred words over the host and the chalice, transforming them into the Body and Blood of the risen Christ. I could not ignore the fact that I loved this man, who was also a priest sworn to celibacy. I had asked him about this earlier in the year, before the clouds gathered and the dangers threatened. He had been teasing me about my bold eyes and purposeful poise.

'How,' I'd retorted, eyes fluttering like any dainty maid, 'can you be so attracted by the flesh when you are sworn to chastity?'

Demontaigu glanced sadly at me, blinked and looked away before turning back to kiss me fiercely on the forehead.

'I am sworn to chastity but not forbidden to fall in love.' He smiled. 'There is no vow or oath against that.'

On that particular morning I remembered those words as Demontaigu finished his mass. Afterwards I helped clear away the sacred vessels, which he kept concealed in a locked iron-bound coffer. I would have loved to discuss the matter of his priesthood again, but Marigny's words about my mother were beginning to nag and tug at my soul. Demontaigu was also more concerned about his brethren and Ausel's determination to discover the Judas amongst them.

'Four of our comrades died after the attack on us in the Chapel of the Hanged.' Demontaigu acknowledged my surprise. 'Eternal rest be given them. One died suddenly; he had a weak heart. Others received wounds which turned rotten. Either that,' he sighed, 'or like other brothers they just lost the will to live. I have prayed for them. Other priests have sung the requiem. Now,' he placed the keys of the coffer in his wallet, 'Winchelsea hungers for New Temple Church.' He opened a leather satchel, and fishing amonst its contents, drew out and unrolled a finely drawn map of London. Head close to mine, he pointed out the location of New Temple, with its frontage on the Thames. He described how a curtain wall circled the church, hall, barracks, stables and other outbuildings. I stared fascinated as he explained how the church was circular, a replica of the Temple in Jerusalem; the long chancel beside it had been added later. Staring at that map, I immediately recalled Chapeleys' drawing of a circle with a letter P in the centre.

'Pembroke,' I whispered. 'Winchelsea claimed that the Earl of Pembroke's ancestors are buried in the Templar church.'

'True,' Demontaigu replied, 'but not his direct family; rather that of William Marshal and his descendants, who first held the title of Pembroke.'

'And when was New Temple Church seized?'

'Last January.'

'And Langton, when was he arrested?'

'Earlier in the autumn.'

'So your king died in July last, and Langton was his treasurer.' I tried to curb my excitement, my thoughts pressing in. 'Who was in charge of New Temple Church, its preceptor, its master?'

'You know that, Mathilde! William de la More: he is now under house arrest at Canterbury.'

I bit my lip to hide my excitement at the first crack of light piercing the vaulting black mysteries around us. Demontaigu could see I was absorbed but I dared not speak, a skill my uncle taught me: to reflect, plan and never act hastily. I kissed Demontaigu absent-mindedly on the cheek and left his chamber pretending, as I often did, to be carrying a pannier of documents from one of the queen's clerks. I went down across the yard. A cool, calm day was promised. The sun was strengthening, the sky freshening. I heard my name called. Robert the groom, dressed in dark fustian, a leather apron flapping about him, hurried out of an outhouse. He explained how he had been inspecting horses' hooves. Drying his mud-strewn hands on his apron, he asked if he could speak to me. I nodded. He was sweaty-faced beneath his tousled hair. Breathlessly he thanked me for my help, gingerly feeling his neck.

'I thought I'd hang, mistress.'

'You were fortunate, Robert. You drew a dagger on a royal official in the king's own palace; that's treason.'

Robert cheerfully conceded his own stupidity but begged me to come into the outhouse as he had a present, a gift for me. Still distracted, I agreed. We walked into the warm, musty darkness, past the stalls into a small enclosure with its crude pieces of furniture. On an old barrel that served as a table, a battered lantern horn glowed. Robert drew his dagger and, inserting it between two wooden slats fixed to the wall, prised up the bar behind. He grinned over his shoulder at me.

'I know how to do this.' The small recess beyond, built into the stone wall, served as a secure coffer. Robert took something out and slammed back one of the slats then the other on which the wooden bar was fixed. I watched curiously as he used his dagger to pierce the gap to ensure the bar had fallen down on to its clasp. I recalled those window shutters at the Secret of Solomon. Robert, intent on his gift, opened his hand and offered me a carving of a horse, small but exquisitely rendered, lifelike in all its fine detail.

'I did that myself.' He waggled his shoulders in embarrassment. 'I could be a carpenter, mistress.'

'Its beautiful,' I smiled, 'thank you.'

'A gift, mistress, it's the best I could do.'

'And Anstritha?' I teased. 'Is she sweeter towards you?'

Robert blushed.

'There's something else, mistress.' He accompanied me out into the yard. 'On the night Rebecca was murdered,' he stammered, 'I was looking for her. I crossed the Old Palace Yard near the door to the stairs where that clerk,' he nervously cleared his throat, 'the one you know. He has his lodgings in the corner?'

'Demontaigu?'

'Yes, and where that other clerk was found hanging from the window-door.' Robert licked his lips. 'On that night everybody was getting ready for the feast. The yard was deserted; I glimpsed a shadowy figure . . .'

'Man or woman?'

'Oh, definitely a woman. She wore a cloak but I glimpsed the kirtle beneath. She went in through the door to the staircase leading to your clerk's chamber.'

'You have a description?'

'Mistress, the light was fading. I just noticed how swift she was. I had troubles of my own. I forgot it, I was more concerned about Rebecca, it's just that . . .'

'What, Robert?'

'What's happening here, mistress? I mean, who was that woman, and what about those workmen going in and out of Burgundy Hall?'

'What about them, Robert?'

'Mistress, as you know,' he smiled ruefully, scraping his mud-caked boots on the cobbles, 'I'm hot-tempered. Everyone knows that! A year ago, around Martinmas, I was drinking in the Pot's Yard, a tavern near the Royal Mews next to the Queen's Cross. I stabbed a man. He was only lightly wounded but I fled to the sanctuary; you know, the enclosure north of the abbey where the sheriff's men cannot pursue . . .'

I knew all about the sanctuary enclosure, an ancient privilege where malefactors, wolfsheads and outlaws could shelter unscathed, free from the reaches of the sheriffs and their bailiffs. A place of villainy. A melting pot of wickedness, it still is. I was surprised that Robert should be in such company. I half listened to his story, then he paused, fingering the leather apron.

'Strange, mistress! Some of those workmen in Burgundy Hall, I've seen them before in the sanctuary.'

'Are you sure?'

'Mistress, you never forget some faces: the cast in the eye, the scar, the way a man walks or sits, but there again, I might be mistaken.' He shrugged. 'After all, I have been in sanctuary; now I work in the royal stables. Perhaps they too have secured honest employment.'

I thanked him and walked across the palace yard, down alleyways and narrow paths. I took a wrong turn and came out on to the broad field that separates the palace from the abbey. Apparently it was Laver Day, when the chancellor of the abbey had to provide fresh straw for mattresses and bath mats as well as supply wood for the calefactory, the warm room, where the monks would bathe in tubs of oak; this was preceded by the head-shaving, when the monks sat in two rows in the cloisters awaiting for the attentions of the barber. Labourers were now organising all this. Carts full of fresh straw, linen towels, jars and pots were lining up outside the south door of the abbey. I was caught by the beauty of the massive soaring stone, the buttresses, pillars, gleaming new stonework and precious glass glinting in the windows. I walked along a path, just stopping where the carts turned as they trundled down towards the abbey. A bell clanged. I was about to walk away when I smelled a flowery fragrance, almost the same as I'd noticed in that water glass Guido had drunk from. I hurried after the cart from where the smell seemed to originate. The lay brother sat half asleep, clasping the harness straps; he glanced in surprise but, at my insistence, reined in.

'Brother?'

'Yes!' He smiled at the silver coin between my fingers. 'How can I help you, mistress?'

'This cart is sweet-smelling.'

'Why, yes, it carries herbs for the monks' baths; always get the best they do.'

'What herb?'

'Mistress, I am a carter by trade, a lay brother by profession, I am no—'

'Apothecary?'

'Yes, mistress, that's where I've been, down to the spicery on the quayside.'

'Do you have a list of what you are carrying?'

'Of course.'

Someone shouted at the lay brother to move his cart; he just raised a hand, fingers curled in an obscene gesture. He gave me the parchment. I handed over another coin. I unrolled the spicery scroll, noting the various herbs listed: rosemary, violet, lavender, dry hops and others. I memorised as much as I could, then thanked him, returned it and hurried down a lane that would lead back into the palace grounds. At the entrance to Burgundy Hall, I asked Ap Ythel if all was well. He replied by asking why it shouldn't be. I enquired about the workmen. He shrugged and said they came and went; the latrines and garde-robes had apparently become heavily clogged. They had been cleaned and the refuse taken down to the river. Some of the workmen, he admitted, were lazy and tended to wander off if not properly supervised.

'The king indulges them,' he declared in that sing-song voice. 'Anyway, mistress, you have a visitor.' He shook his head. 'A messenger, but first the queen dowager has left strict instructions that you must go and see her. Master Guido is not yet fully recovered.'

Guido, in fact, was still pallid-faced and weak. He leaned against the bolsters with Agnes on his left, the queen dowager sitting on the bed feeding him broth. She welcomed me with the sanctimonious expression she had developed to such perfection. Agnes looked solemn, lower lip jutting out, lost in her own thoughts. Guido stretched out his hand and grasped mine.

'Mathilde, the physicians came to bleed me. No.' He let go of my hand. 'I refused. Mathilde, what poison was it? Have you discovered?'

'I don't know. Some herb or flower with a perfumed smell. I've consulted the leech books, but as you know, different powders can smell the same.'

'Henbane, foxglove, belladonna,' he held his stomach, 'it could have been any of those. Thank God for you, Mathilde. I remember now,' he smiled, 'sitting down at Gaveston's chair. I had not taken my wine; his water glass looked full and untouched.'

'Didn't the odour alarm you?'

'No, no, I took a deep draught. True, I smelt the perfume,' he shrugged, 'of flowers, or herbs. I thought it was a fragrance from the feast. I'm recovering, Mathilde, still weak but I wish to thank you, as well as beg you,' he licked his lips, 'to discover what the poison was.' He leaned back against the bolsters. 'Her grace thinks I may not have been the intended victim but the Lord Gaveston—'

'Never mind that,' the queen dowager interjected. 'Once you've recovered, we shall all, including Agnes, go on pilgrimage to give thanks to the Lord's Precious Blood at Hailes Abbey. Do you know, Mathilde, the Abbey itself . . .'

I fled that sick-chamber as soon as I could and hastened along to Isabella's quarters. In the waiting hall clustered servants and men-at-arms; Ap Ythel's archers sober-dressed in their dull brown and green livery compared to the flame-haired members of Gaveston's Irish mercenaries, with thier flamboyant garb and long hair. All these gathered in window alcoves, enclosures and entrances or just squatted on the ground with their backs to the wall, eating, drinking and dicing, waiting either to be called for some task or to be relieved of their duty. The passageway leading down to the queen's chamber was guarded by a cluster of household knight in half-armour, swords drawn, resplendent in their blue and gold livery. I stared round, looking for the messenger, and glimpsed a grey-haired man, his high-heeled boots mud splattered, the hood of his green cloak pushed back to reveal weatherbeaten skin, deep-set eyes and a neatly clipped beard and moustache. The kindly face was familiar. I went towards him. He glimpsed me, smiled and rose. I remembered Raoul Foucher, a neighbour of my parents' farm near Bretigny, a landowner and trader in skins and leather goods, a righteous man who often visited my mother. We clasped hands and exchanged the kiss of peace. Raoul, beneath all the pleasantries, was anxious to speak alone. I took him beyond the bar, and one of the royal knights escorted us down the passageway to sit on the quilted seats in a deep window enclosure. I asked Raoul if he needed something to eat or drink. He just grasped my hand.

'Mathilde de Clairebon.' He spoke slowly, as if I'd forgotten my own patois. 'Mathilde, it is good to see you. The guards told me how close you are to the queen.' He winked. 'You always were clever, Mathilde. Now listen. I am in London only one day. I must return to Dover by the end of the week when the cog *La Cinquième* returns from Wissant. I have brought no letter from your mother; she thought that might be dangerous. No, no,' he shook his head, 'your mother is well. She sends her love. Like all of us she is getting older, but my sons help on the farm. All was quiet.' He shrugged. 'Season followed season. No one knew where you'd gone after the arrest of your uncle and the chaos in Paris. It was the same out in the countryside. Templar houses and properties were seized and ransacked, their communities arrested and carted off to prison. Tales became common about the torture, degradation and cruel execution of Templars. Royal proclamations described them as sons of Satan, sodomites, idolaters, heretics and warlocks. Few people believed such lies. This was a matter for the king, his lust for gold, his greed for power.' He paused. 'You sent a message to your mother that you were safe, yes?'

I nodded.

'No one believed the stories about men like your uncle, but we considered that a matter for the Great Ones of the land. I never thought your mother was in any danger until last month. Groups of horsemen, black-garbed mercenaries called Noctales, appeared in Bretigny. They proclaimed they were there to hunt down fugitive Templars, though according to common knowledge, very few had escaped. To put it bluntly, Mathilde, for at least ten days, using royal warrants, the Noctacles requisitioned your mother's farm.' He let go of my hands and rubbed his face. 'The experience was not pleasant. You know the law: royal troops, armed with writs of purveyance, can quarter on any chateau, village or farm.'

'My mother wasn't hurt?'

'No. I went down there. The Noctales were bully boys, the dregs of the slums. They helped themselves to food and wine, roistering and sleeping in the stables and barns. I did my best. I objected, asking why Catherine de Clairebon should be their sole host.'

'Was their leader Alexander of Lisbon?'

Raoul pulled a face. 'No, the leader of these crows was a Burgundian called La Maru. He was, is, I think, a defrocked cleric. He was different from the rest, cold-eyed with a weasel soul. He rejected my plea, saying I should complain to the king at the Louvre or, if I wanted to, Mathilde de Clairebon sheltering amongst the Goddams at Westminster. I understood from your mother that La Maru made this reference time and again before he left, promising they might well return before midsummer.'

I tried to control my fears. Raoul knew, I knew, my mother knew, and so did Marigny, the root cause of such abuse, hence that unfinished threat in the abbey gardens. I was being punished, warned through my mother because of my hostility towards Philip and his minions from hell. I questioned Raoul most closely but he could say no more. Perhaps he was being kind and wished to save me from the litany of petty cruelties and indignities inflicted upon my mother. He was nervous, anxious to be gone from such strange surroundings. I told him to wait, hurried to my own chamber and brought from my precious store two small purses of silver coins. I explained that one was for him, the other for my mother. He refused. I still thrust both into his hands, and begged him to reassure her of my love and tell her that I was well but, for the moment, could not return to France as it would be too dangerous. He listened carefully, promised me he would do all he could and left.

Un bon homme, Monsieur Foucher. I have a

special Book of Hours, once beautiful, its vellum cover now tattered, aged with use, stained and frayed. At the back, like any good bedeswoman or chancery priest, I have a list of those souls I pray for. People who did what they could when there were so many reasons why they should pass by on the other side. Raoul is one of these. After he left, I fled to my own chamber and crouched in the corner, staring at the light pouring through the lancet window. I sat huddled, seething with fear, hate, revenge and a deep, cloying sense of despair. When would this all end? I stared at the bleak crucifix and prayed for an end to my heart bubbling like a cauldron, full to the brim with disorderly, dangerous humours. My gaze wandered to a triptych of St Anne, mother of the Virgin, bending over her precious child. I prayed to her even as I recognised the words of Augustine: how demons can cloak themselves in thick, moist bodies such as steam from a pot or foul gases from a marsh. Did such demons prowl now, wrapped and wafted in the perfumes of this palace, drifting along its corridors and galleries, sliding like a mist, searching for the gaps and crevices in the armour of my soul? I prayed to St Anne and breathed in deeply. Images of my mother floated through my mind. I'd always been closer to my father than to her. I believed I was more the expression of her love for him than the object of her love. Nevertheless, the ties of the womb are the strongest. I wept for how her gentleness must have suffered at the hands of the Noctales. God forgive me, I seethed with hate for Marigny, Alexander of Lisbon and La Maru.

A tap on the door roused me from my reverie. A pageboy, hair all tousled, pushed his cheeky face through.

'Mademoiselle Mathilde, you must come, the queen waits for you.'

I rose to my feet, straightened my dress and hurried after him into the gallery. The queen was in her own private chamber. She was sitting on the edge of her hung bed, its gorgeous tapestries bundled back over the rods above her. She was dressed in a linen shift gathered high at the neck, her feet pushed into silver-gold slippers, her long hair hanging free down to her shoulders. She was humming to herself as she arranged the playing cards Marigny had brought her from France, sorting them into sections: hearts, trefoils, pikes and squares. She sat as if immersed in this, unaware of anything else as I closed the door behind me. By then I knew her. Isabella was at her most dangerous when she looked the most innocent!

'What is wrong, Mathilde? You've been back some time, I understand? Yet you did not hurry to see your mistress.' She gestured at a stool close to the bed. I sat down and told her everything that had happened. She kept playing with the cards and, after I had finished, continued to arrange them into sets of four.

'Do you know, Mathilde,' she gathered one set into her hand and clenched them tightly, 'while you were gone, I went across to the abbey; the good brothers, I understand, are preparing for their head-shearing. Anyway, I examined the misericords, the carvings beneath the stalls where the monks sit. Grotesque scenes! A witch riding a cat, a man fighting a dog, a mock bishop, Samson tearing a lion's jaws, and next to that, a jackal devouring a disinterred corpse. I wondered, Mathilde, do such paintings reflect the humours of our tangled souls? Let us forget about our problems here.' She stared at me with those icy blue eyes, her lower lip clenched between her teeth. 'Your poor mother, Mathilde, what shall we do about her?' She threw the cards on the bed and lifted a finger. 'I shall certainly write to my father. What I don't want is to be like Herod in that play we are preparing for Easter. You remember?'

I nodded, though I scarcely did. Isabella had a love of such mummery and liked nothing better than to hire players and watch their comic antics. She was a keen reader of their texts and had learnt some of the lines, which she would mouth with the leading characters.

Isabella closed her eyes. 'Remember Herod's line? "Out, out, out! I stamp. I stare. I look about! I rant! I rage! Now I am mad. The brat of Bethlehem? He shall be dead."'

'Mistress?' I queried.

'Mathilde,' Isabella opened her eyes, 'we must

not rant and shout but sit and watch. This is the waiting time. We must be subtle, as full as trickery as our opponents. So, let us think, then let us prepare . . .'

Two days later my mistress, clothed in shimmering cloth of gold, her chair of state strewn with blue silk tapestries boasting the gorgeous lilies of France, invited Enguerrand de Marigny and Alexander of Lisbon to share sweet wines from Spain and honey-coated cakes. The ostensible reason was to thank the Portuguese for accepting Gaveston's offer of battle as well as commiserate with him for injuries received. Isabella, the perfect minx, her hair and beautiful face framed by a snow-white wimple, a gold circlet round her head, had issued the invitation and received the Lord Satan and his imp, as she called them, in her inner chamber. Marigny, of course, dared not refuse. Moreover, he was full of curiosity as well as diplomatic questions about whether Isabella was enceinte. He came clad in the dark, rich robes of a lawyer, except for a froth of white around his throat and wrists; rings glittered on his fingers; around his neck was a silver chain carrying a large gold fleur-de-lis – a sign that he enjoyed his royal master's personal favour. Alexander was clothed in the usual black cotehardie and leggings, a white cambric shirt beneath. He looked unaffected by his fall except for mild purple bruising on the right side of his face, a sprain to his wrist and a slight limp. Both were ingratiating to my mistress. I was ignored. The Lord Fox, his sharp, pointed features frozen in a smile, red hair combed and coiffed, darting green eyes full of malice, did glance sharply at me; his thin lips twisted in a smile before he returned all adoringly to my mistress with a litany of false flatteries. Alexander of Lisbon, dark face smouldering, tried to ape such subtle deceit but found it more difficult.

I served goblets of sweet wines and silver dishes of sweetmeats and frumentaries. My mistress was a born actor, playing the part, the gracious queen, the gentle hostess. I recalled those accounts I had drawn up for the plays to be staged at Easter: 'Pontius Pilate paid five shillings. Demons one shilling and fourpence. The man who imitated a cock crowing, fourpence. The drapers who acted the end of the world, three shillings. The person who kept the fire at hell's mouth, fourpence.' I reflected on these as I watched my mistress closely. She was acting. She saw everything as a play: the various parts were assigned, the roles to be played, and she had to deliver her lines. She was a mistress of the moment, the dramatic change, the subtle tone. She allowed Marigny to treat her as if she was some infant babbling away, then abruptly put her goblet down and leaned back in her chair.

'My Lord Marigny, tell my father I may not be enceinte. I deeply regret, but perhaps I will not bear a child, at least this year.'

Marigny's eyes fluttered. He slurped noisily at

the goblet and glanced sharply at me as if wondering whether this had been a trap all along.

'I wish now,' Isabella's voice became hard, 'to move to another matter. Alexander of Lisbon, are you enjoying that wine?'

'Yes, your grace.'

'Do you know it is poisoned?'

The Portuguese almost dropped the goblet but grasped it in time. Marigny leaned forward, hand extended; Isabella fluttered her fingers and he quickly withdrew.

'Your grace,' the Portuguese gabbled, 'you are joking?'

'Think, sir,' Isabella continued, 'Mathilde here poured the wine. She distilled a concoction in yours.' She sipped from her own goblet. 'Do you feel the effects, an irritation in your stomach?'

Alexander of Lisbon's dark face creased in concern. He licked his lips and put the goblet down.

'Your grace would not poison me?'

'Why not?' Isabella retorted.

Marigny sat, eyes darting from Isabella to me then back again.

'Your grace, what is this? I am your father's envoy.'

'So you are, Monsieur Marigny. You wage war against my husband and his favourite, as do I, you know that.' Isabella smoothed over the lie. 'You bring this man here to do your bidding. Is that not so, Alexander of Lisbon?'

The Portuguese nodded. He was now clutching his stomach, staring agitatedly at my mistress.

'I think we should talk about Mathilde, Monsieur Marigny,' Isabella continued. 'You are her enemy. She is yours. We both know the reason why. Last month, Alexander of Lisbon, your men, under a Burgundian named La Maru, were quartered in her mother's farm: Catherine de Clairebon of Bretigny, do you remember that? Swiftly now, and I might tell you how to heal yourself.'

Alexander of Lisbon nodded quickly.

'That must stop,' Isabella said quietly. 'Do you understand me, Monsieur Marigny? That shall stop! You, sir, if you have dealings with Mathilde de Clairebon, deal solely with her, like two warriors in a list, but her mother, an ageing widow – surely, sir, the rules of combat exclude her?'

Marigny half smiled. 'And my companion,' he asked, 'Alexander of Lisbon? Is he to fall ill like Master Guido, to vomit and retch? How would your husband explain that? What does that say of you, mistress?'

'Do I have your word,' Isabella insisted, 'that Catherine de Clairebon of Bretigny will not be abused or ill treated?'

'I cannot say ... I ... I do not know ...' Marigny paused. Alexander, white-faced, was clutching his stomach in apparent discomfort.

'Yes you do,' Isabella insisted, 'as will my father in my next letter to him. I will tell him that is my wish. Catherine de Clairebon is to be treated most tenderly and fall within his love as she must within yours, Monsieur de Marigny! Do I have your word? If I do not, your friend and companion will certainly fall ill. I shall still write to my father explaining how you frustrated my wishes. Do I have your word?'

Marigny shrugged. 'Your grace, provided your father agrees, you have my word.'

'And you, Monsieur Alexander?' Isabella turned, all smiles, and the Portuguese, hand on his stomach, stared fearfully at her. 'Do I have yours?'

'Yes, your grace,' he gasped.

'And this La Maru – he has now come from France? He is with you here in England?'

'Yes, your grace.'

'He is to be dismissed from your company immediately, without stipend or payment. Do you agree?'

Alexander of Lisbon looked quickly at Marigny, who nodded imperceptibly.

'Yes, your grace.'

'Good.' Isabella rose to her feet, walked across to a side table and poured a beaker full of water, then took it back and thrust it into the Portuguese's hand. 'Drink, Alexander.' She patted him gently on the shoulder. 'You have nothing more than a mustard paste in your stomach. No, no.' She daintily held up a hand to fend off his protest. 'The point I am trying to make is that this time what you drank was innocent; it will cause some discomfort, but it will pass. Next time, Alexander of Lisbon, if you try to hurt Catherine de Clairebon or any of her family and friends in France, the potion you shall drink will be deadly.'

Isabella sat back on the throne-like chair, hands folded across her stomach. She smiled sweetly at her two guests.

'You see, Monsieur Marigny, I too have power and influence. If I cannot protect those I love, what princess am I? What queen am I? Reflect carefully on what I have said and done today. Moreover, what can you do: protest to my father in Paris? He'll be angry, but in his secret chamber, he will reflect and laugh behind his hand at what happened. And you, Master Alexander – do you want to tell your company how you were tricked and deceived by a mere girl and her maid?' She shook her head. 'I don't think so. You delivered a warning to Mathilde. I have delivered one back. I have drawn a line; cross that line and we will be enemies. Observe the truce, and so shall I. You see, Monsieur Marigny,' Isabella held her hands up, clasping them together as if in prayer, 'what my husband and Lord Gaveston do is one concern; what happens in my own household is another. You must observe the division, you must observe the line. Do I have your word?'

Marigny cocked his head to one side and stared impudently at my mistress as if assessing her for the first time.

'Your grace,' he leaned forward, 'do you wish to

have further words with us? My companion, as you can see, is distressed and we should retire.'

'I have spoken what I wish, Monsieur Marigny. You and Alexander of Lisbon may withdraw.'

Marigny and the Portuguese rose to their feet. The Lord Satan bowed. He was about to turn away but, of course, he had to say it, end our meeting with some subtle flattery.

'Your grace,' he smiled, 'now I can see you are truly your father's daughter.'

'And so I am, Monsieur Marigny,' Isabella replied, 'and you must remember that. I tell you this.' Her voice thrilled slightly. 'Monsieur Marigny, you should look to yourself and to your own. You tie yourself to my father's belt, and if he rises, you rise with him, but have you ever thought what happens when he falls, *if* he falls?'

Marigny looked shocked, as if he had never contemplated such a possibility.

'You should be careful, Monsieur Marigny. The world is changing, and so must you. I bid you adieu.'

Once they had gone, Isabella leaned forward, face in her hands, and giggled quietly to herself. She let her fingers fall away.

'Well, Mathilde, did we do well?'

'Very well, your grace, very well indeed.'

Isabella took a deep breath and sighed noisily.

'Mathilde, what I said to Marigny is true. Everything is changing. This is a time of weeping and waiting. Yet I'll confess this to you. One day my Lord Gaveston must go. He cannot remain dancing on the green for ever.'

'You oppose him, mistress?'

'No, Mathilde, I do not. I have studied Edward most closely; I must control him as any woman must a man. Edward and Gaveston,' she locked two fingers together, 'they are not two but one: one body, one soul, one heart. Some day, tomorrow, next week, next month, next year, the Great Lords will seize Gaveston and kill him. Once he dies, Edward will retreat like a hermit into his cell. He will hide deep within his soul and plot vengeance. Anyone who had anything to do with Gaveston's fall or destruction will rue the day. When that happens . . .' Isabella half smiled, 'I want to ensure that my name is not on that list of those who caused his fall.'

'So you will not move against the favourite?'

'I did not say that, Mathilde. All I will ensure is that my name is not on that list. Now come.' She got to her feet. 'What is that magpie riddle? Let's dance to it. How does it go, Mathilde?'

'One for anger, two for mirth . . .'

'Ah, that's right.' Isabella took it up. 'Three for a wedding, four for birth, five for rich, six for poor, seven for a bitch, eight for a whore, nine for burying, ten for a dance, eleven for England, twelve for France. You see, Mathilde, I have learnt it well. Now come . . .' She spread her hands. 'Show me the dance.'

My mistress was in a strange mood. When we

had finished, she collapsed on the bed, laughing, begging me to bring some fresh water. She straightened up, drained the cup and handed it back to me.

'Mathilde, let us go to St Stephens' Chapel and pray for your mother. After that,' she gestured across the tables strewn with manuscripts, 'my lord wishes to entertain me and the Lord Gaveston. I will be absent this evening. You need not be in attendance.' She peered at me. 'I will leave you to your own thoughts. Perhaps it is time, yes, we try to thread this maze.'

CHAPTER 11

He who dwelleth on high and looketh down
on low things hates pride above all things.

Vita Edwardi Secundi

Later that evening, my mistress left to join the king and Gaveston for a private supper party. I was always excluded from such meetings. The Evangelist be my witness, Isabella rarely talked about what happened there. On that night, I recalled what she'd said about staying close to the king. God knows how she did that. Perhaps Edward welcomed unreserved support for his favourite when no one else gave it. Perhaps her friendship for Gaveston confirmed the king's perception of his own morality. If Isabella, his beautiful young queen and wife, accepted the favourite, then what fault was there in it? The chroniclers have written about Isabella as the Virago, the Jezebel. They talk of her arrogance, her adultery, her wickedness – that is only monks feeding on their own pleasures. Isabella had many virtues; chief amongst these was her patience, tried and tested long before she ever came to England. She could wait and watch. She would accept insults and jibes with the sweetest smile, then smile and smile again. 'A time and place under heaven for everything,' so says Ecclesiasticus; it could well have been Isabella's personal motto.

On that particular evening, once the queen had left, I was closeted in my own chamber, warm and secure, the doors and shutters locked, a brazier crackling, a copper chafing dish fiery with charcoal nearby. I wrapped a cloak about me, prepared my writing tray and reflected like any good student of physic on the symptoms I had observed.

Primo: the Poison Maiden, Ancilla Venenata, La Demoiselle Venimeuse. Who was she, he or it? An actual person, or more than one? An event, as Guido had suggested, such as the king's marriage to Isabella, or even Gaveston's liaison with Edward? The old king had certainly fulminated against the Poison Maiden, raged about her very existence, but why? Was she a spy or some hideous obstacle or weakness at the English court that Philip of France could exploit? The connection between the Poison Maiden and the Louvre Palace was definite. Edmund Lascelles, commonly known as Pax-Bread, had fled from France bringing privileged information, perhaps about the Poison Maiden, which had eventually proved to be his death warrant. The same was true of Chapeleys. He might have had his own theories about the Poison Maiden, and he too had died. The Poison Maiden, however mysterious, certainly existed. The old king, Edward, Philip of France, Isabella, Pax-Bread and Chapeleys had all made clear reference to this.

Secundo: the King and his idol. Edward and Gaveston were literally besieged at Westminster. The exchequer was empty. They had some troops but little support amongst the Great Lords. Were they waiting for the earls to exhaust themselves, to utterly deplete their treasures? But then what? How would the stalemate be broken? Did Edward anticipate help from some unexpected source? Yet where would such assistance come from?

Tertio: the Great Lords. They were camped in Westminster and its surrounding fields, but for how long? Did they have a spy at the royal court? Did they know more than they pretended? Who was secretly supporting them? Philip of France, the papacy? How could they continue to sustain the swollen retinues they had brought south?

Quatro: Philip of France and his Spiders. The French king was certainly fishing in troubled waters. Ostensibly to protect the interests of his beloved daughter, but what else? To provoke Edward to turn in fury on his lords? To weaken the kingdom with civil war? Was Philip hoping eventually to abandon the Great Lords and force Edward to rely solely on him, as well as force the English king to support his own cruel attack on the Templars? Or was there something else? Did

Philip hope to create civil war in England so as to seize the wine-rich province of Gascony and bring it under Capetian hegemony once and for all. Did he plot to remove both Edward and Gaveston? But that would jeopardise Isabella and, surely, weaken French influence. And Philip's present alliance with the Lords, would that last, or was he simply playing a game? Had the Poison Maiden assumed a role in this? Would the king's enemies eventually move into open warfare? That reference to assassins: *les ombres*, or the Tenebrae? Had the king's enemies hired killers, professional assassins to deal with Gaveston? If so, who were these, and where were they? When would they attack and how?

Quinto: Pax-Bread's letter. Most of it simply confirmed the real dangers confronting the English king as well as the existence of the Poison Maiden, but those references to *Jean*, *Haute* and *Mont*: what did they mean? Was the 'Jean' mentioned in that letter the person Pax-Bread had referred to in his conversation with Alvena about 'old Jean' and the hymn he sang?

Sexto: Pax-Bread's murder. According to Alvena, Pax-Bread was anxious and fearful. He had fled from France and sheltered in London, but someone had hunted him down. He had lodged at the Secret of Solomon but left the safety of that noisy tavern to meet a mysterious Agnes, allegedly sent by Gaveston, who in turn claimed to have no knowledge of such a messenger. Why had Pax-Bread, so openly fearful, gone out into the dark to meet that stranger, and why was his chamber stripped of any trace of him? The doors and shutters all locked from within? Who was Agnes? How could she kill a man like Pax-Bread, already wary and vigilant against any attack? I studied my cipher and wrote on. Pax-Bread could have gone straight to Westminster but delayed at the Secret of Solomon, which meant French agents might have been scouring the city for him. Pax-Bread, I concluded, had made a hideous mistake – he must have thought he was safe as long as he never approached the palace.

Septimo: Chapeleys. He had been Langton's clerk and wished to escape from the Tower, allegedly with information useful to the king. Langton had been most dismissive about him. Nevertheless, Chapeleys had fled to Westminster and lodged in a secure chamber, where he should have been safe. Yet though that room was locked from the inside, he had been found hanging from a window-door. The suicide of a man frightened witless? But he had seemed very determined to approach the king, and had shown no sign of that numbing fear that prompts a soul to take his own life. Yet if it was murder, how was it done? Chapeleys might have been a clerk, but he was alert and would have fought for his life. There was no sign of any violence or anyone seen approaching that chamber, except for that mysterious cloaked woman glimpsed by Robert the groom. What had happened to the contents of Chapeleys' chancery bag? Stolen, burnt or both? And that scrap of parchment with the word 'basil', a circle with a P in the centre, surmounted by a cross and the phrase *sub pede*, underfoot. What did that all mean?

Octavo: Rebecca Atte-Stowe. Who did kill her? Why? Was her murder part of this mystery or just an unfortunate occurrence, the result of some vicious in-fighting amongst servants?

Nono: Agnes d'Albret. Why was she so withdrawn, so anxious to enter Isabella's household? Was it simply fear at being returned to France? What did she mean by her question: are you not suspicious? Did she have a secret relationship with Gaveston? If so, why, and to what purpose?

Decimo: Guido the Psalter. Was he the intended victim of that poisoning? If so, why? Or was it Gaveston? How was that water glass tainted? What poison was used? I reflected on the trick Isabella had played on Marigny and Alexander of Lisbon, and smiled. Nevertheless, the potion Guido had drunk seemed more noxious. I had searched my leech books, but as yet could find no trace of a poison with that distinctive perfume.

Undecimo: the Templars. Would Edward persecute them in return for Philip's patronage and support? Was there a traitor amongst the brethren? How did Alexander of Lisbon know so much about that secret meeting at the Chapel of the Hanged? And New Temple Church? Why was Winchelsea so eager to gain possession of it? What was so special about it? Why had he referred to Pembroke's ancestors being buried there? Was Winchelsea acting for himself, the Great Lords or his fellow bishops?

I smiled and put the pen down. Prince amongst the bishops was Langton! I recalled what Uncle Reginald had taught me. 'Mathilde,' he told me on one occasion, 'always go back to the prime cause, the very first instance. I remember, *ma petite*, a powerful merchant from Dijon. He was lodging in Paris and came to the Temple because of violent pains in his stomach, a loosening of the bowels. I asked him to list precisely what he had eaten and drunk. He assured me it had been the best meat, the freshest bread and the most fragrant wines. I was puzzled. I asked him what had happened since he came to Paris. He told me he had received some very bad news and I wondered whether the humours of the mind had interfered with those of the stomach and bowel. The cause of his sickness might be worry rather than rancid meat.'

I recalled those words as I sat huddled in that chair studying my cipher. *Go back to the prime cause.* Langton was the prime cause! The murder of Chapeleys occurred only after we had visited the good bishop. He might well be one of the principal causes of the mysteries and murders surrounding us. I sat, reflected and plotted. Midnight came and went. I reached my decision. Could Langton be trapped?

★   ★   ★

We arrived at the Tower mid-morning. A royal barge, oared by eight stout boatmen displaying the royal livery, shot like an arrow through the turbulent waters of the Thames. A veil of mist hung heavy, thick and threatening. A page boy in the prow blew harshly on a hunting horn to warn all other craft to pull aside. Above me in the canopied stern flapped a broad pennant boasting the royal arms, golden leopards on a scarlet background. On my left, through the shifting mist, I glimpsed the might of the city: the gabled, red-tiled mansions of the merchant princes; the spires and towers of churches and monasteries, nunneries and chapels; the various quaysides piled high with goods and thronged with crowds. Alongside the wharves was a glorious display of ships: merchantmen, Venetian galleys and Hanseatic cogs. These moved majestically among herring ships, fishing boats, oyster smacks and coracles. Now and again, glimpses of the horrid cruelty of life caught my gaze. Gallows, black and stark. River pirates hanging by their necks from quayside rings. The corpse collectors, dispatching skiffs and punts to bring in the cadavers floating amongst the bankside reeds or bobbing mid-current, turning and twisting, rising and falling as if in preparation for the final resurrection. The air was rich with a variety of smells and odours, the corruption, refuse and rottenness mingling with spices, wood smoke, salted fish, spilt wine and dried seaweed, as well as the fragrances from the precious cargoes nestling in the foulsome holds of the various ships.

I reflected on the day's beginnings. I had met my mistress early. She'd not even murmured her Matins, still heavy-eyed after her rich supper with the king and Gaveston. She heard me out patiently, smiled understandingly and agreed. Demontaigu was summoned, I could tell by his wine-rich breath how he had just celebrated the Eucharist. Isabella sleepily dictated a short letter and instructed him to accompany me to the Tower to tend to Walter Langton, Bishop of Coventry and Lichfield. Demontaigu acted the faithful clerk. Once the letter was finished, he strapped on his war belt, threw his cloak around his shoulders and accompanied me across the mist-filled palace grounds to King's Steps and the waiting barge. On reflection, it was a sombre start to a sombre day. Murder would greet me. Blood would be spilt. God be my witness, I tremble at my sins, scarlet red, but what else could I do?

I suppose the terrors of the day stretched back to the start. Even as our barge pulled away from the quayside, I glimpsed that cowled figure hurrying down the green-slimed steps to the waiting wherry. The mist closed in, but later, just before we reached the starlings and arches of London Bridge, I glimpsed that wherry again. I was certain it was the same one, but kept my peace. Demontaigu sat huddled beside me, praying his beads. We landed safely at the Tower wharf, teeming and bustling like a hive in summer. Memory still holds fast from that day. Glimpses, scenes, pictures like those miniatures in a psalter that catch your eye as you thumb its pages. Four old soldiers begged for alms, dressed in black with red crosses daubed on their foreheads. They shouted how their eyes had been removed and the skin stitched tight by infidels in Outremer. Beside them a madwoman sang the Salve Regina, those prophetic words ringing out: 'Hail Holy Queen, Mother of mercy. Hail our life, our sweetness and our hope.' Prisoners, roped by neck, hand and foot, shuffled in filthy rags towards the dungeons beneath the Tower gate. Men-at-arms and archers were busy imposing order with their staves. A king's knight, astride his caparisoned warhorse, watched them closely. A lady perched daintily on a palfrey trotted by across the cobbles, the hooded hawks on her wrists eager to be free, their jesse-bells tingling above the raucous cries of fishermen, oyster wives, fruit traders and tinkers. An old man pushed his infirm wife in a wheelbarrow, bawling at everyone to stand aside. A market bailiff followed a peasant, live fluttering poultry tied to his back. The official was waiting for the man to place his bird on the ground so he could charge him stallage. Beadles were grasping a squealing fat-bellied sow so as to cut its tail as a punishment for wandering into this marketplace. Smoke and fumes from tanneries and lime-burners drifted across. The stinking badness of the air caught at nose and throat. A dog nudged at two corpses dragged from the river. Three madcaps, bells sewn to their clothes, hastened up to offer a dance. Demontaigu pushed them aside and, one hand on his sword, the other on my elbow, guided me through the soaring, gloomy gateway. Officers and serjeants mailed and helmeted, thronged about us, faces almost concealed by coifs and cowls. The stink of leather, sweat, tar and salt was all-pervasive. Torches guttered in the breeze; above us, the sharp-toothed portcullis hung like a threat. We went along narrow lanes and alleys watched by hooded archers, arrows notched to bows. We crossed baileys, cobbled yards and muddy enclosures where engines of war reared up, ghastly, threatening shapes against the sky. A place of contrasts. Yards full of children playing amongst mastiffs, chickens pecking at the ground, geese strident in their screeching, cattle bellowing. All the noises and smells of the farmyard and stable mingled with those of the kitchen, washtub and bathhouse. In the distance, however, dull roars from the royal beastry sounded, whilst above us, as if watching our every footstep, black-winged ravens floated like demons.

At last we reached the great four-square Norman tower. The serjeant explained how Lord Cromwell, the constable, was out provisioning stores in Petty Wales. He offered Cromwell's apologies and led us up the steep steps, unlocking doors on to the landing and Langton's comfortable chamber. Some of the shutters had been removed from the lancet windows to allow in air whilst the good bishop was warming himself over a brazier. He exclaimed in surprise at my arrival but seemed welcoming enough. Demontaigu murmured how he was only my escort and left for the nearby chapel of St John. I hurriedly excused myself and followed whilst Langton shouted at the serjeant to bring fresh wine for his visitor as well as some sweetmeats from the Tower kitchen. I followed Demontaigu across the narrow passageway and asked what troubled him. He undid his sword belt, let it slip to the ground and explained how Ausel might come to the Tower quayside. He wondered what news he might bring. Demontaigu's voice echoed hollow even as Langton's instructions to the serjeant rang out through the opened doors. I stood still, listening carefully, recalling our first visit to the bishop.

'Mathilde, what it is?'

'Nothing, *mon coeur*.' I smiled. 'Just memories.'

I returned to Langton's chamber. He was now wrapped in a heavy fur-lined cloak; he sat enthroned, gold pectoral winking in the light, fingers fiddling with his episcopal ring. To be sure, there was little priestly about Langton: thick, solid and squat, an untidy mat of iron-grey hair now hiding his tonsure. He looked, in truth, what he was in fact: a clever bully boy. He would have made an excellent captain of the rifflers, those violent gangs in London's underworld hired by powerful merchants who wished to trade in dagger-thrust and violent swordplay. A clever man, despite his slobbery lips and wine-flushed face. My uncle often quoted the old proverb: 'You can tell a man's health by his eyes.' As I took my seat on the quilted stool, I recalled one just as accurate and ancient: 'You can also tell a man's soul by his eyes'; Langton's, hidden in folded creases of fat, were young and clear, full of arrogant mischief. Gaveston called him a bag of poison or something similar, but Langton was wily and astute. He would have made Edward a cunning ally; instead the king had made him a venomous enemy.

We exchanged the usual pleasantries. I handed over Isabella's courtesy letter and decided to follow the path I'd chosen. I chattered like a sparrow in spring. How Guido was ill. How both the king and my mistress were concerned about the bishop's health, particularly the ulcers on his legs. I talked as if highly nervous, spilling out court gossip, and all the time those young, clever eyes in that old, weathered face studied me carefully. I needed to touch Langton, examine those ulcers. He claimed his legs were now healing beautifully. I immediately replied how the danger was not the ulcers but the fresh skin: it must heal completely and not be broken. Langton continued to study me. I undid the clasp of my cloak and the laces to the neck of my gown gathered tightly around my throat. I did so daintily and prettily, leaning forward and smiling at that fox, who truly thought he was hosting a capon for dinner. He asked me to pour some wine and invited me to join him. I did so. I slurped at the goblet and bit into a sweet-meat, dates coated in honey. The sweetness filled my mouth. I cleared my throat and gossiped on, giggling when Langton leaned forward. He gently squeezed one of my breasts, then caressed it admiringly. Eventually he agreed that the ulcers, perhaps, should be inspected. He stood up, threw his robe on to the chair, lifted the linen shift beneath and pulled down his hose as if he was a boy stripping for a swim in the river. He waddled over to the bed and threw himself down, leaning back against the bolsters and patting the coverlet beside him. I went across and pushed back the quilt. The ulcers had healed beautifully to faint red-purplish marks. I examined these, letting my fingers knead the vein-streaked flesh beneath his knee. Langton's hand came out again and grasped my breast, stroking the nipple. I laughed coyly. Still chattering about the court, I moved from one item to another.

'The king still pursues the Templars,' I murmured, hiding my revulsion at that old man's touch. 'He believes that New Temple Church conceals their wealth; he is determined to search there.' Immediately, Langton tensed. I could feel the muscles in the leg go hard and rigid, and his hand fell away. 'And there is a great to-do amongst the chancery clerks,' I continued. 'They are searching for a man, someone who served the old king: John Hot . . . or High . . .'

'John Highill.'

'Yes, that's right!'

The name had slipped out before Langton could stop himself. Again there was that tension. I stood back and stared down at those fleshy legs.

'My lord,' I smiled, 'you are correct: the scars have healed. You are very fortunate. Can I recommend that you wash your legs daily in hot water and some precious soap from Castile, then rinse well. Keep as much irritation as you can off the skin.'

I continued my chatter about the joust between Gaveston and the Portuguese knight; the king's feastings; what the Court would do at Easter, but I could see I'd hit my mark. Langton was no longer interested in me. He sat on the bed, eyes staring, lips murmuring, lost in his own thoughts. I hastily made my farewells. Demontaigu joined me outside. I put a finger to my lips. We hastened down the steps and out on to the green, where the waiting serjeant escorted us back to the great cobbled yard beyond the Lion Gate. I was excited, pleased at my own cunning, forgetful of danger. Ah well, arrogance is a slippery plank and I paid the price. We'd hardly gone through the gate when I glimpsed Ausel, dressed like a friar, his head shaven, standing on a small barrel lecturing the crowd, drawing them in with the power and oratory of his sermon: 'May the day perish when I was born. Why did I not die newborn? Perish when I left the womb? If that had happened, I should now be lying in peace, wrapped in restful slumber with the kings and high lords of earth who build themselves vast vaults crammed with precious jewels. Down there in death, bad men bustle no more! There the weary rest for ever . . .'

Demontaigu tapped me on the shoulder. 'Stay here, Mathilde.' I stood and watched the people mill across the great cobbled expanse. A group of city bailiffs led prostitutes found touting for custom down to the thews. The poor women's heads had been completely shorn, and they were forced to wear striped gowns, their humiliation emphasised by two bagpipe players who screeched noisily, attracting a crowd to shout abuse and hurl offal, bones, anything they could lay their hands on. I watched them go even as the Gabriel bell tolled from nearby churches summoning the faithful to say one Pater, Ave and Gloria, as well as stop work for the noonday drink. Scavengers arrived, the great iron-rimmed wheels on the slung carts crashing across the ground. The scavengers, burly men dressed in motley rags, always had an eye for profit: they quickly seized a goose, wrung the bird's neck and immediately dropped it into a sack hanging on the inside of the cart. The owner ran up protesting, but the chief scavenger referred to the city ordinances: how a goose found wandering where it shouldn't forfeited all rights; its neck could be wrung and its flesh belonged to the man who found it. The great market area began to empty as people made their way to taverns and alehouses for the noonday refreshments. I stood on tiptoe, wondering where Demontaigu had gone, wishing I had accompanied him. I abruptly felt a presence behind me. I looked over my shoulder and glimpsed a sharp nose and glittering eyes, even as I felt the dagger prick my skin just beneath the shoulder blade.

'Mathilde de Clairebon?'

'Yes?' I tried to control my panic. 'I am Mathilde de Clairebon. I carry the queen's warrant.'

'For all I care, you can carry God Almighty's!'

I caught the accent and tried to turn; the dagger dug deeper.

'Very well, Mathilde de Clairebon, do exactly what I say. Walk on. Attempt to scream, run, fight or struggle and this dagger will be through you in less than a heartbeat.'

We went down a ribbon-thin alleyway leading to the Customs House, which fronted the Wool Wharf. I was ordered to keep my hands hanging by my sides and attempt no mischief. My attacker had chosen well. The runnel was narrow and dark, with recesses between the crumbling houses on either side: the path to the underworld, inhabited by spitting cats and thin-ribbed mongrels. Small, shabby alehouses fronted it; gloomy entrances led into deeper darkness; there was the occasional makeshift stall manned by rogues who watched us pass. Counterfeit beggars squatted in nooks and crannies counting their ill-gotten gains.

'A plump, pleasant capon for the plucking,' a

voice rang out. 'Remember us when you're finished!'

My assailant pushed me on; halfway down, he shoved me violently into a small enclosure to my left, a gap between two houses sealed off by a soaring wall. I was pushed against this so hard the stones scored my back. My assailant, one hand holding the dagger beneath my heart, tipped back his deep cowl to reveal a young face, smooth-skinned, eyes glinting with malice. He pressed on the dagger, his ale-soaked breath hot on my face.

'Mathilde de Clairebon, I am La Maru, formerly a member of Alexander of Lisbon's entourage. That Portuguese turd, that by-blow of a sow, has now dismissed me. He claimed he had to on the orders of your royal bitch of a mistress. Yet Mathilde,' he sighed noisily, 'I was only carrying out orders. I came to this water-drenched cesspit, and after a few days I am turned out of my lodgings, away from my companions.'

He spoke Norman French fluently with that particular Burgundian tone, slightly nasal. My fears passed. I felt cold and watchful. This man had terrorised my mother; now he hoped to do the same to me. He searched me roughly, snatching off my wallet and small purse, a ring from my left hand, a brooch from my gown, a bangle from my wrist. I recalled Langton and acted all simpering, the pretty distressed damoiselle. I know the words and actions to perfection. I pleaded. He thrust his mouth to my ear and whispered some obscenity about my mother. I recognised a killer. He would show me no mercy. La Maru's soul was full of gloomy halls and sombre rooms; he was whittled away like a rotting tree, the poison deep-soaked. He grew excited, clawing at my breast. I struggled weakly. He lifted the hem of my skirt, his hand searching beneath. My hard cloth belt hindered him. One hand holding the dagger, the other searching my skin, he was trapped.

'I shall undo my belt,' I stammered. He agreed. My hands fell to the buckle, then to the narrow sheath, cleverly hidden, holding an Italian blade, long and thin like a bodkin, with a razor tip and sharp serrated edges. I grasped it. La Maru was intent on his pleasures. I thrust deep into the right side of his belly, just beneath the ribcage, a hard upward cut. The shock alone made him drop his dagger. He staggered back, eyes startled, mouth gaping, a hideous gargling at the back of his throat. I followed up and struck again swiftly, deadly.

'God knows,' I breathed, 'I never sought your death.'

La Maru stood shocked, blood spilling out of his nose and mouth like water from a cracked pot. He stared at me, eyes glazing over in death, slumped to his knees and lurched on his side on to the filth-strewn ground. I knelt down, hastily gathering my possessions and his dagger. A shadow moved to my right. I whirled round. A hooded, venomous face peered down at the two daggers I held.

'The choice is yours!' I hissed. 'The same for you,' I gestured with my hand, 'or you can take what you want and escort me out of here.'

I have never seen a corpse plundered so swiftly, so expertly just like a pillager on a battlefield. My unexpected visitor, stinking of the alleyway, stripped La Maru's body, bundling everything into the man's cloak. I gestured with the daggers.

'Monsieur, after you.'

He smiled thinly. I brought up the daggers. 'Others wait for me on the quayside.' He led me out back down the alleyway. He kept his word. Dark shapes moved out of doorways and recesses but he had drawn his knife, so they slunk back. I gathered he must have made enough profit for a month, let alone a day! When I reached the end of the alleyway, he mockingly waved me forward then disappeared back into the gloom. I went across the cobbles. I was unaware of anyone around me. My body was clammy with sweat, my heart thudding. My dress and gown were dirty, unbuttoned and loosed.

'Mathilde!' Demontaigu appeared before me.

I just leaned against him, letting everything slip from my hands to the cobbles. He embraced me, shouting at a beggar man to stay well away. He crouched down and picked up what I had dropped. He helped me lace my dress, put back the bodkin knife and gently escorted me to a nearby alehouse, where he ordered wine and food. He didn't eat – I recalled that on certain days Demontaigu fasted – he just fed me like a mother would a child. After a while the coldness went. The shivering terrors and fears receded. On reflection, I had no choice. My words to La Maru were the truth. He had brought his own death upon himself. I told Demontaigu what had happened. He listened, and then, as if eager to divert me, said he had been with Ausel, who had told him the rumours amongst the brethren how the Temple still held great treasures. A similar story had originated from Canterbury, where William de la More, master of the Templar order in England, was incarcerated. I nodded in agreement.

'I know what treasure it is,' I forced a smile, 'and where it is hidden.'

Two hours later, washed and changed, I knelt on a cushion decorated with silver asphodels in the king's own chamber. Edward lounged. Isabella sat to his right, Gaveston on his left, leaning against a table staring intently at me. I had told the queen about my suspicions and she had immediately sought this audience with her husband. Edward's opulent chamber was littered with boots, spurs, baldrics, belts, cloaks, a knife, even pieces of horse harness. He seemed more interested in the sleek peregrine falcon perched on his wrist, its sharp, neat head hidden by a hood. As I talked, he played with the little bells attached to the bird's claws. However, when I began to describe my suspicions, he handed the falcon to Gaveston, who put it on a perch near the oriel window at the far side of the room. The king leaned forward, head slightly turned as if he couldn't believe what I was saying. Gaveston simply nodded in excitement. Isabella, as usual, kept her face impassive, though when I caught her gaze, she winked slowly and smiled in encouragement. Once I had finished, Edward turned in his chair, staring at Gaveston as if disbelieving every word I had uttered.

'Mathilde speaks the truth,' Isabella declared sharply.

I held her gaze and glimpsed the change. Just that remark, the tone of her voice, a mere shift in her eyes, a fleeting expression. She was now growing openly tired of Gaveston's pre-eminence, of her husband's slavish dependence on his favourite.

'Mathilde is a good student of physic,' she continued. 'She notes the symptoms and searches for the cause. My lord, order Ap Ythel and my Lord Gaveston's Kernia immediately to the New Temple Church Find the effigy of Pembroke. Have the flagstones, *sub pede*, near or beneath the feet of each monument lifted. See what can be found. Search must also be made for this John Highill.' She laughed quietly. 'Pax-Bread was too clever: *Jean*, *Haute* and *Mont* – John High Mountain. Langton gave us the correct translation: John High Hill literally, John Highill in fact. He must have been a clerk, an advocate or *peritus*.'

'I agree.' Gaveston tactfully intervened. 'I am sure he was one of your late,' his voice was laced with sarcasm, 'beloved father's clerks.'

Edward shook his head. 'I don't know,' he murmured, 'I cannot remember.' He straightened in the chair, stared down at his feet, then rose quickly. 'Searches,' he murmured, 'careful but swift searches must be made. Madam,' he bowed to Isabella, patted me gently on the head as if I was a pet dog and walked to the door, clicking his fingers at Gaveston to follow. Isabella sat like a statue, only starting as the door slammed shut behind her husband and his favourite.

'How long, Mathilde?' she whispered, her gaze shifting to me. 'Gaveston at Matins! Gaveston at Prime! Gaveston at Terce! Gaveston at Nones! Gaveston at Vespers and Gaveston at Compline! What do you advise?'

'Wait, your grace.'

'Wait, your grace,' Isabella mimicked. Her expression changed and she smiled dazzlingly at me. She slowly rose to her feet. 'Wait, Mathilde.' She stretched out a hand and helped me up. 'We'll wait, but in the mean time, we will dance. I have also written a play.' She grinned mischievously. 'It's a dialogue between two souls on the theme: is it easier to love those far away than those closer to you?' And, laughing and teasing, she led me out of the chamber back to her own quarters.

The late afternoon passed in the tolling of abbey bells. Noises from the courtyards drifted along the gallery. We heard shouts and listened to the clatter of horses leaving the stables. Isabella and I tried to divert ourselves, but the queen declared she was tired and retired to her private chamber saying she wished to be alone. I was about to return to mine when I received a message that Demontaigu was in the waiting hall. I went to meet him. We sat, I remember, under a tapestry depicting the Lady of the Lake grasping Excalibur. It was certainly a time of war; news that something was afoot had swept the palace, courtyards and baileys of Burgundy Hall. Ap Ythel was assembling his men. Cohorts of Kernia also gathered under the watchful eye of knights of the royal household, the king's bully boys all coiffed and armoured, warhorses snorting as they stirred restlessly under a forest of pennants and banners. Gaveston himself was to lead the cavalcade in a show of force along the Westminster bank and into New Temple. Demontaigu and I watched them from a window. Ap Ythel came bustling by. He stopped and explained how the Great Lords, thinking the king was moving against them, were also summoning their forces. Edward had sent Ingelram Berenger to give his personal assurances that the royal array was only on royal business involving the Templars. Demontaigu stiffened at this. After Ap Ythel left, I explained what I had haltingly informed him of on our return from the city.

'God and his Angels.' Demontaigu clasped my

hand. 'Of course. The old king died in the summer; Langton must have known he was for the fall. He secretly hid his treasure hoard in one of the safest place, New Temple, the principle house of our order in this kingdom. The Templars,' he added bitterly, 'bankers as well as warriors.' He laughed sharply. 'Langton must have thought it would be the securest place on earth, protected by knights whose allegiance was more to God and the pope than any earthly king. What a spin of Fortune's wheel! Langton falls but so does the Temple, suddenly, savagely! Few people would know about any hidden treasure.' He sighed. Most of those are probably dead, fled or in strict confinement like our master.' Demontaigu laughed, put his face into his hands then glanced up. 'Like rivers rushing into one,' he murmured, 'the old king dies; Langton panics! He hides his money away with the Temple. The Templars fall; Langton is imprisoned in the Tower. That old fox must be beside himself! He still plots,' Demontaigu looked at me, 'from prison. Langton the spider cannot rest, he knows it is only a matter of time before that treasure is discovered. So he offers it, or at least part of it, to Winchelsea, who is already inflamed with righteous anger that one of his fellow bishops has been imprisoned. Of course, Winchelsea would be only too willing to agree. The king is starved of money, whilst the Great Lords' retinues are becoming costlier by the day. Such a treasure, if it fell into Winchelsea's hands, would eventually force Edward to come to terms.'

'So,' I replied, 'Winchelsea attempts to secure New Temple, a reasonable demand, as surety of the king's good faith, a property in that misty twilight that separates the ecclesiastic from the secular. Edward would be tempted to agree. What use to him an empty church, barracks and hall already looted and pillaged of any treasures?'

'And of course,' Demontaigu added quickly, 'the surrender of New Temple would be seen as a public move against the order whilst Winchelsea, Langton and their allies seized the treasure hoard.'

'I believe . . .' I stopped, half listening to the armoured clatter below, 'Chapeleys knew about this treasure and wished to barter such information, amongst other things, with the king. Langton must have been furious at Chapeleys' escape. He may have had a hand in his murder.'

'But how?'

'I don't know. Somehow Langton discovered Chapeleys had not left on some errand but had deserted him. He sent a message, God knows how or when, but it must have been shortly after we left the Tower.'

'To whom?'

'To the Poison Maiden or others hostile to the king. Chapeleys was murdered. The assassin made it look as if it was suicide, but that was because he, or she, didn't want to provoke suspicion that Chapeleys may have had something very valuable to sell. I am sure whatever was in that chancery bag was seized, read, then destroyed.' I stared across the hall at a shield fixed between two of the lancet windows emblazoned with the brilliant blue and white colours of Norfolk.

'How,' I murmured, 'could Langton act so swiftly? Ah well.' I turned and edged closer to Demontaigu. 'You wished to see me?'

'To apologise.' Demontaigu blinked. 'This morning at the Tower wharf? I should not have left you.'

'You said you were sorry,' I fluttered my eyelids, 'at leaving a damsel in distress.' I joked and flirted, trying to blot out La Maru's ugly face, the dagger, his crawling touch, the blood bubbling out of his mouth.

'Brave face hides anxious heart,' Demontaigu teased back.

'Brave face hides hard heart,' I retorted. 'You are a warrior, I'm a physician of sorts . . .'

'Of sorts?'

'No,' I held my hand up, 'I know what I am. God knows, Bertrand, sometimes a bridge is reached and you just have to cross it. This morning La Maru came determined to kill me. Whenever that happened, wherever, it would have been him and me. It would have ended in a death, his, mine or both.'

'I bought you a present, a *consolamentum*.'

Demontaigu drew from his jerkin a psalter bound in calfskin, its cover studded with precious stones to form a Celtic cross and Ave beads. The pages were gold-lined and of the finest parchment, the writing in an elegant script, the letters black and clear. A collection of prayers, poems, songs and psalms; the first letter of each verse was decorated in a miniature bejewelled picture displaying exotic creatures from Celtic legends. I scanned the opening lines of the first poem, 'St Patrick's Breastplate': 'I rise up today, God's power with me.' I read on to hide how deeply touched I was by the gift.

'Reparation,' Demontaigu murmured.

'I wish it was adoration!' I teased back. 'It's beautiful.' I kissed him on the cheek, cradling that book, now tattered and worn, as I do every night as I lie on my bed. I clasp it and close my eyes. I'm back in Burgundy Hall. Demontaigu is beside me, his face, his warmth. I vividly recall him as a comforting light in the murderous murk gathering around us. Embarrassed at the time, I went to return the book.

'My gift,' Demontaigu insisted. 'It is the last produced by the scriptorium of my order.'

I had planned to go down to tend my herbs, which I'd begun to cultivate in the palace gardens. I was about to ask Demontaigu to join me when a page boy came hurrying up to breathlessly inform me that the queen dowager wished to see me. Demontaigu raised his eyes heavenwards. I kissed him on the cheek and, hiding the psalter under my cloak, followed the page. The queen dowager was in her usual poise of a devout nun. She was sitting by Guido's bed feeding him watered wine. Nearby, Agnes, who looked drawn and tired, avoided my gaze and tended to the queen dowager's baby sons, Edmund of Woodstock and Thomas of Brotherton. The boys, apparently exhausted after their play, were lying on cushions half asleep. I greeted Guido, who looked stronger, a full colour returned to his face. He was apparently impatient to return to duties, though the queen dowager dismissed this, saying a few more days' rest would help. Queen Margaret patted her wimple and asked what all the excitement was about. Had any progress been made? I decided on the truth, or at least part of it. I told her how the king had decided to investigate certain rumours, that a great treasure lay hidden in New Temple Church, close to one of the Pembroke effigies. She and Guido expressed their joy, gabbling how such treasure would assist the king. Did I know, Guido asked, how the king had come by this information? I shrugged and said he was searching for many things, including an old clerk named John Highill. Did her grace recall that name? She pulled a face, and replied that she'd heard the name but couldn't recall the face or person.

'I suppose he was one of my husband's old servitors,' she murmured. 'But Mathilde,' she smiled; this time those cold, beautiful eyes crinkled in amusement, 'Guido, *Deo gratias*, is better. I thank you.' She sighed and gestured lovingly at her red-faced, heavy-eyed baby sons. 'I've little time for anything, going backwards and forward between the palace and here. Little time for politic, even less time for prayer, but,' she patted the coverlet, 'Guido, you must stay here until you are better. The countess will visit you and so will Agnes and, if she is not too busy, dear Mathilde.'

CHAPTER 12

Give peace in our days, Oh Lord, and let the king be in accord with his barons.

Vita Edwardi Secundi

I left the chamber bemused by the queen dowager and Guido, but I was too agitated to reflect. I had assured Demontaigu that La Maru's attack was simply a strand of the tapestry I wove. By the gospel, it was not! Now alone, I felt sick and tired. My belly bubbled. My mind flitted like some sparrow caught in a room. I needed to soothe my humours. I have confessed how I pick out events in the same way candlelight draws your eye to a certain scene, colour or thread in some tapestry or painting. Or better still, I felt like a watchman on the parapet walk of a castle. One minute follows another. Hours drift by. Days, weeks and months merge into one. A whole series of menial tasks is begun and finished, then abruptly the watchman sees the far beacon flare, signalling danger. The hurly-burly time has arrived. Armed men are ready, bowstrings tightened, quivers filled, daggers sharpened, war belts strapped on. Yes, that was me. Daily routine tasks until the perilous days gathered like an ice-cold mist seeping under doors, finding its way into my life through cracks and crevices. One comfort I treasured, which soothed the soul: my love of physic and knowledge of herbs.

I was still curious about the poison fed to Guido, so on my return to my warm, welcoming chamber, I opened my book coffer, that treasure chest of various treatments: Palladius' *De Agricultura*; the Monk of Cerne's *Nomina Herbarum*; that famous Latin poem by Macer, 'De Virtutibus Herbarum'; the Herbarium of Apuleius; Isidore of Seville's *Etymologiae*; and that erudite woman Hildegard of Bingen's *Liber Subtilitatum Diversarum*. My uncle had owned all of these and used them to educate me as keenly as my theologian would depend on the canon of scripture or the teachings of the fathers. When he had been arrested, these manuscripts had been seized, but Isabella had brought copies from the Louvre library, and when various monasteries and abbeys asked what present they could give her, she always asked for a certain book, manuscript or thesis, be it the legends of Arthur, a collection of Goliard songs or a medical treatise. She admired the latter, having a deep interest in herbs, particularly, as she ruefully remarked, those 'nine dark shades of night' that calmed all humours and healed all ailments, *per omnia saecula saeculorum* – for ever and ever; in other words, poisons!

I leafed through the manuscripts, taking careful note of certain entries. I then decided to go to my own small herbarium in one of the palace gardens. Now Burgundy Hall has gone, and Westminster has changed as if it is some living thing. However, in those spring days of 1308, the king's private palace, guarded by its own curtain wall, consisted of a long hall with buildings added on so small courtyards and gardens were formed. Edward had entertained ambitious plans for these, hoping to develop orchards, vineyards, lawns for peacocks and sprightly herons, and a rabbit park, build small watermills and dovecotes, as well as sink fish and stew ponds to house fine pike and whiting. All, of course, remained unfinished. Parts of the garden were fox-ridden, with weeds and gorse growing almost waist high. Now according to Albertus Magnus, a sophisticated herber should include a trellised loggia, a walled area of square herb beds, a flowery mead with arbours and a hedged garden containing a fountain. There were none of these. My physic garden did not have the required sixteen beds; it was makeshift and rough. I had dug the soil myself and planted what I could.

I left my chamber and went out through a small postern door into the garden. Ghostly smells of both summer and autumn greeted me, the sweet odour of rotting apples mingling with the fragrance of wild flowers thrusting up beneath the blackthorn hedges, which heralded the change in season with their own whitening flowers. I had brought a list of the herbs I needed: the rich, mildew-like blue gromwell, which flowered on limestone walls and was so useful in curing irritations of the skin; ground ivy, found winding its way about the orchard trees, so healing of congestion and the rheums; harebell, which flourished in the long wild grass, very valuable for staunching bleeding and compressing wounds. I stared round that wild overgrown place, the birds skimming over bush and grass, the flowers flashing in colour, the full richness of spring making itself felt. I walked over to my herber and stared down in desperation at the weeds clogging the soil, clawing around it like the fingers of a miser would precious stones. All about me the palace lay silent. The garden, however, was alive with the chirping of birds hunting among the fertile foliage. Small insects hovered noisily over a weed-encrusted carp pond. I glanced up abruptly and glimpsed a shadow at one of the arrow-slit windows. I smiled to myself, looked again, but there was nothing. The garden lay beneath the royal quarters. I wondered if the shadow had been that of Isabella, or even the king, but why the mystery?

I decided to calm my agitation by weeding the soil before I went searching for herbs. A derelict outhouse built against the palace wall was used to store picks, hoes and shovels. I went in and grasped a hoe that was standing in a cobweb-filled corner.

As I pulled it out, I glimpsed the leather sack pushed hard against it. I cut the cord around its neck and peered in. The sack contained three arbalests, heavy Brabantine crossbows. I pulled one out. The wood was thick and polished, its powerful twine cord supple, the lever oiled and easy to move, the groove smooth, ready for the barbed bolts, pouches of which lay at the bottom of the sack. Alarmed and curious, I hid the sack away and hurried back into the palace.

Ap Ythel had gone into the city, but I found his lieutenant, a sandy-headed Welshman named Ap Rhys, dicing with some of his comrades in the small guardroom near the gatehouse. I begged him to come with me. His companions whistled and joked in their lilting voices. Ap Rhys was about to refuse, but he caught my fearful expression so he shrugged, put his dice back into his wallet and followed me across the garden to that small outhouse. I pulled the sack out, Ap Rhys helping me. He emptied the contents on to the soil and crouched down.

'Arbalests,' he exclaimed, 'and pouches! Do you know how they got here, mistress?'

I shook my head. 'Do you?' I asked.

Ap Rhys made a face.

'Tell me.' I crouched down beside him. 'If I was to attack the king or this palace, how would I do it?'

He scratched his head. 'Mistress, I'm an archer, a bowman, not an assassin. You think these were left here for such mischief?'

'Perhaps.' I recalled Robert the groom's words and that sinister reference to the Tenebrae.

'Don't be alarmed.' Ap Rhys put the pouches back into the sack and tied the twine around the neck. 'I will take these.' He got to his feet. 'I'll not tell anybody.' He caught my curious look. 'Mistress,' he grinned, 'this may not be the work of some enemy hostile to our king; more likely a thief. We have stores here. It is not unknown for soldiers to try to make a quick profit. They steal bows, daggers, crossbows, hide them away, then take them into the city markets.' He kicked the sack, then picked it up. 'You'd get a pouch of silver for these.'

'Ap Rhys?'

'Yes, mistress?' He walked back.

'When Ap Ythel returns, tell him what we found and where.' I held my hand up. 'And ask him this. If the three of us were planning to attack his grace the King, or my lord Gaveston, or both, how would we do it? Please.' I grasped his hand. 'In this, favour me?' Ap Rhys nodded, adding that he'd do anything for a pretty face, then sauntered off.

I decided to leave the herbs. I was tired, still agitated. I returned to my own chamber, drank half a goblet of wine and tended to the braziers. I took off my shoes and upper gown and lay down on the bed, wrapping myself tightly in its coverlet. I only intended to sleep for a while but it was dark when Isabella shook me awake.

'Quick, quick, Mathilde,' she urged. 'His grace the king and my lord Gaveston need to see you.' She was garbed in a fur-lined cloak with a deep hood. She shook me roughly, the capped candle in her left hand dazzling my eyes. I climbed out of bed and made myself ready as swiftly as possible. Ap Ythel and some of the archers were waiting in the passageway outside. Ap Ythel's expression told me everything. They had found something in the church at New Temple. Isabella confirmed this in hushed, excited whispers as we went along the shadow-filled gallery.

The king and Gaveston were waiting, swatched in costly night robes. Both were rejoicing, sharing a two-handled loving cup between them. The chamber was bathed in candlelight and the cause of their joy was plain to see: coffers, caskets, chests, boxes and bags all open to reveal a king's ransom in gold and silver coin, jewels and an array of precious goblets, belts, necklaces, rings, pectoral crosses and costly gems, all sparkling in the bright light. Edward and Gaveston had drunk deeply. Once Ap Ythel had withdrawn, Edward roaring at him to keep close guard outside, both men embraced me, hugging me close and smothering me in their exquisite perfume. Edward scooped up a pile of gold and silver coins and pressed them into my hands.

'What else do you want?' he asked.

Still sleepy, I went down on my knees as I slipped the coins safely into a pouch on the inside of my robe.

'A title?' Gaveston teased.

'Pardons,' I answered quickly. 'Your grace,' I gestured round, 'what happened?'

'As you said.' The king dragged a chair across; he sat down and waved at Gaveston and Isabella to make themselves comfortable.

'My lord?'

Edward turned to Gaveston. The favourite took another deep drink and passed the cup to the king. I glanced quickly at Isabella. She sat there all docile, a fixed smile on her face, but I could see anger in those light-blue eyes as she played with the tendrils of her hair. Gaveston whispered to the king, and the loving cup was passed to her. Isabella drank quickly, not taking her eyes off me. Gaveston explained how he and Ap Ythel had arrived at the Templar church.

'The postern door was sealed and locked. We of course had the key. Strange,' Gaveston wagged a finger at me, 'I shall return to that. Inside, Mathilde, well it was the first time I'd ever been there. A solemn place, full of ghosts and ancient memories, beautiful paintings on the wall and nine stone effigies on the floor. At first I was reluctant. I felt as if I was committing blasphemy. Ap Ythel examined the paving stones just beneath each of those effigies which bore the title of Pembroke. We found nothing, and then I remembered what you had told us: *sub pede* – seven letters in all. I counted the paving stones from the feet of William Marshal, the premier Earl of Pembroke; the

291

seventh stone was loose. To the naked eye, nothing was amiss. We used bars and levers. The paving stone came up, and beneath was a wooden slat expertly placed there to keep it firm. The slat was wedged tightly in. We removed it, and underneath was a rope ladder, neatly coiled. We loosened and unrolled it. Ap Ythel, holding a torch, went down; I followed. The cavern beneath was square, formed on each side by rough ancient stone, airless and musty but definitely used as a treasure hold. We lit the cresset torches in the walls,' Gaveston gestured round, 'and found Langton's hoard. Drokensford and his exchequer clerks calculate a treasure of at least seventy thousand pounds sterling.'

I gasped in astonishment.

'There could have been more,' Edward intervened testily, 'but someone had been there before us.'

I glanced at Isabella. She had curbed her anger and smiled tenderly at me.

'Who, we don't know,' Gaveston retorted. 'We entered by the corpse door; it was locked and sealed. The other doors were barred and bolted.' He shook his head. 'To my memory, the seals were unbroken before we entered.'

'Was New Temple guarded?' Isabella asked.

'A few men-at-arms.' Edward shrugged. 'I and my council thought it held no treasure.'

'Your grace,' I bowed, 'how do you know the treasury had been entered?'

'One coffer had been forced,' Gaveston replied, 'two large sacks emptied. Drokensford believes five to six thousand pounds has been removed. But . . .' He handed the loving cup back to the king and rubbed his face.

'Langton will be beside himself with rage. He must be told.' Isabella's voice turned harsh. 'He may have removed some of that treasure himself after it was placed there.'

'Yet when he was arrested,' the king remarked, 'he proclaimed himself penniless. His chambers were searched, and nothing was found.'

'He may have given it to someone else. But in the mean time,' Isabella continued, 'my lords, I beg you. Be prudent, be cunning! Use this wealth to entice the likes of Pembroke and Lincoln into your camp. To quote the great Augustine: "*flectamur nec flectimur*" – "let us bend before the storm lest we break under it". We must concede more to the Great Lords, even if it is only for a time.' Her words sobered Edward and Gaveston, who glanced sheepishly at each other like boys being lectured by their mother.

'Lincoln and Pembroke,' Isabella continued, 'are the most susceptible, or at least so I understand.' She smiled thinly. 'They are certainly beginning to baulk at my father's envoys over their long stay and their meddling in what they call the affairs of the English crown.'

'I suspected that,' replied Edward, cradling the loving cup, 'but how do you know it?'

'My lord, they have spies in Burgundy Hall. I certainly have mine amongst them. My lord Mortimer has listened to the chatter; a few more days and the cracks will appear, but,' she clenched her hands in her lap, 'we must be cunning. We must plot, use this treasure to our advantage. However, rewards to those who have earned them. Mathilde has asked for pardons.'

'For whom?' Gaveston leaned forward.

I took a deep breath.

'The truth as always.' Isabella glanced warningly at me.

I confessed my help and assistance for Templars, the true identity of Demontaigu and others. Gaveston nodded in approval. Edward, in truth, didn't really care. My mistress confirmed Demontaigu's loyalty, his hostility to Philip and all the power of France. Edward, however, was bored, eager to return to his revelry. Since Demontaigu was loyal, the enemy of his enemy, and patronised by his queen, there was no need to discuss it. I stared at a glorious tapestry hanging on the wall behind the king. It showed scenes from the Romance of Alexander, the great conqueror on the battlefield or in his pavilion receiving the spoils of his enemy. The silence deepened until Edward softly clapped his hands, a common gesture to show he had reached a decision, and shrugged lazily.

'Demontaigu is no threat to me or mine. I cannot issue a pardon to him or others for being Templars;

that would go against the pope's instructions.' He bared his teeth like a dog. 'However, I will issue general pardons, letters of protection at the behest of the queen, so Demontaigu and two of his comrades can be brought into the king's peace.' He gestured at me. 'The clerks of the chancery will draw these up, to be issued under the Privy Seal.' He clapped his hands again and whispered to Gaveston. The favourite rose and crossed to the huge chancery table. He brought back a thin scroll, which he thrust into my hands, then stood over me and stroked my hair. I held his gaze; those lazy, good-humoured eyes were marble hard, as if he was assessing my loyalty. He stroked my hair once again, tipped me lightly under the chin and rejoined the king.

'John Highill,' Gaveston sighed, taking his seat, 'that scroll tells you all. Highill was a master from the schools of Cambridge, a principal clerk in the office of the secret seal in the old king's reign. He and Chapeleys were a pair, both apparently trained for the priesthood, knowledgeable in Latin, Greek and other tongues. Anyway, in 1299, after he had passed his sixtieth summer, Highill became witless. He was given a pension and dispatched to Bethlehem Hospital outside Bishopsgate.' Gaveston leaned forward. 'You know the place, Mathilde? Good.' He flicked his hands. 'Take your silver and gold. Collect your pardons and go. But first, tomorrow morning, discover what Highill knows, or might have known.'

Isabella, as if to emphasise her own authority, asked me to wait outside. The gallery, despite the late hour, was packed with Ap Ythel's men waiting for orders about the treasure. Its find had caused great excitement amongst them, as the archers realised they were not only to be rewarded but would also receive their long-awaited wages. Ap Ythel plucked me by the sleeve and took me away from the rest.

'Ap Rhys told me,' he whispered, 'what you found and what you asked. Mistress,' he looked over his shoulder, 'our discussion could be construed as treason. An attack upon the king and my lord Gaveston would be impossible during the day. They are closely guarded, even if they go into the gardens or baileys.' Ap Ythel pointed to a window. 'They are protected. If they hunt, a *comitatus* of royal knights, mounted men-at-arms and archers accompanies them.'

'And at night?'

'Mistress, you have seen the gatehouse to Burgundy Hall? The curtain walls are patrolled, windows are bolted and barred. The only weaknesses are three postern doors: you use one for the garden; the other two are further along, both leading on to galleries that run beneath the royal quarters, but again, those doors are bolted, barred and regularly checked.' Ap Ythel patted me on the shoulder. 'Ap Rhys is probably correct. The arbalests were stolen from the armoury to be sold in some city market. *S'avisera*, be advised.' He grinned. 'The demons that stalk by midnight and the terror that lurks by noonday will not strike you.'

I watched him go. Ap Ythel might have been a skilled archer, a loyal retainer, an excellent singer, but he was certainly no prophet!

A short while later Isabella and I were escorted back to her quarters, down the long galleries, torches and lanternlight sending the darkness dancing. Once inside her private chamber, Isabella dropped her cloak and immediately knelt on the cushioned prie-dieu before a triptych of the Virgin Mary and Child.

'You'd best leave, Mathilde, I will call the maids.' Isabella spoke without moving. 'Send a message to Demontaigu. He must accompany you tomorrow morning. Oh, Mathilde! Outside, the season changes. The blackthorn flowers and the seeds burst into life; so it is here, Mathilde, the season of change is thrust upon us.' Her voice rose. 'I am queen, the descendant of kings and saints. My son will carry the sacred blood of both Plantagenet and Capet.' The rest came as a hiss. 'Soon there will be no room for Gascon upstarts, remember that!'

I did so, as Demontaigu and I shivered on our journey to Bethlehem Hospital the following morning. We left the palace while the stars hung heavy in the rain-washed skies. Demontaigu advised we take horses and journey round the old city wall rather than risk a river passage through the darkness. He had not celebrated his dawn mass but murmured how the Matins we were about to attend were, for the moment, more important. A cold, hard ride. During it I told him all that had happened. When I'd finished he pulled down the muffler protecting his face.

'As regards to Langton's treasure, our master might have well agreed to that. New Temple and its halls have many secret places. I am sure,' he sighed, 'Edward will send Drokensford and his exchequer clerks to ransack every nook and cranny of the grounds. As to that theft . . .' He blew out his breath and stroked his horse's neck. 'Langton may have been given a key or even taken the treasure himself. And the arbalests?' Demontaigu reined in, turning his horse slightly to face me. He leaned forward and grasped the reins of my palfrey. 'What you discovered, Mathilde, is very serious. I don't think those arbalests were stolen from the armoury. The garden is ringed on all four sides by walls?'

'Yes, but there is a gate connecting two wings of the palace.'

'Someone could climb over it?'

'Oh yes,' I replied. 'The garden is overgrown, a desolate, tangled place.'

Demontaigu cleared his throat. Pushing back his hood, he stared up at the sky. On the cold breeze floated the sound of barking dogs and the cock-crow from some nearby farm. The first light of dawn was beginning to dim the stars. He let go of my reins and turned his horse's head, and we rode on in silence. To our right was the old city wall, to our left the open heathland stretching up to the dark mass of St Bartholomew's hospital. We passed St Botolph's Church in Aldersgate and turned north towards Cripplegate. An eerie grey morning now coming to life as farmers, their carts piled high with produce, cracked whips, urging their horses along the rutted tracks towards the city markets. On the open moor, a swirling mist made our journey more difficult, shrouding trees and hiding the path in front of us. Demontaigu hung his sword and dagger belt from his saddle horn; his gauntleted fingers kept moving to this as dark shapes emerged abruptly from the murk: wandering tinkers, a Dominican friar holding a cross before him, city bailiffs with an escaped prisoner shackled between them. Outside Cripplegate, the huge stocks were full of drunken miscreants and whores caught soliciting in forbidden areas. They screamed and yelled a torrent of abuse at their tormentors; the city beadles stood around grinning as clasps were fastened imprisoning heads, legs, wrists and ankles. The six-branched scaffolds close by had apparently been used the day before, the corpses now ripening to full-blown. The stinking carts of scavengers clustered by the city ditch emptying their filthy mixture of rubbish, offal and human waste, all coated in a foulsome slime, along with the bloated corpses of dead animals: dogs, cats and farmyard birds. A funeral procession, ghostly in all its aspects, capped candles glowing and bells ringing, emerged out of the murk; the sombre voice of the priest chanted the 'Dirige' whilst the mourners, cloaked and cowled, seemed like lost souls crossing the bleak landscape of hell.

I thought Demontaigu's silence was due to all these distractions, but eventually he grasped my horse's reins and led me into the courtyard of one of those taverns that serve the roads leading into London. We stabled our horses. Inside the spacious taproom, Demontaigu secured a table close to the roaring fire and ordered bowls of oatmeal, steaming hot and mingled with milk and honey. Such occasions I recall: the fire, the warmth, the hot food, the savoury ale in leather tankards. Demontaigu put his spoon down, blowing on the oatmeal, and grinned quickly at me.

'I've been thinking about what you said about Ap Ythel. When I served in Outremer, one of the great dangers was the Old Man of the Mountain; you must have heard of him. He and his followers lived in a secluded castle deep in some valley in the desert. He would choose his victim, then send them a warning: a sesame cake, usually placed in their private chamber to show that they could never be safe. Now and again this assassin turned his attention to us Templars, particularly before the fall of Acre.' Demontaigu picked up his horn spoon. 'One thing we learnt: never flee, but wait. The Old Man's murderous emissaries, drugged and armed, would come stealthily enough. Our

300

task was to trap them. Perhaps the same must be done at Westminster yet.' He sighed. 'Leaving the arbalests in such an open way was very clumsy. I shall certainly have words with Ap Ythel. However,' Demontaigu leaned across the table and grasped both my hands, 'for the matter of the pardon, I deeply thank you. You are right, Mathilde, sooner or later, today or tomorrow, I will have to confess my true identity. Pardons or letters of protection will afford some defence to myself and Ausel.'

'And if the king moves against the Templars?'

'I suspect he would give us clear warning, perhaps ten days to leave the kingdom.'

I caught my breath.

'Don't worry.' Demontaigu picked up his horn spoon. 'For the time being,' he winked at me, 'I'll stay close to your apron strings.'

We continued our journey around the city. Church bells were summoning the faithful to the Jesus mass. Beacons flared in steeples. The mist began to thin. It was still freezing cold, so we were pleased to reach the high curtain wall of Bethlehem Hospital. A lay brother admitted us; others took our horses, and we were ushered into the waiting chamber. For a while I sat half asleep. Demontaigu remained lost in his own thoughts. Now and again he would get up and walk around the room as if inspecting the limewashed walls, or stand tapping his boot against the polished red tiles on the floor. A bleak chamber, stripped of all ornament except for the roughly carved cross and the sturdy makeshift furniture; clean and sweet-smelling, warmed by braziers. I had explained to the lay brother who greeted us that we wished to see the master about John Highill. The lay brother looked at us perplexed, but nodded and, fingers to his lips, hurried away. Now there was a knock on the door. The lay brother re-entered, apologising for the delay but saying that the master would be with us shortly. However, he had a visitor for Master Demontaigu; did he wish to see him? Demontaigu looked at me in surprise and nodded. The lay brother disappeared and returned escorting an old man slightly stooped, skin burnt almost black by the sun, head almost bald except for a few tufts of hair above the ears and at the back. He rested on a stick, tapping it on the tiles as he made his way over, scuttling like a beetle towards Demontaigu. He stopped and stared up.

'Master Bertrand Demontaigu, you do not remember me?'

Demontaigu stepped back, staring in disbelief. 'Joachim Hermeri!' he whispered. 'Joachim Hermeri, by all the saints.' He went forward, clasped the old man and brought him to the stool next to mine so he could enjoy the warmth of the brazier. Joachim stared shrewdly at me with watery eyes. He waited until Demontaigu took his seat, then cackled with laughter, shoulders shaking.

'I heard the lay brother, he came into the refectory. He said there was a visitor from the court, a young mistress escorted by a military clerk called Demontaigu.' He rubbed bony knuckles on Demontaigu's knee. 'Oh, I've heard how our order is finished, but I remember you, Demontaigu.'

'And I thought I was safe.' Demontaigu smiled.

'Oh, I know all the news,' Joachim whispered, 'all the names, but I'm safe here. Who'd think of coming to Bethlehem Hospital, a house for the witless and the moonstruck? Who would believe my ranting and ravings? You see, mistress, once I was a Templar, wasn't I, Demontaigu?' He didn't wait for a reply, but hurried on. 'I was at the fall of Acre. I was a serjeant, a standard-bearer. When Acre fell, I and others escaped across the desert. I tell you this, mistress, I saw things that brought me here. The good monks at Charterhouse who first cared for me thought it best. They didn't believe me. I told them about young Fulk; he came from Poitou, also a standard-bearer. He was bitten by a basilisk. He hardly felt any pain from the bite, and his outward appearance was normal, but the poison stole through his blood secretly! A creeping fire invaded his marrow and kindled flame in his innermost parts. The poison sucked up the moisture next to his vital organs and dried his mouth of saliva. No sweat flowed to relieve his body. He couldn't even cry. He burnt all over and searched desperately for water.' Hermeri leaned on his stick. I glanced across at Demontaigu, who just shook his head. 'Then there was Beltran, bitten by a basilisk in the leg, he was. The basilisk left a fang there. Beltran had to tear it away but the flesh near the bite broke up and shrivelled until it laid the whole bone bare. The gash grew wider and wider, and before long Beltran's calves dissolved and his knees were stripped of skin. Neck, thighs and groin dripped with corruptive matter, trickling down into a puddle of filth. That is all I can remember.' He peered up the ceiling, lower lip jittering. 'Those basilisks lord it over the desert, their wings carry them high. No creature is safe from them, mistress, not even elephants; I understand the king has one of those at the Tower. Ah well, such is my story.' And without further ado he got up, bowed at both of us and shuffled out.

Demontaigu rose and followed. He opened the door, looked swiftly outside and closed it again.

'Is that true?'

'He was lucid enough to remember I was a Templar.' Demontaigu sat down. 'I recall Hermeri; his eyes, lips and gestures. When Acre fell, many Templars died. Others were taken prisoner by the infidels; a few did escape across the desert. Perhaps Joachim was telling the truth. He must have seen things, experienced fears we don't know of, but who believes him? I have met Templars found lost, wandering in the desert. They are never the same again; they have bouts of lunacy as if struck by the moon. They jibber and jabber, then become as rational and clear-thinking as the next man. What I suspect is that Joachim has been visited by some of our brethren. They would come to a place like this for shelter and protection. They may have talked to him about me and others and so freshened his memories of his Templar days. Ah well, he is harmless enough.'

I gazed at the crucifix. Joachim's story about the basilisk reminded me sharply of the word Chapeleys had written. Had he been referring to a basilisk, or something else? A tap on the door and the grey-faced master of the hospital entered. He was garbed in the dark robes of an Augustinian friar. He sketched a blessing, studied me carefully, then turned to Demontaigu.

'I understand you have come to see Master Highill?'

'He is here?' I asked, forcing the master to address me.

'He was,' he replied, 'at least until yesterday.'

I rose to my feet. 'Brother, we are here on king's business. We carry warrants and letters if you wish to see them. Master Highill, where is he?'

'He is in his chamber.' The master looked me up and down. I curbed my temper.

Demontaigu half drew his sword and let it fall back. The slither of steel startled the friar. He closed his eyes and took a deep breath.

'I apologise. I have been up most of the night.' He opened his eyes, turned to the crucifix and blessed himself. 'Yester evening, Master Highill was visited by a Franciscan nun, or so she claimed to be, from the House of Minories. He had been ill and was in his bedchamber. The Franciscan was closeted with him, then left. Later, when one

305

of the brothers was doing his rounds before the candles were doused, he knocked at Master Highill's door, and receiving no answer he went in. At first he thought Master Highill was fast asleep, but feeling for the blood beat in his neck, realised he had died.'

'At what hour did this nun come?'

'Oh . . . just before Compline. She said she wished to see Master Highill. She claimed to be his distant relative and had heard he was ailing, which was true. We took her down to his chamber and left her there. I mean . . .' the master spread his hands, 'what harm could a nun do?'

'Do you think Master Highill was murdered?' Demontaigu asked.

'I don't know,' the Master replied. 'There was no mark of violence. The cup he kept on the table beside the bed was dried and cleaned. Master Highill liked his wine. You'd best see yourself. Oh,' he turned at the door, 'there is something else. Master Highill was old and frail, so when he died, little suspicion was provoked. However, when we began to list his possessions, we found virtually everything gone. We know he had a psalter, some ledgers, the bits and pieces an old man collects over the years, all missing . . .'

He led us out of the small chamber and down clean, lime-washed passages. The master was an excellent physician. No rushes cluttered the polished floorboards; everything was clean; herb pots and sweet-smelling pomander hung against the walls or from rafters. We turned a corner, and I paused. I caught the same smell as I had from Guido's breath, that flowery, sweet odour.

'Master, what is that smell?'

He came back. 'Lavender . . .'

'Yes, yes, I recognise that, but beneath it, another?'

'Crushed violet,' the master replied. 'We had some left from last summer. We find it very powerful against malignant odours and foul stenches.'

'Of course!' I smiled at him. 'Violet!' I thanked him and we walked on.

The hospital was built round a cloister garden. Highill's chamber was just off this, really nothing more than a narrow closet. Like the rest of the place, the floorboards were clean and polished, the walls whitewashed and hung with dried herbs. A narrow cot-bed stood in the corner. There was some paltry furniture and a coffer, its lid back, the clasp broken. On the bed, covered by a sheet, lay Highill's corpse: an old man, obviously frail, his cheeks sunken, white hair brushed back, the lower part of his face covered in untidy stubble. He wore the dark-green gown of all inmates; his head rested slightly back, his nose sharp and pointed, lips half open. To all intents and purposes an old man who had died in his sleep. However, when the master showed us more coffers, small caskets and chests piled in a corner, he explained how various items that he knew had been there were now missing. He suspected that the previous night's mysterious visitor had taken them.

'Why was Master Highill placed in Bethlehem?'

The master pulled the sheet back over the dead man's face.

'He was a senior clerk in the secret chancery,' he remarked, 'or so he told us. We know he had been in royal service, but his wits had wandered. Sometimes he talked about his days with the old king as if he was very close to him, though few believed him. Mistress, many men and women are brought here because of their delusions. Master Highill could be quiet, but sometimes he'd burst into song, something that always frightened me a little. You know the "Salve Regina" sung at the end of Compline? Well, Master Highill would sing that, but a blasphemous version. I cannot remember the exact words: instead of "Mother of Mercy" it was "Mother of Discord". I ordered him to stop this. He did, but on occasion I found him writing the same words.' The master pointed to a painting, a piece of vellum in a wooden frame, which hung on a hook from the wall. 'Ah yes, that's it.' He took down the painting, an Agnus Dei surrounded by the Five Wounds of Christ, and showed me the marks beneath.

At first I couldn't make them out. I took a candle and, holding it against them, studied the scrawl. I stared in disbelief: they struck a chord, a memory. I asked Demontaigu to copy down what was written there: *Salv. Reg. Sin. Cor. Ma. Disc.*

Once he had finished, I asked the master for a description of the nun who had visited the night before, but he shrugged and shook his head.

'She was wimpled with a deep hood. No one took much notice. She came in the dark, asked to see Master Highill, then left.' He pulled a face. 'Who cares about an old man, or a nun visiting him to give him solace?'

Distracted, I thanked him and left. We collected our horses from the stables and made our way back to Westminster, riding along the busy tracks following the city wall down towards the Thames. My mind was a blizzard of thoughts and memories. Even as I read those scratch marks out to Demontaigu, I realised I had discovered something important, though I couldn't fully comprehend it. Demontaigu tried to draw me into conversation, but I shook my head. I gathered my cloak about me, grasped the reins and let my horse plod on. I was totally unaware of the day or the people around me. At last Demontaigu, exasperated, reined in outside the entrance to the Gate of Antioch, a prosperous-looking tavern just past Bishopsgate.

'Mathilde, for the love of God at least talk to me.'

We stabled our horses and took some food and jugs of cantle in the warm taproom. Although absorbed, I was also excited, on the verge of resolving sinister mysteries. Those arbalests still bothered me, as well as Demontaigu's words about a trap. Over bowls of hot potage I questioned him further. At last he put his horn spoon down, tapping the table with it.

'Mathilde, why are you questioning me about this?'

'I'm stating the obvious.' I replied. 'If you were to plot a secret attack on the king and Gaveston in Burgundy Hall, would you use such heavy arbalests?'

'No,' he replied quickly, 'they are ponderous, heavy to carry, slow to load. What are you saying, Mathilde?'

'I was meant to find them.' I told him about the shadow I'd glimpsed at the window. 'The king shelters behind the walls of Burgundy Hall. He believes he is safe. We know there are those who wish to do great hurt to either him or Lord Gaveston. So what do we do? We look beyond Burgundy Hall for the attack. We expect weapons to be hidden away so secret assassins can come crawling over the walls, seize them and carry out their assault. But that's not going to happen. We are looking for the enemy beyond the walls when the enemy—'

'Is already within?' he asked.

'Precisely!' I replied. 'The enemy is already inside, but who are they and where are they hiding? I don't know. It is time we returned to Westminster.'

CHAPTER 13

So the Lords, exhausted by the trouble and expense they'd sustained, went home.

Vita Edwardi Secundi

I remember that ride back. The sky had clouded. Peals of bells rang out as protection against the impending thunder and lightning. The day's business was well underway, shops open, stalls laid out, water-bearers, ale-sellers, butter wives and herb wives all selling their wares. Tinkers and pedlars accosted us, eager to do business. A red-faced market bailiff strode about proclaiming the recent injunction against the use of stubble, straw or reeds in any house or tavern, as they were inclined to flare and burn easily. We continued our journey back to Westminster, taking the road that wound down to the royal mews, past the exquisitely carved cross to Queen Eleanor, along King's Street and on to the Royal Way. The crowds were busy, people moving up and down to the palace and abbey, and the sheer throng, clamour and chaos forced us to pause now and again. A line of lay brothers from the abbey were bringing in the corpses of three beggars found frozen to death in the nearby meadows. The hue and cry had also been raised. People shouting, 'Harrow, harrow!' and armed with any weapon they could lay their hands on, were chasing two fugitives who'd robbed a shop near Clowson Stream. As we turned into Seething Lane, a group of bailiffs from Newgate had cornered an escaped felon hiding in some ruins; he was being dragged out to suffer the immediate sentence of death, forced to kneel, his head pressed against a log whilst a bailiff armed with a two-edged axe hacked at his neck. I turned away. Demontaigu whispered the 'Miserere'. Such a scene agitated my mind, teeming as it was with images, pictures and memories. I had concentrated on one path, totally ignoring other evidence until I had read those etchings on the wall of John Highill's chamber.

Once back at Westminster, I asked Demontaigu to accompany me to Burgundy Hall and immediately asked to see Isabella. She was entertaining leading aldermen of the city, resplendent in their scarlet robes. Only when they left could I see her alone. Demontaigu waited outside. Isabella looked magnificent in cloth of gold, her beautiful hair hidden under a white veil held in place by a green chaplet. She looked strangely at me as I knelt before her like a penitent waiting to be shriven. I clasped my hands, placed them in her lap and stared up at her. At first my words came haltingly, but I soon gained confidence. I told her everything I suspected, and what must be done. Now and again she would hold up her bejewelled fingers, ask me a question, then tell me to continue. When I had finished, she sat staring down at me and shaking her head in disbelief. 'Impossible, yet probable,' she whispered, then leaned forward and kissed me full on the lips. She took my face between her hands, pressing gently, staring into my eyes.

'Mathilde, I have always seen you as my alter ego, my soul, my confidante. Do you remember the teachings of the school? If a hypothesis is true in part, then it is possible that it is true in all aspects. Well, let us test it.' She asked me to summon Demontaigu and Ap Ythel to her chamber. When they arrived, she swore them to secrecy. Ap Ythel objected to this, saying his first duty was to the king. Isabella countered this. 'No, sir, your first duty is to the Crown, and I am part of that. If what I say is the truth, then the king will be pleased. You are to search Burgundy Hall from its rafters to the cellars, every nook, every corner, every cranny. You must look for anything out of place, not just a weapon hidden away or a damaged bolt on a door, but anything where it should not be. Then come back and report to me.'

Once she had dismissed them, she sent a page boy for the supervisor of the king's works, the clerk responsible for the cleaning of the latrines and cesspits. The man came all nervous and fell immediately to his knees. Isabella assured him all was well.

'I have one question, sir. You must keep that and your answer confidential until I speak to my husband.'

The man swallowed hard, nodding vigorously.

'What was the cause of the blockage to the latrines and sewers?'

The clerk shrugged and spread his hands. 'Mistress, you know how narrow the runnels are; they become easily clogged. What is lying down there is rotting but bulky enough to create a blockage.'

'And?' Isabella asked imperiously. 'What did you find? Sir, I do not wish a full description of what you dragged from the sewers and cesspits; just what caused the blockage, the foul smells in this palace.'

'Simple enough, your grace,' he replied quickly. 'Cloth, coarse wool, some wire, hardened parchment—'

'Except,' I intervened, 'surely it is rare for so many sewers and latrines to become blocked at the same time, unless they feed into the one pit?'

'Yes, I did wonder about that,' the clerk mumbled, 'how different latrines became blocked at the same time, but there again, it can happen. Page boys, squires, maids,' he smiled nervously at me, 'they could do it deliberately. Now they are cleared and run clean, flushed with water.'

My mistress thanked and dismissed him. After

he'd gone, she asked me to help her undress. Once finished, she stood on a turkey carpet in the centre of her chamber dressed only in a bed-robe, her long hair falling down almost to her shoulder blades. She looked older, her face drawn; the way her eyes kept moving from left to right to left betrayed her agitation, her nervousness at what she had to do.

'Mathilde, it is best if you retire to your chamber. I wish to be alone.'

I bowed and left. Of course, I visited Guido, but he was now out of bed, dressed and shaved, his hair oiled and crimped. He explained how the queen dowager and her children had returned to their own quarters in the Old Palace. I asked him about Agnes. Guido raised his eyes heavenward.

'My mistress sent her to Marigny on some errand; that was yesterday evening, and she has not returned. Why do you ask, Mathilde?'

I replied that I wished to speak to her, thanked him and left. He called after me how he hoped to visit me, as he would soon be joining the queen dowager. I returned to my own chamber, locked and bolted the door, prepared my chancery desk and started to write down my thoughts, this time more coherently, in a logical form, like a *peritus* in the chancery drawing up a bill of indictment.

Demontaigu and I had returned to Westminster as the bells rang the Angelus, so it was late afternoon before a page boy asked me to join my mistress in her chambers. She seemed more calm and poised.

'Mathilde, we must wait upon Ap Ythel and Demontaigu. If they discover what we suspect, then I must approach the king, not you. It is my hour, my day. So tell me again.'

I did so, sitting opposite her as if telling a story, my words no longer stumbling. I had hardly finished when Ap Ythel and Demontaigu, dirt-marked, their clothing all stained, asked for an audience. Once the door was closed and both were seated on stools before the queen, Demontaigu glanced at Ap Ythel, who nodded.

'Your grace, Mathilde, I must apologise. We found other weapons in the gardens, daggers and swords, but nothing else until we came to the cellars. In Burgundy Hall,' Ap Ythel used his hands to demonstrate, 'the cellars are dug deep and stretch virtually from one end of the building to the other. They are small rooms, each cut off by a jutting wall; they not only serve as storerooms, but also support the building above. Wine casks and other provisions are kept there. We found something else: bulging skins, sacks full of oil tied tightly at the neck, pushed behind barrels or wedged tightly into corners.'

I closed my eyes and murmured a prayer.

'There was more,' Ap Ythel continued. 'Small casks of saltpetre, fire powder, your grace. I served with the late king four years ago when he besieged Stirling. I saw him use such oil and powder to crack the hardest stone.'

'And these lie throughout the cellar?' Isabella asked.

'Yes, your grace. Once sworn to secrecy, the master of the stores, the cellarer, and the master of the pantry and the kitchen were questioned, but no one knew anything about these things. In fact, as we interrogated them, I could tell they were concerned. One candle, one torch . . .'

'And what would have happened?' Isabella asked.

'Burgundy Hall would have been turned into a roaring inferno,' Demontaigu replied. 'The oil and powder together with the dry wood, wine and other stores in the cellar would create a fire hotter than a furnace. Some of the hall is built of wood. The flames would simply roar up, bursting through one floor after another whilst draughts would sweep the fire the length of the building. Within a few heartbeats, your grace, and I do not exaggerate, Burgundy Hall would become hell on earth. I have seen such fires spread; it doesn't wait, it actually leaps, the smoke itself can choke you.'

I stared at the tapestry on the wall: a gift to the queen from the scholars of St Paul's. It described the legend of Medusa, who lived in the furthest extremes of Africa where the hot earth is burnt by fire at sunset. Medusa cradled her own severed head whilst from her neck swarmed hissing serpents, their flickering tongues spitting blood. Vipers hung loose around her body as those awful eyes in that severed head glared out. The picture caught my mood of horror.

'They meant to kill us all,' I whispered. 'If that

cellar was lighted at the dead of night, the fire would spread, and the king, my lord Gaveston . . .' I stared at Isabella. She sat, face hard, eyes bright with anger. 'No one would have survived, or very few.'

'I thought of that,' Demontaigu murmured. 'Your grace, every man and woman would have had to look after themselves. Can you imagine his grace the king, Lord Gaveston, yourself, Mathilde? Even if you did escape, stumbling out, shocked, burnt, coughing and spitting, any assassin lurking in the dark would find it easy to strike.'

'And these hellish cellars?' Isabella asked sharply.

'They are now being secretly cleared,' Ap Ythel declared, 'the oil and powder loaded into carts. Tonight these will be taken into the meadows south of the abbey where they will be closely guarded. My men are under oath, no one is to know!'

'Good.' Isabella rose to her feet; immediately we all did the same. 'I have learnt enough.' She turned to me. 'If a hypothesis be true in one part, then it is probably true in all its aspects. Mathilde, gentlemen, I shall return.' She swept out, shouting for pages and squires to escort her to the king.

Demontaigu and Ap Ythel went out into the gallery. I followed, closing the door behind me and summoning a page to stand on guard. Ap Ythel shook his head.

'The enemy within,' he murmured, 'that's how my people were conquered by the great Edward, the enemy within!' He and Demontaigu left, determined to conduct one more final search and ensure that what Isabella had called those 'hellish cellars' were clear of all danger. I returned to my own chamber, locked the door and crouched over a small brazier, gathering warmth from the glowing coals. I picked up a coverlet and wrapped it around my shoulders. I found myself cold, shivering as the horror of what could have happened dawned. My uncle had told me about fire powder. Even a farmer's lad would know the danger of blending oil, wine, dry wood and saltpetre; the flames would have raced through those cellars and up, turning Burgundy Hall and all within it into a living torch. Eventually I calmed my soul. I heated some wine, drank the hot posset and returned to my own studies. There was a gap, one piece of evidence I needed, but for that, I would have to wait. I dozed for a while; the abbey bells tolling for Vespers woke me. Shortly afterwards Ap Ythel, now dressed smartly in the royal livery, knocked on my door. The king had summoned me to his own chambers, where the queen was waiting.

As I walked along the galleries, I could sense the change. Virtually every man in Ap Ythel's *comitatus*, together with the Kernia, stood on guard. Ap Ythel whispered how all the gates and postern doors to the hall had been locked and secured. No one was allowed in or out without the king's express approval. Inside the royal chamber,

Edward was pacing up and down like the leopard I'd seen in its cage at the Tower. He was full of rage. Dressed only in a cambric shirt, hose pushed into a pair of black boots with the spurs still clinking, a jacket of tawny fustian around his shoulders, he kept pacing up and down. Gaveston, dressed more elegantly, lounged in a window seat, left hand covering the bottom half of his face. Isabella sat in the king's great chair, like some effigy or statue of the Virgin. She never moved, not even when I entered. The king snapped his fingers and ordered me to kneel on a cushion beside her. For a while he just raged, a torrent of filthy abuse. At last he calmed himself, came over, stroked my hair, patted me carefully under the chin then strangely enough – but that was Edward – knelt down before his queen, leaning back to sit on his heels.

'ApYthel will search this palace,' he commented. 'I've had the treasure taken to the Tower. Cromwell can look after it. Mathilde, you have given my lady good advice and counselling; your reward will come.' He held up a hand, fingers splayed. 'The prisoner will be brought here in the early hours, confined, chained and securely guarded. You will question him, but first, my lady,' he turned to the queen, 'you will issue a summons to Marigny and the others for an audience with you shortly after the Jesus mass tomorrow morning. You know what to say?'

'And afterwards?'

Edward shrugged. 'Do what you have to, but do it swiftly. We can only risk one more night. The decision is yours. As I have said, no blood. Let time be the executioner.'

Afterwards Isabella, still hard of face and sharp of voice, came to my chamber. She described Edward's rage at what she had told him, particularly about the plot to fire Burgundy Hall. She also reported, with some satisfaction, Gaveston's fear.

'Our noble lord is wary, much more so than I thought. You know his friendship with Agnes is because he uses her as a spy on his wife, the Countess Margaret, though,' Isabella sighed, 'she is so benighted, she'd scarce notice anything untoward. My lord will leave Burgundy Hall soon,' she continued, 'move well away from London. He and Gaveston will probably take shelter behind the walls of Windsor Castle, where Edward will find it easier to summon the shire levies. He is still determined on war. Gaveston has already sent secret messages and bribes to Lincoln and Pembroke. Langton's wealth is being well used. Both earls are to be admitted to Burgundy Hall tonight for secret talks with the favourite.' Isabella chewed on her lower lip. 'I shall take advantage of that to return to my lord. I need to lecture him about his duties to me and the governance of this kingdom. Mathilde,' she leaned forward and stroked my face, 'you have done well, but as in any hunt, I must be in at the kill. Remember that!

Pray and prepare that tomorrow our forced guest confesses the truth. Any further delay will only alert the enemy. The hours pass; soon the gossip will begin.'

I slept little that night, Burgundy Hall lay wrapped in silent darkness, broken occasionally by faint chanting from the abbey, the tolling of bells or the calls from the guardsmen and watchmen. I wondered if the king's vigilance and the deployment of troops would warn our enemy, but there again, such alarums were common. Nevertheless, time was of the essence. We had to strike hard, and as swiftly as possible. I returned to my writing until I grew restless and wandered the galleries and passageways like some ghost. The threatened thunderstorm swept up the Thames, blocking out the moon and stars. Stark flashes of lightning illuminated the shadow-filled galleries, bringing to life the grotesque faces of the babewyns and gargoyles carved on corbels and lintels. I stopped and closed my eyes, suppressing a shiver. On a night like this, in those hellish cellars, torches would have been thrown; a conflagration caused which could have ended it all. I walked quickly back to my chamber, closing the door, pulling across the bolts. I continued my reflections, fell asleep and was roused by a pounding on the door. Demontaigu and Ap Ythel had returned. They were both dressed in half-armour, war belts strapped around their waists, hoods and cloaks saturated with rain. Demontaigu made a mock bow.

'Mathilde, my lady, your guest has arrived.'

They took me along the galleries. I peered through a window. The grey light of dawn revealed that the thunderstorm had swept on, the clouds were breaking. They took me down to the cellars, and a small adjoining room used by the clerks of the stores; it was secured by a heavy oaken door with bolts and lock. Inside was a red-brick wall with a grille high up to allow in light and air. On a ledge beneath this sat Langton, seething with rage. He was swathed in a heavy cloak, hands and feet manacled. He was about to curse at Ap Ythel, but as the Welshman placed down the lantern horn, Langton saw me and smiled, drawing in his breath so his nostrils flared. He slouched back against the wall.

'The cause of my destruction,' he murmured as Ap Ythel and Demontaigu slammed the door shut behind them. He lifted his manacled hands and shook a finger at me. 'You, Mathilde, represent my great weakness. I have little regard for women, and it has been my undoing. I realised that as soon as you left. I understood why you wanted to examine my leg, and those references about New Temple and Master Highill. Very clever! And I was warned about you, Mathilde! They did warn me. Ah well, pride has its own fall. Arrogance is a sin.' He beat his breast mockingly. 'I confess, I confess, *peccavi, peccavi* – I have sinned, I have sinned.'

'My lord,' I stood over him to show I was not frightened, 'my lord, I wish to make you an offer.'

Langton's shrewd eyes crinkled up. 'An offer? I never thought I'd sit in a cellar and be questioned by a maid, a scullion wench.'

'My lord, insults are like the patter of the rain: they fall but don't remain. Do you wish to go back to the Tower, spend your time in confinement? The king has your treasure and a full understanding of your secret doings. If you confess—'

'If I confess!' Langton mocked.

'If you confess . . .' I continued remorselessly, 'freedom, the return of your temporalities, restoration to your see, no fine, no disgrace. Re-admittance into your king's love. What can you lose, my lord? The friendship of the Lords and other bishops? They will see your release as just vindication for their pleas. Who else?' I cocked my head, staring at him; his glance told me he knew exactly who I was talking about. He stared down at the floor, then back up, his face drained of all arrogance, eyes watchful, lips slightly pursed.

'Mathilde, I apologise for my mockery, for my bullying of you. I am supposed to be a man of God, though I often fail. God gave me sharp wits.' He held both hands up as if in prayer. 'I will hear your confession, and if you tell the truth, you have my word, as sacred as if sworn on the Gospels, you shall hear mine.'

In the end, I heard Langton's confession as he first heard mine. He sat throughout, a half-smile on that podgy face, those cunning eyes shifting from anger to admiration then to self-mockery.

A tortured soul, Langton! Once I'd finished, he beat his breast again.

'I have sinned, I have sinned,' he mocked. 'Pilate asked what was truth and didn't wait for an answer, but you will, won't you, Mathilde?'

An hour must have passed before I hammered on that heavy door for it to be opened. I nodded at Demontaigu, put a finger to my lips and returned to my own quarters. I stripped, washed, dressed and prepared myself. A page came whispering that her grace was now ready, whilst the Lord Marigny and other French envoys were also assembled. When I reached my mistress' private chamber, she had prepared it well. All was cleared; a chair for herself, a stool beside it for me. Four other chairs, taken from the chancery room in the palace, high-backed with soft quilted seats, were placed before us. Isabella had dressed most demurely in a dark-green gown, her hair piled up beneath a wimple, almost in mockery of a certain fashion. She was nun-like in manner, her face all coy and simpering. She rose, nodded at me and gestured at the page to bring in Marigny and the others.

Isabella acted the part beautifully. She greeted her father's emissaries, waving them to the seats, asking if they wished anything to eat or drink. Of course Marigny, full of curiosity, refused, eager for the business in hand. Isabella sat down, gesturing that they do likewise. Four demons in all: Marigny, Nogaret, Plaisans and Alexander of

Lisbon. He sat slightly to one side, the other two fiends either side of Marigny, all dressed in the official livery of the French king, elegant blue and silver robes, rings of office glittering on their fingers.

'Madam?' Marigny, one hand on his chest, bowed and smiled. 'We received your invitation yesterday evening. I understand the queen dowager is also here. Your grace wishes to see her?'

'My good aunt,' Isabella replied, 'pursues her own business. Monsieur, I've asked you to come to answer one question and one question only.'

The smile faded from Marigny's face.

'Oh yes,' Isabella added, 'I also want to tell you something.'

'Your grace?' Marigny spread his hands.

'First, where is Agnes d'Albert? The lady-in-waiting from my beloved aunt's retinue?'

'Ah.' Marigny closed his eyes.

Plaisans and Nogaret moved uneasily; Alexander of Lisbon looked perplexed. The great demon's lieutenants had sensed something was very wrong.

'Why are you interested in Agnes d'Albret?' Marigny asked softly.

'Because I am,' Isabella replied. 'She petitioned to join my household. She went to see you in your quarters and has not returned.'

'Agnes d'Albret,' Marigny replied, choosing his words carefully, 'is not well, Madam, an evil humour.' He tapped the side of his head. 'It would be best if she returned to the French court. The queen dowager herself has admitted that, perhaps, her presence is no longer required here. In fact, Madam Agnes has already left for Dover; a French cog waits there.'

'Ah well.' Isabella stood up.

The look of surprise on the faces of Marigny's companions was almost comical.

'Your grace?' Marigny rose to his feet. 'Is that all?'

'I asked you a question,' Isabella retorted, 'where is Agnes d'Albret? You have answered it. What more can I say?' She gestured at the door.

Marigny and the rest hurriedly recollected themselves and bowed.

'Oh, messieurs, I almost forgot.' Isabella took a step forward. 'When you return to France – and perhaps you may be leaving earlier than you think – tell my good father how my husband, his grace the king, knows who the Poison Maiden is.'

Marigny paused, mouth gaping. Oh, the sight was sweet revenge! He stared like a man hit by a club, hands halfway up, mouth opening and closing, eyes darting.

'My lady, your grace,' he stammered, 'what is this?'

'Messieurs,' Isabella replied sweetly, 'our audience is over. My pages and squires will show you out.'

Marigny would have stayed, but Isabella flailed her hand. 'Monsieur, I have other business.'

Once they had gone, the door slamming shut

behind them, Isabella sat down, fingers to her face, and giggled like a girl. 'Oh Mathilde,' she took her hands away, 'for years I have wished to do that! Now, my sweet,' she turned to me, 'my revered aunt and her imp Guido the Psalter; let us talk to them.'

The queen dowager sensed something was wrong as soon as she took her seat. She stared in suspicion at her niece, dressed so mockingly in the same attire and fashion as herself. Beside Margaret, Guido, in red and gold jerkin and blue hose, looked uncomfortable; he kept staring back at the door where Isabella's squires and pages had plucked his dagger from its sheath.

'Beloved niece,' the dowager began, 'something is wrong? Guards are everywhere, there is gossip of great danger . . .'

'Beloved aunt,' Isabella retorted, 'there is, but it will pass.'

'So why have you invited me here?'

'To accuse you of treason, vile and heinous, against me, my husband and the power of England.'

Margaret made to rise.

'Please stay!' Isabella warned. 'Leave this chamber now, and you and yours will be arrested.' She gestured at Guido. 'He'll be hanged out of hand. I have the power; just a few heartbeats and you, the Poison Maiden, will be incarcerated, whilst you, sir, assassin, spy, a truly treacherous soul, will be hanging from the gatehouse beams.' She spread her hands. 'The choice is yours.'

'I will protest!'

'Of course you will! The Lord Satan does eternally.'

'My lady, your grace . . .' Guido squirmed in his chair.

'Keep your peace!' Isabella snapped. 'You, sir, are before justices of oyer and terminer. You are on trial for your life. Outside men gather who will be your executioners. Will you resist or listen?'

Guido slouched back in the chair, but the shock of his predicament flushed his face, eyes bright and startling, a sheen of sweat glistening on his brow.

'There are two people missing,' Isabella declared cheerfully, 'Margaret, Countess of Cornwall, but she is not needed for these matters, and Agnes d'Albret. Margaret, where is she?'

The queen dowager gazed solemnly back. Guido made to speak.

'Langton has confessed all,' I interjected. My words stung like the lash of a whip. Margaret started in horror. Guido groaned openly.

'The indictment?' Isabella spoke softly. 'Mathilde?'

'Madam,' I tried to catch and hold Margaret's gaze, 'you are Philip of France's sister, very close to him. Your brother occupied English-held Gascony and forced a peace treaty on old Edward of England. He was to marry you; his son, the Prince of Wales, your niece Isabella. Philip was determined that the throne of the Confessor, which stands so close to this place, be occupied by a prince of the Capetian blood. He was ruthlessly set on it. The marriage took place but the old king had taken a viper to his bosom. You were his wife but you were also Philip's spy at the heart of the English court. Now in ancient times, a female assassin, the Poison Maiden, was sent into the enemy camp, to wreak as much damage as she could. You were, are, Philip of France's Poison Maiden. You betrayed your husband's secrets to his arch-enemy—'

'What proof do you have of this?' Margaret yelled, no longer the pious widow, the nun-like dowager; more like some furious harridan from the slums of St Denis or Cheapside.

'Very little,' I agreed. 'Except that the old king, your husband, must have warned you, probably in a letter that no longer exists, transcribed by his faithful servitor John Highill. Or perhaps, in a moment of weakness, he confided his anxieties to that clerk of the secret seal. Your husband enjoyed the romances about Arthur and the great Alexander. In one of the poems about the Conqueror of the World, the King of India sent Alexander many precious gifts, including a beautiful maiden whom he had fed and poisoned until she had the nature of a venomous snake. Seduced by her loveliness, Alexander, according to the story, rushed to embrace her but her touch, her bite, even her sweat, the poem declares, would have been fatal to him. He would have been killed except for the intervention of his wise adviser, the philosopher Aristotle.' I paused. 'That is why your late husband used the phrase Poison Maiden to describe you, only in his case he had embraced you!'

The queen dowager was staring full at me, her face strangely younger, more beautiful, eyes rounded in anger. I could see her attraction to the old king, who must have been torn between anger and lust. Guido kept his head down, fingering with the buckle on a wallet strapped to his belt.

'As I said, in the old king's eyes you were the Poison Maiden, sent to seduce, to betray. He lusted after your body, determined to seek his own revenge through pleasure, but he never really trusted you.'

'He loved me!' Margaret hissed, her face pushed towards me.

'I do not doubt that, madam,' I replied, 'but he had been cuckolded, trapped in a marriage with the sister of his enemy.'

'He was no cuckold.'

'In a sense he was. You put your brother the King of France's interests before those of your husband, Edward of England. He knew that, but like any cuckold did not wish to proclaim it abroad. What could the old king do? He was bound by solemn treaty and the bonds of holy marriage. He could do nothing except fulminate. Two other people knew the full truth. The old king's treasurer and confidant Walter Langton, and the clerk John Highill. The latter grew old and witless and expressed his sorrow at his royal master's plight by composing a mock version of the "Salve Regina" – the ancient hymn to the Virgin.'

Margaret, violent with rage, would have lunged at me, but surprisingly, Guido grasped her arm while Isabella leaned forward.

'Kinswoman, I do not wish to summon Ap Ythel to restrain you.'

'Highill,' I resumed, 'became witless but his veiled attack on you meant he was committed to Bethlehem Hospital, where he continued his rantings, even scrawling on a wall.'

Guido's head came up, eyes all fearful.

'Oh yes,' I declared, '*Salve Regina, Mater Misericordiae*. In Highill's confused mind this became *Salv. Reg. Sin. Cor. Mat. Dis.*, or, in full, *Salve Regina sine corona, Mater Discordiae*. Instead of "Hail Queen of Heaven, Mother of Mercy" his version, translated from his clerkly cipher, was: "Hail Queen without a crown, Mother of Discord", his perception of you. The old king must have been furious with him, yet what crime had Highill committed except tell the truth? Hence, Bethlehem Hospital. Chapeleys also knew something about this, though perhaps not the whole truth. He had the wit to keep silent, but he made a reference to it on a scrap of parchment found in his chamber: an unfinished word, "basil". I thought he was referring to a basilisk. Chapeleys, however, like Highill was a scholar of Greek. In that tongue the complete word, *Basilea*, means queen.'

'Rantings and ravings!' scoffed Margaret, glaring hot-eyed at my mistress.

'Wait, wait,' Isabella murmured.

'In a sense, the old king had his revenge,' I continued. 'You were never crowned, were you? Almost nine years in England but never taken to Westminster. No crown lowered on to your head. Your skin never anointed with the holy chrism. I thought of that when I was close to Eleanor's tomb in the Abbey. Did you hate your late husband, madam? He died at Burgh-on-Sands last July. You were there tending to him.' I let the implied accusation hang in the air before continuing. 'After his death, your role as the Poison Maiden did not end, but came to full flower in the new king's reign. You acted as your brother's spy, informing him about Lord Gaveston's pre-eminence and the new king's confrontation with his Great Lords. Philip of France must have been delighted. He made one mistake: the royal pastry cook Edmund Lascelles, commonly known as Pax-Bread, overheard his secret conspiracy and somehow discovered that the Poison Maiden was again bent on mischief. I do wonder if Pax-Bread actually knew the identity of the Poison Maiden. Or just that Philip greatly relied upon her to do great mischief against the power of England. Now Pax-Bread was a spy. He'd served the old king but he'd also served Lord

Gaveston, changing horses, as it were, mid-stream. He must also have learnt something about Highill and written a letter warning the king and Gaveston about the dangers facing them.' I paused. 'We'll never fully comprehend how much Chapeleys and Pax-Bread really knew, because you had both murdered.'

'Pax-Bread,' Margaret scoffed, 'who is he?'

'Oh, you knew! By the February of this year, madam, you were playing the two-faced Janus: the sanctimonious queen dowager trying to mediate between the young king and his opponents—'

'Nonsense!'

'And Philip of France's sister,' I declared, 'determined on assisting him in all his subtle schemes.'

'What is your proof?'

'Langton has truly confessed,' Isabella intervened. 'He hopes for a pardon for all offences and the restoration of his temporalities.'

'Traitor!' The word escaped Guido, now torn between fear and anger.

'You were no mediator,' I declared. 'Langton was your secret ally before he was arrested late last autumn. He'd already moved treasure from his hoard at New Temple to assist you. You used that to bribe the likes of Pembroke and Lincoln. You met those Great Lords at banquets in your private chambers, and bribed them with wine, silver, gold and flattery.'

'And anything else?' Isabella whispered.

'How dare you!' Margaret was now beside

herself with rage. She sprang to her feet but a clatter outside the door forced her back. 'My children?' Her voice turned weary.

'They are safe,' Isabella retorted. 'Safer than we would have been in Burgundy Hall.'

'What do you mean?'

'In a while. Continue, Mathilde.'

'The Great Lords and Langton were delighted by your secret sustenance and comfort. You reached an unwritten agreement with them.' I paused, watching those hate-filled eyes. Margaret's hands fell to the cord around her waist, and I wondered if she had a knife concealed.

'You would act as mediator but advise them on as much as you could about the king's secret councils.'

'But surely in time the Great Lords,' Margaret jibed, 'would inform Edward about my so-called deviousness? I was vulnerable to any of them betraying me.'

'Nonsense,' I replied. 'What proof did they have? I suspect you dealt with only Langton, Pembroke and Lincoln and no one else.' I paused. 'You would negotiate with them individually. Why should Langton expose you as the Poison Maiden? No one would believe him, whilst he would lose a valuable ally. As for Lincoln and Pembroke – oh, you'd play the wise woman who wanted to help your stepson, whom you so admire, whilst fully understanding the Great Lords' aversion to the favourite. Moreover, why should Lincoln and

Pembroke confess to plotting against the king? They would hardly wish to incriminate themselves, so they scarce would mention you. They would understand your role. You portrayed yourself as the pious queen dowager, deeply concerned by her stepson's actions, alarmed at the rise of the Gascon favourite. Of course, Langton's fall from grace, his sudden arrest, the attack on the Templars, the seizure of their estates, particularly New Temple Church, was an obstacle. However, you clearly tried to resolve that by pleading with your stepson to cede New Temple to Winchelsea so the Lords could gain control over Langton's secret hoard. They could then have continued their opposition indefinitely whilst working hard for Langton's release.' I paused, planning my next words carefully. 'Now the royal prosecutors,' Margaret started at the implied threat, 'will argue that your ultimate plan was to weaken the king and his kingdom, make it more malleable for your brother to eventually subdue. The Lords might sense this but, of course, blinded by their hatred for Gaveston, tolerate such meddling. In truth they were unaware of your real plot.' Guido muttered something in the patois of the Paris slums. A prayer? A curse? I could not say, but those few words assured me I had struck to the heart.

'Plot? Real plot?' The queen dowager was flustered, her face snow white, eyes desperate.

'Oh yes! The Great Lords and Langton did not fully understand Philip's subtle moves on the chessboard. He dreams, doesn't he, of being the new Charlemagne, dominating kings, princes and popes? He hopes to control everything through marriages. My mistress married her husband and Philip used Lord Gaveston's rise to meddle more deeply in the affairs of this kingdom. In the beginning he hoped Edward would become his client king, but now to the real plot.' I leaned forward. 'What if both King Edward and his favourite disappeared, were killed in a fire or assassinated soon afterwards? To whom could the Lords turn? Which prince has Plantagenet blood? Edward has no sons; that only leaves, madam, your infant offspring, Edmund of Woodstock and Thomas of Brotherton. My mistress, if she survived the plot, would be dispatched back to France, the poor widow. You, however, madam, would enter your glory. The queen mother of future kings, possibly regent of the kingdom guided, of course, by brother Philip and his minions! Little wonder you became so agitated at the possibility that your niece might be pregnant; that would have posed problems!'

Margaret sat tense, shaking her head.

'Sweet kinswoman,' Isabella's voice thrilled with sarcasm, 'is that why I was to die as well?'

Margaret refused to meet her gaze.

'And you,' I turned, 'Guido the Psalter, Pierre Bernard – you are no fugitive from French justice. You are no supporter of Edward, whatever you pretend. You are a high-ranking member of the

Secreti, Philip's coven of spies and assassins, dispatched to England to assist Queen Margaret. You know a great deal about murder, and such skills were certainly needed. You pretended to be Marigny's enemy when you are, in fact, close to his heart. You act the jester when in truth you're a Judas. You are here to protect, sustain and nourish Philip's great enterprise. However, nothing under the sun goes as smoothly as we would wish; obstacles and problems afflict even princes. You were here to remove such obstacles. Chapeleys was the first. He wished to be free of the Tower, to negotiate with the king. I doubt if he knew the full plot, but he'd learnt where Langton had hidden his treasure hoard and, perhaps, that the queen dowager was not to be trusted. When he came here, Chapeleys brought some proof of his allegations but that was burnt by his assassin. Whiling away the hours, however, he took out a scrap of parchment, and using what he thought was a secret cipher, carefully made note of his intended revelations.'

'But . . .' Guido stumbled over his words.

'Listen,' Isabella replied harshly, 'don't plead, don't lie. You, sir, had me marked down for death!'

'You accompanied Demontaigu and myself to the Tower. You are your mistress' messenger to Langton, who, of course, denies all knowledge of Philip's plot though he would bear witness to your treachery. On that day you acted the skilled physician, a leech conversing with Langton while tending to his leg, but as Langton was talking loudly, you crept back to the door, where you overheard Chapeleys pleading with me. After that clerk had left, you followed me to the Chapel of St John the Evangelist. You were probably already suspicious of Demontaigu. On that day you made a discovery: not only was Demontaigu a Templar, but he was planning to meet with his separated brethren the following evening at the Chapel of the Hanged.'

'I never overheard you,' Guido stammered.

'Oh yes you did,' I mocked. 'I returned to the Tower, as you well know. I left Langton's chamber, re-entered that chapel and recalled the events of that day: talking to Chapeleys, then moving into St John's to converse with Demontaigu. You're an accomplished spy, Master Guido, used to eavesdropping, to listening secretly, as you did that day. I would wager you were suspicious about the preacher on the Tower quayside. The way he approached Demontaigu, who whirled round to face him.' I never waited for an answer. 'You're a clerk from the secret chancery – you would recognise a cipher, a hidden message, when you heard one. In the end you hastened back to warn Marigny. He and Alexander of Lisbon plotted the attack on the Templars at the Chapel of the Hanged. You would take care of Chapeleys and immediately . . .' I paused, listening to sounds outside, and took a deep gulp of fresh spring water from a cup.

'You discovered that Chapeleys was lodged in Demontaigu's chamber. The royal banquet was about to begin. You entered the maidservants' quarters, a shabby, ill-lit room where they keep their cloaks and other clothing. You stole some of these. You dressed quickly in disguise. You're a mimer, Guido, able to act different parts. You did not wish to be glimpsed hastening across the palace yards and up darkening staircases. You made a mistake. You were disturbed by a maid, Rebecca Atte-Stowe. You killed that poor woman and continued with your devious plot. You slipped out into the dark; you'd wait for Demontaigu to go into the banquet. Chapeleys would be alone in that chamber and easily fooled. Did you mimic me or declare that Demontaigu or I had sent you? Chapeleys, lonely and vulnerable, was tricked into opening that door. Again the garrotte string was used and Chapeleys was killed. The contents of his chancery pouch were quickly emptied, studied and burnt. You then dragged his corpse across to the window-door. You took the fire rope; one end was tied to a ring on the wall, the other you lashed tightly around Chapeleys' neck. The rope was thick and coarse; you positioned it so that the weal in the still warm flesh would hide all signs of the garrotte string. You doused all lights, pushed open those window-doors and hanged poor Chapeleys. To deepen the mystery, you locked and bolted the chamber door from inside, compelling proof that Chapeleys simply despaired, burnt his papers and hanged himself. You then used that same rope around the corpse of your victim to clamber down into the darkness. You quickly removed your disguise and hastened to join the banquet in Burgundy Hall. You were the king's special guest. The guards at the main gateway knew you. People were coming and going. No evidence to show that you had just carried out a foul deed.'

Guido sat staring at me. I noticed he had taken a small scroll from the wallet in his belt. I glimpsed the edges of a purple seal. He followed my gaze.

'You have no proof for your allegations.' His voice was quiet, calm, as if that manuscript restored his confidence.

'Sometimes logic is its own proof,' I retorted. 'As I said, nothing goes as smoothly as planned. Edmund Lascelles, Pax-Bread, an English spy in the court of France, had been discovered and had fled to England. The Secreti followed him here. They noted that he'd lodged at the Secret of Solomon, yet they could do nothing and did not wish to provoke suspicion. Instead they passed this information to Marigny and his coven, who informed you, Master Guido. Once again disguised as a woman, with your smooth face and gift for mimicry, you slipped into the night. You approached the Secret of Solomon and inveigled a maid to take Pax-Bread a message. You gave her a copy of Lord Gaveston's seals—'

'How would I have obtained them?'

'Quite easy, Guido: your mistress here has access

341

to all sorts of documents. She has, I know, received letters from Lord Gaveston. You simply detached two of the seals to persuade Pax-Bread to leave that tavern. You sent him a note advising him to flee, taking everything without being noticed. You wanted to make sure that he left no evidence in his chamber.'

'A note?' Guido scoffed. 'In Lord Gaveston's hand? How could I—'

'Very easily,' I said. 'You're a spy, an assassin. Lord Gaveston would not write a note; a clerk would do that. Pax-Bread would notice nothing amiss. The note was one thing, the seals were another. In that note you warned Pax-Bread to take everything. He filled his pannier bags, bolted the door from the inside and climbed out of the window, banging the shutters behind him, first the one on his left then the other to his right so the bar inside fell down into the clasp. I have seen that done; it is quite common. There's a cupboard here in this palace where even a groom could show you how to seal a door by bringing the bar down, as well as opening it by inserting a knife. Pax-Bread thought nothing was amiss. He knew he was being hunted. He was being warned by his patron to leave the Secret of Solomon as quickly and quietly as possible. A spy, he followed that order faithfully, taking all his possessions, fully hoping the king and Lord Gaveston would protect him. I suspect you may have laid a siege ladder against that window to help him climb down.

In the darkness, however, you were waiting for him with your garrotte string, and Pax-Bread paid for his mistakes with his life.'

'Yet I was poisoned!' Guido blustered. 'I was ill. You saw that! I drank what was intended for the Lord Gaveston.'

'Foolishness,' I replied. 'Guido, you are skilled in physic and the potency of herbs. I now know all I need about what Apuleius calls *Violata odorata*. What confused me was the fact that there are so many species of this herb, as well as its distinctive smell. Now the violet's roots and seeds can provoke ill humours of the belly, vomiting, slight breathing difficulties, looseness of the bowels and the occasional skin rash. In a word, sir, you poisoned yourself with a herb that is not malignant but gives every sign that it is. You hoped I would never find out. No wonder you kept asking me if I'd discovered what herb had been used, hinting it must be noxious whilst you used your skills to depict yourself as a very sick man.'

Guido shook his head in disbelief.

'You are a liar!' I accused. 'You peddle stories as it suits your whim. You spread confusion and lies – as you tried to when you took me out into the gallery. You wanted to muddy the waters with your own theories. Langton did the same by declaring Gaveston was really the Poison Maiden, a public insult to the favourite whilst concealing the Poison Maiden's true identity. You also concealed the truth. You depicted Langton as

343

dismissive of Chapeleys. You misrepresented what Chapeleys believed. You were desperate. You said you'd been sent back to the Tower to treat Langton after Chapeleys was killed.' I shook my head. 'You were reporting back to him about Chapeleys' death—'

'I was sent there.'

'No, sir, you, or rather your mistress, asked the king for you to be sent back. Edward, thinking it was of little importance, agreed. What harm was there in that? A clever deception like your so-called poisoning.'

'Lies!' Guido gasped. 'I was ill.'

'You were pretending,' I retorted. 'You needed to stay here in Burgundy Hall. As I said, violet causes stomach cramps, rashes, a loosening of the bowels but nothing dangerous. You pretended it was something more malignant. Your mistress, the queen dowager, persuaded Gaveston to take your chair. You put the violet in the water glass near the favourite's chair and drank it. You were in Burgundy Hall and intended to stay there.'

'But I was the queen dowager's messenger.'

'So?'

'I could come and go as I wished.'

'Master Guido, so you could! Ap Ythel made a strange remark about you. He called you the lord of the garderobes. When my suspicions were quickened, I asked him what he meant. He explained how, when you came into Burgundy Hall, you often visited the garderobes. He thought

344

you might have suffered some stomach ailment. I don't think so. You used hidden cloths, broken pottery, any rubbish at hand which could be concealed to block the holes of the latrines and cesspits, which in turn would provoke foulsome odours.'

'And why should I do that?'

'Master Guido, it would not be the first occasion that latrines, cesspits and sewers have been used against the very place they serve. The Surveyor of the Royal Works was brought in. The cleaning of cesspits and latrines is unsavoury work. He hired labourers. A coven of assassins known as Tenebrae – *les ombres*, the shadows – used this to infiltrate their own members into Burgundy Hall as workmen. Days passed. A stream of labourers went backwards and forwards. The assassins mingled with these, outlaws and wolfsheads recruited from the sanctuary of Westminster. They brought in sacks, covered barrows that concealed skins of oil and barrels of fire powder. Even if these were checked, a Welsh archer might conclude they were simply commodities to be used in cleaning the latrines. I doubt if the wolfsheads themselves realised the full significance of what they were doing. The vigilance of the guards was relaxed. His grace the king, with his well-known love of mixing and talking with labourers, worthy though it might be, did not help matters. The oil and powder were secretly stored in the cellars of Burgundy Hall.'

I stared hard at Guido, who was now fumbling with the parchment held in his hand. 'I do not know the full truth,' I continued. 'Arbalests, swords and daggers were also found. I thought they'd been placed to divert suspicions. I now believe I was wrong. You didn't want anyone to discover what was being planned. I suspect those powerful arbalests were hidden away for the assassins to use against anyone who escaped from Burgundy Hall, powerful weapons, deadly bolts and quarrels that could be loosed in the dark at some unfortunate staggering out against the light of the flames.'

'I know nothing of this,' the queen dowager declared. She moved her chair a little away from Guido, a gesture not lost on her servant.

'Madam,' Isabella accused, 'that is why Guido acted the way he did, pretending to be poisoned, his life at risk; you wanted that!'

The queen dowager stared bleakly back. Isabella turned and nodded at me.

'Madam, you would arrange to leave Burgundy Hall, but Guido would stay. He was recovering; in time he would become accepted. One night he'd prepare a grease wick, as you would for a lamp, only longer and thickly coated with oil. One end would be placed against the fire powder, the other lit by him. The ensuing conflagration would devastate Burgundy Hall. God knows what other devilry he was planning during his stay here: stair-wells blocked, doors wedged shut. Master Guido

346

would escape to plot whatever mischief was required afterwards, including the death of any survivors.'

'John Highill?' Isabella murmured.

'Ah, yes.' I pointed at Guido. 'I have talked about what you planned. Let me return to what you did. A hideous mistake, Master Guido. I tricked Langton into revealing the name of John Highill, an old chancery clerk who ranted strangely and was closeted in Bethlehem Hospital. Apart from the king, Lord Gaveston and my mistress, only you, the queen dowager and Langton knew about my discovery. Highill died mysteriously at the hands of a supposed Franciscan nun. A matter of logic, Master Guido! That nun was either you or your mistress. Cowled and hooded, in the dark, with your talent for mime, you visited Highill. He liked his wine and you mingled a poison in it. Highill died. You cleansed the cup, stole his possessions and slipped away.'

'I was ill here in Burgundy Hall!'

'You were well enough,' I scoffed. 'And as you said, you are the queen dowager's messenger, who could wander as he wished. Indeed, who would notice? Who would care?' I paused. 'The queen dowager comes and goes, sweeping in and out; who would notice the veiled lady-in-waiting carrying her baby sons, perhaps? Who would suspect it was Guido the Psalter? And if you were found missing from your sick-bed? Well, Guido has gone for a walk.'

Guido made to object.

'You're a killer,' I insisted, 'you dispatched those assassins against myself and Demontaigu. You, her,' I jabbed a finger at Margaret, 'and Marigny. We troubled you, didn't we? You tried to find out what we knew! You wanted to stop our prying and snooping! Slit our throats! An unfortunate incident out on the heathland! A clerk and his maid barbarously slain by footpads!'

'And Agnes d'Albret? Isabella's voice was harsh.

'Agnes,' I replied, 'was dangerous. Friendly with my Lord Gaveston, on whose wife she spied, she may have become suspicious. She may have noticed anomalies and contradictions but had little proof, or the status, to make any allegation. She even asked me if I'd observed anything wrong. Agnes first wanted to be safe, to find refuge in my mistress' household. She fell under suspicion, so she was dispatched on a simple errand to Marigny, who knew what to do: seize her and send her as swiftly as possible back to France!'

Guido rose to his feet, not threatening but rather awkwardly. The queen dowager tried to grasp his wrist but he knocked her hand away.

'Madam,' he whispered hoarsely, 'this is finished. We must follow our own paths. I have,' he bowed respectfully to Isabella, 'a commission from your august father. I, Pierre Bernard, commonly known as Guido the Psalter, am a member of King Philip's secret council, a special envoy carrying your father's personal seal. I lie within the jurisdiction of the power of France. If charges are to be brought, I demand—'

Isabella raised a hand. 'No more, no more,' she murmured. 'We expected as much. Go, sir, but as you pass through the hall of attendance, do tell the earls Pembroke and Lincoln that,' she smiled falsely, 'you are hastening to join my Lord Marigny at his lodgings elsewhere in this palace. As God lives, my father will know soon enough about you. I bid you adieu.'

Surprised, Guido gauchely bowed to both Isabella and Margaret, smirked at me and left.

'And you, dearest kinswoman.' Isabella's voice thrilled, and once again I realised how consummate a mask-wearer she truly was. She disliked her aunt intensely and now made this obvious.

'I am the queen dowager.'

'So you are, and so you will remain, madam.' Isabella rose. 'You and your children will be taken back to one of your residences. Preferably,' she mocked, 'as far away as possible from me, but close enough to some mouldering relic. You can babble about them, visit the shrines, but this time it will be genuine, not a cover for your intriguing. As for my father,' Isabella clicked her tongue, 'you can tell him whatever you like. However, this charade of my husband, Gaveston, me and the power of France is all ended. I am Edward of England's queen, crowned and anointed, the mother of future kings. Oh, go!' She sat down, her voice weary. 'In God's name, madam, go!

My husband sees no advantage in publicising your disgrace or humiliating you.'

Margaret rose, sketched a bow, glared hatefully at me and swept from the chamber. Isabella patted the stool beside her as I returned from closing the door. For a while we sat in silence. I went to speak. Isabella took a ring from her finger and pressed it into my hands.

'A gift,' she whispered, eyes smiling, 'one my mother gave me. I now give it to you, Mathilde, with my love.' She put her finger to her lips and walked over to a window. She stood there for a while, then put her face into her hands and stood, shoulders shaking. I made to rise.

'No,' she whispered without turning, 'no, let me weep for what is, for what has been, but above all for what could have been.' She continued to stand staring through the window.

There was a loud knock on the door. Isabella made a sign. I hastened to open it. Demontaigu stepped through. He was dressed in black leather jerkin and breeches. I noticed the blood-stains on his high-heeled boots. He placed his war belt on the floor and knelt.

'Your grace.'

'Is it done?' Isabella asked without turning.

'As you said,' Demontaigu replied. 'Pierre Bernard, known as Guido the Psalter, was intent on rejoining Lord Marigny. Lincoln and Pembroke will bear witness to that. No servant of this kingdom would seize him, but we were waiting.'

Isabella glanced bleakly over her shoulder at him.

'My brethren and I were just beyond the gateway, Ausel and the rest. Guido the Psalter came swaggering out like a cock in a yard. We surrounded him. We gagged his mouth and bound his hands. No one noticed. I don't think anyone really cared.'

'And?'

'We took him into the northern meadow just beyond the Great Ditch on Tothill Lane. We released his bonds and accused him of being what he was, a spy, a traitor and an assassin. At first he pleaded, but then accepted his fate. We allowed him to confess and took him over to a tree stump. Ausel cut his head off. He and the brothers have taken his corpse to the House of the Crutched Friars for burial. I sent money for the requiem mass. Madam,' Demontaigu declared, 'Bernard deserved his death. He brought it on himself.'

'Thank you.' Isabella turned away. 'Please,' she glanced swiftly over her shoulder, 'please wait outside.'

Demontaigu rose, bowed, nodded at me and left. Only when the door closed did Isabella walk back; even then the lengthening shadows concealed her tear-streaked face.

'This charade is over. I am queen; let Gaveston have his day. My husband will concede to the Lords through bribes, concessions and intimations of what Philip of France really intended, which will turn their hearts back to their king. We will

351

move to Windsor. I will persuade Edward to let Gaveston go into honourable exile, perhaps with my Lord Mortimer, the king's lieutenant in Ireland.' She sighed. 'Of course, Gaveston will return, but believe me, Mathilde de Clairebon – or should I say Mathilde of Westminster? This charade will end. Oh yes, I remember the maxim: never go to war unless you have to, never fight a battle unless you are going to win. However, on a day of my choosing, at a time of my choosing, at a place of my choosing, I, Isabella, will end this charade for good!'

AUTHOR'S NOTE

Most of what Mathilde has written here about the crisis of spring 1308 is founded on fact, be it Philip IV, the French envoys in England, Gaveston's warrior skills, as well as his penchant for nicknames! Mathilde's description of Winchelsea and the leading earls is also accurate. Edward II's character is faithfully reflected in contemporary chronicle accounts, whilst Philip IV and his minions were dark, sinister souls. Edward II did prevaricate about the Templars. New Temple Church can still be visited and the effigies on the floor carefully examined. Relics were very important in the Middle Ages. The monks of Glastonbury did 'discover' the bodies of Arthur and Guinevere, whilst the sacred blood at Hailes Abbey was venerated up until the Reformation. On the sacred cloths, see *The Burial Cloths of Christ* by Mark Guscin (CTS Publications). One of these cloths is still kept in Oviedo, Spain. Burgundy Hall did exist, and the political and geographical background to this crisis, as well as the layout of Westminster, is analysed in two of my non-fiction works: *Isabella and the Strange Death of Edward II* and *The Great Crown Jewels*

Robbery of 1303; both of these are based on my Oxford thesis on Queen Isabella. Guido's plot to cause foul odours and miasmas is logical. In 1326 Mortimer tried to kill the imprisoned Edward II in the same way.

Walter Langton's career is as described here – *The Lancercost Chronicle* describes the bishop as 'Gaveston's implacable enemy'. Langton did fall from power and Hemingburgh's chronicle describes the seizure of his vast treasure hoard in New Temple Church.

Mathilde's inclusion in the royal household would be logical and acceptable. Kings and queens often relied on commoners for advice and support. In 1326 Edward II was specifically accused of this. Queen Margaret's treachery is also a fact. The peace treaties of 1296–1298 virtually forced Edward I to marry her. Margaret was never crowned. Edward I certainly acted the loving husband; they had four children. However, Sir Thomas Grey, in his chronicle *Scalacronica*, mentions how Margaret secretly informed her brother that Edward I had bribed a number of Philip's knights to assassinate him, and the French king was so concerned he abandoned the siege of Lille. This was a deliberate trap by Edward I, who left a highly confidential letter on his bed for Margaret to read. Edward could certainly be harsh towards her. In a collection of private letters, edited by Pierre Chaplais (*English Historical Review*, 1962), he told her confessor to gently break the news of the death of her sister Blanche. However, if she was inconsolable, Edward continued, she should be reminded that Blanche was as good as dead as soon as she left France to marry the Duke of Austria! Margaret was certainly active in the crisis of 1308. The Lincoln archives hold two anonymous newsletters (D and C Muniments 11/56/1, nos. 39 and 42) that describe Philip bribing the earls, through his sister, with wine and £10,000. Little wonder that, in May 1308, three of Margaret's castles, including Devizes, were seized whilst Isabella was given fresh estates. In addition, after the crisis of 1308 Margaret appears to have been exiled from Court. She died in 1318, and was buried in Greyfriars, London; hence Mathilde's assertion in the Prologue that the Poison Maiden was not far from her!